A TALE of a TEMPLAR

Daniel Robichaud

Reader Advisory: Some language in this book may not be suitable for younger readers

A Tale of a Templar

This is a work of fiction. Aside from reference to known public figures, places, or resources, all names, characters, places, and incidents have been constructed by the author, and any resemblance to actual persons, places, or events is coincidental.

A Tale Of A Templar

Cover and Interior design by: CS Book Design

ISBN: 9781953247582 (Print)

9781953247599 (Ebook)

True Potential, Inc.

PO Box 904, Travelers Rest, SC 29690

www.truepotentialmedia.com

Produced and Printed in the United States of America.

Dedication

This book is dedicated to my mother, Mary K. Dockery, the best mother a boy could ever have, and to God, for letting me see my dreams become reality.

Contents

Preface: The Crusades

This ancient tale was written on the sacred scrolls of heaven above. The story begins in the summer of the year of AD 1099 in Jerusalem during the time of the First Crusade. There was a great cry in Jerusalem, not one of freedom or liberation, but of fear and pain. The crusaders had successfully taken all the large coastal cities of Palestine away from the Muslim armies—starting with Constantinople all the way to Caesarea. When Jerusalem was sacked, the Christian army slaughtered everyone—Muslims, Jews, and any non-Christians there. The streets ran with blood, and the crusaders tarnished their name in history forever. To be able to govern the land, the knights developed the Latin states to better control the Middle East.

During the sieges, there was a man named Sir Godfrey L'Enfant who helped fight in the First Crusade. Godfrey was from the southern tip of France, born to a family of wealthy stonemasons; his father was a Frenchman and his mother was a converted Jewish woman. His family was large; they were known to be devout Catholics in the local community. He was the youngest male of his family. He had an older brother and three younger sisters. At this time, the eldest son always inherited everything upon the death of his father. So the second-born sons often joined the church, became merchants, or pursued military careers. At this time, the Muslims were pushing ever forward into Europe—in the west, they nearly controlled all of the Spanish mainland; in the east, the remnant of the Byzantine Empire had Muslim armies camped on the eastern side of their capitol, Constantinople. Emperor Alexius of the Byzantine Empire appealed to Pope Urban II for help in pushing the Muslim enemies back. The pope agreed and the Christian crusading knights were established. The call rang out through Europe to repel the infidel from Christian lands and to free the holy city of Jerusalem. Two battlefronts were formed; one army went to Spain and the other marched to rally in Constantinople.

After successfully partaking in the defeat of the Muslims, Godfrey joined the Poor Fellow-Soldiers of Christ and of the Temple of Solomon, better known as the Knights Templar, when they were formed before the call of the Second Crusade. The Templars were an order of warrior monks started by nine veteran knights from the First Crusade to protect pilgrims while traveling back and forth to the Holy Land. After they were established as a religious order, they took orders only from the pope, and could only be tried in papal courts. Anyone who joined swore an oath of secrecy, poverty, piety, and obedience to the pope and no one else. Godfrey swore an oath to the Templars, but inside he did not believe in a Messiah, Deliverer, or anything else of that nature. There could be a God or Supreme Being of some kind, but God did not care about Jerusalem, the human race, or the crooked pope. At least, that is what Godfrey thought. During these times, if you were not Catholic, you were condemned with heresy by the church and excommunicated. This meant you had to act and look Catholic. Pretending to be religious didn't bother Godfrey; everyone had to be religious in order to survive. Godfrey simply saw all the religions as a way to control men, and the Crusades an opportunity to make a name for himself. Being a Templar, he had immunity from a lot of things—like taxes, most laws, and serving kings. Being a Templar made one nearly untouchable.

Chapter 1: Robert O'Sharky

There were two ways that pilgrims arrived in the Holy Land—by sea or by land. Godfrey was assigned to the port of Acre. Whenever a large wave of pilgrims arrived, Godfrey and his men escorted them to Jerusalem from Acre. Usually twenty to thirty fully mounted knights would provide escort; thieves were not organized enough to overcome the strength of the knights. So unless there were a large number of pilgrims to escort, a large number of armed men was never needed. Godfrey had done this for what seemed a thousand times and nothing new ever happened. After the First Crusade, the fighting had calmed down.

Then one day Godfrey met an Irishman by the name of Robert O'Sharky. Robert was a cheerful person, short, husky, pale, bald, with a thick orange beard that nearly covered his whole face. He was a blacksmith and very successful. Robert was in charge of a group of seven pilgrims. When Godfrey and his men met up with the group at an inn called the Little Shepherd's Inn, Robert looked right at Godfrey as if he already knew him with a piercing gaze. Godfrey stared back with slanted, cold eyes, but within he was a bit startled. Godfrey asked if everyone was ready for the trip. Robert assured him that they were and they began their journey to Jerusalem.

Look there, another cheerful pilgrim, heavy in the cheeks seeking forgiveness for sin. This one appears more delighted than the rest of his lot. Let us entertain ourselves a bit and speak to the madman, Godfrey thought.

Godfrey went back to the group where Robert was walking happily. Leading his horse, Zaxos, to walk beside Robert, he said, “Greetings, pilgrim, ready for the journey to Jerusalem?”

“Of course, my good knight; Jerusalem has been with my thoughts many years” Robert responded.

“You and many others say such things,” Godfrey said.

“These things are true and dear to me. I have yearned to see where the Lord was crucified since my childhood in Ireland,” Robert replied.

“I am sure you do, but do you realize the men who had to die for this reality of yours to come true?” Godfrey asked.

“I do not doubt the severity of war and bloodshed, but it must be the Lord’s will if the Holy Father has sanctioned it,” Robert replied.

“You speak truly, Irishman. Wars are sometimes necessary, but they wear down the senses after many toils,” Godfrey replied.

“Your treasure waits in eternity, my good knight, for all that you sacrifice,” Robert said.

“Let me speak plainly to you, sir. If there is treasure awaiting my blood-soaked hands in eternity, then God is not just and neither is this world,” Godfrey said.

“You lack foresight, sir, but soon you will see,” Robert said.

“Perhaps I lack faith, but not foresight. I see plainly the future of this country and all who fight for it,” Godfrey said.

“Jerusalem belongs to our Lord. He will protect it. Even if that means using a hardened and prideful knight such as yourself,” Robert responded.

“Pride is what keeps my lungs full. Keep this truth in your thoughts as well, Irishman; my stained hands and tarnished soul is what protects you,” Godfrey responded, steering Zaxos ahead of the group of Pilgrims.

Godfrey was quite alarmed from the encounter with Robert O'Sharky; he couldn't get away from what the man said. Out of all Godfrey had seen and experienced nothing had prepared him for such an encounter; it was weird, yet it seemed like it was supposed to happen. Was it fate or was it just a random occurrence? Godfrey shrugged it off as just another intriguing conversation.

Oh, Father, what a choice of a man. He is arrogant, stubborn, hard, and does not even believe in You. I know though, that he is the one You chose for an incredible task and purpose, a purpose that is not even known by the angels above, thought Robert with joy in his heart.

Chapter 2: Reunion

Escorting the pilgrims had become an easy enough job for Godfrey because of the defeat of the Muslim armies. Not only that, but with the religious dissent between the Muslim Sunni and Shiite tribes, they couldn't muster a force to retake the land from the crusaders. While running things in Acre, Godfrey received an order to report to the Grand Master of the Templars in Jerusalem. Godfrey was staying at the Little Shepherd's Inn, so he planned to leave bright and early the next morning. Before leaving, he left his subordinate in charge; his name was Philip Beaunox. Waking up before sunrise, Godfrey went down to the kitchen of the inn and had some breakfast. The inn was run by a Jewish man named Jordan Mordecai. A medium-sized fellow, he was allowed to stay in Acre after the takeover because he was so wealthy. Godfrey ate a fresh egg and a slice of bread before leaving. He paid for his meal and headed out the front door. As he stepped out and breathed the dry air, Godfrey looked around at the large fortified city, thinking how beautiful the early morning desert really was. He took a deep breath and headed to the stables to find Zaxos and get started on the journey to Jerusalem. Over at the stables, a young teenage boy named Mussef was in charge of taking care of the horses. He was a good kid; Godfrey enjoyed talking to the young boy. Approaching Mussef, Godfrey said, "Good morning to you, Mussef! It looks like pink skies this morning."

"Oh yes, Master Godfrey, looks like we might have a storm approaching," Mussef answered.

“Some rain would be nice; did you feed and water Zaxos?” Godfrey asked.

“I sure did; he should be faster and fit for travel more than any other creature out there,” Mussef answered.

Godfrey liked the work ethic of Mussef; the young man really did his best when taking care of the horses. Mussef was an orphan; his parents were killed by invading Christian armies. Jordan, the owner of the inn, had taken the boy in and become a father to him. Somehow, Mussef didn’t talk about his parents at all. He was a devout Muslim, and prayed every day.

“Good, good, that is what I like to hear; we might make a warrior out of you yet, son,” Godfrey said.

“Ha! Ah, yes! Maybe, God willing,” Mussef said. “Is it me, Master Godfrey, or does something seem out of the ordinary around here?” Mussef asked.

“Not you as well, Mussef! No, there is nothing wrong around here. I don’t have time to speculate on what the fates dictate; hand me Zaxos’ reins so I can be on my way,” Godfrey replied.

“Sorry to upset you, Master Godfrey, but remember one thing: just because you can’t see it, doesn’t mean it isn’t there,” Mussef said.

“I will see you when I return, Mussef,” Godfrey replied.

Mounting Zaxos and waving to Mussef, Godfrey headed toward the southern gates of Acre. As Godfrey passed through the large sandstone gates, he could see the sun just peeking out of the eastern sky. His light armor was shining in the fresh sunlight, bright and silvering. He had his helmet off to let the wind blow through his short, black hair and feel the chill of the wind on his sweaty skin. Godfrey had grown to love this simple pleasure provided by the desert. He looked around and could see for miles on end. Somehow he felt connected to the desert; it was big and vast and lonely; it reminded him of himself.

Godfrey followed the long desert road and headed toward Jerusalem. There is not a lot to look at in the desert, besides the bleak cliffs, singled out mountains; every once in a while, a pack of wild dogs or a lizard would run by. Godfrey should have brought another knight with him on the trip, but wanted to think about things and just be alone in the vastness of sand, stone, rock, wind, and sun. The road itself was not that well managed; it was built by the Romans back in the time of emperors. By this time, the western leg of the Roman empire had dismantled into smaller factions, and just a few years before the eastern leg of the empire, that is the Byzantine empire, had controlled this road. When they still had stability here, the Roman legions patrolled it and took care of bandits, thieves, or murderers. That time was called the Pax Romana, or Roman peace; it had lasted over two hundred years. When the Muslims became a force to be reckoned with, they had made an example of the Byzantines by carving up their empire piece by piece and army by army. There was one good thing about the road though; any traveler could see the Mediterranean Sea from a good distance, depending on how tall a person was. It was a wonderful sight to see; in a fashion unlike him, for just an instant, Godfrey could see how this could be called God's Holy Land.

As Godfrey and Zaxos travelled casually down the dusty highway, Godfrey thought of the majesty of his horse. He and Zaxos had been together for over six years. He was very large and muscular; he had a rich, solid brown color to him and his mane was an even lighter brown. Zaxos was a good war horse; scars covered his long nose, legs, and sides. He didn't have all his armor on either; it was too much to bear while making the long journey to Jerusalem. By now Godfrey had been on the road seven hours; he broke into a few gallops every once and a while, so Zaxos wouldn't get too bored with the journey.

Looking ahead, Godfrey saw an old well that travelers and shepherds used to water themselves and their flocks. Godfrey had water, but decided to stop and stretch his legs. He was still a good distance away, and while looking at the well he could see two men standing by refreshing themselves.

Godfrey thought, *they don't have horses or camels, and are not shepherds either because there is no flock that surrounds them. Why would two men be way out here? They must be too poor to afford animals to travel with. Or they lost a bet and couldn't pay so they were left out here to die.*

The two men intrigued Godfrey, and he wouldn't mind having a chat with somebody anyway, so he headed straight for the well. From the well, the two men saw Godfrey coming toward them. They saw a man with short black hair, tanned skin, wearing the attire of the Knights Templar—a white cloak emblazoned with a displaced red cross on the front of his chest.

As he came closer on his horse, one of the men said, "Here is the man we have been waiting for!"

"Yes, he's the one," the other man said.

"So what needs to be done?" asked one of the cloaked men.

"All we need to do is introduce ourselves. Let's make an impression on him," Shemiel answered.

Godfrey rode up and dismounted. The two men appeared to be from the Middle East somewhere. One of the men looked oddly familiar, but Godfrey couldn't put his finger on where he had seen him before; his light blue eyes stuck out the most to Godfrey. As Godfrey was giving his horse some water, he started talking to the men.

"Hello, what brings you two way out here?" Godfrey asked.

"We are heading to Jerusalem," Jazrael answered.

"So am I," said Godfrey.

Jazrael stood there leaning on his staff, and asked, "What is your name, Templar?"

"Godfrey L'Enfant," Godfrey answered while drinking some of the cool well water.

"Good to meet you, Godfrey; my name is Jazrael and my companion is Shemiel," said Jazrael.

"Likewise," said Godfrey.

"It appears you have been in the desert a while, Sir Godfrey; it has left its mark on you," said Shemiel.

"I have been here a while. Maybe too long really. I'm actually thinking of going back home one of these days," said Godfrey.

"Maybe it's your purpose to be here, Godfrey," said Shemiel.

"The only purpose I have is surviving this cursed place," answered Godfrey very bluntly.

"You are very bold; I have to hand it to you, friend. You are one of a kind; that choice of words can get you killed around here," Jazrael said.

After filling up his water bag and refreshing himself and Zaxos, Godfrey mounted the steed and talked to the two men a little more before departing. He made sure both of them saw his sword—just in case they were thinking of robbing him.

"It was nice talking to both of you. Have a safe journey," said Godfrey.

"You, too, friend, and the Lord sends His love with you," answered Jazrael.

Before Godfrey could come up with a sarcastic comeback to the Lord comment, the two men began glowing with a golden light. Godfrey squinted his eyes because it was already sunny outside, but the light emanating from Shemiel and Jazrael seemed even brighter. Their cloaks fell to the ground and blew away in a sudden strong wind. Godfrey couldn't see their faces anymore—only golden outlines of large wings and faint figures of gigantic men. As the wind and the light grew even more intense, Godfrey could hear Jazreal's voice speaking through the light. It was echoing and loud—like an orator coming out of an amphitheatre.

Jazreal said, "You're welcome, Godfrey."

With that the two vanished in the air and a giant gust of wind knocked Godfrey off Zaxos. He shot through the air at least twenty feet or so, hitting the sandy ground hard—so hard, in fact, that it knocked him unconscious.

Godfrey woke up to Zaxos licking and sniffing his face. When he got up and gathered all his thoughts, Godfrey looked around and saw he was not in the same spot. As a matter of fact, he was standing about a mile from Jerusalem's outer wall. Instead of sandy desert, Jerusalem's bright green was everywhere. Some pilgrims were passing by singing psalms and looking at Godfrey like he was crazy because he was just lying on the side of the road being licked by his horse.

What in the world just happened? Okay, let me think—two guys just disappeared right in front of me. I can't blame it on being drunk; they were there, and then they weren't. I guess that's why he said you're welcome; he knocked a few days off my trip.

As Godfrey was thinking about what Jazreal said, he had a flashback of an accident he had as a child. Godfrey's mother had sent him to the well that was in the middle of his village to get water. He was a small child then, maybe eight or nine. He had gone outside and grabbed a wooden pail and run as fast as he could to the well. It was an adventure for him at that age. He was running so fast that it was hard to slow down. By the time he got to the well, Godfrey tripped over a rock and went over the side of it. The well had a circumference of five feet, and had a stone wall about two feet high from the ground. Godfrey smacked into the stone surface as his body gracefully went over the side. The well was thirty feet deep, and the fall, depending on how Godfrey landed, would have killed him. In just seconds that felt like an eternity as Godfrey went over the edge, he felt a strong hand grab his ankle and hold him in midair. The man had pulled him back over the edge with incredible strength. Godfrey had taken a deep breath and looked up at the man as he regained his balance and got back on his feet. The man was tall and well built. He looked to be someone who was in the military. His eyes were light blue and seemed to have a lot of wisdom in them. The rest of his body was covered by a blackish cloak.

"Are you okay, Godfrey?" the man had asked.

"Uhhh...yes," Godfrey had mumbled.

"It must not be your time yet, young man. I think I hear your mother calling you. You're welcome," the man said.

"Thank you, sir," Godfrey responded.

Godfrey didn't know why this came into his remembrance, but Jazreal and the blue-eyed man had the same voice and eyes. The sudden revelation came to Godfrey that it must have been the same man. Everything in Godfrey's life here of late started getting very odd all of a sudden—first the meeting with that fat Irishman, then Mussef talking like a mystic, and then the pinnacle of it all, men with wings disappearing into thin air and transporting him and Zaxos to Jerusalem. Godfrey did not know what to make of this, but he had a feeling he would find out very soon.

Chapter 3: The Fallen

Godfrey cleaned the dust and sand off of his white attire. He mounted Zaxos and approached the western gate of Jerusalem. The Christian knights standing watch recognized him and let him through. Godfrey walked under the massive stone walls of the city and headed uphill to the mount where the newly founded headquarters for the Templars was. The city was alive. Merchants from around the world had their tables set up to sell everything and anything to the never-ending procession of pilgrims, who would buy anything with a cross on it. People walked up and down the narrow streets of Jerusalem. There were so many languages being spoken at once that it seemed as if this ancient place was near the tower of Babel. It was a beautiful city. The sun hit the walls and buildings which gave off a gleaming brightness, and all the hills surrounding Jerusalem shone with an almost translucent emerald green.

In the backdrop, gray clouds rumbled from storms coming off the coast of the Mediterranean. Sometimes a rainbow would appear and stretch from one end of the city to the other. There was no city in Europe that had a history like that of Jerusalem. Rome had been a mere village when the prophets of old walked the streets of David's capital. Godfrey always thought there was, and would be, more blood spilled for this plot of land than any other spot in the world. Godfrey had already experienced his fair share of war and bloodletting for the Holy Land.

Godfrey finally arrived at the headquarters of the Templars. The headquarters were quite humble-looking. They were located in the sub-basement of the temple mount. The area was called Solomon's stables, but hadn't been used as stables until the knights took it over. The Templars had plans to start excavating the area for artifacts for the church once the order had more funds. As Godfrey arrived, one of the guards approached and grabbed Zaxos' reins from Godfrey.

"I'll take your horse, sir," the servant said.

"Thank you. Is the Grand Master here?" Godfrey asked.

"Yes, sir, but he is in his prayers right now. He should be finishing up soon though," the servant responded.

"Good. I will get something to eat and drink," Godfrey said.

"Very good, sir," the servant responded.

Godfrey dismounted and let the guard take him to the stables. He walked over to the barracks that were close by and went into the kitchen to get something to eat. Normally he would have been famished from eating rations and being on the road, putting up with the unforgiving sun. He wasn't though; because of the two vanishing he had somehow reached Jerusalem in a day. He wasn't angry about it; he had seen a lot in his day, but never anything like this. He wasn't going to tell anybody about what happened. No one would believe him anyway. If he did, he might be accused of witchcraft, or having too much mead. The Grand Master would realize that Godfrey was three days ahead of schedule for being here. *I'll just tell him I was already on my way to Jerusalem and was intercepted by the order carrier. That would work; nothing more would be said about it.*

After finishing up his food, Godfrey headed back to the command post to see if the Grand Master was ready for him. He was, and the squire told him to go ahead and enter. Godfrey walked into the small office and stood in front of the commander's desk. Standing at attention, he reported in.

"Good afternoon, sir, Sir Godfrey L'Enfant reporting as ordered."

The old knight looked grave. He was bald on top, with long white hair around his head. He had a white shaggy beard to go with the hair, and old, green eyes. He looked up at Godfrey and nodded his head.

"Hello, Sir Godfrey. I didn't expect you quite so early. Go ahead and have a seat," the Grand Master said.

"Thank you, sir," Godfrey said.

"How was the trip? How did you get here so quickly?" asked the Grand Master.

"The trip was good and uneventful, sir. I was on my way to Jerusalem and intercepted the order carrier," Godfrey said.

"I wanted to inform you that there is talk of another Muslim force raising banners," the Grand Master said.

"The Muslims are gathering men again?"

"Our spies tell us the Muslim forces are coming together politically, like we did with the Byzantines. The problem with that, I'm sure you know, is that we don't have enough men to sustain another attack," the Grand Master said.

"I know, sir; everyone except a few went home after the victory we achieved. Surely Europe and the pope haven't forgotten us, sir," Godfrey responded.

"I wouldn't bet on it; I'm sure that eventually there will be another crusade. If there is though, it will be after we are all dead and the Latin states are lost," the Grand Master said with a sad, but realistic tone.

"This is grave news indeed, sir," Godfrey said.

"Nothing is official yet, so don't spread anything around. I wanted to let you and the rest of the captains know, so you can prepare Acre for any surprise attacks," the Grand Master said.

"Yes, sir, of course," answered Godfrey.

"Godfrey, I would say take a day's rest here in Jerusalem, but you need to get back as soon as you can," the Grand Master said.

"Right sir, I will get back on the road immediately," said Godfrey.

"Make haste and may God be with you," the Grand Master said.

"Yes, sir," Godfrey responded.

With that, Godfrey stood and said good-bye to the Grand Master, and left to find Zaxos. Godfrey walked over to the stables and the servant went to get his horse. The servant went into the stables and brought Zaxos back out.

"Here he is, sir; he has been fed and watered," the servant said.

"Thank you," Godfrey said.

"Yes, sir," the servant said.

Godfrey patted Zaxos on his strong, thick neck and mounted the horse. He turned him around and rushed through the crowded streets of Jerusalem, heading with speed and haste back through the gates he came through. Zaxos' hooves pounded hard on the road, leaving a dusty trail behind them as they rushed out of the city.

"Heyahhhh! Ride fast, Zaxos, we have to get home," Godfrey exclaimed.

I guess we have another war brewing in these lands. I thought I was going to go home, but not now. I can't leave these guys behind. If I make it through this war, I'll go home then.

It was past midday and the sun would be going down in a couple of hours. Godfrey had already been travelling for a few hours. A chill was coming in the air; the hot sun was losing its strength in the land. The wind was not blowing too hard, and there wasn't anybody on the road for miles each way. Godfrey didn't feel right; there was an eerie feeling in his gut. This was a dangerous road, especially for just one person; Godfrey scolded himself for not bringing another knight with him. He pushed his worry aside, and started thinking of the events that had happened that day.

This has been the weirdest day in my life. It seems like everything is happening for a reason. There have been stories about men vanishing into thin air, especially around this area. I can't believe that happened to me—very strange indeed. Two days ago I didn't believe any of this was possible. I think I'll tell Mussef about it when I get back to Acre; I think it will interest him.

Godfrey was starting to nod off from the silence of the peaceful quiet desert, so he looked for a place to sleep. He noticed a spot located not far off of the road. It had a few trees for cover. He led Zaxos over to the area and tied his reins to one of the trees. The sun was just about down by now. Godfrey started a small fire and pulled out some wrapped bread he brought from Acre and ate some of it. After the small meal, he wrapped himself in his white cloak, leaned against the tree, and closed his eyes. Godfrey quickly crept into a deep sleep, and was soon dreaming.

He was dreaming of when he was a little boy when he nearly fell into the well. This time though, he did fall. Once he hit the cold, deep water, he started screaming for help. He looked up to the top of the well, and there was the most gruesome creature he had never seen staring at him. The creature had black, scabby-looking skin. It looked as if it had been burned in a fire. The creature's eyes were bright red. His head was round and fat; its ears were large and uneven. Godfrey could smell the brimstone on the creature.

"You're mine now, boy," the creature said.

His voice was low and deep. He closed the well and Godfrey's surroundings went dark. Godfrey was staying afloat in the water. Then something grabbed his foot and took him down into the well. There wasn't an end to the depth; he just kept going deeper and deeper and deeper.

"Ahhhhhhhhhh!" Godfrey screamed.

Godfrey woke up screaming. Sweat was pouring from his body, and his breathing was fast and rapid. Godfrey's chest was vibrating from his frantic heart. His sweat brought a chill on him from the cold desert night. He looked around and saw a crowd of men on camels staring at him. There looked to be about ten of them. He couldn't tell because his fire was just embers now, and his eyes were still adjusting to the night. The men were dressed in black—they looked like Saracens. Saracens were the sworn enemies of the Christian knights. They were brutal in their tactics, and had no mercy for their enemies. They were most likely a scouting party for a larger force. Godfrey knew what was going to happen. They were not going to allow him to live. Especially after seeing the red cross on his chest. The men stared at him, not moving or making a sound. Godfrey was sitting up against the tree. He had had his sword on his chest while he was sleeping, and he kept a dagger at his side. This was going to be a very interesting conflict for Godfrey. He knew he could take a few of them, but they weren't like common thieves. Saracens were trained killers. Godfrey took in a deep breath and leapt to his feet. Grabbing the handle of his sword, he took a defensive stance. Two of the ten men hopped off their camels and drew their swords as well. Their swords were curved in a rounded fashion. The only light that was shining was the full moon and bright stars above. Godfrey swung his sword in the air, warming up his arm and screaming.

"Come on you dogs! Do you honestly think you can take down a lion?"

One of the men charged, raising his sword in the air. The man brought the sword down with deadly force. Godfrey brought his sword up, connecting with the other one. The two parried back and forth, blocking each other's blows; the men in the background encouraged their comrade to finish off Godfrey. The Saracen took the bait and swung his sword hard and with all his might at Godfrey's head. Godfrey out of muscle memory ducked the blow and twisted himself around, bringing his sword to the man's leg. Godfrey's sword went through the man's leg with ease. The man screamed and fell over and grabbed his freshly made nub. Godfrey came out of his spinning move and turning around, and aimed at the man's chest. Godfrey's eyes met with the fallen man's eyes as he rammed the sword through his heart. Godfrey put his boot on the man's chest and forced the sword back out. He stood back with fresh blood dripping from his sword, and took another defensive stance. On the ground, the fallen man was still gurgling and groaning from his wounds.

Another Saracen looked up from his fallen friend and charged at Godfrey. He was swinging his sword violently and full of emotion. Godfrey parried the blows, backing up at the same time. Godfrey felt the tree he had been sleeping against hit his back. He lowered his guard so the Saracen would go in for the kill. Like clockwork the Saracen went in for a stabbing kill to Godfrey's chest. As the sword came closer, Godfrey jumped out of the way, causing the sword to dig into the tree. The Saracen, realizing his mistake, tried vehemently to pull it back out. Godfrey raised his sword up and brought down on the man's arms. The sword went through both of them right above the elbows. The man screamed and backed up with his arms swinging, blood pouring out each end. Godfrey charged with his sword, puncturing the man's throat. It went all the way through, coming out of the back of his neck. Godfrey pulled it out as the man fell forward on his knees and then on his face to the ground. Breathing hard, Godfrey looked up to see who was next. No one was getting down; they all had arrows pointing at him.

"Enough," one of the men said on the camel.

When the leader said that, bow strings were released, sending arrows directly into Godfrey's pathway. Before Godfrey could think, seven arrows entered his body, all hitting him in the groin and chest area. Godfrey stumbled back from the impact. For one last effort, Godfrey picked up his sword like a spear and threw at the closet Saracen to him. The unlucky Saracen tried to get out of the way and block the sword with his arm, but the gleaming weapon lodged itself into his left shoulder. The man's camel kicked him off. Godfrey dropped to his knees because his body was going into shock. From behind one of the Saracens got off his camel and kicked Godfrey hard in the back making him fall forward on the arrows. The arrows went further into Godfrey's body before snapping from the dead weight. Godfrey rolled to his side from the pain the fall had caused. The one who kicked him in the back came over and tied his hands behind him. He forced Godfrey to his knees. Godfrey's life was slipping away slowly; his eyesight was getting more blurry every second. Godfrey felt himself wanting to leave his body. He saw their leader walking toward him.

"You were in the wrong place tonight, crusader," the leader said.

"Go ahead and get it over with you pig-eating dog," Godfrey said.

Godfrey heard the man behind him unsheathe his sword. The leader made a gesture with his hand. Godfrey closed his eyes and waited. The man raised the blade and came down on the side of Godfrey's neck. Just for an instant, he felt the sharp, forceful pain as the blade forced itself through Godfrey's flesh. Then it all went black. Godfrey's headless body fell forward; blood was squirting out of his neck. His severed head rolled over near the leader's foot; Godfrey's mouth twitched a bit. The men, before leaving searched Godfrey's things for anything worth taking. They grabbed Zaxos and headed into the dark desert night. Godfrey woke up, but when he stood up, his body stayed on the ground. Godfrey examined the bloody scene. He looked at his hands and they were transparent. He still had sensations, as if he had a body.

I must be dead.

As Godfrey finished the thought, a hidden force grabbed him and threw him into the air. Godfrey tried to fight the force, but it was useless. He looked down to the earth and saw the distant landscape. He saw giant wind tunnels that looked like tornadoes stretched across the surface of the earth. He floated above the quiet, serene planet. Then one of the tunnels started sucking him toward it with an extreme amount of force.

Godfrey was pulled into the violent tunnel; once in, he descended into the earth. Godfrey looked around terrified and realized that it wasn't just him, but there were other people being pulled in too. Everyone was screaming, and trying to get of the tunnels. Godfrey noticed that there were demonic creatures chained to the walls of the tunnels. They were every shape and size—some were black, some were brown, some scaly, some hairy with large horns, some with small horns, and all seemed to have an abundance of sharp teeth. They were wicked in appearance and in speech. They were screaming and cursing and laughing at everyone as they fell deeper and deeper. The farther Godfrey went the less light he could see. The darkness was thick like a witches' night. It was getting really dark, and the air was too hot to breathe. Godfrey kept falling and finally couldn't see anything anymore. *Oh God, please help me.*

Chapter 4: Hell

Godfrey woke up, the ground pounding like he was resting on top of a drum. *Boomba! Boomba! Boom! Boom! Boom!* The harsh ground moved to the beat, causing all of the new souls that had arrived into hell to bounce up and down. Godfrey watched as giant demons with huge bones ran around hitting the ground; they swatted the poor souls that had just arrived like careless flies. Godfrey watched his unlucky neighbor get crushed like a baby bird in a dog's mouth. The soul's smeared remains stuck to the bone and made a squishy sound when the oversized demon pulled his weapon up, laughing hysterically. Godfrey looked around and at himself. His body was a pale gray flesh. It was dead. He didn't have any clothes on; he was completely naked. There were worms crawling out of his skin. He stood up, but barely, because he had little strength to do so. It was dark and hot. He was sweating the stench of a corpse, and was beyond thirst. There were screams of pain and agony everywhere. He looked ahead of him and saw a massive gargoyle head. It was larger than any mountain he had ever seen on earth. The face was alive and breathing; every time that it inhaled more people fell from above. Godfrey could barely see them, but he heard them fall. The people were scared, and so was Godfrey.

The only light was from the huge fires in the distance. Godfrey looked down at the dirt that was below him and could see the dry, cracked, lifeless surface. It looked like a desert that had been in drought for hundreds of years. There were worms, spiders, snakes, scorpions, and ants, both large and small, crawling around and attacking and biting the helpless souls that had arrived. The smell was horrible—it was like a mix of blood, rot, and sewage all in one. It reminded Godfrey of a battlefield full of dead warriors after a week of being in the sun.

Where am I? Is this the end? Oh my God, what have I done to be here?

Godfrey was pulled to the ground by an invisible force; he couldn't move. A large black figure walked up to him, carrying a chain. There were spikes and razors all over it. The figure had red eyes and large bat-like wings. About ten feet tall, his skin was a mix of hair and scales. Evil emanated from the creature. Suddenly it started kicking Godfrey hard on his sides repeatedly. Godfrey cried in pain as he heard his ribs breaking. The creature picked Godfrey up with ease. It put a shackle around Godfrey's neck; he felt the spikes and razors tearing at his neck. Then the creature tied Godfrey's hands behind his back with some type of sharp razor wire. Godfrey's flesh was ripping and tearing, but no blood came out of his body. Godfrey was weakened by the immense pain and powerless to do anything. Godfrey's life was at the mercy of this terrible creature. After binding Godfrey, the creature looked at him with his evil, dead eyes and said, "Welcome to hell; enjoy your stay. We supply all the modern comforts of life here. If there are complaints about your stay, then do tell the one in charge. She loves a good laugh."

With that the creature kicked Godfrey in the stomach. Godfrey flew through the air. Before hitting the wall, the demon pulled the chain connected to his neck and slung Godfrey hard through the air into a jagged black rock. It felt like his spine broke. The pain was throbbing. Death would not relieve him of this torture.

The demon started dragging Godfrey on the hot ground by his neck with the chain. Godfrey's face was scratching against the rough ground. The large insects kept jumping on him, trying to enter his mouth.

"Come, my dear guest; there is someone you need to meet," the demon said.

Godfrey wanted to die, but couldn't. He looked around as he was being pulled around like a feather blowing in the wind. He could hear the nonstop screams of thousands and thousands of people all around him. He could feel the harsh heat and the continual pounding from the distant drums of his surroundings. His neck was killing him; he couldn't breathe at all. The demon was purposely pulling hard to choke Godfrey. The razors and spikes were embedded into his throat, slicing, cutting, tearing his ragged flesh.

No one could survive this and live; they would be dead instantly. I have to get of this place. This is hell. It is real—my parents, the priests, they were not lying. Oh God, Jesus, save me from my torments.

The two were climbing up a round spiral of stairs. Godfrey felt the stairs hitting him on his face and back as he twisted around. The demon was ruthless; he had no mercy while pulling Godfrey. Godfrey tried to stay on his back as much as possible, because that position gave him the least amount of pain. He looked up and saw nothing but darkness—a darkness that was so dark, it was alive. It appeared to be breathing and looking back at Godfrey with a satisfied stare. There were dragons and large vultures flying around, breathing fire and acid onto the victims below. Godfrey watched as the vultures flew over to people chained to a wall of brimstone and ripped their insides out as the people screamed in agony and begged for them to stop.

All of a sudden as Godfrey and the demon went further up the stairs, the ground started shaking violently like a volcano about to erupt. The demon started screaming in adoration, waiting to see what was going to happen. Fire engulfed the entire place, as far as the eye could see; it literally came out of nowhere. Godfrey's entire body was covered with flames. His flesh melted away to nothing but a burnt skeleton and a misty gray soul inside of what was left. Godfrey tried to scream, but a large albino snake came crawling out of his mouth, choking him. After the fire stopped, he noticed his lifeless flesh came back. It was like watching a body decay in reverse.

"You got to love the baptism of fire! Did it feel good? Ha ha ha ha," the demon exclaimed while stomping Godfrey on the side of his head.

But even in all the pain, loneliness, hatred, and the terrible place he was, Godfrey could still remember looking at the sunset on warm summer nights at home. He could remember playing with his sisters and brother as a child. He remembered his first kiss behind his cottage in France. The love that he had for his family, brothers-in-arms, and his country were all still too real. Godfrey wanted nothing more than to tell everyone to stay away from this wretched place.

The demon stopped and Godfrey forced his eyes open to look and see why they did. The demon jerked him up with a rapid force. They were at a high and towering palace. The walls were made out of brimstone. There was lightning and thunder continually raging in the background. Light came from the windows of the palace. He could tell hell was very large, but he couldn't tell exactly how large because of the way the darkness ate the light. There were hordes of unhappy souls chained together, building onto the massive structure. There were thousands of slaves working around the clock, on the ever-growing palace. They were never given rest nor water, but had to look forward to torture and terror. Demons were slapping them on their backs with whips to make them work faster. Little demons were throwing balls of lava at the slave's feet to make them move faster.

As Godfrey and the demon approached the palace, large black doors in the front opened slowly, making a long echoing sound. There were stairs two stories high that led to the opening. The demon forced Godfrey to stand up and walk into the palace. Inside it was surprisingly beautiful; it almost looked heavenly. Giant pillars of gold reached the high ceilings. Paintings of mythical creatures and landscapes were hanging on the walls. The walls were made out of pearl, which glowed majestically. A long red velvet carpet spread all the way to a throne ahead. The throne was very large and mystical. Demanding all the attention of the vast room, it was in the shape of a large serpent's mouth, and made out of bones and skulls.

A woman was sitting in the middle of the mouth of the serpent chair. She was the most beautiful woman Godfrey had ever seen. They walked closer so that Godfrey was only about ten feet from her. She sat on the throne with her back straight and her long legs crossed. She had black, silky long hair that went down her back. Her body was perfect—slender, long, and toned with dark olive skin. On her head was a golden crown adorned with many different jewels, but in the shape of a crown of thorns. Her eyes were green with black slits like a snake. She was almost naked, and had golden scales covering her breasts, back, and neck. She had a red cloth that gently covered her waist. There were little green imps around her throne, kissing her hands, face, and feet constantly. She was enchanting and could easily entice any man who came near her. Her fingers, neck, and ankles were covered in shiny gold jewelry adorned with precious stones. Her nails were black, long, pointy, and curved like animal claws.

Behind the throne, there was a large wall full of prison cells sitting out like bricks. Each one was filled with suffering souls. They all stood up like a cord of wood and were forced to continually worship the ancient woman. Her chest would rise up as if filled with power each time they praised her unholy name.

"Lilith, our holy queen. Lilith, our beautiful queen. Lilith, our loving goddess," the souls said repeatedly.

Green imps with wings were flying around the cells, stabbing anyone with a spear who wasn't participating in the chant and screaming. "Say it like you mean it!"

"I am Lilith, the queen of hell. Bow and worship your goddess, human," Lilith demanded.

Godfrey stood and looked around at the worshiping imps and the beautiful interior of the palace. The low agonizing chanting in the background bothered him deeply. Out of all of that had happened to Godfrey so far, he realized that he still had the right to choose to worship her.

How could such a lovely place exist here?

"No. I will not worship you, you foul creature of the darkness. You are nothing but a fallen disgrace of the Creator. Don't you think you have enough people worshiping already?" said Godfrey defiantly.

The demon beside him pulled the chain and slung Godfrey against the hard marble walls. His head hit first; he felt his skull crack open, making a crunching sound. Godfrey fell to the ground; he could see his gruesome reflection in the diamond floors. The chain pulled again, but with even more force this time. He went up and came down, smashing his back against the carpet. Godfrey hurt very badly, and still couldn't breathe. The queen stood up and walked over to look down at Godfrey. She placed her foot on the side of his face, pushing it hard against the carpet. His necked was stretched so far that he felt like the tendons were almost popping.

"So we have a fighter, huh? We have ways of dealing with hard-headed people like you, Godfrey. You will have extra special attention here in hell, your new home. Everyone will know your name here. Take him to his cell; let him get used to his new home," the queen said.

Lilith pushed Godfrey's face hard with her foot and kicked him; her sharp talons dug into his cheek. She sat back down on her throne and the imps continued to take special care of her. The slaves in the background never skipped a beat with their worshiping. Godfrey spun around on the carpet as he was being dragged again by his neck, while he watched the queen as she waved with an evil smile on her face.

Godfrey noticed that they were not returning the same way they had come, but were going down another spiral of stairs. Godfrey's body caught every step going down. He had so much momentum that he fell off the side of the ledge. He sat there dangling and choking. The demon didn't bother with him; he just let him hang. Godfrey, struggling to breathe, looked down and saw people in a long row being impaled by long metal stakes that came from the cracked, dry ground. There was a group of demons watching with pure enjoyment. Eventually with Godfrey blacking in and out, they finally arrived at his cell. The bars were made out of brimstone, like everything else. The cells were chiseled into the rocky, brimstone walls. Godfrey looked around and saw prison cells with screaming people everywhere; they went on forever as far as the eye could see.

The demon opened the cell and took the shackles off Godfrey's neck and ripped the razor wire off his hands. He pulled them off mercilessly, ripping and tearing the flesh Godfrey had left. The demon grabbed him by the neck and picked him up into the air. When the demon's flesh touched him, it burned like hot metal.

"You will worship our king and queen, because you, whether you like it or not, are their subject. You can thank your precious God for that," the demon said squeezing Godfrey's neck.

He threw him into the cell and slammed the door. Godfrey met the stone walls with a harsh impact. Godfrey fell down, lifeless, with no hope in sight. He could feel creatures crawling in and out of him. Rats as large as stray cats were inside the cell with him. They bit him, tearing and feeding off his flesh.

Oh God, does it ever stop? Please, just let this stop. I just want to go to sleep and die.

Godfrey lay in a corner of his cell; he was hot, naked, alone, with every pain imaginable reminding him that it was still there. He tried to sleep, but the fear was so great and constant that he could not. He was thirsty and hungry, but he knew that he wouldn't be eating or drinking anymore. Hell was never quiet; the screaming was continual, and the drumming never skipped a beat. *Boomba! Boomba! Boom! Boom! Boom!*

The smell was the worst. The stench rested inside of your nostrils, never leaving. Godfrey was so scared, the pain was always there, but death was not. No matter how harsh the torture was, he could not leave his body like when he was on the surface of earth.

God, I am so sorry for not believing in You. I was a fool; I was stupid and ignorant. Please, oh please, help me out of here.

Chapter 5: Reflection

Godfrey was sitting in his cell trying his best to deal with the everlasting pain. He could still feel the effect of time down in hell. The demons were always sure to remind Godfrey how long he was there. Godfrey sat rotting in his cell for what seemed like years, because in eternity there is plenty of time. Godfrey noticed that every time whenever the lake of fire raged through hell, he would get another brand-new body for the demons to try to destroy. He tried talking to others, but they couldn't. Godfrey watched one of his neighbors eat the flesh off his own fingers and begin scratching pictures into the brimstone with the bone. Everyone was trapped inside their own world of torment. Godfrey tried a couple of times to look out of the cell to see what was going on; but every time he tried, an imp was there to stab him with a spear to push him back.

The demons came in different degrees and sizes. It mostly depended on what their specialty of torture was. The large ones that had wings were the ones in charge of all the other smaller creatures of hell, such as imps, snakes, worms, scorpions, spiders, and other contorted demons. The large demons with wings received their orders from Lilith the queen. She ran hell from her large, wicked palace. Satan was not always there, because he was busy tricking mankind to come here. There was such a vast number of fallen creatures that Godfrey couldn't understand how it all ran and what everybody's jobs were.

Hell ran like an efficient machine, never stopping for anything. It kept going constantly, like a methodically wound clock. It was always expanding to make more room for souls. Godfrey did learn one thing coming here—it was that God the Creator was real, and that these demons took their anger out on mankind because of His love for man. They cursed and blasphemed the name of Jesus on a regular basis. Godfrey prayed to Jesus constantly; nothing ever happened, but it felt a little better doing it. Godfrey held out a sliver of hope that someone heard his prayers.

Godfrey sat alone in the darkened cell, his ears pierced by the nonstop assortment of screams, laughter, and drums. His memories were flooded with what his life was like on earth. He couldn't get them out of his mind; the memories were just another form of torture—probably the worst. Suddenly three dark gray, hairy imps appeared beside him. They laughed with a horrid anticipation of what they were going to do him. They grabbed Godfrey by his arms, dragged him to the bars and tied his hands to them. He was standing up, arms spread, and chest against the cell. The imps started ripping his back open with their little claws. They were eating his insides from his back slowly and carefully to make sure it was going to hurt. Godfrey's legs were shaking, and his bloodless veins bulged out. Every time he tried to scream some kind of insect or reptile would clog up his throat so he couldn't. Every time they crawled out, another one would be coming up.

Godfrey could feel one of the evil little creature's hands coming through his chest from the other side. It brought its hand up to Godfrey's face and pushed in his eyes with a terrible force. They were so strong; they had the strength of a hundred men easily. The bigger the demons the more powerful they became. The more they hurt men, the more powerful they became. They all worshiped Satan and his queen with great adoration and piety. Satan was their god. After the imps had their fun with Godfrey, they disappeared, leaving him tied to the bars almost fleshless. Another blue flying imp came by and started stabbing Godfrey in his throat, eye sockets, chest, and groin area repeatedly. Godfrey could do nothing but take it. His mind wouldn't go crazy; it just stayed on the brink of it constantly. The pain was all too real, as usual. He had to stay awake, even though he was beyond the worst exhaustion. Sleep was not possible. Every second of every day, a massive presence of fear and loneliness pervaded the atmosphere. He could not get used to it; hell was a brand-new experience every minute. Hell was such an unimaginable horror that mere words could not describe it. There weren't words evil or dark enough to describe the beast of Hell.

Godfrey stood there with the imp stabbing, cutting, ripping, and stabbing some more of his lifeless body. When a large brown, hairy demon with green, reptilian wings walked up and smacked the imp with his long, skinny arm, the imp flew away, laughing and moving on to the next cell. The demon's face was long and narrow. Its head looked liked a demonic version of a stork. His eyes were sunken into his small head. When he spoke, it sounded like a slithering snake, whipping out its tongue to smell something.

"We have some fun planned for you, Godfrey. I promise it will be memorable. The queen herself might even show up to grace you with her fallen presence," the demon said.

The demon opened up the cell door and pulled Godfrey down from his bondage. Godfrey could barely move. He had just enough strength to do what the demon told him to do. It grabbed Godfrey by his wrists and wrapped razor wire around them behind his back. Godfrey's cell was very high up; it was a mile or so above the main torture area at the center of the massive prison at the bottom of the spiraling stairs. The demon snatched Godfrey by his hair and raised him into the air. He walked over to the steep ledge, holding Godfrey over it.

"I was wondering, Godfrey; can humans fly? I don't think they can, but let's see anyway," the demon said sarcastically.

"Please…no, no, please don't drop me!" Godfrey begged.

The demon released him like he was a pebble or coin being tossed into a well. In hell, the very ground, dirt, and stone itself is alive, and an active part of the whole. It will try to torture any tenant of hell if it is at all possible. It will lash out at a prisoner at random moments, surprising its victims. This increases the fear—not knowing when something bad will happen. As Godfrey was freefalling and spinning around helplessly, one of the ledges manifested a large metal hook to catch him. The sharp edge of the hook caught Godfrey's stomach and slid in nicely because of the force of his fall. Godfrey was upside down. The jagged hook was all the way through his stomach. He hung there, dangling. Drool and worms poured out of his mouth, falling to the bottom. Godfrey couldn't pick up his head to look at the horrific scene. He felt the hook inside of him. It burned immensely. Godfrey's bound hands were hanging back parallel to his head because he couldn't hold them up. The demon who dropped him was hollering something to him, but Godfrey couldn't hear him because of all the other loud sounds. The large demon jumped off the ledge and grabbed Godfrey's bound hands as he came barreling down. Godfrey's arms were definitely out of their sockets now. The only thing holding the two up was Godfrey's lower body. The pressure was so intense on Godfrey's lower half that he prayed he would fall apart to take the pain away.

Godfrey's lower half eventually gave because the demon was pulling and jumping up and down to cause it to rip. Godfrey screamed as loud as he could; he didn't care about the worms coming out of his mouth. They fell from the hook, moving very fast, hurling toward the ground. Godfrey looked at the ground and saw that there were jagged spikes with smaller spikes on them to catch his fall. The demon started flapping his wings and caught Godfrey in midair. They stopped abruptly. Godfrey looked hopeless; he had little or no gray flesh left on his body. His back was torn open and a large rugged tear went from his stomach through to his groin. He looked at his body, wanting cry it all away, but knowing he couldn't. His arms hurt badly from the ungodly amount of stress they had been through.

Godfrey raised his head to the demon and said, "The only power you have is what is allotted to you from your fallen coward king, Satan. You are nothing but a tool at his disposal."

The demon became furious; that was blasphemy to talk about Satan that way. He spun Godfrey around in a circle a few times and threw him to the spikes. Godfrey hit them hard. His left leg caught one in the thigh at an angle. The right side of his chest caught another high into his armpit. He felt it coming through his shredded back. Another was smashed against the right side his face. The smaller spikes were caught in the side of his temple and cheek. Godfrey could feel each and every one of the spikes in him. He could also feel every bit of pain that he went through since he arrived here. The demon landed lightly near the spikes.

"That must hurt; I bet you wished you were not in that jam, huh? Poor Godfrey, bless your tender little heart," the demon said sarcastically.

He walked away, laughing at the atrocious torment he had executed on helpless Godfrey. Godfrey lay there, pinned to the spikes; he could feel the ground starting to shake. He knew what that meant—the unquenchable, ferocious living fire was coming. He could do nothing but prepare for the worst.

"Pull him off those spikes," someone said off in the distance.

Godfrey could recognize the voice; it was the queen. Godfrey was ripped off the spikes and thrown to the ground. He lay on his back as the fire consumed him.

"Ahhhhhhhhhhhhhh! Ahhhhhhhhhhhhhhhhh! Stop! Please stop it, it hurts so bad! I can't stand it anymore! Please just stop it!" Godfrey and every prisoner of hell screamed at the top of their lungs.

Godfrey shook violently and convulsed like he was having the mother of all seizures. The demons laughed hysterically at everyone's endless torment. Godfrey knew that he had a new body now. Lilith would enjoy destroying it again. His hands still bound, he turned over on his side to see who was near him. He looked and saw the queen standing there close to him, waving. She was wearing something different now. She had a thin see-through black cloth wrapped tightly around her body. It showed her flawless curves. Her jet black hair was tied in a bun with bones holding it in place. She had long black boots on. They had spikes on the toes, and razor sharp spurs on the back, most likely used for kicking insubordinate imps and human slaves. Around her neck was an ancient looking necklace that had an Egyptian style. It was gold with small hieroglyphic symbols on it. The shape of the necklace was a bird with its wings wrapped around her neck. She was very tall—at least eight feet or so.

The queen looked at Godfrey with prideful eyes. The slits narrowed as she focused on him. His body rose from the ground as if he did it by himself. He was floating in front of the queen. Godfrey could not look away from her; she was absolutely beautiful. She was perfect looking in every respect. His eyes were locked with hers. Standing around were her personal imps and large demon bodyguards at attention, waiting for her to give a command. Around them was darkness, except the lightning in the distance and the leftover embers from the fire.

"Godfrey, my dear, you have been here for nearly five hundred years now. A lot has happened on earth since your unfortunate passing. Yet still you refuse to worship me as your sovereign goddess. I am second in command in this kingdom, and it is your duty to please your goddess. This is your home now; you are not going anywhere else. This is it; judgment has been passed," Lilith said.

Her eyes were blank and satisfied with the way she was and what she had said. She stood confidently with one hand on her curved hip and the other holding a black scepter, shaped like a dragon standing straight up. It was the scepter of hell. Godfrey could feel the worms and other creatures moving around in his body. If they could not get out through the mouth, they would eat their way through the skin.

Even if I do worship her, she will just increase my punishments for the sake of it. If I have lasted this long without willingly worshiping her, I should go for another five hundred years. Godfrey's mind had been made up; he would deny the lovely cursed queen again.

"Well...Lilith, queen of hell, lawful sovereign of hell and its subjects, goddess of demons, I, Sir Godfrey L'Enfant of the Knights Templar, renounce any claim you have on my soul. May you burn like the rest of us in the end."

The queen didn't become enraged; at least she didn't show it. She just smiled nonchalantly and caused Godfrey to fall to his knees. She kicked Godfrey right in his jugular. Her boot went all the way in. She twisted it around to catch anything possible to cause more pain. She pulled the boot out. Godfrey sat there, agonizing from the severe hole in his throat. He couldn't move because of the invisible force. The queen looked at him; she was pleased by the pain she had caused.

"Godfrey, I have another punishment for you. You will be banished to the pit to feel the constant burning of the lake of fire from now on and until eternity's eternity. Take him to his final home; Judas Iscariot will keep him company," the queen said.

A demon shackled Godfrey around the neck and tossed him all the way across hell, and then took him down to the lowest pit, the one that is reserved for Satan, his son, and his prophet when the time comes.

Chapter 6: Saved

Godfrey was in a large, very deep pit in the shape of a cone that was pointed down and etched into the stone floor. The walls were the hottest brimstone in hell. The fire burned forever; it never stopped, not even once. Godfrey had a massive chain connected to his neck that was strapped to the bottom of the pit. His hands were bound and so were his feet. He was nothing but a black skeleton with his misty gray soul trapped inside. Whenever he screamed, the fire travelled down his throat and burned all his insides. The fire was everywhere; it was impossible to escape. The flames came out of Godfrey's eye sockets, nasal canals, ear holes, and mouth, blazing like a jet engine. Even his thoughts burned when they were born in his mind. Pain, fear, loneliness, and lack of hope consumed Godfrey. He was officially a dead man. He was lost to the world, lost to mankind, lost to heaven, and lost to hell. Even the demons wouldn't descend this low into hell to torment the prisoners because the fire was so hot. If they did, they would risk being consumed themselves. Godfrey had successfully made his way to the worst spot in hell.

Godfrey was down there a few hundred more years with no change in anything. He was in the same pit, burning endlessly by the same intense flame. Inside the pit with him were hundreds of other people from different generations—Jezebel, Judas, Nero, Antiochus Epiphanes, Haman, a few of the popes, and plenty of others—all chained to the middle of the pit, burning to a crisp together. They all looked like Godfrey, frozen by the intense burning flames, sitting lifeless in a roasted skeleton with their tormented souls residing in it.

When suddenly the fire stopped burning Godfrey, all the pain and sorrow he had acquired through the centuries was gone. It was completely gone. His gray flesh had returned, but his body still looked dead. The chains fell off of him and he was raised out of the pit by an invisible force. For the rest of the souls down there, the fire didn't stop; they continued to burn. When Godfrey reached the top, he saw Queen Lilith and her cohorts standing with a majestic being who had six brown, feathered wings. He was taller than Lilith by at least a foot. He was wearing a bright white cloak, with a silver breastplate covering his chest. His hands were covered with silver gauntlets. He had a chiseled face with thick reddish hair. His feet were like shiny bronze. He had a document in his hand and was reading it to Lilith. She was wearing a thick black cloak, covering her entire body except her hands. Godfrey was set down gently by the invisible force that picked him up. He didn't feel the pain anymore; he could think clearly again. He had a sound mind. Godfrey walked up to the crowd.

"Hello, Godfrey, my name is Jazrael. I believe we have met before."

Godfrey remembered Jazrael very clearly and thought, *this guy seems to be everywhere.*

"Yes…yes we have. What is going on here anyway?" Godfrey asked.

"A whole lot of hypocrisy, that's what, you conniving little worm!" the queen screamed in rage.

Godfrey shifted back from shock. He never saw Lilith so angry. He noticed that she wasn't in her usual beautiful form either. He saw that her skin was a deep green, and it was full of scales like a snake. She couldn't hold a counterfeit form around someone as holy as Jazrael.

"Lilith, fallen human, disgrace to mankind, it is all legal. There is one catch though, a minor detail that has to be dealt with," said Jazrael.

Godfrey's soul lit up with an unspeakable amount of joy. He realized he had a chance out of hell. Finally, the torture would be over the pain would cease for him. Godfrey was so ready he imagined himself flying out of hell on his own.

"What is the minor detail?" Lilith asked.

"Godfrey has to accept my invitation freely, by his own choice," said Jazrael.

"Well, ask him; he has already been out of his pit too long. Hurry up! I have damnation to run!" Lilith exclaimed.

"Okay. Godfrey, the Father has sent me to you to offer you a deal," said Jazrael.

"What is the deal?" Godfrey asked impatiently.

"The Lord will release you from your eternal torment if you will fulfill a certain task for Him. I do not know the task, because I am but a messenger. You will have to travel with me to the highest heavens and speak to Him. Do you accept the call to a higher calling, friend?" Jazrael said.

"Absolutely, where do I sign? I'll even kill that witch over there if He needs me to," Godfrey said.

"I like your courage, but Godfrey, it's too late; she is already dead," Jazrael answered.

Lilith slung back her black hood and revealed her giant snakelike head. She tried to attack Godfrey but couldn't; he was out of her jurisdiction now. Godfrey felt relieved because she was definitely a scary sight to see. Her eyes were completely black, and bulging out of her skull. Her mouth was open wide, and hissing like a taunted cobra. She had fangs that were at least three inches long. How she desired to pierce Godfrey's little neck. Instead she turned around and grabbed one of her imps by its head. She tossed the creature into the pit that Godfrey had just left. The poor creature screamed in agony, but his cries were quickly drowned out when the roaring flames overtook him.

"All right, so you accept; that is good. I couldn't really see you not accepting this offer. Godfrey, let's get out of here; we have some travelling to do," Jazrael said.

Godfrey waved sarcastically to Lilith just as she had to him when he had arrived in hell. She looked at him with hatred, but she knew God could do anything He wanted, especially when it came to His beloved men. Lilith and her demons vanished into midair and were out of sight. Jazrael looked up into the darkness above, and a thin white light appeared and shone through the pitch black. The hole of light gradually grew larger. When the light hit Godfrey, his countenance was instantly changed. His body transformed into a perfect version of his body from earth. A bright white cloak wrapped around him and brown boots appeared on his feet. Godfrey felt so happy; he could not believe this was happening. Jazrael touched Godfrey's shoulder and they shot through the bright portal.

Chapter 7: Earth

Godfrey and Jazrael were traveling through a bright, white, illuminating tunnel. Wind was blowing all around them. Godfrey noticed stars, planets, and colorful gases that saturated the outside of the portal they were going through, but they were nothing compared to the intensely warm white to which they were heading.

"This is the way angels travel to hell. When men die, they go through one of the many other portals to hell. There are many of them, too many. It's a shame, you know; hell wasn't created for mankind. It was made as a prison for Satan and his fallen cohorts. Many of those cohorts were my friends, and it kills me to see what they have chosen," Jazrael said.

"You know, I do not know what to think right now; this is all hitting me like a ton of bricks. I am telling you now, Jazrael, thank you so much for getting me out of there. I thought that was it; I didn't think I would ever escape that place. Nothing in life, not the most descriptive words I know can show what that horrid place is like," Godfrey answered.

"Do not thank me, Godfrey; it was our Father who chose you and saved you from that. Thank the Almighty Creator for His tender mercies; He is very kind hearted, you know. It hurts Him, seeing His children, that is, mankind, doing what they do on the face of the earth," Jazrael said.

"I am a fool, Jazrael; I spent my whole life raising my fists at God. I didn't believe in Him; I hated Him. It was terrible. Now everything has changed. Experiencing what I did down there has opened my eyes as wide as they could possibly be. All I want to do is tell my family, friends, and fellow men to turn to this God who has made everything with just speaking it into existence," Godfrey said.

"You sound like a genuine preacher, Godfrey. No one knows why God does what He does. We, the angels, only know so much; we are just servants. I do know this; I would do everything in my power to please our Father," Jazrael said.

"You angels are very beautiful creatures; I have never seen anything so bright and perfect," Godfrey said.

"Thank you, Godfrey; we are direct creations of God. We are His servants and warriors. We were created out of light. Our main job, though, is to protect man, and report to the Father," Jazrael said.

"How come you have always dealt with me? It seems you're the one getting me out of all my monolithic conundrums." Godfrey asked.

"I am your guardian angel; the day you were conceived, I was assigned to you. Since you had such an important purpose, I had to make sure you stayed out of trouble. I am sure you remember the well incident," Jazrael said.

"I knew that was you; by the way, thanks for that," Godfrey said.

"I was just doing my job. We angels can only interfere with man's business so much. Unless the Father allows it," Jazrael said.

Everything has changed now on the earth; it is not the same world you left when you were murdered. Do not worry. I will show you many things on our way to heaven," Jazrael said.

Godfrey and Jazrael came out of the tunnel and were floating high above the earth. Godfrey looked around in amazement. The stars were shining bright through the pitch black of space. Godfrey could see the sun, round and bright orange lighting up the surface of the earth. Godfrey saw the earth in its peaceful majesty. It was a giant ball just floating on nothing. He could see the vast blue oceans and the green and brown land. White clouds were easing around just above the earth.

Godfrey saw the moon was a ball too; he always thought it was the size of the sun. He now realized it wasn't; it was much smaller than the earth.

"I always thought that the earth was flat," Godfrey said.

"It was the knowledge and understanding that man had at the time," Jazrael answered.

"If anyone had a chance to see all of this, they would have a totally different perspective about God and life," Godfrey said.

"That's why you get the privilege, Godfrey; you have questions and they will be answered. Believe me when I tell you this, you have not seen anything yet, friend," Jazrael said.

"I believe you, Jazrael, and I am kind of scared to see it," Godfrey answered.

"Now you are starting to understand a little more about our Father," Jazrael said.

Godfrey could also see other angels flying very fast from the earth, going upward and eventually disappearing. He could also see evil-looking spirits similar to the ones in hell, floating above the Earth. They were laughing with a sinister sound and pointing at Godfrey. They somehow knew who he was. Godfrey wasn't scared; he felt protected with the awesome presence of Jazrael near him.

"Godfrey, I want to show you some things on earth; we will travel as fast as a thought." With that they vanished and reappeared outside of a city.

The city looked vaguely familiar. It was night and the wind was blowing. *This has to be Jerusalem.* It was much different than what he remembered; the walls protecting the city were gone. The roads around it weren't dirt anymore. They were a black hard substance with yellow lines in the middle of them.

"I believe we are in Jerusalem," Godfrey said.

"Yes, we are, but it looks much different then what you would remember," Jazrael said.

"It does; who controls it now, the Muslims or the Christians?" Godfrey asked.

"Neither," answered Jazrael.

"Neither? Who else would want it? It looks very prosperous, and I don't see any armies camped out beside it," Godfrey said.

"It belongs to the ones God gave it to—the offspring of Abraham," Jazrael said.

"The Jews? They weren't even allowed to own land in my day. If they control the city, then why is there a mosque in the heart of it?" Godfrey asked.

"Godfrey, the times are much different than what you remember. A lot has happened; a thousand years have passed here on earth while you were in hell," Jazrael said.

Godfrey sat there, astonished. Godfrey realized that time kept moving when he was in hell, and it continued moving despite what man wanted. If a thousand years had passed, then that meant that all his family and friends were all dead. He hoped they had not received the same fate that he did. No one should go through all the burning and torment that was down there.

"Godfrey, Israel is a nation now. It is sovereign, and is controlled by Abraham's decedents. It will stay like that from now on. God loves these people; they are the apple of His eye. They have a special destiny just like you with God. My general, Michael, is the one who protects them," Jazrael said.

"I never thought that Israel would be a nation again. I only heard stories about Israel from the Scriptures; this is truly amazing. We men really do not know anything, do we?" Godfrey asked.

"No, you're wrong. The Father has revealed everything that must happen on earth. It is His righteous son, the Christ, who has given man an opportunity to be sons of God. Only through Him can you understand the mysteries of God," Jazrael said.

"I don't know what to say. It is inconceivable to me that such a Creator would care about an insignificant soul like me, or the rest of mankind for that matter," Godfrey said.

"You will understand in due time, Godfrey; God will open your eyes to see what He has in store for you," Jazrael answered.

They stood a little longer and then vanished again. They reappeared near a massive crowd of dark-skinned people. Godfrey recognized them; they were Africans. They were singing and yelling and dancing. Joy and happiness was thriving in the atmosphere everywhere. Godfrey saw angels walking through the crowds—touching the people and pouring oil on them. There were large angels surrounding the group of people; they looked like they were protecting them from something or someone. Up ahead there was a stage with men talking into something that echoed their voices. The men could be heard from far away. The one speaking now was passionate and full of surety of what he was saying. He was telling all the people about Jesus. How He died for everyone, and wanted everyone to be saved. The crowd loved what they were hearing. Godfrey could see wicked looking spirits coming off some of the people. These spirits screamed and flew away as quick as lightning.

"What is this? Some sort of peasant revolt?" Godfrey asked.

"This is what Christians call a crusade nowadays. This is where a lot of people gather to hear about Jesus, and learn how He can change their lives," Jazrael answered.

"A crusade! This isn't a crusade. Nobody has weapons and armor; there is no fighting going on between the people," Godfrey said, dumbfounded by the term.

"You're right. There is no battle in the flesh going on, but there is one going on in the spirit. Christians have learned much since your time. They are led by the Holy Spirit, not the pope. This is what the true church was called to do: Help the poor, heal the sick, cast out devils, and preach the gospel of Jesus," Jazrael answered.

"Things have changed. So this is the real church—spiritual warriors," Godfrey said.

"Godfrey, the wars you fought were necessary. You had to fight to protect your lands from the Muslims. Everything that happens has a purpose, but only God knows the full purpose. All of these lovely people are becoming believers in Jesus; they are being accepted into the family of God as we speak. This is the thing that makes our Father the happiest," Jazrael said. "It's time that we leave, Godfrey; we must be on our way to heaven. Many are waiting to see you."

Godfrey looked around at all the joyous people. He could tell they were all very poor, but it did not matter to them. They were new people, new creations of God. They were in love with Him; the singing, dancing, and praising was all for Him.

"Let's go, my friend, I am anxious to meet the Creator," Godfrey said.

In the twinkling of an eye, Godfrey and his companion disappeared and shot to the heavens.

Chapter 8: Failure is Unacceptable

Lilith sat nervously on her throne. She was in her beautiful human form again. Her fingers were tapping anxiously on the armchair of her throne. Her heart was beating irregularly and faster than normal. Her eyes were staring blankly ahead without blinking. Her mind was moving a mile a minute, trying to figure out this serious situation. She was angry and scared about what happened. She was angry because Godfrey never willingly worshiped her; even in hell that little man wouldn't bow to her. She hated Godfrey; if she could, she would torture him personally for the rest of her free days. She would make his pain and suffering so agonizing that the demons themselves would feel mercy for him. Somehow, some way Godfrey had been allowed to leave hell freely. God was up to something, and whatever it was, He was the only one who knew about it.

The only way Godfrey was allowed to leave legally was that it was written in heaven for him to come here for a time. It was all very legal; everything in creation ran with some kind of order to it. The trouble was that none of the fallen angels had access to heaven anymore—except Lucifer. When Satan heard about this, he would be down here demanding to know what happened. He would hear about it quick enough; his wicked little servants would get the news to him as fast as possible. Lilith knew Satan would take his anger out on her. He would torture and punish her for not knowing about this before it happened. She laid her head back and closed her snakelike eyes. She took a deep breath and wondered what would happen to her. She never personally experienced the tortures of hell. She had been chosen on earth to carry

Satan's child to start his bloodline. When she accepted, he told her she would be his queen forever. So when she died, she was the only one who had this life of luxury in hell.

What am I going to do? There is nothing that I can do. He will be here soon, and I know he will be angry. Maybe he won't react too badly, Lilith thought.

She lifted her head back up and opened her eyes. The large doors in front of her swung open violently. Wind and screams came through the door surrounding Lilith. All the imps in the chamber stopped pampering the queen and bowed on their faces. The human slaves were silent and also bowed. Lilith gasped; her breath left her. She jumped out of her throne and fell to her face, sobbing. In the doorway, there stood a tall, dark figure. His silhouette lit up as lightning struck in the background. It was the prince of darkness, the fallen one, the father of lies, the great devourer; it was the king of hell, Lucifer, now Satan, the sworn enemy of God. He walked casually toward the frightened Lilith. Fear, death, sin, and iniquity suddenly came into the atmosphere.

"Why are you so sad, my dear? You act as if something bad has happened. Get up, my queen; embrace your king and tell me what is wrong," said Satan with tenderness in his voice.

Lilith stood up; her whole body was shaking. She wiped her flood of tears from her eyes. She waited as Satan came closer her. Lilith trembled more the closer he came. His hair was short and pitch black; small ivory colored horns curved outward and then inward on his forehead. His skin was dark blue; it had a weathered, leathery look to it. Small horns came out of his elbows. He had large bat-like wings—six of them altogether. His face was clear with no facial hair, but there were bumps forming all over his body; they were little horns in the process of coming out. He was wearing no shirt; his chest and back were chiseled perfectly, except for the horns coming out of his skin and his large, curved spine sticking out. He had on a long black kilt that went down to his feet; it looked fluorescent and shone vaguely. On the kilt was a large black belt that had black jewels, trimmed in gold wrapped around it. His legs and feet were covered in black and brown fur; his feet were shaped like a five-pointed hoof.

His eyes met Lilith's sad countenance. Satan's eyes were the only thing that was left the same after his fall. They glowed with a faint white light. Anyone who looked into them would feel hope and love. Lilith embraced him. She hugged him tightly; his skin was clammy and cold. He had no emotion whatsoever, except hate, revenge, and love for himself.

"I'm sorry, master; I didn't know anything about this! Hell was in the dark about that disgusting man. Please forgive me; do not hurt me, oh great one! Don't I do everything you ask me? I have never disobeyed you, have I?" Lilith pleaded.

Satan had her in his arms and rubbed the side of her left cheek gently. He kissed her softly on her forehead and lips. Lilith felt at ease when he kissed her and looked in her eyes again.

"Now, child, it's okay. Everyone makes mistakes; you're only human. You are the mother of my children. I would never hurt you. Who is this man, Godfrey, anyway?" Satan asked.

"He was a fallen crusading knight who was beheaded by Muslims. He then came here. He was brought into my palace to worship me as his goddess and queen. He refused to and I put him through all the most excruciating torture I could. After many, many centuries he would still not submit willingly to me as his goddess. Then an angel named Jazrael came and retrieved the little rat by orders from the courts of heaven. I tried to stop him, but there was nothing I could do. Please, please, my sovereign and most worshipful god, you must believe me!" Lilith said.

Satan grabbed her face with both hands; they were as hot as brimstone. The pressure became more and more forceful on her head and face. There was no way she could escape his grip. His wings shot out and stretched to full capacity. The talons at the tip of them were straight out. His eyes were burning red hot now. Lilith could see the tension and anger glowing on him. His skin became as hot as hell fire when he was angry.

"You mean to tell me you could not get a soul that is in my prison to bow and worship you? You are the queen of hell! This is the most terrible, frightening, horrific damned place in the universes! You are an insubordinate witch I should have never kept! I should have let you rot in the land of Nod with Cain! You don't even deserve the crown that you wear! I will make you regret all of this, Lilith! I do not like failure; it is not allowed in my kingdom. You, Lilith, scum of man, have failed me. No one leaves hell; don't you understand that! If I am going to dwell here, then so will everyone else!" Satan exclaimed.

Lilith was grabbing Satan's wrists, trying to relieve the pressure on her head. He just kept squeezing her harder. He picked her up into the air and started shaking her rapidly. She was screaming and crying, but there was nothing she could do. Satan was grinning with extreme pleasure. The muscles tensed in his back, arms and neck as he shook her harder. Satan yelled at the slaves in the cages to start worshiping him. They started chanting his name immediately. He commanded them to yell louder and louder as he shook her harder and harder. He was laughing without pity as Lilith started choking for lack of breath. Her lower body moved back and forth like a rag doll being played with by a dog. Lilith felt her neck and spine start to break and sever.

"What am I going to do with you, my dear wife? I will think of something for you!" Satan exclaimed.

Satan finally stopped shaking her. She was limp, and lifeless. Her hands by now had let go of his wrists. He sat her down gently in her chair and rubbed her forehead with his finger, moving the hair out of her face. Her eyes were rolled back into her head. Her neck looked twisted and contorted. The skin had ripped at the bottom of her neck near the chest. Satan looked at her, and his facial expression suddenly changed from anger to sympathy. He reached down and grabbed one of her hands delicately and kissed it.

"I am sorry, my dear, for doing that. You know how I get; I was just angry. You know the rules, and the rules have to be followed. The law has to be enforced. The law in this kingdom is me, and when something goes wrong, I will enforce it," Satan said.

Satan closed his eyes and sent a thought to one of the demons in charge of transporting souls to come get the queen. Within seconds a large demon lumbered in the chamber with a chain and a bag full of torturing devices. Satan looked back at the door and motioned for the foul creature to come forward.

"The queen has committed a crime against our beloved kingdom, so she has to be punished for a season. Take her to my personal chamber of treats, and begin the punishment immediately on arrival," said Satan.

Lilith woke up as a large brown, hairy demon approached her. She looked up at Satan and begged again for him not to do this. She couldn't move because her neck and spine were broken. The demon reached out and grabbed her by her messy, long black hair. She was picked up in the air with ease. Her legs were dangling in midair. He threw her down to the floor hard on her face. She felt her nose smash and her mouth bust when she hit the ground. He then stomped her hard on the back of her neck. She made agonizing whimpers from the pain. The demon opened his bag and grabbed a collar; he bent down and clasped the collar around her neck.

"Here you are, my queen; this won't hurt a bit, I promise," said the demon sarcastically.

It was just like the one that Godfrey and so many others had worn; there were jagged spikes on the inside of it. The spikes slowly pierced her skin as the demon closed the collar tightly around her withered neck. She screamed in agony until the spikes were all the way in. After they were in, she could not make a sound come out of her mouth. The demon bound her hands behind her back with shackles. Then he connected the shackles to the collar on her neck with a small chain; he pulled it tightly so her arms were pulled up as far as they could go up her back. The demon put her legs together and shoved a large spike through both of her heels. She could not move as the demon overpowered her; her body was still shaking from it all. Once the spike was deep enough and all the way through, he bent it into a circle. Then he grabbed an even larger spike and shoved this through her knees, and also bent it carefully into a circle. She cried and cried because of the pain. There was no blood coming out, because just like all the other humans, she was just a soul; she too was already dead. She was just like a regular prisoner of Hell. The demon finished up by putting a chain on the rounded spike at her feet.

"It is all done, my king; she is ready for transport," the demon said.

"Good, good. Take the long way there, so she can savor the long journey just like Christ carrying His cross," said Satan.

"Yes, my lord," the demon answered.

Satan bent down and grabbed Lilith by her hair, pulling her battered face up. One of her eyes was blackened, and they both had tears in them. Her nose was large and flat looking, and all her white front teeth were knocked out.

"Don't worry, my queen; you are still beautiful in my eyes. The punishment will be over soon enough. Be of good cheer; I still love you, my darling," said Satan.

He let her hair go and motioned for the demon to take her away. The demon pulled the chain and started walking to the door. Lilith looked up as she was being dragged along on her stomach, trying to find mercy, but there was none. He sat down on her throne and smiled at her. He snapped his fingers and Lilith suddenly caught on fire. She started shaking violently from the burning. There was a trail of embers and ashes as they exited. Satan sat there, pleased by the punishment that had been inflicted.

"Now that's done. I have to see what is going on with this Godfrey character. He is going to wish he never left my kingdom," said Satan.

Chapter 9: Entering Heaven

Godfrey and Jazrael appeared in a huge, bright, white area. There was no sky or stars, only a white light emanating from everywhere at once. It was like a nostalgic dream of some sort; everything seemed to shine, even Godfrey and Jazrael. Godfrey could see a set of massive gates that were open. The gates shone bright and looked like they were made of gold. The walls were fluorescent like pearls; they went upward and sideways as far as the eye could see. There was a crowd coming out of the gate toward Godfrey and Jazrael. They were all wearing white cloaks that gave off a majestic glow. The people in the crowd were laughing and singing as they approached. It was the most joyous group of people Godfrey had ever seen.

Godfrey looked at Jazrael and asked him, "Who are all these people?"

"They are your family members, friends, and people who were used in your life to teach you something. There are here to greet and welcome you into heaven. I have to go and report all that has been done. There will be someone sent to you to show you around. I will see you soon, friend," said Jazrael.

After Jazrael finished his sentence, he walked in the gates in a hurry. Godfrey noticed how great he felt here. All of his senses were heightened to capacity. He was feeling only good emotions—love, happiness, kindness, warmth, safety, security, charity, and adoration for his surroundings. There were colors of every kind, glowing with happiness. Many of the colors Godfrey had never seen before, but his mind seemed to understand everything with no problems. There was music playing; it enveloped the entire place. It sounded like millions of voices and instruments playing in perfect harmony all at once. The music soothed Godfrey's soul; he could tell the melodies were holy. Godfrey stood in awe as the crowd came. At once, he began recognizing faces; he saw his mother, father, grandparents, sisters, brother, friends, aunts, and uncles. They all hugged and kissed him and asked him what he thought about heaven. His family and friends seemed to be totally concerned about his welfare. There was no loathing or guile in them; they all looked as perfect as could be.

Godfrey recognized one face in particular—it was Robert O'Sharky. He had a large smile on his face as he came and hugged Godfrey. He gave a bear hug of an embrace. Godfrey hugged him back and they shook hands. They all started heading for the gate as Godfrey was talking to Robert.

"I knew you would make it," Robert said.

"I sure did, and am glad for it too," Godfrey answered, relieved.

"I was told to give you a tour of heaven. I will show you some of the wonderful things here," Robert said.

As they went through the tall gates, Godfrey saw two very giant angels standing guard at each end of the entrance. They were both huge and intimidating. One had brown feathered wings and the other had white. They were covered in gold armor from head to toe. They each had gold swords that burned with a white fire. As Godfrey walked through, they both smiled and welcomed him to heaven. When they walked through, Godfrey was shocked by even more beauty and tranquility. There were buildings everywhere; they were the biggest Godfrey had ever seen. The streets were pure gold; they were so bright that Godfrey could see his reflection in them. Angels and people were walking around doing daily tasks, happy with what they were doing. One man wearing a golden crown was passing out cups of water. He looked to be some type of elder or ruler here. Other heavenly creatures that Godfrey couldn't recognize were walking around. A large lion approached Godfrey, purring and rubbing against his side. He petted it graciously.

"I have always wanted to do that," Godfrey said.

"This is heaven; everything and everyone are friendly and can speak to each other through thoughts or speech. That was the original intent of God for earth. Go ahead, think about asking the lion how he is doing," said Robert.

Godfrey did as he said and asked the lion how he was doing using his thoughts.

Hello, majestic creature, how are you doing? Godfrey thought.

I am wonderful; I love this place. God is great, don't you think? The lion asked.

He sure is. He saved my life from ultimate despair. I am grateful for it too. It was a pleasure talking to you, Godfrey thought back.

You too; enjoy the scenery, the lion said.

The lion left the two standing there. Godfrey looked around. Buildings of all kinds and mansions were on the side of the golden streets. They went on and on forever. There was a gigantic mountain in the distance; on the top of it were large golden pillars that went around in a circle. In the middle of the pillars there was a throne that had a large misty cloud above it. Lightning and thunder could be heard from the cloud. A crystal-clear river flowed down the mountain from the throne. The river went through the city. Godfrey automatically knew that it was Jesus' throne, and the cloud above was the Father's Spirit.

I want to go up there and meet Jesus, and thank Him for what He has done for me.

Suddenly a thought came to Godfrey's mind and said, *we will meet soon; look around and enjoy heaven.*

"Let's go and take a drink of the river," Robert said.

The two continued onward down to the river. They passed by a lot of houses and entered into a bright green forest. There were flowers all over, and they were moving with the music of heaven. The trees were dancing too, and birds of all shapes and sizes were singing along with the music. They walked through the forest and came to a large field. In the middle of the field, there was a giant tree that had fruit all over it. The tree reminded Godfrey of some type of oak, but much bigger. All kinds of people were eating the fruit. Right near the tree was the river; people were also drinking from it. Godfrey and Robert came to the bank of the river and knelt down to get a handful of water. Godfrey had never seen water so crystal clear. The water was more perfect looking than a diamond. Robert took a sip first; Godfrey watched him as he took a sip. When Robert drank, his body started glowing even more than it already did. Godfrey liked what he saw and took a gulp too. As soon as the water entered his mouth, his spirit leapt with joy, and the experience of heaven became even more real than before.

Godfrey loved this place; he was happy that it existed and that he had the privilege of being a part of it. One thing in particular that Godfrey noticed was the surrounding, powerful presence of God; His spirit was always close. Godfrey thought that heaven itself stayed together because of the presence of God.

"How do you like the river of life?" Robert asked.

"There is truly nothing like this. I feel even better than I did before drinking from the river," Godfrey answered.

"It just keeps getting better, Godfrey," Robert answered.

They sat there on the green field and enjoyed the constant bliss around them. Godfrey looked at all the others drinking from the river and saw that they were just as happy as he was. He looked over at the giant tree and saw a large crowd eating from it. Godfrey hopped up and started walking over to the tree to see what everyone was eating. Robert ran behind him and grabbed his shoulder. Godfrey turned around, perplexed.

"What…what is wrong? I'm just going to eat from the tree," Godfrey said.

"You can't eat from it yet, Godfrey," Robert replied.

"Why not? Everyone else around here is," Godfrey responded.

"God does not want you to eat from it yet; if you do, it will make your new body eternal," Robert answered.

"Why doesn't God want me to be eternal?" Godfrey asked.

"You have to return to earth. I don't know why, but it is God's will," Robert said.

"I don't want to go back to the earth; I want to be here in heaven," Godfrey said.

"You must. You made a deal with God that you would fulfill a task for Him. Returning to the earth must be a part of the task for you," Robert answered.

"I guess I should talk to God about it then. He did save me from hell. I will do anything for Him that's within my power," Godfrey said.

"Say, do you want to see your mansion?" Robert asked.

"Yeah, of course, let's go!" Godfrey exclaimed.

Godfrey and Robert headed off again, this time toward Godfrey's mansion. Godfrey noticed that traveling in heaven was fast and efficient. It was not troublesome like a march in the military or a long ride on horseback. One had the option of walking, flying, or traveling by thinking of the place you desired to go. It was the ultimate convenient way of going to and fro. They walked through the forest and came to a large cliff; it was thousands of feet in the air. The river of life turned into a waterfall running off the cliff. Godfrey and Robert walked to the edge of the cliff and looked at the scenery. Below, the river stretched through a valley of vast mountain chains. The mountains were peaceful and serene. The valley was green with a rainbow going across it. Godfrey saw large golden eagles flying above the mountain peaks. Robert looked over the ledge and jumped off; instead of falling, he started flying. Godfrey looked at him, shocked. Robert motioned for Godfrey to jump off and join him. Fear doesn't exist in heaven, so Godfrey didn't feel any. He closed his eyes and jumped into the air. He imagined himself flying, and when he opened his eyes he saw that he was.

Robert had already started flying, so Godfrey sped up to catch him. The eagles saw them and joined them. The closer the eagles came, the more Godfrey realized that they were massive creatures. They flew around with the eagles and played racing games with them. Godfrey felt like a little child again. When they flew over the mountains, Godfrey saw a large body of water. The river of life flowed into it. Robert started descending lower toward the sea, so Godfrey followed him. They landed on the beach. Instead of having sand, the beach had tiny diamonds and pearls as sand. There were angels playing with children alongside the sea. The children were swimming in the water. Animals of all kinds were cuddling and playing with the children too.

"Who are these children? Why are they not full grown?" Godfrey asked.

"These are the children who have died or have been killed prematurely. Godfrey, when you go back to earth, you will see that it is a lot more evil than you remember. God gathers the little ones up and charges his angels to raise them and give them a proper childhood," Robert answered.

"God doesn't seem to forget anyone does He?" Godfrey asked.

"No, He knows every single detail that goes on in His creation," Robert answered. "Come on, Godfrey; your mansion is not too far from here."

They walked further down the shore. Up ahead on a small hill there was a huge mansion. The shape of it was like an old Roman villa house. The walls were white, and the roof was red and made out of ceramic clay. The backyard was a huge open field. On the border of the field was a dense, dark green forest. Mountains could be seen further into the distance. Beyond that the largest mountain in heaven could be seen from anywhere; it was the one where the great throne was. All kinds of animals were walking around Godfrey's new yard. The sea crashing against the coast made the scene completely peaceful and perfect for Godfrey. They walked closer to the house and entered in. Godfrey saw jewels, gold, and fine jewelry lying around in his house. There were paintings of heaven and space hanging on the walls. They walked back outside onto the front porch of the villa. Below was a long table full of all kinds of food. There were plenty of seats for all his family and friends to come and eat.

"Godfrey, this is what God has given you. It will never be taken away from you. It will always be yours and yours alone," Robert said.

Godfrey took in a big breath of fresh air and looked around at all the lovely things; then he looked at Robert and gave him a big hug. Godfrey's heart was full of thankfulness. They stood there laughing and talking, enjoying each other's company. In the distance a loud horn started blowing; it became louder and louder.

"That is the horn to remind all of us that we have been summoned to the court," Robert said.

"So what do we do?" Godfrey asked

"We grab a gift from our possessions, and meet in the court," Robert answered.

"You can have anything of mine to give; let's hurry up and grab something and get going," Godfrey said.

The two grabbed some jewels to give and transported to the court of heaven. When they got there, a very large multitude of people was already there. They all had some kind of gifts to give. The court was at the foot of the mountain of God. The singing was even deeper and could be felt with more power in the court. The music seemed to penetrate through Godfrey with waves of heat. It made him feel renewed like the river did. Godfrey looked up and noticed a rainbow above the throne. The music became so powerful that a mighty wind started blowing on everyone. The presence of God became so strong that everyone got on their knees and bowed their faces to the ground. When everybody bowed a large cloud descended. This was when the Father came and visited all His creation together.

The spirit of God consumed Godfrey completely. His body was lifeless, and electricity shot through him. As Godfrey lay there, a powerful voice started speaking to him. When the voice spoke, his body vibrated.

"Godfrey, you have finally made it to Me. I see you enjoy all that I have made."

Yes Father, I do love it. Thank You for saving me.

"Godfrey, you were chosen to do what you have done and for what you must still do. I know all things; nothing can escape My eyes. I know the beginning and the end at once," the Father said.

"Yes, Father, please accept my gift," Godfrey said.

"It is well received, little one. I require you to travel up My mountain and talk to My Son. You have much to learn, and much to do," the Father said.

"Yes, Lord," Godfrey answered.

After that everything went white; it was so bright that Godfrey couldn't get up or open his eyes. When the light dimmed enough, everyone got up together. Godfrey noticed all the gifts were gone. He walked over to Robert and said, "I have to go up the mountain and talk to the King."

"It seems that it is time for you to go already; I will see you again, friend," Robert said.

"I don't want to leave, but I must do what I am called to do. Tell everyone I'll be back soon enough; so long, my good friend," Godfrey said.

Robert and Godfrey hugged each other and parted ways. Godfrey walked to the immense mountain. There were golden stairs that went all the way to the top. There were colorful torches lit in tall poles, going all the way up the stairs. Every fire in each torch was a different color. There were purple, yellow, blue, green, red, orange, and many more colors lighting his way. Godfrey walked up the stairs and noticed the higher he got the more of God he could feel. Thunder and lightning was rumbling in the large clouds above. The wind was blowing more fiercely the higher Godfrey went. Godfrey could hear what sounded like water gushing forth above him. When Godfrey got to the top, the presence of God was so strong he had to get on his knees. Godfrey didn't want to go any further until he heard the most humble and peaceful voice he had ever heard say, "Godfrey, stand up and come here. We have much to talk about."

Godfrey got up and covered his face because of the blinding brightness. He walked further and bowed near the throne. The light dimmed so he didn't have to cover his face anymore.

"Look up, child," Jesus said.

Godfrey looked up and saw Jesus. He was smiling and laughing with a joyous laugh. The throne where He was sitting was large and golden; it looked too big for Jesus. There were large golden pillars surrounding the throne. They were connected at the top, but there was no roof. The elements were at their most powerful around the throne. The wind that was so powerful was really the very creative breath of God. Jesus was holding a large golden scepter in His right hand; it glowed bright with authority. He had a white cloak that radiated with beauty. His feet were in sandals, but they shone like fiery bronze. On His head was a golden crown. It was round like a wedding band, and there were different colored jewels going around it. His hair was brown and went down to

His shoulders. His beard was brown and well trimmed. His eyes were so bright and holy that they would pierce through anything they gazed upon. His hands and His feet still had holes in them. His whole body glowed with power. Godfrey knew He had all authority in heaven and on earth.

"Godfrey, My son, how are you?" Jesus asked.

"I am wonderful, Lord; Your creation is indescribable," Godfrey answered.

"I like to impress My children," Jesus answered.

"Godfrey, you have been through a lot for a man, but it was your destiny to go through this. I planned it for you to bring you to Me," Jesus said.

"Lord, I do not understand; I didn't serve You while on earth. All I worried about was myself," Godfrey said.

"When you were a child, you believed in Me, and prayed to Me often. One night you prayed for Me to come into your heart; when you did that, I did come into your heart. As you grew older and colder, because of religious oppression and constant war, you quit praying to Me. I never left your heart though. I was there the whole time, just a whisper away," Jesus said.

Godfrey fell on his face and started crying. Jesus stood up and picked him up and hugged him firmly.

"I'm sorry, Lord; I lost my faith and trust in You. Will You please forgive me?" Godfrey cried.

"Of course, you are forgiven," Jesus said.

"Lord, what is it that I must do?" Godfrey asked.

"You must return to earth, to a foreign land. There you will be given another life to live as a man again. I have a servant who has a most important message to speak, but will not because he is frightened to say it. I am sending you to him to encourage him. This is the biggest task for you, but there will be many while you live on earth. When on earth, you will have to live by faith, just like everyone else. Remember I am always near, no matter what happens. Jazrael will teach you what you must know, and will escort you back to earth. I know you will do well there," Jesus said.

"I will do anything You ask me, Lord; thank You for giving me a chance to serve," Godfrey answered.

As Jesus hugged Godfrey, the bright white light came back and consumed Godfrey. When the light faded, he was outside the gates of heaven. Close by, Jazrael was waiting.

Chapter 10: Ministry

Sitting outside against the wall of the famous studio known as OBN was the young, rebellious, and beautiful daughter of John and Meredith Maxwell. Her father was a famous preacher who had a successful television ministry called OBN, or Our Blessed Network. He was the biggest, most well-known preacher in America. He had met presidents, prime ministers, kings, queens, capitalist giants, and all the great men and women of the day. If a politician wanted Christian votes, all he had to do was go on John's weekly show. John's daughter, Tabitha Maxwell, did not like her father's lifestyle or his popularity. She argued that it had ruined her life and her family's, too. She tried to go to college, but it didn't work out too well for her. She got into the drug and party scene and couldn't keep her grades up anymore. Eventually the college had to kick her out; with that happening, she came back home to Georgia and started working for her dad. She ran cameras, did some editing on videos, and did odd jobs around the set. She didn't want to, but it was decent money. Despite her hating the family business, everyone who worked for her dad was paid a good wage, and it was enough to keep her supplied with pot.

Tabitha was not a Christian like her parents were. In college, she had officially given up on the faith. Tabitha was angry with God because of her fake family who had to always look perfect for the sake of television. The image they all had to portray daily was sickening to her. If and when she finally got away, she vowed to leave it all behind her. It worked somewhat, until people recognized her. Some people loved her, but a lot of people hated her and her father. Tabitha did her best to deal with all the problems and tried to fit in as much as possible. She found the best way to cope was doing a lot of drinking and doing a lot of drugs.

The money that her father gave for school expenses was spent on her party life. Once John found out what his daughter was doing, he wouldn't give her extra money anymore. After getting canned from school and coming back home, Tabitha calmed down a little. She wasn't drinking as much, and had given up most of the drugs she was on. Well, some of them anyway.

It was around 10:30 at night; they had finished up doing the live show on Sunday evening. It was the most-watched time slot for them. The wind was blowing outside; the moon was full and bright. Tabitha was sitting outside alone in the dark, thinking of what she was going to do that night. Nobody was around outside, so she lit up a cigarette and smoked it casually. She was average height—5 feet 4 inches. Her skin was slightly bronze from living in the South all her life. Tabitha wasn't the glamorous type; she liked dressing casually and comfortably. She was wearing a pair of blue jeans with brown sandals, and a regular fitted blue T-shirt. The logo on the shirt was in white writing and said, "Kill Your Television." Her hair was light brown with blonde and red streaks in it. It went slightly past her shoulders; it was curly with a couple of braids going around her head. Her eyes matched the T-shirt she was wearing. Tabitha was slim and petite. She looked like a girl with a wild streak in her; the boys loved her and her dad couldn't stand the way she acted.

After finishing her cigarette, she got up and headed back inside the studio to tell her father that she was leaving for the night. She walked over to the back entrance to go in as her dad was walking out.

"Honey, where have you been? We've got work to do," John said.

"Dad, I'm tired. I'm gonna call it a night and go home. I'm too beat to do any more tonight," Tabitha said.

"All right, honey, if you're sleepy than head home and go to bed. Tell your mom I will be here all night. Make sure you are here tomorrow morning; we have to get prepared for my next show," John said

John reached over and hugged his daughter, and gave her a kiss on her cheek. She reluctantly submitted to his affection.

"Bye dad," Tabitha said.

"Bye honey, don't forget to tell your mom I'll be here all night," John said.

"Whatever, dad," Tabitha answered.

John watched his daughter walk to her car. She got in and started it up, and exited out of the security gate. John headed back inside the studio. He walked down the long corridor. There were large black doors lining all the way down the walls on both sides. The walls and ceiling were a bright white. John walked all the way down the silent hallway; the only noise was his expensive brown loafers making a loud clacking sound. He turned left and headed to the taping and editing room. He opened the door and told the guys inside to go ahead home. The four men didn't argue and made their way out. John headed to his office, which was further down the same hallway. John opened the door and turned on the lights. It was a large and somewhat luxurious room. There were two desks—one against the wall that had his computer, the other was in the middle of the room with a computer chair in between them. They dominated the room like the president's desk in the White House. They were both carved out of mahogany. On the middle desk, there was a picture of his family on the left corner. On the right, there was a bundle of papers and a couple of pens. Facing the desks were two brown leather chairs. They were soft and puffed out like feather pillows. Along the wall stood a bookshelf with all sorts of books on it. It was a collection that only a pastor would have—commentaries of the Bible, the writings of Josephus, maps of the Holy Land, concordances, Greek and Hebrew lexicons, and a few different translations of the Bible itself.

Against the other wall was a soft couch that matched the comfortable chairs. That particular couch had been a bed for John many times. He had grown accustomed to sleeping in the office. It was easier for him just to stay at his office; he and Meredith, his wife, were having marriage problems. He would never get a divorce though; it would destroy his image and ministry if he ever did. John knew he couldn't do that. Their problems really arose when John became so popular. All the fame and spotlight was difficult for Meredith to deal with. She liked it at first, but it soon started to bother her conscience. She noticed a change in her husband, and saw the effect of it in all the trouble that her daughter had caused because of the ministry.

Everyone in the family wanted out, even John. The ministry had turned into a massive monster of satellites, TV stations, channels, and all the most popular shows on Christian television. John went over to his desk to write down some plans for the next show. He had an idea in his head that he wanted to write down. The idea was to have a painter to come on the show and paint a huge picture of heaven for the new OBN set. He would announce it on the next show, and would ask painters to send in pictures of their work by e-mail. John liked the idea; it seemed out of the ordinary. The actual painting was going to be huge, at least forty to fifty feet long and at least twenty-five to thirty feet high. It was going to be an arduous task. John sat back in his office chair, pleased with himself.

"This is going to be fun, I can't wait to see the reaction of the viewers on this one," John said.

John thought about calling his wife and telling her, but it was late and figured she had already gone to bed. John was tired too, so he set his alarm for six o'clock a.m. He took off his shoes and lie down on his couch, and fell into a deep sleep.

Tabitha pulled into the driveway of her parents' house. It was a large two-story brick house. There was a three-car garage for everyone's vehicles. In the front, a white gravel ring driveway surrounded a fountain of two naked cherubim spitting water from their mouths. The estate was on ten acres of land with trees all around the back of the house. On the front of the house were four large, square windows—two on the second story and two on the first. The front door was tall and wide, and a light brown color. There was a large metal lion on the door to use for knocking. The porch had a few concrete stairs leading to the door. The steps gradually grew larger the further away they came from the door. Tabitha pulled into the garage and headed inside. She walked into the kitchen and turned some lights on; her mother wasn't downstairs. She must have gone to bed. Tabitha grabbed a soda from the fridge and went out through the back door to the deck. The deck was a light wooden color with lawn chairs and tables arranged around it. It had tiki torches set up at the corners of the deck to keep mosquitoes and other annoying bugs away.

Tabitha went over and lay back in one of the lawn chairs. She sat her soda on the table next to her and pulled out a bag of freshly rolled joints. She pulled one out and lit it up with a cigarette lighter. When the effect of the drug hit her she lay back and closed her eyes. She sat there stoned, letting her mind relax and her imagination soar. Tabitha felt like her entire body's senses were being turned on like several light bulbs. There was no sound around her outside except for the chirping crickets and frogs. Tabitha had started smoking pot in high school; she always told herself it helped her mellow out. Her parents still didn't know that she smoked; at least she thought they didn't know.

Inside the kitchen, Meredith Maxwell stood staring at her daughter through the door outside. She saw a cloud of smoke above her, and could smell the distinct smell of marijuana all around her. Meredith came down because she heard her daughter come in. Now she stood silent and sad; seeing her daughter staying high all the time killed her inside. She tried talking to her daughter about the drugs, but it was useless, because she would deny using them every time. Meredith had her arms crossed like she was hugging herself. She had on a night robe; it was light purple and made from a silky material. She was also short and petite; her daughter had the same figure. Her skin wasn't as dark as her daughter's though; she had a paler complexion. Her hair was shorter too; it came above her shoulders. Instead of curly, it was neatly trimmed and straight. As she stood there, Meredith said a prayer under her breath.

"God, please save my daughter from herself. Heal her, and heal my family. Bring us together, and let us be happy again like we were a long time ago," Meredith prayed. With a tear running down her cheek, she went back upstairs to go to bed.

Chapter 11: Dreams

Inside John's office there was not a sound; all was quiet and peaceful. John lay there on his couch sound asleep, but he didn't look at peace. His eyes were moving back and forth rapidly, like he was having a dream or nightmare of some kind. Standing above John was a man in a white robe. He was translucent like a ghost, and he glowed like a bright summer day. He was dropping gold dust on John's head. The angel was sent to give a message to John. God was speaking to John through a dream.

Insides John's dream, he was standing on a beach. The wind was blowing very hard. He looked around and saw a huge tidal wave coming to the shore. It didn't look real; it looked several stories high. Behind the wave, a hurricane was brewing. The clouds in it were black; lightning and thunder were rumbling inside of it. The hurricane covered the whole sky; it didn't look like a natural storm. John became terrified, he looked beside him, and all around him were families of people lying on the beach like nothing was happening. They were laughing and joking; their kids were running around without a care in the world. All of the people had cash in their hands; they were giving it to each other and filling up their pockets at the same time. They looked at the money with loving eyes; they looked at it like it was very important to them. Some people started kissing the money and worshiping it. John looked further inland and could see skyscrapers everywhere; they were very tall and seemed to be growing more and more as the people worshiped the money. John fell to the ground when he heard a loud thunder clap; it felt like it went through him when he heard it. He opened his eyes and saw a huge black horse with red eyes charging vehemently out of the storm. The rider on the horse was carrying scales; the sound of the horse's hooves was getting louder and louder. John was terrified and closed his eyes, because he didn't want to look at the terrifying sight anymore. John heard a voice all around him, and suddenly, it was peaceful and just above a whisper.

John, tell My people judgment is coming. Tell them that the world is about to be shaken like never before. Tell them to trust Me and not their goods, for it is Me who supplies all these things. It is time to get prepared for judgments. The seals are being broken; tell My people I love them and to come back to Me. John, you must tell them.

John woke up in a cold sweat; he was trembling. His mind was racing from the dream he just had. He stood up and staggered over to his desk; he started writing down all that he had seen. The dream was still very vivid in his mind. After he had finished writing it down, he sat there and pondered.

Judgment, everybody is prospering. No one will believe me if I tell them this. My ministry is built on prospering, not doom and gloom. If I tell people this, they will stop supporting me, and I will lose my popularity and status. That black horse sounds familiar; I think it was in the book of Revelation. I remember him being about inflation I think. Who will believe me? This isn't what people want to hear.

John looked at his piece of paper to make sure he had all the details. He went back over to the couch and tried to go to sleep.

Chapter 12: What Is He Doing Now?

Deep in the caverns of hell, where no light dwelled, sat Lucifer in his chambers. He was sitting on his large black throne. It stood twenty feet high, with spiked arches at the top. Written at the top was *lord of flies*. There was a guard to each side of the throne; they had their heads bowed and held large scythes. They were wearing gray cloaks; their faces were hidden in pitch-black darkness. They both had a pair of large reptilian wings gently resting behind them. The throne room was dark and mysterious. Inside was very dull; it seemed no life was there. Only death and evil were felt around the place. An eerie quietness filled the room, except for an occasional scream from Lucifer's personal torture arena. Lilith was still in there; she had not yet finished her punishment for failing Lucifer. He sat bent over, with his elbows on his knees and his chin in his open palms. He was thinking about Godfrey; he wondered what God was planning, and what this plan had to do with some Templar from the crusades.

What does He want with this useless human; why is he so important? If I can get my hands on him, I will sift him like sand. I will make him wish he never even heard of hell because I will show him the darkest and deepest pits of my kingdom. Who dares to leave my kingdom without my permission? I am god here. I am the sovereign lord of all here! thought Lucifer.

Lucifer leaned back in his chair and clasped the chair arms. He dug his large hands into them until the black charred stone started cracking slightly.

I will ascend into heaven and see what God is up to. I will ask about this Godfrey and try to bring him back home where he belongs.

He stood up and walked out of his throne room and headed into his torture chamber. He wanted to let off some steam on his frightened subjects.

Chapter 13: A New Life

Godfrey walked up to Jazrael and greeted him. They hugged and shook hands.

"Hello, Jazrael, how are you doing?" Godfrey asked.

"Very well; how about you?" Jazrael responded.

"I feel great; I have received my assignment from the Lord. He told me you have some things to show and teach me," Godfrey answered.

"Yes, there is a lot to learn. Luckily in heaven you can understand things a whole lot better. Your mind in heaven works to its full capacity; on earth, you barely use ten percent of it," Jazrael said.

"Wow, that's amazing! God really is magnificent! So what do you need to teach me?" Godfrey asked.

"Well, let's see, you're not going back to the Middle Ages, and you're not going to be speaking a mixture of Latin and French anymore. The language that you will be speaking is American English," said Jazrael.

"A new language, huh? What else?" asked Godfrey.

"You will need to know a lot about history and all the things that have happened since you left the earth. Oh yeah, you need to know how to paint like a professional too," said Jazrael.

"Is that it?" asked Godfrey, feeling overwhelmed.

"It is for now," said Jazrael.

Jazrael stepped in front of Godfrey and placed his huge hands on the sides of Godfrey's head. Jazrael started speaking in an ancient tongue that Godfrey didn't understand. Godfrey felt tons of information, knowledge, pictures, and visions enter his mind of people and places he had never seen before. They penetrated his thoughts gently and peacefully. Jazrael let go of Godfrey and stepped back. Godfrey shook his head; he had a look of amazement on his face.

"I wish to stay. Are you sure that I have to leave?" Godfrey asked

Jazrael laughed because of Godfrey's enthusiasm.

"You have a job to do, so yes, you have to go back. We should be on our way," said Jazrael.

"If we must, we must," Godfrey responded.

Jazrael reached out to grab his hand. Godfrey took it, and the two vanished in an instant. The two appeared somewhere in Israel, close by a major highway. It was nighttime, and the sky was lit up by the moon and the Milky Way. Godfrey wasn't totally sure where they were, but he had a feeling.

"Is this Israel?" Godfrey asked, looking at Jazrael.

"Yes, this is Israel in modern times. This particular spot where we are standing is where you were killed, Godfrey," Jazrael responded.

"That must have been what I was feeling—dread and familiarity," Godfrey said.

"I'm sure it is not a good memory, but watch this," Jazrael said, as he began blowing the sand with his mouth.

At first Jazrael looked ridiculous, blowing the sand, but the wind quickly picked up. The sand started blowing and scattering in a frenzy of what look like small tornados. Godfrey and Jazrael began sinking as more and more sand was blown away. Godfrey watched as Jazrael blew one last gust of air and all the extra flew away in an enormous dust cloud. What lay before Godfrey's feet was an old skeleton with some rusted armor. The skull of the skeleton was not far from the main body. Godfrey instantly realized it was his body they were looking at, still here—preserved in sand.

"I can't believe my skeleton is still here," Godfrey said.

"We had to make sure nothing happened to it, so it was buried deep as soon as you departed from it," Jazrael said.

"Why are you showing me this?" Godfrey asked.

"It has to be resurrected," Jazrael said.

"Really? That is interesting. How do we do that?" Godfrey responded.

"You have to speak life into it, Godfrey," Jazrael said.

"I have to speak life into my own body?" Godfrey asked.

"Yes," Jazrael responded nonchalantly.

"Well…okay…here goes nothing," Godfrey said as he knelt down to his skeleton.

Godfrey put his hands over his body and began to say, "Body… bones I command you to come back to life and to resurrect from the dead."

Nothing happened. Godfrey just sat there wondering what to do next. He looked back at Jazrael with a perplexed look on his face. Jazrael looked at him and said, "You forgot in whose name to pray."

"Oh, I forgot. In Jesus' name I pray this," Godfrey said.

Suddenly, Godfrey's bones began to move. The skull rolled over to the body and connected back to it. The skeleton started moving its limbs around, making creaking sounds as it did. Then flesh began to appear, tendons, muscles, and then skin quickly enveloped the moving skeleton. Godfrey watched as his face came back together—green eyes and short black hair. Before Godfrey could say anything, he felt himself being pulled into the body. Next thing he knew, Godfrey was lying on his back with all of his old, slow sensations. Godfrey stood up like he was a newborn, and found that he was naked. Jazrael snapped his fingers and Godfrey had on a pair of jeans, tennis shoes, and a blue T-shirt. Godfrey sat and looked at himself for a while.

"This is awesome," Godfrey said.

"Yes, it is; now we must be off to your destination," Jazrael said, as they vanished into thin air.

Chapter 14: Earth Again

On the back roads of Georgia way out in the country, the stars were shining bright—crickets were chirping, frogs croaking, and owls hooting. Up in the sky a faint white light made its way to the surface of the earth. It was Godfrey and Jazrael. They landed quietly and easily in a large, grassy field not too far from a country road. Godfrey fell to the ground, suddenly fatigued from the travel. He was back in his body, so gravity became all too real again. Godfrey could feel the air go through his lungs; it sent goose bumps up his arms. The wind was blowing through his black hair. He stood back up to look around; he saw that Jazrael wasn't there.

"Jazrael, where are you?" Godfrey asked.

Then a thought streamed into to Godfrey's mind that wasn't his own.

I had to leave you, but don't worry I'll be around. Walk to the road, and head to the city. Look for an inn or hotel to stay in, Jazrael answered.

Godfrey looked down and noticed a large brown, leather bag beside him; it had money, art supplies, a Bible, and a pocket knife in it. Godfrey reached down, picked up the bag, and started walking to the road.

These must be my supplies.

He looked ahead and faintly saw the road. Godfrey walked casually through the grassy field and made his way there. When he reached the road he saw a sign that said, "Athens 20 miles." Godfrey saw it as a divine sign to tell him to go to Athens, so he started walking that way. The road was quiet and the air moving slightly. The only light was from the bright stars above. In the middle of nowhere with no soul in sight

Godfrey felt at peace. He knew where he was, though, because of the massive amount of information Jazrael had given him before he brought him back to earth. His memories of all that had happened to him were playing in his head like a movie reel.

After all that, he still felt at peace because of the one who saved him. Godfrey heard a low rumbling sound coming from behind him. He turned his head to see what it was and noticed the headlights of a vehicle coming toward him. As the vehicle approached, the driver turned off his bright lights and pulled up beside Godfrey. The driver of the truck was an older man. He looked about 65 or 70. His skin was tanned and sun beaten. He had a straw hat like old farmers wore. White sideburns came down the side of his face. The driver had his left arm resting on the door of his old truck.

"How are you, stranger?" The man asked in a southern accent.

"I am doing fine; I have a long walk ahead of me," Godfrey answered.

"Well, where you heading to?" The man asked

"Uh…I believe Athens," Godfrey answered.

"Hot damn son, you're in luck; Athens is up the road a ways. Why don't you hop on in? I'll give you a ride into town. I'm heading that way anyway," the old man said.

"Thank you, uhhh…I'm sorry, what is your name?" Godfrey asked.

"Clyde, Clyde Birdie is the name. And just who might you be, son?" Clyde answered.

"Godfrey," Godfrey answered.

"Well, hop on in, Godfrey," Clyde said.

Godfrey thanked the stranger and got in his pickup. The two began driving toward the town of Athens.

Chapter 15: Ascending

In the realm of eternity, Lucifer transported himself from hell to the gates of heaven. For him, there were no family members to greet him, or angels rejoicing that he had come. Heaven did not dazzle him; it held only remnants of his past. Everything looked the same, alive and vibrant. Inside Lucifer's heart was different; it was cold and calloused. The father of lies had no heart; he lost it when he fell. Lucifer walked up to the golden gates to inquire from the guards. The two giant angels that were standing there stood in front of Lucifer and crossed their spears. The two fixed their gaze on Lucifer and did not flinch.

"I wish to have an audience with the Lord; I need an answer on a particular problem of mine," Lucifer said.

"Denied; your presence is not welcome before the highest throne," they said together with deepened voices.

"What? I have the right! You two fools cannot stop me; I was once your sovereign!" Lucifer exclaimed.

"Lucifer, Lucifer, calm down. God has sent me to you to answer your questions. So tell me what burdens your little black heart?" Jazrael asked, as he stepped out of the giant golden gates. He had a smile on his face that caused Lucifer to grow even more agitated. The two angels guarding the gate went back to their posts, laughing as they went. Jazrael walked closer to Lucifer to hear what he had to say.

"Where is my soul?" Lucifer asked.

"You gave that up long ago, if I remember correctly," Jazrael said.

"Not me, child! I am speaking of Godfrey. The little worm who was able to leave his infernal resting place," Lucifer said.

"Oh, Godfrey! Now I know who you are talking about. Godfrey belongs to the Lord, not you," Jazrael said.

"Then why was he allowed to rot in hell for hundreds of years?" Lucifer asked.

"It is a part of his destiny; we do not presume to know the mind of God," Jazrael said.

"Where is he then?" Lucifer asked.

"Why are so you worried about where Godfrey is?" Jazrael asked.

"He is back on earth, isn't he?" Lucifer asked.

"You're so smart Lucy; yes, he is back on earth. This time, though, he knows the Lord, and he is quite the formidable opponent," Jazrael said.

"I will break his little spirit, and make him renounce God. He is mine!" Lucifer exclaimed.

With that, Lucifer vanished. Jazrael stood and prayed for Godfrey. "Lord, give Godfrey the wisdom and knowledge to fight his enemy. Amen."

Chapter 16: Day One

Godfrey was dropped off at the nearest hotel by Clyde Birdie, the friendly stranger. He waved to the old man as he drove off in his old pickup. The name of the hotel was Weary Knight's Inn. Godfrey reached in his bag and pulled out a couple hundred dollars. Godfrey couldn't believe he knew what all these things were just because Jazrael had touched him in heaven. When Godfrey was alive before, men used gold and silver; now they used paper. *What a world this is.*

He walked in the hotel and asked for a room. The hotel was like many others. It had a front desk with bulletproof glass going all the way up the ceiling. It had the cheap, colorful carpet covering the floor. There were three green chairs resting against the wall beside a couple of drink and snack machines down the hall. It was late, so Godfrey was the only customer in the lounge except for the employee across the desk. Godfrey walked up to the window to speak to her.

"Hello ma'am, I would like a room please," said Godfrey.

Behind the desk a middle-aged black lady looked up from organizing some towels below the desk. She was short and her hair was tied back in a bun. She had a white collared shirt that said Weary Knights Inn. Her eyes were light brown and had a sparkle about them. She smiled, and Godfrey noticed her perfect white teeth. She rested her arms on the counter and leaned forward to get a better look at Godfrey.

"Let me see what we have, young man," the woman said in a smooth southern accent.

She leaned back up and started typing away on her computer and asked, "You want a single bed, right?"

"Yes, please," Godfrey answered.

"How long are you staying, honey?" the woman said.

"I'm not sure, really," Godfrey said.

"Why don't you pay for a couple of days, and we'll go from there then?" the woman said.

"Sounds good; let me pay for two days then," Godfrey said.

"Okay, that brings your total up to a hundred and twenty dollars and thirty-five cents. Cash or credit?" The woman said.

"Cash," Godfrey said.

Godfrey counted out some money to give to the lady. He slid it across the hole in the bulletproof glass. She then grabbed his key card and handed him back his change and the card. Their hands touched slightly when he grabbed his items; when they did, Godfrey had pictures of the lady flash before his eyes. In one of them, she was a child; in another, she was a teenager singing in church; then came another one of her standing by her father's grave; and finally there was one of her praying beside her bed for her husband to be healed of lung cancer. Then a voice came to him: *Tell Grace that her husband will recover from his sickness*. Reality came back to Godfrey and he could see again. The lady just stared at him, perplexed.

"What's wrong, honey? Did you see a ghost?" the woman asked.

"Grace, your husband will recover from his sickness," Godfrey said.

The lady's skin color turned paler as if she had been the one to see a ghost. She gasped for air and put her hand on her chest.

"My Lord, I knew there was something strange about you. Are you an angel on assignment?" Grace asked.

"No, I am not an angel, but I am on assignment," Godfrey said smiling.

The lady started to cry and weep for joy that her husband would be fine. She came out from behind the front desk to give Godfrey a hug. When she did, the hug was so tight that Godfrey lost his breath for a bit. She backed up and put her hands in the air and yelled, "Thank You, Jesus, for healing my husband; thank You, Jesus, for saving me! And thank You, Jesus, for sending me Your angel!"

After all the praise and commotion Godfrey finally headed for his room. The card had the number 7 on it, so he walked down the first walkway to find room 7. Once he found it, he opened the door and went inside. Godfrey put his bag on the small table near the entrance and pulled each item out—money, pocket knife, paintbrushes, tubes of paint, and various other paint supplies, and finally a copy of the Bible—the *New Living Translation*. He was tired so he stripped down to his boxers and T-shirt to go to bed. He turned on the lamp and pulled out the Bible. He rubbed his hands across the leather surface. He flipped open the pages and smelled the smell of a new book that's never been touched. Godfrey opened it to Genesis and read all night until he fell asleep.

Chapter 17: Day Two

Godfrey woke up early in the morning; the sun had just come up. The sunlight was glimmering through the blinds. Godfrey felt refreshed and new. Everything looked and seemed new to him. For the first time, he was enjoying life on earth. He looked to the side of him on the bed and saw his Bible open; he had read all the way to chapter ten in Genesis. He marked where he stopped with the flyleaf and closed it up. Godfrey went ahead and took a shower, shaved, and cleaned himself up a little.

As Godfrey was shaving, he examined himself in the mirror and wondered if all of this was real. He wondered about heaven, hell, God, and everything that had happened. It was starting to overwhelm him. As he thought about it more and more, he realized this didn't make sense at all. It got his nerves so bad, that his stomach started growling. He didn't have any food in the hotel so he walked outside to see if there was anywhere to eat. The morning was warm and pleasing to Godfrey. He examined his surroundings and saw various cars in the parking lot. He could hear morning traffic. The town wasn't that big so there was not a lot of noise. A cleaning lady walked by, pushing a cartful of towels and toilet paper. She was short and plump. She looked up at Godfrey and addressed him.

"Good morning," the lady said.

"Good morning to you," replied Godfrey.

She smiled as she walked by. Godfrey looked up and saw a big, bright red sign that said, "EAT HERE." *Well, that is an easy enough sign to see.*

He walked over to the little country breakfast diner. The place was small and quaint. There were a good many people inside, especially truckers. Godfrey walked in and scanned the place and met the eyes of a waitress.

"Good morning, just have a seat and I'll get to you in a minute," the lady said.

Godfrey found a spot near a window and sat down. The lady soon came up and gave Godfrey a menu to figure out what he wanted.

"What do you want to drink, honey?" the lady asked in an especially drawn out southern accent.

"Coffee and orange juice please," Godfrey answered.

"I'll be back in a second with your drinks, and to get your order," the lady said.

"Okay, thanks," Godfrey responded.

Godfrey opened up the menu to see what he wanted. Godfrey felt like he was starving so everything on the laminated menu looked good to him. The lady was back quickly with Godfrey's coffee and orange juice.

"All right, have you decided what you want?" the waitress asked.

"Yes, I would like to have the steak, scrambled eggs, and grits. With a side of maple sausage too," answered Godfrey.

"Darn, honey, you must be starving," the lady said.

"Yeah, I guess you could say that. I feel like I haven't eaten in centuries," Godfrey said with a smile and a chuckle.

The waitress laughed with Godfrey and put the order in for his food. As Godfrey waited for his food, he started thinking again about everything that had happened. To get his mind off the subject, he picked up a napkin and asked the waitress if he could borrow a pen. She gave it to him, and went on with her tasks. Godfrey had an image in his head and felt like he needed to draw it. He spread out the napkin as much as possible and started drawing. He had to be careful because the pen would tear the thin napkin. He scribbled here and there, and a picture started forming as if out of thin air. He was completely and utterly focused on what he was doing. Godfrey had never felt a passion like this; it was amazing to him. Before he knew it, his food was ready. The waitress brought it over to him.

"Watch out, it's hot now," she said.

"Thank you," answered Godfrey.

"What are you drawing there? It looks like the crucifixion," she said.

"Yeah, I guess it is," Godfrey responded.

"Enjoy your food, honey," she said.

"Thanks," answered Godfrey.

Godfrey took in a giant whiff of his food. He loved the smell of the hot greasy mess. He began eating a little and continued to work on his picture. He sat at the table over an hour, eating and drawing. When he was finally finished, he got up and paid for his food and headed back to his room. When he got there, he used the bathroom. Then he pulled out his art supplies and painted the picture that he had drawn at the diner until it was finished. It was a detailed painting of the crucifixion. It looked so real and vibrant that it appeared as though Godfrey painted the scene in person. Godfrey was exhausted from painting; his hand, eyes, and head were killing him. It didn't matter how much pain or fatigue he felt, the picture was inside of him and it had to come out. It was almost like a child ready to be born. With a sense of accomplishment, Godfrey sat back on his bed and began reading his Bible again.

As he was reading, he heard a voice deep inside his chest guiding him to turn on the television and put it on channel 12. Godfrey did as the voice told him and grabbed the remote and turned on the television. When he turned it on, there was a guy on TV talking about painters sending in pictures of their paintings for a contest to paint the new studio. Godfrey was shocked, and thought, *that must have been God talking to me.*

Then he heard the voice again: *It is Me; contact that man, and show him your paintings*.

Godfrey wrote down the contact information, turned off the television, and started reading again. Soon after, Godfrey faded into a deep sleep. He woke early in the morning. He had been dreaming all night. The most prevalent dream he had been having was one about heaven. The images his mind had created were still fresh in his head. He sat up in his bed and was examining his painting that he finished the day before. It was really good; the detail was perfect, and the colors just came together flawlessly. Godfrey didn't even want to eat; he had another painting cooking inside of him. This time the subject would be heaven. Godfrey stood up and stretched a little; he then gathered his paint brushes and cleaned them up. He set up his canvas and stroked away like a madman. Godfrey painted all day and all night. He didn't stop to eat until he finished.

Chapter 18: Conflict

John Maxwell was sitting in his office looking over pictures of paintings that had been sent in via email. They were all good paintings, but none seemed to catch his eye. He was waiting for a quickening of his spirit to pick one, so it would be the right one. As John was diligently examining the paintings, he heard knocking at his office door.

"Who is it?" John asked.

"It's your wife," Meredith responded.

"Come in, dear," John answered.

As Meredith came in John got up and kissed her on the cheek. Meredith was wearing a white jogging outfit; she had just finished her morning run. She usually ran when she was upset. Her hair was in a tight pony tail. Little strands of hair were sticking out on her forehead. Meredith loved staying fit; she always had John interview doctors and other health experts on the show. Meredith had something on her chest; she was worried. John could tell by the expression on her face.

"What's wrong, honey?" John asked.

"It's our daughter, John; she is worrying me to death," Meredith responded.

By this time, they were both seated—John was in his office chair, and Meredith in one of the leather chairs in front of the desk.

"What did she do this time?" John asked with a hint of sarcasm in his voice.

"I saw her smoking pot in our house again last night," Meredith responded in an aggravated tone.

"I don't know what to do, babe; I've told her repeatedly not to do it in the house. She told me that she had quit smoking, and altogether denies it," John said.

"Well, she lied to you; she definitely hasn't quit. John, she doesn't listen to you or me. I'm surprised she even entertains the idea of halfway listening to us in the first place," Meredith said.

"I'll have to talk to her about it," John said, trying to calm Meredith down.

"Talk to her? When? While you're here working on this show? You don't even come home at night!" Meredith asked.

"Meredith, don't start with me here. You know I'm busy," John responded.

"John, you are so full of it. Tabitha is this way because you have been busy her whole life!" Meredith exclaimed.

"You just hold on a minute! I can't help I was called into the ministry! This is my calling! And you are supposed to be helping me!" John countered.

"This isn't a ministry! This is a popular TV show teaching fake Christians how to get rich! This has nothing to do with God or salvation! We are a bunch of hypocrites!" Meredith screamed.

John stood up, speaking with his arms. His face was red hot with anger. "What do you want me to do? Just give up? Quit? Throw in the towel and tell God I couldn't finish the task?" he replied hotly.

Meredith stood up and pointed her finger directly at John. "I want my husband back. I want you to come home and hold me. I want a daughter who loves me and loves God. I want peace again, not Christian politics," Meredith said in a low voice.

Meredith started crying; John put his head in his hands and let out a breath of despair.

"So do I, Meredith, so do I," John desperately answered.

Meredith wiped her tears, looked at John, and said, "John if something doesn't change, I am getting a divorce. I can't take it anymore; God knows I can't take it anymore. I am at the end of my rope."

She walked out of the door, and closed it gently. John sat there, stunned. He knew life was not the greatest for them, but Meredith had never mentioned divorce before. When she said that, it stung John right in his heart. The worst thing of all was that he had to go on the air in two hours and pretend that everything was fine.

Chapter 19: Disruption

At the hotel, Godfrey woke up late in the morning. When he sat up, he saw the painting he had done the night before. He had painted three pictures. One was the gates at the entrance to heaven. The second one was of the great city with its golden streets. The third was the top of the mountain where God's throne was. The colors of the paintings glimmered brightly. Godfrey's detail was impeccable.

Godfrey took a shower, cleaned up a bit, and went to the diner again to get something to eat. As Godfrey walked out of the diner, the thought came to him to get in contact with the man on the television and to show the man his paintings. At first Godfrey figured he would just call and talk to the man, but he felt that he needed to go see him in person.

Godfrey thought, *I know that the guy's ministry is in this town, but I don't know where. I'm sure somebody does; let me go ask Grace.*

Godfrey went outside and walked toward the hotel office. The weather was humid; the sky was overcast with the wind slightly blowing. When Godfrey came inside the office, the same lady Godfrey had the prophecy for was working. Her eyes lit up when she saw Godfrey. She came around the counter as quick as she could and gave him a huge hug.

"Thank You, Jesus, for using this man! Thank You, Lord!" Grace exclaimed.

"It's nothing really, ma'am; I didn't even know that it was going to happen," Godfrey responded.

"My husband has been healed from his cancer; the doctors don't even know what to say! Listen, I don't have much to give you for this. So I paid for your room for the rest of the week," Grace said.

"Thanks! You didn't have to do that; I have the money to pay," Godfrey said.

"Oh nonsense; it is already done," Grace said.

"Thank you very much, Grace," Godfrey said.

"You're welcome, honey," Grace responded.

"Grace, I was wondering if you could tell me something?" Godfrey asked.

"What is it, honey?" Grace responded.

"Do you know where John Maxwell's office is located— the place from which he does his broadcasting?" Godfrey asked.

"Ohh, him, that money-hungry hypocrite. That guy makes all of us look bad. Yeah, I know where his office is, but I don't know why an angel like you would want anything to do with him," Grace responded. Grace had her hands on her sides and her head was swaying side to side as she told Godfrey about John Maxwell.

"Well, it's not complicated, but I can't reveal too much at this time. I know that I have to go talk to him though," Godfrey responded.

"Man on assignment; you are a strange one, Mr. Godfrey. I guess I can take you there if you want me to," Grace said.

"That would be great; what time can we go?" Godfrey asked.

"In just a few minutes. I'll get one of the girls to take over here in the office," Grace answered.

"Sounds good. Let me go get a few things before we leave," Godfrey said.

Godfrey stepped out of the office and headed to his room. Inside he grabbed his paintings and stacked them together with paper covering the front of them. Godfrey carried them out; Grace was waiting outside in her car.

"You ready?" Grace asked.

"Yeah," Godfrey responded.

He got into Grace's vehicle, and they headed out of the parking lot onto the main road. There wasn't a lot of traffic. After they passed two stop lights, the surroundings changed to open fields and trees. Unaware of what was watching them, the two continued to drive casually to their destination. Above the vehicle, a wicked spirit was levitating in the sky and following Godfrey and Grace. The spirit was a very high-ranking one. Lucifer himself assigned this fallen angel to disrupt Godfrey as much as possible until Lucifer had more time to deal with him himself. It had the face of a jackal, but its eyes were small slits and completely white. The lining of the being's skull could be seen, trimmed in white, through the dark brown fur. Its mouth was like a black hole, with flies going in and out of it, while its tongue hung lifeless out of the side of its mouth. The demon was wearing a dark red cloak that covered all of its body. The cloak had the texture of what looked like large shiny, oily scales. Besides the cloak, the only things that could be seen was its face, hands, wings, and the spikes coming out of its back. It had two wings covered in brown feathers. There was barely any skin on them; mostly bone could be seen through the feathers. Its back curved over like an old man, well along in years. Ripping through the back of the cloak were the creature's long, sharp spikes. They started at bottom of his neck and ended at the tip of his spine. This particular fallen spirit had multiple talents; it was an expert in disrupting plans. His rank was Belial, so that was the name he went by. In the old world he had had an angelic name, but that had all changed now.

Belial was told by his king, Lucifer, that he had the authority to disrupt the two, but he could not kill them. If he tried, angels would come and cast him into Tartarus. No one wanted to go there. As Godfrey and Grace were driving, Belial reached down and touched the hood of the vehicle. His long, bony, furry hand went through the hood and down into the engine.

Belial then chanted, "I curse you vehicle; you will not work this day or any other day ever again." When Belial said that, black mist poured out of his mouth like steam escaping a kettle. The mist surrounded the vehicle. When it did, the car's power turned off.

Grace asked, "What in the world is happening?"

Godfrey answered, "I don't know."

Grace hurried and pulled the vehicle over to the side of the road. There was no power whatsoever, and the steering wheel was as stiff as a board.

"There shouldn't be anything wrong with this car! It's only a couple of years old," Grace said.

"Something is definitely wrong, that's for sure," Godfrey said.

They stepped out of the car and popped the hood open. As they opened the hood, steam came up ferociously as if the engine was overheated. The two backed up and started coughing. Belial was pleased with his work, but he wasn't done yet. There was a tractor trailer coming up the road just behind them. Belial flew over to the truck and touched one of the tires. The front right tire popped, causing the driver to veer directly toward Godfrey and Grace. Godfrey looked up and saw the truck coming. He frantically grabbed Grace and jumped off into the ditch on the side of the road as the truck smacked right into Grace's car. The car flew over Godfrey and Grace just as they landed in the ditch. The truck driver regained control of his truck, and halfway stayed on the road as he slid further up the road. Belial started laughing hysterically—so much that his sides were hurting. Then he disappeared from the scene.

Dust and metal landed on Godfrey and Grace. The smell of burnt rubber saturated the air. Godfrey covered Grace as much as he could from the blast. He was lying on top of her back.

"Grace, are you okay?" Godfrey asked.

Grace was face down in the dirt with her hands over her head. She wouldn't even open her eyes.

"No! I'm not okay! I just about died! I feel like I'm about to have a heart attack!" Grace responded.

Godfrey stood up and surveyed the scene. He wiped the dirt and debris off his clothes. Grace's car was flipped over to the left of them. A couple of the wheels were spinning from the impact. The tractor trailer was up ahead, hanging on the edge of the ditch. If the driver hadn't stopped the truck from going over the side of the road, Godfrey and Grace would have been crushed. There was debris from the accident lying everywhere. People had stopped and left their vehicles to see what had happened. Police and emergency vehicles' sirens could be heard coming toward the accident. Godfrey helped Grace up; she started crying when she saw her vehicle turned over; it was completely totaled. Godfrey put his arm around her, and comforted her as best he could. Before going up the ditch, Godfrey reached into one of the car's broken windows and grabbed his paintings. When the two got onto the road, a crowd of people gathered around them. The trucker who wrecked was the first one. He was very tall, about six feet or so. He had a large beer gut protruding in front of him. He had on black cowboy boots with blue jeans and a short-sleeved plain white T-shirt.

"Are y'all alright? I don't know what the hell happened," the trucker said.

"Hell, that is what happened," Godfrey responded.

"I'm sorry, y'all; my tire popped out of nowhere," the trucker said.

"It's all right; at least we're still alive," Godfrey said.

"It ain't all right; my car is destroyed!" Grace exclaimed.

By now, police and an ambulance had arrived. The paramedics came over to Godfrey and Grace to check them out. They brought the two over to their ambulance. Godfrey was fine, but Grace was still really shaken up about the ordeal. The police sat and hounded them for a while to see what exactly happened. The truck company was going to take care of all the expenses. The insurance company was already talking about giving Grace a nice lump sum to keep everything quiet. The company didn't want the bad publicity.

Godfrey was standing off away from the crowd of officials talking to Grace and the trucker. There was still a traffic jam from the accident, so people were standing around their cars waiting. A young woman who was snooping around came walking up to Godfrey to ask for a light for her cigarette. It was Tabitha Maxwell. She was on her way to work. She had on her normal attire—blue jeans, sandals, and a black fitted T-shirt. Her hair was tied back in a lazy bun.

"You have a light?" Tabitha asked.

"No, sorry, I don't smoke," Godfrey responded.

"That's okay. I should quit anyway. My dad would be really happy about that," Tabitha said.

"Well, it is really bad for you," Godfrey said.

"Oh, please do not start preaching, I hear it enough already," Tabitha said. "So, were you in the wreck?"

"Yeah, I was the passenger in the car that's flipped over," Godfrey said.

"Nothing like this ever happens in this town. I'm glad you are okay," Tabitha said.

"Yeah, I am grateful to be alive…I'm sorry, where are my manners? I'm Godfrey, nice to meet you," Godfrey said.

Godfrey reached out with a formal handshake. Tabitha answered back with a handshake.

"Likewise, Godfrey, I'm Tabitha…Tabitha Maxwell," Tabitha answered.

"Your dad isn't by chance John Maxwell?" Godfrey asked.

"Yeah, that's my dad," Tabitha said with a sigh.

"I was trying to get to his office. I have some paintings I wanted to show him. You know, for his contest," Godfrey said.

"Oh yeah, I remember him mentioning that. Are they any good?" Tabitha asked.

"Is what any good?" Godfrey asked.

"Your paintings, are they any good?" Tabitha asked again.

Godfrey suddenly became offended by what she said. It was the artist rising up in him. He felt his face turning red.

"Yeah, they're good," Godfrey responded.

"Calm down; there's no reason to get mad about it, I was just asking," Tabitha said.

"I'm not mad," Godfrey answered, feeling his cheeks burning.

Tabitha started laughing, seeing how angry Godfrey became about his paintings. It was the first time she had laughed in a while. It felt good. Godfrey quickly forgot how mad he was when he heard Tabitha laughing. When he had first seen her, Godfrey had thought that Tabitha was very beautiful. She was even more pleasing to him when he saw her glow from giggling.

"I'm sorry. I shouldn't have questioned your talents," Tabitha said, still giggling. "I can give you a ride to his office if you want. That's where I am heading anyway."

"All right; that works for me. Let me go and tell my friend that I am leaving," Godfrey said.

"Okay, that's fine," Tabitha said.

Godfrey walked over to Grace and told her that he found a ride. He let her know that he would check on her later tonight. Godfrey grabbed his three paintings and walked back over to Tabitha.

Chapter 20: The Ride

Tabitha and Godfrey walked through the traffic and found her car. They hopped in and waited to be waved through the long line of vehicles. Godfrey noticed that Tabitha did not keep a clean vehicle at all. Before getting in, Tabitha had to grab a pile of papers, fast food bags, and a couple of bottles off the seat so Godfrey could sit down. There were cigarette ashes everywhere. It was a nice car. It had leather seats, but they were dirty and stained from the continuous smoking. She really didn't pay attention to the road either. He could tell she was a daydreamer.

"So, Godfrey, you don't even look like you're bothered at all by the accident you just had," Tabitha said.

"Well, yeah, I guess you could say that death is no stranger to me," Godfrey responded hesitantly.

"Really, death no stranger, huh? You had a hard life or something?" Tabitha asked.

Godfrey could tell that she was digging as much information as possible out of him. *She is a nosy one,* he thought. Godfrey didn't want to reveal where and what all he had been through to anyone yet, especially not the young, cute, and inquisitive Tabitha Maxwell.

"The beginning of my life was not so great, but I don't really want to talk about that right now, if you don't mind," Godfrey responded, trying to be polite as possible.

"Oh I see, you're playing the quiet guy. The one who has a dark hidden past that you can't expose or something bad will happen," she said, as if quoting a line from a movie.

Tabitha started giggling at her own joke. The laughter was contagious and Godfrey soon joined her. They had just met, but both of them felt as they had known each other each other for a long time.

After the laughter stopped, Godfrey asked, "So what's your deal? Do you work for your dad or something?"

"Yeah, I bummed out of college and had to come home. My dad pays me decent money, and the work is not too hard. I've been helping him for a couple of years now," Tabitha responded.

Godfrey nodded his head, showing that he understood what she said, and responded, "Oh, okay"

Tabitha went on talking, "Personally though, I don't much care about the preaching, Christianity, or God, for that matter. The only thing God has done for my family is break it up."

Godfrey, not really sure what to say, answered, "I can tell something has hurt you in your past."

Tabitha, expecting Godfrey to be like all the other Christians she had encountered who judged her right away, was shocked to hear one who actually had a little love and understanding toward her instead.

"My family was great before my dad went into his TV ministry. It has done nothing but bring us problem after problem," Tabitha said as she threw the remnant of her cigarette out the window.

"If you feel this way about your dad's ministry, then why are you helping me?" Godfrey asked.

"You know, I really don't know? For some reason I feel like I have to. You're different for some reason; you're strange like me," Tabitha answered with a small chuckle.

"That's a good enough reason for me, I guess," Godfrey responded as they both laughed together again.

Godfrey had a warm feeling when he thought of Tabitha. She was a hard case, but he felt connected to her in some sort of way. It felt like a deep spiritual knitting in his heart. He liked it. The two continued to chat away as they drove up the road. They finally made it to the studio grounds. Tabitha pulled up to the security gate. The guard waved her past and she parked the car.

Tabitha said, "Welcome to Our Blessed Network, my dad's precious baby." Godfrey noticed the huge sign that read "OBN." It was a large white circular shape, trimmed in blue on the edges. It stuck out more than the diner's sign. The two got out of Tabitha's car and went inside. They walked down the corridor to John's office. Tabitha knocked on the door and said, "Dad, it's me, Tabitha. Can I come in?"

John was sitting at his desk, checking his e-mail. He heard the knock and responded, "Come in, dear."

Tabitha and Godfrey walked in. John stood up and hugged his daughter. As he did, Tabitha introduced Godfrey, "Dad, this is Godfrey. He's a painter, and according to him, he's a good one."

John looked Godfrey in the eye and reached out and shook his hand. John thought he was seeing things, but he swore that Godfrey's eyes sparkled at him when he looked at them.

"Hello, Godfrey, it's nice to meet you." John said.

"You too, sir; you must be an important man," Godfrey said.

John chuckled a little and asked, "Why do you say that?"

"Because I have been through hell and high water to get here," Godfrey said.

John, not really sure whether to take Godfrey seriously or not, just smiled and said, "Well, I'm glad you made it." John returned to his desk, and said, "You two have a seat." Godfrey and Tabitha sat down in the brown leather chairs. John leaned back in his chair with his hands clasped together, resting under his chin. "All right, so you are a painter?" began John.

"Yes, I have them here if you want to see them," responded Godfrey.

Tabitha sat up a little with excitement and said, "Dad, he says they are really good."

John noticed that his daughter was acting a bit strangely. She seemed happier. Usually she moped around with a depressed countenance. Seeing this caused a little burst of hope in John's heart.

"Go ahead and pull them out, Godfrey; let's see them," John said.

Godfrey lay out the three paintings. He handed them over to John, one by one. When John looked at them, his eyes lit up with imagination and wonder. Jon couldn't believe the detail in them. He felt like he was really there as he examined the paintings.

"Wow, these are breathtaking. They look real; it's as if you went there and painted them," John said, handing them to his daughter to look at.

"Dude, these are awesome!" Tabitha exclaimed.

Godfrey responded, "Thanks."

"You are modest for a master painter with works like these. You should be teaching at some kind of university," John said.

Tabitha had both her legs pulled up into the chair. Her arms were wrapped around them. After looking at Godfrey's paintings, she suddenly realized that there was something special about Godfrey. She couldn't take her eyes off of him. He was like an intricate puzzle that she had to find out about.

"You are hired, my friend, but what can I pay you?" John asked.

"All I ask is that you provide me the necessities—a roof, a bed, food, water, and a bath. That is all I need," Godfrey responded.

"Well, I'll have to talk to my wife. But I would love it if you stayed at my house," John said.

Tabitha smiled slightly and blushed. Godfrey leaned forward in his chair and agreed. The three sat and talked for awhile. John showed Godfrey where he would be painting. Godfrey let John know what supplies to order, so that he could get to work as quickly as possible. Images still burned in his heart, so he needed to get back to painting and release them on the canvas.

Chapter 21: God's Chosen

Belial was floating above a small country bar outside the town limits of Athens. It was night and all the most beautiful of people had shown up. There were mostly motorcycles outside, with the exception of a white van and a couple of cars. The parking lot surrounded the front and side of the bar. The parking lot wasn't concrete, but dirt mixed with gravel. The name of the bar was The Bears' Den. It was on an old sign that had a rebel flag raised high above it.

I need someone; I want to put some fear in the Maxwells for harboring an escaped convict...I am sure there is someone to fulfill my task in here, Belial thought.

Belial levitated down into the bar. He went right through the ceiling. No human saw him, but the familiars and demons did. They also recognized the authority Belial carried. He just wasn't some demon trying to survive; Belial was a fallen angel who had fought with Lucifer in the angelic rebellion. Belial was one of the highest of the fallen angels, and not known for his kindness.

"Whoever is the highest rank here, bring your ass here now and give me a report!" Belial gurgled.

There were just a few spirits inside the bar. One that had the appearance of a chimpanzee came floating toward Belial. Bowing his head, he kissed a ring on Belial's right hand.

"What can I do for you, master Belial?" the imp asked.

"Which one of these humans in here has the guts to murder? I have a task for him," Belial responded.

"I have one over here, sire; his name is Carlo Rainone. He's a biker; he used to be in the military, and he's a nutcase," the imp said.

Carlo Rainone was sitting by himself at a table in the corner of the bar. He was tall, a little over six feet or so. His head was bald, and there were flames tattooed on both sides of it. He had on a black leather jacket; his jeans wore torn in some spots. He wore black combat boots with red shoe strings going down them. He was working on a large pitcher of beer by himself, and also had a couple of lines of cocaine laid out for him to snort.

"He should be just fine, master; he killed quite a few in Iraq—even more in Afghanistan," the imp said.

"Yes, he'll do. Now get back to work and fill hell's mouth with souls!" Belial exclaimed.

As the imp and all the other demons went back to work, Belial floated toward Carlo until he was behind him. Carlo had his head down because he was snorting his lines of cocaine. When he jerked from the rush, Belial seized his head with both his hands. Carlo couldn't move; his eyes couldn't even blink. Belial put his mouth beside Carlo's left ear and said, "I have chosen you; you are my vessel."

Carlo responded, "Who are you?"

"I am god," Belial responded.

"God, what do you want with me?" Carlo responded.

"Do you dare question me, you fool; I will kill you right here and now," Belial responded.

"No, I'm sorry. I didn't mean to question you," Carlo responded.

"Get up, get on your bike, and drive where I tell you to go!" Belial demanded.

"Okay," Carlo answered.

Carlo did as Belial said; he went outside and got on his bike. Belial gave him the directions to John and Meredith Maxwell's house. Carlo looked in his bike satchel and pulled out his Colt .45 to examine it. He released the magazine to see if it was full; it was, so he inserted it back into the chamber. Carlo grabbed his motorcycle helmet and slid it on; it was black with a screaming skull on it. After Carlo was suited up, he headed down the road toward the Maxwell home.

Chapter 22: Meet Your Maker

John, I do not want anybody staying with us right now," Meredith said.

Meredith was on her cell phone, talking to John. She was on her way home.

"Meredith, I am telling you there is something special about this guy. I feel that this is God's will," John said.

"Is it God's will for me and you to get a divorce? Because that feels right to me," Meredith snapped.

"Please, honey, I'm begging you, stop talking about divorce. I have enough to worry about," John contended.

"That's the problem; you worry about everything except me and Tabitha," Meredith said.

Meredith was driving down an old country road which led to the Maxwell house. It was night; no one was on the road except for Meredith and someone not too far behind her. It looked like the headlights of a motorcycle. Meredith thought John was being really sweet and sincere on the phone about this guy Godfrey, so she felt kind of bad for acting the way she was. Plus John said that it looked as if Tabitha liked him, so she figured she would give him a chance.

Meredith exhaled and then said, "All right, John, I'll let him stay, but you are not off the hook. We need to do some serious talking about our future."

"I know, hon; we will. I promise you will not regret it," John said.

"I'll talk to you when you get home," Meredith said.

"Okay…love," before John could finish the sentence Meredith had already hung up the phone.

Meredith turned into the driveway, lighting up the house as she turned in the circular gravel driveway. She could barely see though, because the headlights she saw on the road behind her followed her into the driveway. The light was shining into her rearview mirror. *Well, they might need help.*

Meredith turned her car off and opened the door to step out. She put her hand over her eyes because of the blinding headlights. "Can I help you? Is there something wrong?" Meredith asked as she stood.

A silhouette walked closer to her and answered, "Yes, as a matter of fact, you can help."

Out of the light, Meredith suddenly realized the barrel of a Colt .45 was touching her forehead. The holder of the weapon was lightly pushing her. With each push, there was more force.

"What do you want?" Meredith asked, as she instinctively put her hands in the air.

The figure responded, "Let's go in the house."

"I have money; please, don't kill me!" Meredith exclaimed.

"Don't worry. I'll take the money later. Now turn around and go into the house," Carlo responded.

Meredith did as he commanded. Carlo was holding the gun in his right hand; in his left he had a roll of duct tape. Carlo had the barrel nudged in the crevice of Meredith's back; every time she slowed down, he pushed her with it to remind her of what was happening.

God, I'm going to die tonight; please God, don't let me die tonight. Let me see my family one more time before You let this man kill me.

Meredith nervously unlocked the front door. She noticed that her hands were shaking. Carlo did too, laughing because of it. They entered and Carlo told her to turn on the lights. She did. Meredith got a good look at Carlo. She could tell he was no angel. The two were in the living room. Carlo motioned her to come closer to him. She did, but started to sob the closer she came.

"Come on, I'm not gonna bite, or maybe I will," Carlo said mockingly.

"Please, don't hurt me. I'll give all my jewelry and money; please just let me live," Meredith begged.

When she was in front of him, Carlo leaned down to her and said, "Turn around, and put your hands behind your back and for God's sake stop that damn shaking. You're starting to piss me off."

Meredith did as he said; she could hear duct tape making that sticky, tearing sound it makes when somebody pulls a piece off. Carlo grabbed both her frail wrists with one hand and started wrapping them together with the tape.

"Close your eyes," Carlo said.

"What, why?" Meredith asked.

"Close your eyes! Now! Don't make me say it again!" Carlo exclaimed as he grabbed a handful of Meredith's hair. She winced in pain.

"Okay! Okay! They're closed!" Meredith screamed, as she cried from the pain.

Carlo then wrapped tape around her eyes and mouth. He pushed her hard to the ground on her stomach and taped her ankles together. Her nose and chin were hurting from the impact on the ground. Meredith was now laying on the floor, bound and scared to death. She did not know why this was happening, but knew that it was real and this guy meant business.

"Now, that wasn't so hard was it?" Carlo asked, as he went into their kitchen.

He opened the fridge and looked in. Carlo started moving stuff around, trying to find some kind of alcohol, but there was none except some red wine.

"Ya got any booze? All I see in here is communion wine," Carlo said.

Instead he grabbed a soda and came back into the living room, grabbed the remote, turned off the lights, and turned on the TV. He put on the guide to find something to watch. He finally settled on a channel, and watched a gory sci-fi flick.

"Now we wait for the target," Carlo said, and he opened the soda and took a sip.

He looked down at Meredith; she was face down on the white carpet that she and John had personally picked out when they had the house built. It was wet from her crying and bloody from where she hit her nose. Meredith was scared, thinking he was going to kill her at any moment. In her heart, Meredith did not feel like this night was going to end well for her. She remembered, as she was sobbing on the floor, that she hadn't even told John that she loved him.

"Hey you, crybaby, let me ask you a question. Are you ready to meet your Maker tonight?" Carlo asked as he leaned back on the cozy couch, laughing and enjoying every moment of it.

"Ah! Look! Someone just got killed by an alien beast!" Carlo exclaimed, laughing and spewing soda out of his mouth.

Chapter 23: Overboard

Godfrey and Tabitha were on their way to the Maxwell house. It was late, around eleven o'clock, and pitch black outside. The two were talking casually. The road was quiet, and they had their windows open because of how warm and humid the summer night was. Godfrey had his hand out the window, waving it up and down like it was flying through the air. *This is nice and peaceful. How time has changed men and technology; it's amazing.*

"Man, I'm starving; I hope mom made something to eat," Tabitha said.

"Yeah, I could eat something too," Godfrey said as he rubbed his belly.

"My mom can cook really well. She doesn't cook as much as she used to though. I think she is depressed," Tabitha said.

"I've been there—depression, I mean. That is a pit I never want to visit again," Godfrey responded as memories of hell came back to him. *I am so glad God delivered me from the torments of that place. I remember it well, but the side effects of it do not bother me at all now. Thanks for that, Lord.*

"Our lives have been pretty hard since my dad has had the ministry. He and my mom's marriage has taken the biggest beating from it. Then you have me, the heathen daughter who doesn't believe all of their religious crap," Tabitha said.

"Yeah, the enemy doesn't play fair; believe me, I know," Godfrey said.

"Let me guess. You blame the devil for all your problems," Tabitha said, looking at his profile.

"No, just the big ones," Godfrey said with a smile.

Tabitha responded by smiling. The two pulled into the driveway of the large brick house. Tabitha noticed that a motorcycle was behind her mom's car.

"Who is that?" she asked herself.

At first, Tabitha thought it could be one of her old boyfriends—one of the relationships gone wrong from her past. Godfrey knew something was wrong; he could feel it in his stomach. It was a feeling one gets when watching a brutal murder for the first time.

Godfrey said, "Something is not right here. I feel something evil around."

"What do you mean, you feel something evil?" Tabitha asked, feeling perplexed.

She parked the car behind the motorcycle. Godfrey grabbed her by the hand and stared into Tabitha's eyes and said, "Listen, I want you to walk into the house like you are alone. When you do, I will come in quickly behind you."

"What are you talking about?" Tabitha asked, getting scared.

She noticed a change in the way Godfrey looked too. Instead of the peaceful glow, his face looked cold and stern. His eyes were blank.

"Just trust me on this; I will explain everything to you. I promise," Godfrey said.

Tabitha started breathing hard, "Okay, I'll trust you on this," Tabitha said.

"All right; let's get out of the car and do this," Godfrey said.

The two stepped out of the car. They shut their doors quietly; Godfrey stayed hidden behind the vehicle as Tabitha walked toward the house.

The only sound that she made was from her feet hitting the gravel. A whippoorwill was singing its melodious tune in the surrounding woods. Tabitha walked up to the door first. Godfrey hid in the shadows away from the house so no one would see him. The door was unlocked.

That is strange, thought Tabitha.

Her mom always locked the door at night, especially when she was alone. Tabitha slowly pushed the door open. She forced herself to walk in the house. The hallway was dark; the only light in the house was in the living room coming from the TV. She crept up the hallway as quiet as a mouse. She could feel and hear her heart beating. She finally asked, "Mom, are you here? Where are you?"

Tabitha stood still in the quiet hallway, expecting her mom to answer. Instead she was answered by the sound of the safety switching off on Carlo's gun behind her.

"Don't turn around; momma's not gonna be answering for a while. She's a little tied up right now," Carlo said. "Put your hands up," Tabitha did as the voice told her, and felt her skin go cold. "Where is your boyfriend?" Carlo asked.

"Who's my boyfriend?" Tabitha answered.

"Don't play dumb…" *Smack!* Before Carlo could finish his sentence, Godfrey hit him on the back of the head with a large rock he had found outside. Carlo bent over from pain and turned to shoot Godfrey. But when he turned around, he was answered by a knee in his face. Carlo heard his nose make a crunching sound as he spun in the air backward, falling hard on his back on the ground. Godfrey took the magazine out of the weapon, discharged the round in the chamber, and threw the gun past Tabitha who stood stunned.

Then Godfrey grabbed Carlo by the feet and dragged him outside. Carlo felt his head hit every step as they went with a repetitive thump. Before Carlo could respond or get up, Godfrey started stomping Carlo on his head and throat. Tabitha ran out and screamed for Godfrey to stop, but Godfrey kept going; his face had a cold blank expression. The only movement was from the tremors of his foot hitting Carlo. By this time, Carlo couldn't defend himself anymore. His hands were at his sides. His face was a mess of blood and mush. Godfrey grabbed another large rock and straddled Carlo. *I am going to kill you.*

He picked the rock up with both hands. He was about to bring it down on Carlo's forehead until it cracked when he was interrupted by Tabitha screaming, "What you are doing, Godfrey? Stop! That's too much!"

Suddenly Tabitha watched a bright white light appear behind Godfrey. A figure of a man with wings could be seen, standing in the white light. It was Jazrael. Tabitha's eyes opened wide. Jazrael commanded, "Stop, Godfrey. You are not in the war anymore. Put the rock down and call the police. Get up and go help Tabitha and her mom." Godfrey snapped back into reality and looked down and saw what he had done. Carlo was barely breathing. Jazrael looked at Tabitha and said, "Peace be upon you, child," and disappeared. Godfrey got off Carlo, and looked at amazed Tabitha.

"Tabitha, go find your mom," Godfrey said.

Tabitha shook her head, as if it brought her back to reality. She ran inside to find her mom. Godfrey followed. Tabitha found her mom on the living room floor, face down and bound. Tabitha and Godfrey took the duct tape off her. Meredith sat up, rubbing her wrists, face, and neck.

She asked, "Is he gone? Where is that evil man?"

Tabitha gave her mom a tight hug, started crying, and responded, "He's outside, and I think he's dead."

Godfrey answered, "He's not dead; we should go ahead and call the police."

Tabitha grabbed the phone to call the police while Godfrey went outside to keep an eye on Carlo to make sure he didn't try to escape. By the look of him though, he would not be budging for a while. Meredith and Tabitha hugged each other until the police and ambulance came. Meredith was in shock; she was glad she was alive. Tabitha called her dad to tell him what had happened. When John heard the news, he ran to his car and sped home.

Chapter 24: Confession

Several hours later, when the police were through questioning everyone, they left and the bloodied and beaten Carlo Rainone was in an ambulance on his way to the hospital. John was home and trying to comfort Meredith as she tried to calm down from her ordeal. It was late now, getting close to morning. Tabitha and Godfrey were still up and talking. Meredith and John finally went up to their room. John was nearly carrying her, because she was so weak and scared from her terrifying ordeal.

Tabitha and Godfrey sat on opposite ends of the couch. Godfrey was staring off into space, and Tabitha was facing him. She said, "Godfrey I don't know what is going on, but you have some explaining to do."

Godfrey exhaled deeply, and then reluctantly responded, "I know I do."

He leaned back onto the couch, looked at Tabitha and said, "Tabitha, I need you to listen carefully to what I am about to tell you, because believe me, it won't sound believable to you at all."

Tabitha was balled up on the couch—arms wrapped around her legs. She put a hand up in the air as if to put a stop sign there, and said, "Hold on! First off, who was that guy who appeared out of nowhere?"

"That was Jazrael, my guardian angel," Godfrey responded.

"Guardian angel? You have got to be kidding me," Tabitha responded, shaking her head in disbelief.

"No, I am not kidding you. He is very much real, as you saw," Godfrey said.

"Well, yeah, I can't question that he is real; I did see him with my own eyes," Tabitha answered.

"Do you mean that we all have guardian angels, or are you special?" Tabitha questioned.

"I don't know for sure, but I believe we all have angels assigned to us. Jazrael has been with me since I was a child. He saved me from drowning in a well," Godfrey said.

"How did you end up in a well?" Tabitha asked.

"Well, you see, Tabitha, I am from a different time," Godfrey tried to answer.

"Are you nuts? Did you escape from the loony bin? What you mean—a different time?" Tabitha asked with both her hands in the air.

Godfrey started to get aggravated with trying to explain everything to Tabitha. Godfrey stood up and said, "I am from southern France. My father was a stonemason. I was in the Knights Templar, and I served under them in the Crusades. I saw Jerusalem during the time of the Crusades when it had been conquered by Christian armies. I had my part in the murder of thousands of innocent people."

Tabitha gasped and said, "What?"

"It is all true. I was killed by Saracen assassins and descended into hell. I was there for centuries. Then God released me, and He brought me back to this time. I know it sounds crazy, but believe me, it is true. That's why my paintings are so good; I have been to heaven. I have walked the streets, and seen all the buildings, and I have met the Lord face to face," Godfrey said.

"Godfrey, you are nuts! Do you expect me to believe all of that?" Tabitha questioned.

Godfrey sat back down, "You modern people are a lost cause. God could come down right now, and manifest himself before everyone, and you would still doubt the very sight of your eyes," Godfrey contended.

Tabitha became a little offended. She then stood up and responded, “I’m sorry if I don’t trust something that someone says that sounds like it came out of a book of fairy tales. I mean, just think about it, there is no way that could be possible. Not even in the mind of the craziest storyteller.”

“I know, Tabitha, but you just have to believe me,” Godfrey contended.

Tabitha had her hand on her forehead, shaking her head with her eyes closed and said, “All right, Godfrey. I am tired and need to sleep this crazy night away. Let me show you where your room is. We’ll talk more about it tomorrow.”

Godfrey stood back up and agreed. All he wanted to do was sleep too.

Chapter 25: I'm Not Done with You

The ambulance that Carlo was being transported in was heading down the road at a quick speed. Carlo was beaten up pretty bad, but nothing that was life threatening. Carlo was a strong guy; he would pull through. There was one EMT driving and two paramedics in the back with Carlo. One was short and round—his name was Timmy; the other one wasn't so round and just a little taller—his name was Clark. The guy driving was the new guy—his name was Ryan.

"Man, that guy really beat this dude up," Timmy said.

"Yeah, I know, look at his face. It looks like he was stung by a bunch of bees," Clark answered.

"Can you blame him though? He had that poor woman tied up, threatening to rape and kill her at gun point," Timmy said.

"This guy got what he deserved. Once he heals up, you know where he is going," Clark said.

"It looks like he has been to prison before; look at those tattoos he has," Timmy pointed out.

"Yeah, I know. I wouldn't want him waiting for me at my house," Clark said.

The two carried on in conversation and continued examining Carlo. Carlo, on the other hand, was lost in dreams. The dream started by Carlo opening his eyes and noticing he was lying on a hospital bed. He was strapped down by three large brown belts connected over his chest, waist, and legs. He could barely see, because someone had a bright light in his eyes. The room started spinning, and Carlo had a hard time focusing on anything. He could barely keep his eyes open. Then, someone started speaking to him; the voice felt as if it was inside him and outside him at the same time.

"You couldn't even get a simple task done, could you?" the voice said.

"What? Who are you?" Carlo asked.

"I am your god, you fool, and I am very displeased with you," the voice said.

Carlo was feeling bad, because he could hear the pain inside the voice that was speaking. He responded, "I'm sorry; I will not fail again."

"You better not. If you do, I will tear you apart and feed you to the hounds of hell," the voice said.

"What do you want me to do, my lord?" asked Carlo.

"I want you to allow me to enter you, so that we can share our thoughts and be one with each other," said the voice.

"Uh…okay, I allow you to enter me," said Carlo.

The last thing Carlo remembered was his mouth being forced open, and a cold breeze blowing down his throat. Then everything went black.

The ambulance was barreling down the highway on its way to the hospital. Clark was reading a magazine while Timmy was staring off into space. Carlo's beaten body lay still. On his face, though, a wicked grin appeared. Slowly, his eyes opened. There was no color to them, only black. He turned his head and looked at both of the paramedics.

The still quiet broke with Carlo asking in a voice that was deep and rasping, "So…who wants to die first?"

Clark lowered his magazine, revealing his eyes. Timmy focused his eyes, and lifted his head off the wall of the van.

Clark asked, "What the…?"

Before Clark could finish, Carlo popped up like he had risen from an open coffin. He quickly grabbed the throats of both men. They grabbed the wrists of Carlo's powerful arms. The grip wouldn't budge. Timmy and Clark made choking sounds. The grip was so tight that they couldn't speak. Carlo looked at Timmy first; then he began slamming the back of his head against the van until his eyes gave a blank stare. Clark watched in horror. Ryan, not knowing what to do, hurriedly pulled over the ambulance in the parking lot of a convenience store. With little ease, Carlo rammed Timmy and Clark's heads together until the life left them both. With one final connection of the two heads, they made a cracking, crunching sound. Carlo threw the bodies down and reached for Ryan.

Ryan heard someone say his name, but it sounded like many voices all speaking in unison. Ryan turned his head slowly to look. A hand out of the darkness came out and grabbed his face, and violently pulled him into the back of the ambulance. Everything in Ryan's eyes and mind went black, never to be awakened again.

After Carlo had killed the three men, he ate their lunch and drank their sodas. Carlo then said, "Yeah, guys, I don't think you are gonna make it to the hospital. You three are all beat up really bad."

Timmy, Clark, and Ryan's bodies were stacked on top of each other like a pile of dirty clothes. Carlo opened their eyes so they could look at him while he talked to them. After eating, Carlo decided it was best to leave before anyone started wondering why this ambulance was just sitting in a parking lot. The CB radio was going crazy; every minute a dispatch called to ask for the EMT's location.

"It has been a pleasure, gentlemen, but I think I had too much fun and accidentally killed you. Sorry for that, and God bless you," Carlo said, stepping out of the back of the ambulance.

A little kid was eating his ice cream cone walking out of the store and stopped and stared at Carlo. Carlo's face was swollen and he had blood all over himself, so the little boy had reason to stare. As the kid was licking his ice cream, he noticed that maggots were crawling out of it. The little boy screamed and dropped it and ran to his mom's car that was parked at the gas pump. Carlo smiled and walked into the darkness of the woods across the street from the store. Shortly after Carlo disappeared, the ambulance burst into an unquenchable fire.

Chapter 26: Through Fire Comes Peace

The morning following the horrific scenario that occurred in the Maxwell house, Meredith woke up early in the morning. She sat up on the right side of the king-sized bed; she did this carefully so the movement would not wake John. It didn't; he lay in a deep sleep. Meredith's heart was feeling troubled. It was stealing sleep from her. She put on her robe and slippers and went downstairs. When she came down the steps, she looked into the living room to see if Tabitha and Godfrey ever went to bed. They had because they were not down there. Meredith peered out the window to see how the weather was; the sun was just coming up so she decided to make a cup of coffee and sit outside and figure this out, if it was possible.

Meredith made her coffee and stepped outside. The sun was rising; the sky was a pink color with streaks of orange. The air was fresh and cool. Meredith took in a deep breath. *It feels good to be alive.* The birds were singing and flying all around the backyard. Meredith wondered if the reason God had created the birds was to sing, because it caused the plants, flowers, and trees to grow healthier. She started walking across the large field that was their backyard. Her heart was pulsating for an answer from God.

For the first time in her life, Meredith felt terrified and fearful of death. She thought she possessed enough faith to not be scared of death or the grave. But suddenly, everything had come into question. She needed to reconnect and figure out why and what had happened to her.

Why? Why did this happen to me? What did I do to deserve that?

She watched the mockingbirds fly around, defending themselves against the crows. There were a few doves wobbling along, picking at the birdseed that fell to the ground from the feeders. She looked up in the sky and watched a lonesome red-tailed hawk glide with ease through the fresh morning sky, letting out its piercing scream.

As she walked and looked at the ground, she spoke out loud in a low voice, "God, where are You? What is the meaning of all this? There has to be a meaning of some kind. Or was this a cruel scenario like what happened to Job? I know I have not been perfect, and I have not felt alive for a long time. My heart has gone cold and feels dead to the world. What has happened to me, God? I used to believe in You; I used to love serving people for You, but now everything is a burden that never seems to end."

This was the first time Meredith had ever prayed like this. Since the glamour of the TV ministry had begun, she only said short political prayers that the people wanted to hear. How it had become this way, she didn't know. Since the kidnapping though, she knew that only God could help her.

"I just don't know anymore, God; life, it doesn't even make sense anymore. I told my husband I wanted a divorce; I can't believe I did that. I know it's not the Christian thing to do, but I can't take this anymore, God," Meredith said.

She continued to speak to God. For the first time in a long time, she let her heart spill out. She poured it all out, holding nothing back. She spoke, cried, yelled—she did a little of everything. It felt great to her; her words actually felt real. After her heart was empty and all the tears had dried, life sprang up inside her again. She felt as happy as a child; her heart beat strongly within her; she sensed God's love and destiny again. Meredith had once again found herself, and it was with God.

"It's so simple, Lord. As I give You my heart and tell you what's wrong, Your presence and peace make it better. Forgive me, God, for being so calloused," Meredith said.

Chapter 27: Let's Begin

The rest of the Maxwell house woke to the smell of breakfast cooking; Meredith had come back in and begun to cook for everyone. In a sense, her batteries had been recharged. This was a strange setting. For one thing, John was rarely home; Meredith had stopped cooking a long time ago; and Tabitha wasn't high from her usual morning joint. Godfrey, on the other hand, was simply grateful he was alive and not in hell. They all settled at the large dining room table; Meredith prepared everyone's plates and handed them out.

Tabitha was the first to notice something different about her mom. "Mom, are you okay?" Tabitha asked, as she ate a piece of bacon.

"I'm fine, dear, how about you?" Meredith responded.

"I'm great, I guess," Tabitha said.

John wrapped his arm around Meredith's slim waist as she came over and gave him his plate, and asked, "You're not in shock are you, honey?"

Meredith bent down and gave John a long and loving kiss, and responded, "No, I am at peace with what happened and desire to move on."

John, shocked by the kiss from the same woman who told him she wanted a divorce the previous day, said, "Okay, we'll leave it at that then."

When Meredith brought breakfast to Godfrey, she gave him a big hug and said, "I am glad God has sent you to our family, Godfrey."

Godfrey hugged her back and said, “You’re welcome, ma’am.”

They all ate and were full from the large breakfast that Meredith had made. They sat and talked while drinking coffee. The morning carried on and John decided to stay home from work today and spend it with Meredith. Tabitha and Godfrey were getting ready to go shopping so Godfrey could get some more clothes.

Godfrey and Tabitha got dressed and left the house. They got into Tabitha’s car and went into town. Tabitha broke the silence with the question, “So are you going to tell my parents what you told me last night?”

“No, I don’t think it’s the right time to do that, and you have to promise that you will not say anything either,” Godfrey said.

“Of course, I won’t say a word,” Tabitha said. “So you have actually been to hell and heaven? When I woke up today, I thought that I had dreamed all this up, but no, you are here in the flesh,” Tabitha said.

“It’s strange. I don’t know why God chose me for this, but He did,” Godfrey said.

“So what was hell like? Is it as bad as they say?” Tabitha asked.

“It is the most evil and tortuous place ever conceived. Think of the worst imaginable place you could put yourself, and magnify it a thousand times, and you might come close to what it is like there,” Godfrey said.

“Wow,” Tabitha said.

“Hell is for the individual; every fear that a person has is waiting for them in hell. Everyone has personal daily torments. There are group torments also. The demons that run the place love their jobs, and they do their best to make you know it,” Godfrey said.

“You don’t seem bothered too much about all of this; you seem peaceful about everything,” Tabitha said.

"When I was released from hell, Jazrael touched my head so my soul and spirit were healed from all of the effects that it had on me. I still have all of the memories, but that is it," Godfrey said.

Tabitha was feeling a little uneasy inside. Discovering all of this about Godfrey really put her own beliefs into question. She believed that hell and heaven were fairy tales created by archaic, superstitious nutcases. But she had a guy sitting beside her who claimed he was from the past sent into the future by God to save her father's ministry. It was all weighing up inside her. She could just deny it, but she had seen an angel appear and disappear in front of her with her own eyes. Tabitha was standing at a crossroads; eventually a decision would have to be made.

As they came closer to town, they noticed a roadblock had been set up. It was causing the traffic to build up. "I wonder what is wrong now?" Tabitha asked out loud.

"I don't know; it seems that there is always something going on in this town," Godfrey said.

"Yeah, ever since you showed up, I might add," Tabitha said.

"I guess you're right; someone is angry that I am here," Godfrey said.

They eventually made their way to a policeman guiding traffic. Tabitha opened the window and asked the man what was going on. He answered, sweat dripping down his forehead, "There was an incident last night with an ambulance. Some guy escaped from it leaving three dead EMTs. If you two see anything out of the ordinary, be sure to tell the police."

Tabitha sat stone-faced in shock, and answered, "We will, officer."

Tabitha looked at Godfrey. The two were thinking the same thing—it was the guy Godfrey nearly killed last night. He was on the loose with three murders under his belt. Tabitha called her dad and told him; but when she called the police were already at the house providing security for Meredith.

Chapter 28: I Need a Bike

Far into the woods, a few miles away from the burned up ambulance, Carlo sat against a large pine tree. He had his head leaned back. There was a small gurgling laugh coming out of his belly. There was blood all over his hands, and his face was still swollen from his encounter with Godfrey. In front of him lay the carcass of a deer; buzzards and crows were eating away at the animal. The birds didn't seem bothered by Carlo's presence, or Belial's.

"I need a bike; I lost mine to the cops," Carlo said.

Carlo opened his eyes and looked up above the feasting fowls and saw Belial hovering above them. Belial started speaking in a low chant that sounded like many voices at once, "From now on, you will travel at night. You have made quite a mess so far."

Carlo bowed his head and said, "Yes, my lord, but where can I find a bike?"

"There is a spot I have selected for you, but first you must eat and replenish your strength. Then I will show you where to go," Belial answered.

Carlo started laughing; he jumped up with superhuman speed. The birds scattered somewhat. He lunged toward the deer carcass and started ripping away at the rotted flesh. The buzzards and crows continued eating with him.

After Carlo was finished eating, he found a nearby creek and cleaned himself up as best as he could. He ran through the woods for several hours nonstop until came to a small seafood bar and grill. The name of it was Palmetto Seafood. It was a small place out in the country, but very popular place to the locals. At night though, only a couple of people hung out there, having a few drinks at the bar. Carlo watched the place from the trees that were behind it; Carlo just stood and stared blankly with no emotion at the small restaurant. It was another starry night—crickets and frogs chirping loudly all around Carlo.

Carlo waited for the command of his lord, Belial. "Go," said Belial.

Carlo started walking casually toward the place; it was quiet except for the bartender and the two bikers who were sitting at the outside bar. They were carrying on, joking and laughing. The two were obviously drunk. The place didn't close until well after midnight, and it was just past ten. Carlo came around to the front and entered the screened-in outside bar. He opened the door and walked over to the bar. The two bikers and bartender gave Carlo a long and scared stare as he sat down. They were trying to give him a hint that he was not welcome, but Carlo really didn't care.

The bartender, Sam, came over to Carlo as he was washing a beer mug and asked, "What will it be, sir?"

"Two doubles of Jack; I'm in an ass-kicking mood," Carlo said.

"All right, coming up," Sam answered.

The two that were to the left of Carlo were named Club and Diesel. They had on black leather jackets with the Hell's Angels symbol on the back. Club was about 6 feet 7 inches and 265 pounds. He had short brown hair with a long goatee. Diesel was seven inches shorter than Club, but at least eighty pounds heavier. He had a long braided ponytail going down his back; it was blonde with a mix of gray in it. Diesel looked over at Carlo, and watched as he sucked down double after double.

Diesel asked, "Are you all right, brother? You look like you just got ran over."

Club laughed a little as he drank his beer. Carlo didn't answer; he just stared down into one of the large shot glasses. The silence was becoming uneasy. Sam didn't like where this was headed, and said, "All right, guys, leave the man alone; everybody just drink your beers and mind your business."

Club looked up at Sam and said, "Diesel was just asking the man what wrong with him; he didn't mean anything by it. Hell, this guy was the one who said that he was in a kick-ass mood."

Carlo sat down the glass and asked, "You want to be the first one, fatty?"

Sam's jaw dropped; Club started laughing; Diesel, on the other, did not. Diesel stood up and asked, "What did you say, boy?"

Club was still drinking his beer and laughing and said, "Well answer him, tough guy."

Sam's stomach was feeling uneasy and he said, "Diesel, sit down."

Diesel, still standing, piped up and said, "Do you know who we are, boy? We're the frickin' Hell's Angels, and you're about to have a lot more problems than that swollen face of yours."

Club continued laughing, waiting for Carlo to respond.

Carlo had his head facing down so Sam couldn't see his eyes, but when Carlo started answering Diesel, he looked up and stared straight ahead. Sam noticed that Carlo's eyes had changed; they were pitch black.

Carlo said, "Hell's Angels, huh? They say that you guys are not to be messed with."

Diesel nodded in agreement with what Carlo was saying, "Yeah, that's right."

"Let me ask you something. Have you ever met an angel of hell?" Carlo asked as he turned and faced Diesel and Club. When the two saw his black eyes, they started to realize something was wrong. Club set his beer down, because he suddenly didn't want to drink anymore. Diesel backed up a couple of steps. Sam slowly bent down to reach for his shotgun.

"Don't you dare grab that gun unless you want me to take it from you and use it on you," Carlo snapped, not even looking in Sam's direction. Sam stood back and put his back against the wall, not understanding how Carlo knew what he was doing. Carlo was laughing as he stood up. When he did, the tables and chairs that were scattered around in the room lifted into the air, levitating as if they were hanging by strings by a puppeteer.

"What the hell are you?" asked Club.

Diesel jumped up out of his stool and pulled out a .357 magnum revolver and had it pointed at Carlo in just a split second. "I don't care who or what you are, I'm going to blow your head off!" he exclaimed.

"No, you're not, Diesel; instead, you will shoot Sam in the head," Carlo casually answered.

Sam asked, "What?"

Before anyone could react, Diesel was made by an invisible force to point the gun at Sam. "I'm sorry, Sam; I can't stop it," he said.

Diesel pulled the trigger twice. Everyone flinched from the shots, except for Carlo who was smiling. The first one hit Sam directly in the forehead; it caused the back of his head to blow out all over the wall behind him. The other shot hit him in the neck; this one was a little to the right when it hit so half of Sam's neck was ripped off. Sam's eyes were wide as he slid down the wall into the floor.

"Bravo, Diesel, bravo; now shoot your fat little friend," said Carlo.

Club tried to run, but the same invisible force that was using his friend was keeping him in place too.

"Diesel, please man, don't shoot me; we've been friends since we were kids," Diesel begged.

As the gun came casually back over to Club, Diesel said, “I can’t stop it; it’s doing it all by itself.”

Diesel was standing behind Club, and the gun was now aimed at an angle behind Club’s head. Club looked at Carlo; he noticed the nonchalant way Carlo sat and waited as if this was normal. Then Club stared at those black eyes that seemed as old as eternity; there was nothing in them. Maybe a long time ago, the owner of those evil eyes had loving memories of the past. Maybe. Instead, at this moment he was creating horrible new ones to cherish.

“Well, Diesel, let’s go. We don’t have all night, you know,” Carlo said.

Club closed his eyes and tensed up, waiting for the inevitable impact. He then said, “Diesel, I love you, man, and I forgive you for this.”

Diesel had a tear running down his left cheek, but it was like a mannequin crying because he couldn’t move his body. The only movement was from the outside force bending his will as it pleased, and right now it was making his finger slowly pull the trigger. Finally the gun went off and so did most of the front of Club’s face. Carlo watched and smiled as blood sprayed him from the shot. Carlo got up and grabbed the bottle of Jack Daniels from the bar, and watched as Diesel turned the gun on himself. After Diesel was dead, Carlo started walking out of the bar. Before stepping out he said, “Burn, burn to the ground; make ash and memories of what once stood here, and let the memories die and disappear.”

The bar exploded into a blazing inferno, just like the ambulance had. It burnt to the ground almost instantly. Carlo hopped on one of the former Hell’s Angel’s bikes, and road off into the pitch-black night.

Chapter 29: Back to Business

John woke up early the next morning at his house, which was new to him, since he always slept at the office because of his marriage problems. He sat up in bed and looked over at the clock. It was ten after six. The happy memory of he and his wife's relationship rekindling yesterday came back to him. He looked behind him and Meredith lay silently and peacefully asleep. John thought that it looked as if she was smiling as she slept. John finally got up and did his morning ritual before going in to work. He showered, shaved, brushed his teeth, got dressed, had some coffee, and headed off to work. It was exactly seven as he walked out the door.

When he stepped out, he said a prayer before leaving, "God, I pray that You send Your angels to protect my family from all wicked forces that decide to come against us. I pray this prayer in Jesus' name, amen." As John walked to his car, a warm, comforting feeling came over him from the prayer. The police had also dispatched a policeman to keep watch over their house, just in case Carlo felt like returning. John looked down at the white gravel, noticing that the tracks from the motorcycle were still there. It didn't help either, that Tabitha called him yesterday and let him know that the crazy guy who kidnapped Meredith had murdered three EMTs and was now on the loose. This thought made him pray again for the protection of his family. As John drove off he didn't see that his prayer was answered almost instantaneously.

An angel named Zadkiel was sent to the Maxwell household. Zadkiel stood on top of the roof of the house. He had large brown, feathered wings; they arched out like the shape of the letter "M" drawn in Gothic form. The angel had on a black breastplate that was traced in gold. On the front of it there was the profile of a male lion. The shoulders of the breastplate were bright red, and so was the cloak that covered the angel's legs. He had black boots that looked as hard as steel. The laces began at the bottom of the boots, then disappeared up and behind the cloak. The angel had short, black hair. His face was chiseled and fierce. There was a long scar that went over his right eye. He had a smile on his face like he was ready for combat and the very thought of war made him rejoice to be alive. On his side in a sheath was a massive claymore. It weighed a couple hundred pounds, and it was several feet long. It glimmered and shone by itself as if the sword had a life of its own. No one could see Zadkiel, of course, but his presence manifested by the overwhelming sense of peace that surrounded and enveloped the household. The angel had something in his right hand; it was a large rolled up scroll. His orders were to give the scroll to Godfrey.

Godfrey and Tabitha were still asleep and would not be up for a couple of hours. Godfrey was quietly asleep on the guest bed, and his eyes were moving side to side from REM sleep. Zadkiel appeared in the room and came over to Godfrey and touched his head.

Godfrey woke up to someone talking to him, or at least he thought he was awake. It was a large man with wings standing in front of him. This was not unusual for Godfrey; he was beginning to get used to encountering angelic beings. The angel was standing at parade rest, and said, "Hello, Godfrey, my name is Zadkiel; I am from the warrior class of the great angelic hosts, and I have a message for you, so rise because I have to show you many things." Godfrey stood up beside his bed; he noticed he didn't feel his feet touching the ground. Instead, wherever he thought to go, he would go. As Godfrey came over to Zadkiel, he looked back and saw his body still asleep. Zadkiel grabbed Godfrey by the arm and said, "Hold on." The two started floating up. Up and up they went through the roof of the house, continuing to ascend through the clouds and atmosphere. Godfrey actually felt it when they penetrated the atmosphere; it was like a hot bubble popping when they went through. After the two were above the earth, Godfrey looked around and saw how vast the universe was again. He saw angels going back and forth from the earth and heaven. He also noticed large demonic beings fighting the angels, trying to stop them from getting to their destinations.

Godfrey looked at Zadkiel and asked, "So what is it that you must show me?"

Zadkiel answered, "Watch the vision."

Godfrey looked and saw asteroids, large and small, coming toward the earth. He watched as they hit the earth, causing huge craters and cracks on the surface. Then Godfrey and Zadkiel were on the earth, but floating high above the ground. The ground was shaking and rumbling. Continents were splitting into pieces. Godfrey could hear people screaming and yelling. Great earthquakes were causing massive tidal waves to hit the shores; thousands were dying instantly.

As Godfrey watched, his jaws dropping, Zadkiel said, "Natural disasters like these will increase dramatically until the end comes. God will use these things to get the attention of mankind once again. This world is plagued by unbelief and doubt. I know that you have encountered this yourself since you have been back."

"Yeah, they have everything they could want or need, but it's like their souls are dead," Godfrey said.

"Listen, Godfrey, it's not just the natural disasters that will come. No, everything will be shaken—every aspect of men's lives will come under judgment. It will bring fear to many, but it will also bring out the sons of light," Zadkiel said.

"What do you mean?" Godfrey asked.

"You are a one. A son of light is a son of God," Zadkiel said.

"The ones who truly believe in their God and desire to listen to what He wants them to do will be the ones who will become the champions of faith, and it will be faith alone that will protect men," Zadkiel said.

“So what do I need to do?” Godfrey asked.

“You need to tell John, so he can spread the message; the Lord wants His people to know what is going to happen,” Zadkiel said.

“When will all of this begin?” Godfrey asked.

“It has already begun,” Zadkiel said.

“What do you mean?” Godfrey asked.

“Our time is short, Godfrey; write down what you saw and tell John,” Zadkiel said.

As Zadkiel said this, the picture around Godfrey began to fade like a sidewalk chalk drawing washing away from the rain. Before everything disappeared, Godfrey heard Zadkiel whisper, “Pursue Tabitha. God has given her to you.”

As quickly as it happened, it stopped. Godfrey woke up around eight o’clock in the morning. His body was numb. His limbs could barely respond. Godfrey’s brain had a hard time adjusting; it was confused for a minute. Was it now, or was he still in the vision? Godfrey just closed his eyes and let his senses calm down and his thoughts gather.

In the other room, Tabitha woke up to the morning light shining in through the white blinds. The house was peaceful, which was strange because of all that had happened. She sat up in the bed and stretched her arms; she felt full of life. By habit, Tabitha reached over to her nightstand for her pack of cigarettes, but the desire really wasn’t there this morning. She lit one up anyway, but only smoked half of it. She finished up the cigarette as she walked into the kitchen to get a cup of coffee.

Coffee and a cigarette, the perfect match.

Tabitha sat down on the front porch; it was already warm. It was going to be hot. Tabitha stared off into space, lost in daydreaming as she drank her coffee. She starting thinking about the actual possibility of what Godfrey had been telling her. It just wasn’t believable; it didn’t make sense. But at the same time, he was here, and so had been the angel that she saw. She also started to see that wherever Godfrey went, situations started changing for the better. It was like he was a piece of heaven, and wherever he went, heaven manifested in some sort of way. Another thing she noticed was that bad things tended to happen around Godfrey too. With all this happening, she couldn't help but feel close to Godfrey; it really felt like they had always known each other. Plus Godfrey seemed comfortable confiding in her, and that made her feel wanted and important. Tabitha could tell that she was beginning to be attracted to Godfrey. Inside the house, Tabitha could hear somebody walking around; she got up and went inside to check and see. It was Godfrey, and he looked worried.

"Do you have a piece of paper and pen?" Godfrey asked as he sat at the bar in the kitchen.

"Yeah, sure, do you want some coffee?" Tabitha asked.

"Yeah, I'll take some; make it black please," Godfrey responded.

"Okay," Tabitha said, as she went into a drawer and handed Godfrey a yellow notepad and pen.

"Thanks," said Godfrey, and he began to write down the vivid vision he had seen.

"So, what's wrong?" Tabitha asked, as she poured a fresh cup of coffee for Godfrey.

Tabitha sat down across from Godfrey, waiting for him to answer. "Uh, ummm, I had a vision that I need to write down. I have to tell your father about it," Godfrey answered in a nonchalant way.

Tabitha nodded her head in agreement, trying to not look too freaked out by what Godfrey just said. "A vision? What is wrong with you? You have to be the weirdest guy in the world," Tabitha said.

"I know," Godfrey said with a chuckle.

“I have heard of people having visions, but usually it’s the nutcases or the witches or voodoo priests who talk about such things,” Tabitha said.

“Well, that’s just a misconception. Visions are just one of the many ways God speaks to His people,” Godfrey said, looking up at Tabitha’s smiling face. She still had the dreamy glaze over her eyes that happens when people just wake up to a new day and a fresh beginning.

“I don’t hear too many Christians talking about visions,” Tabitha answered back.

“They should be the ones talking about it the most,” Godfrey said.

“Why?” Tabitha asked.

“Have you ever read the Bible?” Godfrey asked.

“A little, I guess; it has been a long time since I’ve picked it up,” Tabitha said.

“If you study how God spoke to His people, especially the prophets, it was mostly through dreams and visions,” Godfrey said.

“Like who?” Tabitha asked.

“Daniel, Ezekiel, Job, Isaiah, Elijah, Peter, Paul, and John just to name a few,” Godfrey said.

“Yeah, but these guys are the holy ones—the patriarchs, prophets, and apostles. They’re different than us,” Tabitha said.

“No, they are just the ones God used at that time. They are examples of what every believer can be today,” Godfrey said.

“I see what you are saying, but it is different now. Modern people do not believe in such superstitious things anymore,” Tabitha said.

“When modern people start believing God for who He is, He just may start speaking to them,” Godfrey said, as he went back to writing down his vision.

“How does it feel to have a vision?” Tabitha asked.

"It's like a dream, but everything is literal, instead of symbolic. It is like having a movie start playing in front of your eyes, and it is all that your eyes can see until it is finished," Godfrey said.

"I would get too freaked out if that happened to me. I think I would go insane," Tabitha said.

"No, you wouldn't, because you know what it is now. You'd get used to it fairly quickly," Godfrey said.

"So what was your vision about?" Tabitha asked.

"It is not that pleasant; this world is about to change a whole lot very quickly," Godfrey said with a stern look.

"How so?" Tabitha asked.

"It is going to get very scary around the globe; fear is going to grip the hearts of men. God is going to show His mighty hand to mankind again," Godfrey said.

"Yeah, I definitely do not want to see any visions," Tabitha said.

After Godfrey and Tabitha had their fill of coffee, the two got ready to go to work. But before going to the studio, Godfrey decided to make a pit stop to visit Grace.

Chapter 30: Visiting Grace

Godfrey and Tabitha were in her car and heading into town. Godfrey hadn't seen Grace since the wreck, so he wanted to see if she was okay. He wanted to thank her for all the generosity she had given him, and he wanted to let her know that he would be staying with the Maxwells now. As Godfrey was sitting in the car, he mentally replayed the pictures in his head of what Zadkiel showed him. It felt like a heavy burden, carrying something so drastic and big; it was almost overwhelming. On a happy note, Godfrey thought about God giving him Tabitha. She didn't know it yet, of course. This made Godfrey happy; in his past life, he had never married so this would be something new. Plus there was something so remarkable about Tabitha—she had this free spirit about her. There wasn't a fearful bone in her body, and anybody who had gone through what this family had been through this past week had a reason to be scared. She thought about everything and questioned everything that most people just blindly accepted. She had a sharp mind and her beautiful eyes seemed to pierce his soul and those of everyone she looked at. Godfrey thought she was completely and utterly beautiful, and he wasn't really sure how to convey his feelings just yet.

"Godfrey, quit staring off into space," Tabitha said as she was driving.

"Oh, sorry, I get lost in my thoughts; it's hard to find my way back sometimes," Godfrey responded.

"I know what you mean—deep, endless thought is so much fun," Tabitha said, smiling, as if reminiscing from a past event.

Tabitha had been thinking a whole lot the past couple of days, especially about the idea of God, the afterlife, and her life in general. She had been wondering about who she was in God's eyes. Ever since meeting Godfrey, it seemed as if God had invaded her life and her family's. For the first time in a long time, Tabitha actually felt like God cared about her, that He loved and worried about her, like a father would a tender, small child. Ever since college, she had seen God as a cold, distant, universal dictator who just wanted to torture His creation and make their lives a living hell. Tabitha began to feel that her heart had gone cold; all the feelings of hate, anger, resentment, bitterness, and rage had caused this. Not only that, but the drug addictions hadn't helped at all along with the mix of sexual relationships gone bad that she had experienced. She longed to go back to when the world was new; she wanted that sense of wonder and curiosity that she used to have as a child. She wanted to ask God questions again about His universe and how it worked. She wished she was a child again. As much as she longed for this, she still didn't want to give her heart over to anyone. She just wasn't all the way ready to give God another chance to love her yet.

"Earth to Tabitha, are you even awake under those sunglasses?" Godfrey asked.

"I'm awake. Look, we are here," Tabitha said, as she pointed to the little hotel.

The hotel was different than before; there was major work being done on it. The whole place was being repainted, and lawn care workers were out planting a large assortment of flowers, roses, and bushes. Not only that, but the place was packed; business looked good for Grace. Tabitha parked in front of the main office, "They are doing some major work around here, aren't they?" Tabitha asked.

"Yeah, they sure are, Grace must have got a compensation check from the trucking company," Godfrey answered.

The two stepped out of the car; the sun was shining with blue skies. The fresh flowers smelled wonderful. Before they could go in, Grace came out and hugged Godfrey and kissed him on the cheek. She was smiling and laughing as she came out; she was wearing a white dress with pink and yellow flowers on it.

"Hello, child, I am so glad to see you again," Grace said.

"It's good to see you too, Grace. Looks like you are not doing too bad either," Godfrey answered.

"Godfrey, you won't believe how much God has blessed me since I've met you. The trucking company wrote me a check for two million dollars to keep me from going to court. Two million dollars! I can't believe it! Thank You! Thank You, Jesus!" Grace exclaimed.

"That's awesome, Grace. I would like you to meet Tabitha Maxwell," Godfrey said as he pointed to Tabitha who was standing with her purse in her hands together, smiling at Grace's happy face.

Grace came over and hugged Tabitha; she would hug anybody because she was so happy. Grace stepped back with her hands on each shoulder of Tabitha and asked, "Are you two a couple yet?"

Tabitha blushed, and Godfrey didn't do anything at all. He already knew what God's plan was for the two of them, and Tabitha was starting to develop feelings for Godfrey. But Tabitha answered nervously, "No, we are just friends."

"Oh, believe me, child, God has a different plan for the two of you," Grace said, as she leaned and whispered into Tabitha's left ear.

Tabitha really didn't know what to say to that, so she just answered, "Umm...okay."

Grace turned around and told the two of them to come inside and get a glass of ice cold lemonade. They did as she said, and went inside and sat down in her hotel office. Grace poured everyone a glass and sat down.

"So Godfrey, what is on your mind, honey?" Grace asked as she leaned back and wiped a little sweat off of her forehead.

Godfrey finished taking a sip of lemonade and set the glass down, and said, “I just wanted to check on you because of the accident; you were pretty badly frightened when I left with Tabitha.”

“It was a little traumatizing, but God turned the bad experience into a good one,” Grace responded, smiling.

“Speaking of bad experiences, did you hear on the news about my mother being kidnapped, and that the guy who did it killed three EMTs and escaped?” Tabitha interjected.

“The whole city knows about that. I’m sure the media will be aggravating your dad about it,” Grace said.

“It’s unbelievable that this murderer is still roaming free,” Tabitha said, as she sat back and let out a disgruntled breath.

“There was another bizarre string of killings at Palmetto Seafood—three dead, and the entire place burned,” Grace said.

“That’s got to be the same person who kidnapped Meredith,” Godfrey said.

“What makes you think that?” asked Tabitha.

“He’s trying to scare us. Lucifer and his kingdom do not like the fact that I am here. So they are going to make my stay as miserable as possible,” Godfrey said, looking at Tabitha and Grace.

“You are right about that, Godfrey; the Devil knows you’re here, and he don’t like it,” Grace said.

“You two are starting to freak me out. I don’t know about all of this Devil’s kingdom stuff. This is just a little too much for me,” Tabitha said with her hands in the air.

“You have to forgive my friend; she seems to disbelieve anything and everything around her,” Godfrey said to Grace about Tabitha.

“It’s all right, dear; she will come around soon enough,” Grace said, smiling at Tabitha. “Let’s change the subject to a better one, shall we?”

"Yeah, let's do that," Tabitha agreed.

"Godfrey, there is something I want to do for you," Grace said.

"What's that, Grace?" Godfrey asked, intrigued.

"Tabitha, I don't know if Godfrey told you about the miracle that happened when Godfrey came to my hotel," Grace said.

"No, I don't think he did. What happened?" Tabitha asked.

"My husband was dying with cancer just a week ago. The medical bills and hospital visits were breaking us. Our hotel business was prosperous, but the cancer was eating us alive. We had reached our limit, I guess you'd say. Whenever it comes to that point, that's when faith becomes real," Grace said.

By this time Tabitha was leaning forward in her chair, listening carefully to every word that Grace was saying. "Go on," Tabitha said.

"Well, I had been praying very hard for God to heal my husband completely. Listen, first off I don't know too much about healing; this is all new to me. But I needed God to heal my husband; I didn't want him to die. He is a godly man, so I thought he didn't deserve to die like this. I prayed and prayed. I even started fasting. I had become very serious and focused about this. When the situation became so bad and so overwhelming that it felt as if all my hope was lost, God came through," Grace said with her hands in the air, lifted up before God.

"How so?" Tabitha asked, still intrigued.

"Just the other day, when my husband and I were preparing for the worst, Godfrey showed up at my door, asking for a room. I knew there was something strange about him; he seemed to glow with a white light. I could tell he was a believer. He asked for a room, and I took his money. Our hands touched, and Godfrey told me my husband was healed from his sickness. I was shocked, of course; anyone would be. I called my husband; he said he felt heat all over his body. He said he had never felt this good before. The next day, we took him to the doctor to get him checked. The doctor said that the cancer was gone. None of us could believe it, but the evidence was in front of us. The doctor didn't know what to do; he was just as astonished as we were," answered Grace.

"No way! You're saying that God healed your husband of terminal cancer?" Tabitha asked.

"Yes, and He used Godfrey to do it," Grace answered.

"That's unbelievable," Tabitha said, with her mouth wide open.

"God is real, child; ain't He, Godfrey?" Grace said.

"Yes, yes He is," Godfrey answered, with a deep and comforting feeling of peace.

"What I want to say, Godfrey, is this—God has laid it on my heart to give you two hundred thousand dollars, and I don't want to hear any disagreement about it. I have to do this," Grace said.

"Two hundred thousand dollars! Grace, I don't need that money," Godfrey responded, shocked.

"You may not need it, but I want to give it to you; God has used you in a profound way that has changed my life forever," Grace said.

Godfrey sat there for a minute; he was astounded by what Grace said. He hadn't seen this coming. Since he'd been back on earth, he usually knew what was going to happen before it did. He could tell she was not going to take no for answer, so Godfrey finally responded, "Thank you, Grace, for this gift; I will responsibly and wisely use it."

"Good," Grace said.

Then she reached down beside her and brought up a silver briefcase and sat it on top of the desk. She popped it open; the money was neatly laid out in twenties. "I knew you probably didn't have a bank account, so I thought I would just give it to you in cash," Grace said.

Tabitha and Godfrey stood up, looking at the money. Tabitha had never seen so much cash at once. Godfrey had seen way more money this, but not in paper form. He had been one of the first knights to see the hidden treasures under Solomon's temple.

Grace broke the silence by closing the briefcase and handing it to Godfrey. He took it with special care, as if the briefcase had a bomb in it and the slightest movement would cause an explosion. They all sat back down. Then Grace asked, "So I guess you were hired to paint for the Maxwells?"

"Yeah, they loved my paintings," Godfrey said, still looking at the briefcase.

"Well, I will definitely start watching the show if you're in the background painting," Grace said.

"Sounds good! I give you a shout when I'm on there," Godfrey said.

Grace looked over at Tabitha and said, "So what do you do exactly, Tabitha? Are you on the show or do you do something else?"

"Oh, I am behind the scenes. I help run the cameras, and I help with the editing in the video department," Tabitha answered.

"Okay, that's good; one day I'll bet you will take over the show," Grace said.

Tabitha instantly started shaking her head from side to side, and said; "No, I do not want anything remotely close to being on that camera talking to a bunch of hypocrites."

Grace started laughing hysterically. She laughed so much that everyone else started to laugh. Then she said, "Then you are perfect for the job. God doesn't want the people to hear what you have to say. He wants the people to hear what He has to say."

"TV evangelism is not for me. I would rather join the military than do that," Tabitha said matter-of-factly.

The three sat for a moment, enjoying each other's company, until when one of the contractors came in to ask Grace questions. He needed Grace to come out and to look at a few things, so Godfrey thought this would be a good time to go; they all stepped out and said their good-byes. Godfrey hugged and thanked Grace for the money again. For the last time, he tried to give it back, but he knew she was not going to accept it. They all wished each other luck and Godfrey and Tabitha headed off to the studio.

Chapter 31: A Change in the Message

John Maxwell was sitting in his office, looking at the dream he had written down. It bothered him deeply; this was not good for business, so to speak. America was about prosperity and the easy life. Struggle and pain was not what anybody wanted to hear. The American church was even worse. Nowadays it seemed that every Scripture that was ever written was somehow twisted and tied to a prosperity message. Having dreams like this was new to John; nothing was ever this vivid and real. It felt so real; the pictures were still in his head. John knew he couldn't deny that it was real, and he knew he had heard God speak to him. The message had to be given to the people. The problem was that people would not like to hear this, and whenever doom and gloom was brought up, ratings went down. The other problem would be telling his board of directors about this.

Why me, God? I am not the man for the job; I don't want to be the bearer of bad news. All of Your people will hate me for saying this; they will probably declare me a false prophet or a heretic. This is all very new to me, God—dreams, visions, demonic attacks, my wife was nearly killed. What else? What are You going to put me through? Please God, I don't want to be the next Job. For God sake, I can't take it; I am already burned out completely with ministry.

John continued to think loudly and question God about this, but he knew what he had to do. He had been a Christian for a long time now, and when God wanted you to do something, John knew the easiest way through was to do it. When he accepted this, the burden he felt lifted off of his shoulders. John picked up his phone and started calling the board members to set up a meeting. They were all going to meet in a couple of days here at the studio.

"Lord, I am going to sell it to the board. I hope they listen," John said out loud. He picked up the phone and called Meredith. She picked up after just two rings. John told her about the dream and what God had told him.

Chapter 32: The Time Has Come

Daedriel watched from high up above the clouds. He had just heard John Maxwell make the decision to follow through with what God had revealed to him about the coming days. He stood in the sky as if his feet were touching the ground, but instead he was standing in midair, just beyond the point of the atmosphere, in what man calls the second heaven. Off into the distance, comets could be seen flying through space. The stars, galaxies, and planets lay silent in the vastness of space. Daedriel was nodding his head with agreement; he loved it when men were motivated by the ancient and peculiar ways of God.

The world will change now, with America changing. The world has no choice but to go along with her. It will not be long before Lucifer and his generals know what is going on. We are going to have to really guard John and his family, and especially Godfrey. So many people just do not understand what is really going on in this world; they are blinded by the smallest things and are being dragged to hell without knowing it. America is being judged; she has much iniquity built up in her land, and it has developed a mighty stench in God's nostrils. He is going to wake His church up again in America; and when He does, His power and might will be felt and seen again.

Daedriel had a scroll in his hand; on it was the proclamation that he must speak. He broke the heavenly seal and read its contents with a loud and echoing voice, "Earth, creation of God, your cries and moans have been heard! The stains of blood and fire have echoed loudly in the halls of heaven! You shall be silent no more—shake and tremble your mighty lands, stir your vast waters, and let your heart boil and churn inside; disturb the gates of hell once again! Let the sons of light come forth, and do not let your anger stop until the great and terrible day of the Lord comes!"

As Daedriel read the prophecy, mighty winds blew all around him. High above him a horn was blown—a confirmation that heaven agreed with the prophecy. When the horn was blown, the words that were proclaimed would happen. Daedriel's countenance lit up with an intense white fire that was so bright only the outline of him could be seen.

Daedriel said, "And it shall come to pass now!"

As Daedriel finished, a comet flew by him with supersonic speed aiming toward the Gulf of Mexico. The comet ripped and tore through the sky. Streams of cloud and a slight glint of fire formed a tail on the backside of the comet. From a distance it looked like a shooting star during the daytime. The comet slammed right into the middle of the gulf. At first nothing happened, and then the ocean floor shook terribly, causing a massive ripple effect in the water going in all directions. The first victim of the tsunami was a giant cruise ship called the *Oasis of the Seas*. The ship was hit by a wave that was as tall as the ship itself, causing it to capsize. There were thousands of people scattered in the still green water. All of the passengers that were topside were dragged into the water by the wave before the behemoth ship rolled to its side. The next victim of the terrible wave would be the city of New Orleans.

Daedriel was grieved with what had just happened; it grieved him because he knew how much God cared for mankind. But he also knew the stubbornness of man. They could be very stiff necked and unyielding. Daedriel was assured, though, that out of all of these disasters and those coming, the ones loyal to God would be protected from the judgments near at hand.

I remember when the Father created the earth. We all sat and watched with amazement. The Father was making an extension to His already vast family. Men just do not understand how much they are really protected from the evil that wishes to destroy their dignity and souls. If they only knew.

Chapter 33: The Great Shaking

Meredith woke up around 8:30 in the morning; John had already left for work. Last night the four of them had celebrated because of the blessing that Godfrey had received from Grace. It was another peaceful morning; it felt new to her because of the valley the family had been through lately. Meredith went downstairs and poured herself a cup of coffee; she turned on the small television in the kitchen to see what the weather was going to be like. When she turned on the weather channel, the forecaster was talking about tsunamis around the Gulf of Mexico and all the way down to South America. Throughout the early morning, New Orleans and several coastal cities had been hit by a hundred-foot wave. The exhaustive work that had been done on the pulleys was destroyed by the immense pressure of the waters. Thousands of people were missing; the final death count had not come in yet. New Orleans had barely survived Hurricane Katrina; there was no way they would be able to survive this one.

The weather channel was showing sky views of the city, almost every bit of the metropolitan area was under water. Meredith sat with her eyes wide; she had to sit her coffee cup down because her hand was shaking, causing the coffee to spill.

"Oh, my God, not again. Surely not New Orleans again...those poor people. Lord, I pray, please help them through this tragedy," Meredith prayed.

The weatherman was saying that several spots in the gulf were hit, but New Orleans had been the worst report so far. Witnesses from a capsized cruise ship said that a comet had hit in the water near them;

when it did, the ground trembled. The wave that formed from the impact was what turned the ship over. There were thousands of injuries, and 800 deaths and counting from the ship turning on its side so fast.

Meredith sat there as she watched the video of the big beautiful white cruise ship turned on its side like a dead whale. There were Coast Guard helicopters flying around the ship while smaller ships and boats had arrived to help get people out of the water. It was a giant mess; there were hundreds of bodies floating in the water being eaten by sharks and other fish, along with survivors swimming in the water because of being knocked out of the ship from the wave. On the television, one of the reporters was interviewing one of the survivors; his name was Jim Shultz.

Jim described what happened with a Midwestern twang, "It was like seeing a white ball of fire hit the ocean. Then a huge wall of a wave came right toward us. The only reason I knew was because I just happened to be looking out on the side of the ship when the comet hit. I've never seen anything like that; it was like a wall of water was aiming right for us. It was the scariest thing I've seen in my whole life. I will never leave land again!"

Meredith couldn't blame Jim Shultz for saying that; she would never go on a cruise ship. She was a chicken when it came to that, because John had tried several times to take the two of them on a cruise. Meredith would not do it; now she was glad she never did.

Chapter 34: I'm Done with You

Carlo was riding his stolen motorcycle down an old paved road, full of bumps and potholes. Carlo was weaving side to side on the road, dodging the holes. The engine of the bike was roaring. The recently fallen Hell's Angel had really taken care of the bike. Carlo had a devilish smile on his face. He laughed to himself, thinking of all the lives he had taken; it brought him much pleasure. He loved killing; he felt that it brought out the best in him. He thought he was born to kill; this was his calling in life. Other men started families, had businesses, and led quiet peaceful lives, but not him. He existed for the sole pleasure of the underbelly of this world—what he meant by underbelly was the dark secrets that men kept from their loving wives and children. He was one of the creatures of the night that did the things that had to be done that nobody wanted to admit. Carlo, lost in his thoughts, heard the voice of Belial; he was calling his name.

"Carlo. Pull over and go into the woods. There is something that I need to show you," Belial said. Carlo did as the gurgling voice instructed and pulled over. "Take the rope with you," Belial said.

Carlo picked up the neatly tied rope and started walking into the woods. The birds started chirping and giving off alarms that a man had entered their domain. Sticks were breaking and leaves rustling as Carlo walked into the woods.

"Where are we going, my lord? Is there another mission for me?" Carlo asked.

"You have made a mess of things, Carlo, and have brought way too much attention to yourself. So it is time for you to depart," Belial answered.

"No, we can't separate. What will I do without you?" Carlo asked.

"I have made my decision; now start making a noose out of that rope. Now! I command you!" Belial ordered.

Carlo made the noose, and then climbed a large rock that was overshadowed by a tree. He threw the rope over the branch and looped it. He pulled on it a couple of times to make sure it was secure enough.

"Lord, I don't want to do this. Why are you making me do this?" Carlo asked as he put the noose around his neck.

"Don't worry; you will be well taken care of where you are going. Trust me; I promise you will be welcomed with open arms," Belial said.

Off in the distance, a county cop named Henry Adams saw Carlo's motorcycle parked on the side of the road. He recognized it as belonging to one of the dead men from the restaurant; it was the only thing missing at the crime scene. Henry looked in the saddle bag and noticed a .357 magnum revolver and a pack of cigarettes. Henry pulled out his gun and began sneaking into the woods to find the driver of the bike. Instead Henry found Carlo's lifeless body hanging from the tree, still twitching. Perched on top of the branch that he was hanging from sat an albino vulture; it didn't budge or fly away. It just sat and watched the young cop as he called in the suicide.

What is that? We don't have vultures around here, only buzzards. Especially not white ones.

Henry had a feeling that something was not right about the bird so he kept his distance from it until everyone showed up to the crime scene. When more police finally arrived, they cut Carlo down, causing the large white vulture to fly away. The policeman confirmed that this was the suspect who kidnapped Meredith Maxwell, killed three EMTs, and escaped. With the motorcycle they found, they also linked him to the murders of the three men at the small bar and grill.

"I wonder why in the world he would kill himself. It doesn't look to me that he was a depressed kind of guy," Henry said to the cop standing beside him. His name was Roger Clemmons. He had been a policeman at least fifteen years longer than Henry. Henry had only been on the force for two years now.

"Yeah, rookie, this is weird. This man has committed more murders in just a few days than we have had in years. Hell, I'm glad he killed himself, because I am sure he would have taken a lot more with him before we would have got him," Roger said.

"You know, there was a white vulture perched over his body the whole time until you guys showed up and cut him down," Henry said.

"A vulture? We don't have vultures around here. You must be seeing things," Roger assured Henry.

"I know what I saw, and I know we don't have vultures, but I'm telling you there was one here today. It was right there in front of everybody; you didn't see it?" Henry asked.

"No, didn't see a thing. Say by chance there was one. So what, what does mean anyway? Is there some kind of voodoo magic going on?" Roger snickered.

"You are not going to believe me, Roger, but when I walked up to the body, I felt a very dark and evil presence around here. Call it intuition or whatever, but something wasn't right about all of this," Henry said.

"Can you see dead people too?" Roger mocked. "You need to go home and rest a few hours. I think this whole thing has been just a little too much for your little rookie mind," Roger said.

Henry could tell it was useless telling Roger anything. "I guess you're right. I'll get home and write a report on what I found and bring it to the station," Henry said.

"Make sure you keep the albino vulture and the grim reaper out of the report will you? This is a crime scene, not a horror movie," Roger laughed.

"Yeah, I'll do that," Henry said, as he thought about flipping Roger off.

Henry got in his squad car and headed for his house. As he was driving, he thought just how weird the crime scene felt. He had never actually felt evil before; he had seen evil, but that was it. When he did feel it, it caused his stomach to turn upside down. It felt as if acid was going up and down his throat—quite an uncomfortable feeling. Henry lit up a cigarette while driving; he was not supposed to smoke in the squad car, but who cared? Who was going to find out anyway?

Henry was an average sized man, around 5 feet 9 inches or so, and he was in really good shape. He had come out of the army as an MP, and decided to further in his career by joining the police force. He had deployed once to Iraq, but his job mostly revolved around patrolling at the head of convoys. He had lost a couple friends while over there. Dealing with death was not that hard for him anymore, he figured, as long as he didn't allow anyone close to him. Then he wouldn't be hurt or affected by such things as death. It always amazed Henry just how easy dealing with the idea of death had become—if it happened, it happened. He could tell that war had left a very deep scar on his soul. It had changed who he was completely. Sometimes he envisioned himself as one of the ones who was lost from God, one of the ones who was separated from the sheepfold and chosen to be exposed to the grim, evil, dark things of this world that most people never had to see or experience. But he had to carry it all and pass it on to warn the later generations. Henry missed the desert; something constantly called him back to it. How could something so desolate and hostile be so beautiful to him? Everything in the desert was dangerous and deadly—the animals, insects, the heat, the cold, and the people. Henry didn't know why but he loved it and wanted to go back someday.

As Henry was cruising down the road, he noticed something up ahead, flying right above the road. It was at eye level with him. It was that white vulture again. It was flying directly in front of him. His eyes stayed transfixed on the object, almost mesmerized by it. Suddenly it turned around and was flying toward him. The massive bird aimed right for him. In just a couple of seconds, it was on him. Before it hit the windshield, Henry slammed on the brakes and veered into the grass. Before Henry could gather his thoughts or catch his breath, the white vulture was perched on his hood with its wings spread out. The bird was huge with a wingspan of at least ten feet. Its eyes were completely black. Henry could smell that horrible smell of death again. It reminded him of old food mixed with an animal carcass that had been in the sun for a couple of days. Henry didn't know what to do; his body was feeling lifeless and numb around the bird. Then the vulture opened his mouth and let out a blood curdling scream. Henry felt the sound waves of the screams go through him. The glass around him shattered; as it did, little pieces hit him in the face. Henry noticed that the world around him was changing; everything began to catch on fire. Black shadows were circling the car as the vulture kept screaming and screaming. The car began to melt as Henry sat locked in the seat of the cruiser. The black shadows put their hands on Henry's head. Henry looked down at his hands and watched his skin peel off. Seeing this, Henry started to panic and scream; he banged his head back and forth against the seat with his eyes closed; he couldn't look at this anymore. When he finally did open his eyes, he was back in his car driving down the road as if nothing happened. He could smell something burning though—the smell of brimstone.

"What the hell was that?" Henry said out loud.

Henry was feeling his face and looking at his hands to make sure they were back to normal. "What was that, a dream? How is it that I was driving and dreaming at the same time?" Henry wondered.

Henry could feel his heart beating rapidly. Beads of sweat were pouring down his whole body. The fear was thick; it felt like a cloud full of rain wrapped around him. Henry's world finally came back to him when dispatch called him over the radio to tell him to ride by the Maxwell house to let the family know that Carlo Rainone was dead.

As soon as I leave their house I am making an appointment with a priest or psychologist to tell me what the hell I am seeing.

Chapter 35: Follow the Way of the Light

Not too far from town, there was a small white church that was located right off the main highway leaving town. The building had been around for nearly two hundred years. The front doors were tall and the color of burgundy. The church had a steeple in the front of the building with an old bell that chimed every hour on the hour. It was obviously an old church, so old that it had a cemetery that surrounded the whole left and back side of the building. Woods surrounded the back side of the church. Children who lived around the church swore up and down that the property was haunted; sometimes they would see the pastor going into the woods at night. The church used to be packed every Sunday, but everything changed when the son took over after his father's mysterious death. When the son took over, he changed the name of the church to The Way of the Light.

The locals could not stand the pastor's son. His name was Alex Levonson. He was a short, bald, chubby fellow. He had dark brown eyes that almost looked black. He had a thick brown goatee. He was an evil looking pastor if anybody ever saw one. He was a weird little man too; the church's congregation was around thirty or so people on a good Sunday, mostly loyalists of the poor boy's dad. Alex was not an everyday pastor; when he preached, he just rambled about the light. He rarely ever used the Scriptures to back up what he was saying. The congregation just sat there like zombies and listened to him. The boredom was stifling; you could cut it with a knife whenever he preached. One of the old women who went to the church was quoted as saying, "I hope the grave is more exciting than this guy's mouth."

Alex was a dark and secretive man, and very intelligent—especially when it came to book knowledge. But the problem was that he didn't spend all his free time reading about God and the Bible. Instead at a young age, he had been enticed and drawn by the dark arts; evil was interesting to him. When he first got his hands on the Internet, it was all over. Alex now considered himself a Luciferian priest. He saw Lucifer as the true light bearer, not Christ. He thought the world had Lucifer all wrong; he was not as bad as everyone said he was. Alex thought he could get revenge for his god, Lucifer, if he led astray a whole flock of stupid Christians. He would indoctrinate Luciferian practices in his little flock, and they wouldn't even see them coming.

He had been doing this very thing for quite a few years now, having a very strong sense of the shallow Christianity of the present culture. Alex had grown accustomed to his life of wickedness. From time to time, he sacrificed animals in his mostly made-up ritual practices. That was as far as he would go, though. He did this in the basement of the church. No one was allowed in the basement; it was totally off limits to the congregation. There was a huge pentagram carved into the floor, and another smaller one in front of the big one. That was for incantations, and for protection from any spirit that might materialize in front of Alex. He had done this for some time, but nothing had happened yet. Whenever Alex practiced his spells, he waited until late at night to do them, so he would not be disturbed. If Alex was anything, he was a wannabe; he had grown up as an introvert, so he embraced darkness to reinforce his seclusion.

Alex was moving around in the church basement, lighting candles in readiness for one of his incantations. He had a black cat in a cage that he was going to use for the sacrifice. It was meowing and sticking its paws out of the cage, playfully swiping at Alex every time he went by the unsuspecting creature. After his candles were lit and the pentagrams were surrounded in salt, he pulled out the cat. It was vibrating and purring loudly, but this didn't faze Alex. He held the cat down and reached for his freshly sharpened machete. Raising it, he was just about to bring it down on the cat's head when it started growling—a deep, menacing growl that sent chills down his spine. He froze in confusion, still holding the machete up in the air. The cat turned its head, glaring up at him. Suddenly it hissed, baring its razor teeth, its eyes beginning to glow red. Of all the animal sacrifices he'd carried out, Alex had never experienced anything like this. *It must have rabies or something.* Before he could even finish the thought, a mighty wind began blowing through the basement, creating a vortex, with Alex in the center. In an instant the candles were out, save for the ones that directly surrounded him. The cat, still being held down under his firm grip, broke free with unnatural, predatory strength. With another venomous hiss, it sprang towards Alex's face, sinking its claws right into the top of his forehead. A blood-curdling scream came from his throat as he felt the cat's dagger claws digging into the bone. Feeling the warmth of his own blood as it trickled over his eyes and down his cheeks, he struggled fiercely to remove the cat, but to no avail. By this point it was sinking its teeth into his flesh as well. After more growling and hissing, it finally released its grip before springing off Alex and disappearing into the shadows. Alex tried to recite the correct chants, but the struggle to regain his composure left him completely spent.

The wind started to die down; Alex could hear his heart pounding.

"You bring me the blood of felines, and you expect me to be *pleased*?" a voice said.

Alex couldn't believe what was going on; the Devil had actually shown up. Nothing had ever manifested itself to him before. Still in the center of the pentagram, Alex opened his eyes in just enough time to see it burst into green flames all around him. A piece of his cloak caught on fire. With a small scream of panic, he hastily put it out.

"Look up, you fool; your god is present," the voice said.

Alex trembled and hesitantly looked up. When he did, he saw a man standing—he had six wings, and they were a golden brown. The man reminded Alex of the statue of David that Michelangelo had sculpted.

His hair was thick and curly; it was the same color of his wings. He stood with pride and arrogance. *He is the most beautiful man I have ever seen.* The armor the man was wearing was red, trimmed in gold. There was a symbol of a black dragon on the front on his chest. He was the perfect mix of pure evil and angelic beauty. He had a rolled-up scroll in his right hand.

"Master?" Alex mumbled.

"Yes, your master. Sign this scroll," Lucifer said.

Lucifer handed the scroll to Alex; his hand was shaking as he grabbed it. When he opened it, the page was blank. Suddenly the page was lit up with fire, and letters appeared one by one on the scroll. It was written in some kind of unknown tongue. Alex tried to pull his hands away from the fire to avoid being burned, but couldn't. It felt as if his hands were being held down by shackles.

Alex asked, "What is this?"

"It is our contract, Alex; you and I are making a blood pact. You are my slave," Lucifer said.

"Yes, lord, I will do this," Alex said, watching his ultimate dream come true.

"Good, I knew you would," Lucifer said, with the voice of a caring father. "Your blood will be signature enough."

Alex's right palm sliced open, and blood dropped on the bottom of the page of the contract. It then was engulfed in flames and disappeared. The wound in his hand healed right before Alex's eyes.

"You also need my mark, to make it official," Lucifer said.

"I accept, my lord," Alex responded.

Lucifer reached down and put his hand on Alex's head. Alex snapped back violently. In his head, a vision of Lucifer falling from heaven engulfed him, and visions of lightning striking his body caused him to lay on the ground in a fetal position. His eyes were rolled back into his head; his body was trembling all over. Alex began mumbling some kind of ancient tongue.

"Stand up Alex," Lucifer commanded.

As the command came out of Lucifer's mouth, Alex's body began levitating in front of Lucifer. Alex finally came back from his intense trance.

"I am sending my servant, Belial, to you; he will give you instructions on what to do," Lucifer said.

"Yes, my lord," Alex said in a dry, monotone voice.

"When you sacrifice, I demand human blood—especially the blood of Jews and Christians. You will worship me with only blood and fire," Lucifer said.

"Yes, my lord," Alex responded.

Lucifer vanished from the basement. The candles that had gone out before lit up again and the air calmed. Alex sat there on his knees, dazed. His chest was burning intensely, so he stood up and took off his cloak to look at it. When he did, he found there a scratch that went from his left shoulder all the way down to his right hip. Alex realized that it was all real; he now carried the mark of the dragon. He went to bed; it had been a busy night.

Chapter 36: It's Showtime

It was nearly time to start the show. Godfrey had all his painting supplies out and had already begun painting. Tabitha and the crew were manning the cameras; they had just a couple of minutes before they were live. John and Meredith were sitting on the set, talking with each other. John was worried about the message he had. He was going to tell America that times were going to get hard. Meredith was sitting across from John; he had a couple of pieces of paper in his hand.

"I don't want to do this, Meredith; we are going to lose all of our viewers because of what I am about to tell them," John said, as he leaned toward Meredith.

"John, I know this is hard, and very different from what we are accustomed to, but if this is what God wants you to say then you should say it," Meredith said peacefully.

"It's easy for you to say; you're not on camera," John responded.

"John, don't worry. Whatever happens, happens. We will survive this; if we lose our show, then we will be okay," Meredith said, as she leaned in and kissed John.

"You're right, honey. I am not going to worry any more about it. This has to be God, because the board totally agreed that I should tell the viewers," John said.

"That is nothing short of a miracle. Those guys never agree on anything," Meredith said, smiling.

"Yeah, I know," John answered, exhaling.

"I wanted to let you know that the guy who kidnapped me is dead," Meredith said.

"Really? When did that happen?" John asked, relieved.

"A policeman came and told me today. He was a young guy, but he didn't look too well. I guess he was the one who found him; he looked like he'd seen a ghost," Meredith said.

"That's good he's dead. That guy was evil," John said. "How did he die?"

"Suicide; he hung himself in the woods," Meredith said.

"Strange things are happening," John said.

"The policeman asked me if he could speak to you sometime about some spiritual advice. He looked so distraught. I told him that you would speak to him; I told him to come by the house tomorrow around noon," Meredith said.

"That's fine, honey; I will probably be jobless tomorrow anyway," John said.

"Oh, John, stop it," Meredith said.

"Dad, we are live in twenty seconds!" Tabitha yelled.

"Let me get off the set, love. Good luck," Meredith said, as she leaned down and kissed John.

Meredith walked off the set as the cameras started to roll. Godfrey was in the background, lost in his own world painting away. He was working on the gates of heaven. Godfrey painted with intensity, and was extremely focused while working. Watching the precision Godfrey used with his paint brush was like watching a surgeon. Stroke after stroke, the massive image was coming to life. John looked back at Godfrey and then turned around to greet his worldwide audience.

"Good evening, God's beloved. We have a good show for you tonight. If you look behind me, you will see a good friend of mine, painting. We hired this young man to paint us pictures of the Lord and heavenly images during every show we have. His name is Godfrey L'Enfant, and trust me, beloved, he is a genius when it comes to painting." John said.

John went on with the show, giving updates and announcements about the ministry. Then he gave a quick briefing on things going on around the world. The tension was high and thick in the air; it could have been cut with a knife. Finally, when the show was nearly at its end, John announced, "Beloved I have something to share with you. Something the Lord has put on my heart to tell you about things to come. Listen up and tune in. God spoke to me about America; we are in great trouble and turmoil. The Lord revealed to me that His American church has been led astray by prosperity and love for money and materials. He showed that the stench of idols has reached His nostrils, and He has to judge us to save us. He showed me that America has become careless as a nation, drunk with money and material things. She has thrown the Lord out, and accepted the intellectual gods of this world and their philosophies. The writings of Nietzsche, Marx, and Darwin dictate what America does, not the Word of God. America murders her children in the womb every day, but lets murderers live. You pray for Him to bless this nation, but you do not honor Him. He sends you prophets and teachers, but you do your best to try and destroy them and discredit them. You care less that the entire world is against you, but are on the edge of your seats when a celebrity gets married. Your foundations are crumbling, and your infrastructure is collapsing. You claim to be a friend to His people Israel, but force them to give up their land. He tells you this, America; you will lose your land if you do not stop. Israel is His, and His burden to bear, and anyone who is against her is against Him. America, wake up; wake and repent, before your lamp stand is taken away."

As John was saying these words, the atmosphere changed inside the studio. A cool wind was blowing inside, but nobody could tell from where because no door or window was open. A heaviness and weighty presence could be felt. Everyone inside the studio could feel the weight pushing them down. The more John spoke, the more everyone was realizing that it was God speaking through him. No one spoke; they all watched, amazed by the words coming out of John's mouth. After John was done speaking, he came back to reality and said good night to viewers. After they were off the air, John couldn't believe what he just said; it scared him to death. John stood up and looked over at Godfrey and smiled; John looked like a massive burden was taken off of his chest.

"You did a good job, John; this is what God wanted. The people have to be warned, no matter how much they hate it. They have to know," Godfrey said.

"I know, Godfrey, but what will the cost be? I am the most popular preacher in America, and I just told America she is wrong about everything," John responded.

Meredith came up and wrapped her arm around John's waist. The fact that she was standing with him in this made it all worth it to John. Tabitha was still lurking behind the camera. She was in shock; she had never experienced anything like this. She was convinced that what she felt was God Himself.

What does this mean for us? Tabitha thought. *Could America as we know it really crumble? Everything that is life to us really be taken away?*

For the first time in Tabitha's life, she realized that her life and the world she lived in was all really in God's hand. She had a glimpse of God's sovereignty. After everything was taken care of in the studio, the four went home and waited for the onslaught of the religious and secular crowds to tear John's words to pieces.

Chapter 37: The Morning After

It was just after noon the next day at the Maxwell home. Everyone was up and just hanging out around the house. John was looking at the headlines on the Internet regarding what he had said on the program last night. Every one that he read made him feel worse. He was expecting the board to call any minute to say that they were appointing a new host. John was really struggling with all of this. He felt like his faith had been shipwrecked. The very foundations of his being and beliefs felt like they had been shattered. Inside, his heart of hearts was numb. John knew that he had done what God told him to do, but why was it so hard? John felt like this was going to destroy him and his ministry. John really thought of himself as a passive, charismatic prosperity preacher.

Instead of teaching about the coming world leaders and times, he leaned toward the kingdom of God taking over the world. He thought if enough Christians assembled, they could change the entire world and give the kingdom into God's hand. John would never profess this personal belief on the air because most of the American viewers believed that the world was getting worse—that it was being prepared for the Antichrist and his false prophet. Now everything would be different. Instead of being the most loved pastor in America, he would most likely become the most hated. People didn't take kindly to being rebuked, especially by somebody saying they have a message from God. John himself frowned on allowing so-called modern prophets on his show to share their messages from God. He was thinking that now the prophets he had shunned would shun him. John was sitting at the computer while these thoughts flew through his head. His eyes were staring off with a glassy, blank look. Reality hit when Meredith interrupted him and said that Henry the policeman was here to speak to him.

Henry Adams walked into the large Maxwell house; John greeted him with a handshake. Henry had a magazine in his hand, it was one of those tabloids that sit by the register at the store.

"How are you doing, Henry?" John said.

"I am good, sir; thanks for meeting me, by the way," Henry said.

"Not a problem. I'm glad somebody wants to meet me after last night," John said.

"Speaking of last night, I have a headline for you," Henry said, as he held up the magazine so John could read it. The headline said, "Prosperity Preacher Becomes Prophet of Doom."

John cringed inside as he read it; he just knew his life was over now.

"Wow, you know how to get a man's attention, don't you?" John asked.

"Well, I figured it would lighten up the mood," Henry said, with a touch of sarcasm and humor.

"So, what can I help you with today, Henry?" John asked, getting to the point.

"I'm sure you know that I am the one who found the murderer who kidnapped your wife," Henry said.

"Yes, she told me. I'm glad that guy is dead," John added.

"The damage that he did is the worst any of us have ever seen on the force," Henry said.

"I'm sure of it," John said.

"The problem is, pastor…oh, I can call you pastor, right?" Henry asked.

"Sure, why not," John said.

"When I found the guy hanging in the tree, I could feel something in the air. It was something very old and evil. It felt like it was touching me, and going through me. Then I saw a white vulture perched in the tree next to the newly dead man. It just sat there and watched me. Its eyes examined my soul. I didn't really understand what was happening. I just knew that something was not right about it," Henry said, as he sat back in the chair.

"That doesn't sound very good. I am not an expert on the supernatural world. I know you probably thought I would be since I am a minister, but my expertise is in other doctrines of Christianity," John said, with little confidence.

Meredith interrupted the two, bringing them two cold glasses of soda. She handed one to Henry and then the other to John.

"Thank you, honey," John said.

"Thank you, ma'am," said Henry.

"You're both welcome," Meredith said. "Can I get you anything else?"

"No thanks, dear," John said.

"No ma'am, thank you though," Henry said.

"Just let me know," Meredith said, as she walked out of the room.

Henry took a sip of the soda and then went on with his experience. "You see, pastor, that wasn't it," Henry said.

"Really?" John said with intrigue.

"I tried to tell another officer about what I saw, and of course he didn't listen to me. He made fun of me and told me to go home and get some rest. Well, I got in my squad car and headed home. Then I saw the white vulture again. It was flying toward me as I was driving down the road. It came at me and I swerved off the road. Then I believe I had a vision or that something happened to me," Henry said.

"A vision, huh?" John said.

"I looked around and everything started to catch on fire; then these black shadows started walking around me and grabbing me. I was scared to death and started panicking. Then before I knew it, the whole thing was over. I was still driving my car like nothing happened," Henry finished, and looked at John for some kind of answer.

John shook and sat there for a few minutes, silently pondering Henry's ordeal. John was pretty sure what he thought it was. He looked at Henry and asked him, "Henry, what do you believe you saw?"

"To be honest with you, I am scared to even say what it was. I believe what I saw was some type of evil spirit," Henry said hesitantly.

"I think you are right, Henry, but you do not seem too sure of yourself," John said.

"This kind of stuff is uncomfortable for me, pastor; this is like fantasy crap out of a video game. I want it to be just some kind of bad side effect of PTSD from the war. Or maybe a recurring bad drug trip from back in the day. Something logical and understandable, you know," Henry said.

"Listen, Henry, for the past couple of weeks, my life has changed dramatically. I lived for God a long time now, and I thought I knew a good bit about Him. Tragically, I have found out that I really don't. I have been lost in my own ambitions and passions for a long time. Just like what happened to you, the same kind of stuff has happened to my family. I am honored by the fact you came to me, expecting me to know what happened to you, but I am ashamed that I know very little about demons and devils. Being a Christian, I should know something about that," John said.

"So really, we are in the same boat, pastor," Henry said.

John laughed a little and said, "Yes, and we are barely floating."

"I tell you what, Henry; I will pray for you and do some research for you to figure this out some more," John said.

John and Henry both stood up, and John began to pray for him. After the prayer, they shook hands and Henry walked out the door. As Henry entered his car and drove off, Zadkiel stood on top of the house and watched the young man drive away.

"It appears that Belial and his band of minions have shown themselves to this man. They have become bolder. We will have to keep a greater watch on this man. At this point, he could go either way. The enemy will be working on this one," Zadkiel said.

Chapter 38: The Turn Around

Alex Levonson was a changed man. His entire appearance had become one of purpose and illumination. Since his encounter with Lucifer, he felt completely different. Before the encounter, he described himself as a recluse, but now he was invigorated. When he closed his eyes to sleep, visions of power and prestige danced around in his head. He imagined himself as a powerful dictator who could control the masses with his invoking and charismatic speeches. It was like his intelligence had increased dramatically. Thoughts and ideas pulsated through him at a superhuman pace.

I feel like I am invincible! No one can stop me now! Alex thought to himself as he was jogging through the woods behind his church.

Alex had never exercised in his life, but now he wanted to make himself beautiful, like his master was to him. Alex also worked harder on preparing his message for his congregation. He was going to preach tonight.

"These dumb sheep, don't they know that the idol shepherd is before them?" Alex asked. "I don't know what I am going to do with them yet, but it will be a wonderful display, I promise you."

Alex was ripping through the forest like a cheetah closing in on a gazelle on the African plain. The sweat was running down his pale white skin; the air was thick with humidity. The crows were cawing to warn others that a human was in their midst. None of this bothered Alex; the intense heat just made him run faster and longer. He had never been this far into the woods. The trees were so thick that the light was becoming dimmer. Alex saw something strange not too far in front of him. It looked like a mound sticking up from the ground—almost like a small cave that an animal might live in. There was an entrance, but it was black as night. Alex decided to go in. He slowly approached and crouched down to go in the cave. To his surprise, there were steps. He went down them one at a time, because he couldn't even see his hand in front of him.

I wonder what this is? Someone had to have built this!

The steps went lower and lower. Alex kept his hands on the walls as he went down so he wouldn't lose his balance. Both sides were stone; they were cold and rugged. Eventually the stairs ended. As soon as he stepped forward, eight torches equally spread around the walls lit one by one until they were all lit.

"Wow! What is this place?" Alex whispered.

The room was in the shape of an octagon. The walls were gray stone; the floor was nearly all black marble. In the middle of the floor was a circular trap door. Alex walked closer to get a better look. The circle opened like an eye and flames of white and blue fire shot out of the hole. They made a loud roar, causing Alex to fall back and hit his head. He sat back up in amazement and watched as the fire went back into the hole. Alex stood back up, rubbing his head, and went over to the hole to look down it. He could see lava and flames moving, but could not tell how far it went down. He scanned the small room to see what else was in it. There was an old wooden desk with a chair. It looked like it came from the Middle Ages. Beside it was a wide bookshelf full of rolled up scrolls and old books. They appeared to be spells and incantations to perform. On the other side of the room was a typical prison cell with shackles; bones and human remains were scattered all over the floor.

This must be where the previous priests kept their human experiments.

"This lair has to be hundreds of years old. How can that be? I'm in Georgia, and these things look like they came out of a thirteenth century castle! Maybe the myth about the Templar Knights coming to America was true. They were chased out of Europe because of devil worship and human sacrifice. Maybe they came here! I don't know; that seems like a long shot," Alex thought out loud.

Alex went over to the desk and sat down. The wood creaked as he put his weight on it. There was an old feather pen with a container of ink. Sitting in front of him was letter addressed to him. It was written on what appeared to be some type of animal skin. The letter said:

Alex,

The cave that you found has been here for centuries. It is a vital spot for the Luciferian kingdom. It was used by ancient warlocks from the Old World and has remained in the care of men like you from generation to generation. It is one of the many portals of hell, a gateway, if you will, for the demonic to go to and fro from. You are now the gatekeeper and must maintain this cave. Hell is hungry and must be fed quite often. You have been given a great and sacred task; and when it is your time to go, you must enter the hole to settle its cravings until the next darkened soul takes your place. To make it official, sign your name on the line below to accept the assignment has been given to you.

Alex read the letter a few times just to be sure he wasn't seeing things, and wondered if this was some kind of hallucination. He grabbed the feather pen and dipped it in the ink. Alex thought for a couple of seconds, took a deep breath, and signed the letter. When he did, the letter burned into ashes just like the contract that he had signed a couple of days earlier.

Alex stood up from the desk and walked over to the hole in the middle of the room. He always wondered how his life would end; now he knew. His fate was staring him in the face, waiting patiently to consume him. Alex wondered how many men had jumped down into that hole; maybe he would find out on the other side. Either way, there was no going back now.

Alex looked at the books for a while, and then headed back to the church to prepare his message for his flock.

Chapter 39: The Nightmares

Henry was at home now. After his visit with John Maxwell, his inner questions bothered him even more. Henry was sitting in his recliner, his thoughts running a million miles a second. The television was on, but he was not watching it. Henry thought back to the day when he found Carlo Rainone; but when he did, fear began to surround him and he had to shake himself out of it. Fear was not something new to Henry; he had been scared before. One time in particular. When he was on a convoy in Iraq, they were ambushed by the enemy. He was near the front because he was security for the convoy. He watched the vehicle in front of him get hit by an RPG, and he froze from the fear. It felt like an eternity to him, but finally his fire team leader slapped Henry on the back of his head to bring him back to reality, which caused his muscle memory from all of his training to finally kick into gear.

That situation was probably the scariest he had ever experienced, but the fear that came on him in his car was something totally different. It actually felt like a presence, like a thick cloud that surrounded him and breathed on him. While Henry was lying, thinking away, he dozed off and began to dream.

In his dream, Henry woke up in a coffin. He began to panic, because he couldn't breathe. The top of the coffin was nailed shut. Henry started banging and scratching, but to no avail. It felt as if his arms had no strength in them. When he screamed for help, his voice made no sound. When he felt his heart beating rapidly, he stopped moving because he thought it was going to explode. The top of the coffin flew off because of a strong wind. Henry stood up, and his body felt like stone. Around him was a dry, cracked desert. The sky was red; he could see stars, but they kept falling from the sky as he looked at them. Everything around him felt like it would collapse; nothing was stable. He started walking forward, and every movement Henry made seemed to sap all of his energy. Henry looked ahead and saw something on the horizon; it looked like green fields and hills. Henry felt that he should try and reach them. He kept on moving; the wind came from all directions like it was seeking vengeance on him. The cracks in the ground were becoming larger, and fumes of sulfur and gusts of steam spewed out of them. The steam burned, and Henry did his best to avoid it, but he had no choice but to take the heat.

Henry's knees fell out from below him, and he hit the ground. He just wanted to give up, to throw in the towel. To him, that seemed to be the best option. As he thought of giving up, a hole in the form of a coffin formed in front of him. Henry felt that he should lie down it, just to rest a bit and gather his energy. Suddenly, he second guessed himself. *But no,* Henry thought, *this feels bad; something is not right about this. I need to make it to the green land ahead.*

Henry stood up, but felt someone behind him.

"Where are you going?" the voice crackled.

Henry turned around and saw the grim reaper, floating in the air. His cape was brown, and black wings were stretched behind him.

"I'm leaving; I am getting across this desert," Henry said.

"Oh? You are? Who gave you permission?" the spirit said.

"I don't need permission; I go as I please, spirit," Henry snapped back.

The wind was increasing its intensity. The land below was still shaking and fumes continued channeling through the ever-increasing cracks. The spirit grabbed its belly and laughed hysterically. Henry watched the spirit laugh, and as he did, he felt his confidence melt away like butter in a frying pan.

"The green land is for certain people, and you are not one of them. You belong to me. I own you; you were bought and paid for in blood," the spirit said.

"I'm no slave; I am a free man; no one owns me!" Henry contested.

The laughing spirit was not laughing anymore; he began growing taller and wider in front of Henry's eyes. The spirit was becoming angry; Henry's body started trembling from fear. The spirit pointed its finger at Henry; it was as long as Henry was tall. The hand of the spirit looked and smelled like it had been rotting in the sun for weeks.

"You are not free, you ignorant little fool! You, your family, your entire race belongs to me! I say 'jump' and you say, 'How high, master?' Now get back into your grave!" the spirit screamed, as he came face to face with the trembling Henry.

The blow of the spirit's voice was so strong that it knocked Henry back into the coffin that was behind him. He lay there on his back, looking up at the red clouds passing by rapidly overhead. Then piles of dirt started hitting him in the face, but he couldn't reach up to get them off because he felt paralyzed again. There was an old man shoveling dirt on him. He was whistling as he shoveled. He was a tall, skinny man. He had white hair and long, furry sideburns that went down the side of his face. Henry tried to scream for him to stop, but when he did, the old man aimed right for his mouth with the rich-tasting dirt and sand. Henry sat in silence, and felt the old man pack the dirt down with the shovel.

"Rest in peace, brother," the old man said in a southern accent.

Henry opened his eyes, stricken with panic and fear. Sweat was forming drops on his head. Henry felt like he had been swimming because he was so soaked with perspiration. He wanted to get up, but the nightmare had taken all his strength and willpower. All Henry could do was breathe very hard, and he scanned the room with his eyes, fearing someone was in there. Henry couldn't see anyone, but someone was definitely there.

Floating above the house, a small demon was chanting. The demon was sitting Indian-style with its hands outstretched in a position similar to a Hindu god. It was mumbling and humming. Words were coming out of his mouth and going into Henry's head. The demon's assignments were night terrors. As the words were entering Henry's mind, they manifested as thoughts of his fears coming true.

Henry couldn't take it anymore; he finally jumped up and turned on all the lights in the house. When he did, Henry saw shadows run out of the rooms. He was terrified, absolutely terrified. Henry wanted to run, but his legs were lead. He headed down the hallway. Henry kept falling down; every time he got up fatigue hit him harder. Finally, Henry closed his eyes and fell back to sleep.

In his second dream, Henry's eyes were open again. He sat up. It was pitch black, and he was sitting in a cemetery. In front of him was a row of tombstones. Henry examined them closely; they were the names of his family members—his father, mother, three brothers, and one sister. Beside them was an empty grave. The tombstone had his name on it. Henry came closer to read it, and as he did, corpses started coming through the graves. Hands and arms grabbed at Henry's feet. He jumped, trying to avoid them, but fell down. When he did, the rotting skeleton of his mother jumped on top of him. He could see through her head. There were more zombies coming his way. He couldn't get his mom off of him; she was stronger than she looked. She started pounding and screaming, "I love you, son!"

Henry was doing his best to block the blows, but with every connection, his arms got slower and slower. Finally with a shot of adrenaline, Henry reached up with both of his hands and grabbed his mother's head and head butted her with all of his might. Her head crunched like a sack of bones. Liquid, like blood mixed with pus, sprayed all over him. Henry threw her remains off of him.

When he stood up, there were thousands of corpses waiting for him. Henry turned around and started running into the forest. The swarm of zombies quickly chased him down. His father grabbed him by his hair, and dragged him back to the empty grave. The zombies were kicking and stomping on him as they made their way to the grave. They threw Henry into it; standing beside the tombstone was the old man with the side burns.

"Welcome home, boy; now lie down like a good son," the old man said.

Before Henry could respond, the old man brought the shovel down on his face. The impact made a loud "whack" sound. Henry's consciousness quickly faded away.

Chapter 40: The Pursuit

Godfrey was a little anxious today, so he decided to get up early and go jogging. While going through the classes in heaven, he had learned that jogging was one of the favorite pastimes for modern westerners. In the medieval times, where Godfrey came from, people didn't jog. They ran at full speed all the time, and it was usually from danger or by order of a king. Jogging helped Godfrey process his thoughts and put everything into order. It was not just exercise, but a type of therapy for him. One of the issues that seemed to be bothering him the most was Tabitha. Godfrey was having strange feelings about her. There was just something about her that connected to him. She was absolutely beautiful, but it was more than that; it was an inner connection that he felt. Whenever he walked with her or talked to her, he literally felt his heart jump out to her. This was very strange to him, and he couldn't control it. The only conclusion that he could come up with was that he was falling in love with her. Godfrey had never been in love before as an adult.

Once as a child, Godfrey had loved a girl, but it had been nothing more than puppy love. When he grew up and went off to the Crusades, a relationship with a woman never had the chance to fully develop. He had many encounters with prostitutes, but they were just for passing time and fulfilling temporary pleasure. Godfrey knew what the angel had told him, that "Tabitha was his," but he was confident that Tabitha didn't feel the same way as he did. Godfrey didn't really want to bother her about all this now—not with all the things that were going on with her family and all the strange, supernatural occurrences that kept happening. That is what his mind told him, but his heart told him to go to her and confess his love for her. He didn't know what to do. *Where is the middle ground in all of this?*

As Godfrey played out each scenario in his head, the confidence he had quickly dwindled. Truthfully, he just wanted to forget about it. In every scenario, it didn't turn out well. On the one hand, he could tell her and she could accept him—or not. The other option was to just forget about it and never know what would have happened if he wasn't such a coward. At this point, Godfrey had run several miles. He just kept running down roads; as he saw signs, he would turn and run.

It is hot and humid here. "The desert is way more tolerable than this place," he said with a chuckle.

He was focusing on his breathing while he ran; he had learned that the trick to running is controlling your breath. Once that was under control, he could run as far as his mind would let him. It had been hot in France too; he was from a Mediterranean climate. Godfrey wondered what France looked like now. In heaven, it was possible to watch the history of any nation. The way to go about this was to visit the Grand Library of Heavenly Accounts; in it were literally billions of aisles of books. Godfrey went to the earth's nation's aisle and pick up France's book of history. Whenever he opened the book, his surroundings changed from Heaven to France instantly. Then time would speed up or slow down with the command of a thought and he'd watch the nation grow and go through the process of maturing as a country and people. The worst part was that eventually the people would throw God out of the picture totally. This seemed to happen to every nation.

It hurt Godfrey's heart to see his country do that. He knew from seeing from a heavenly perspective that once the Spirit left, death replaced it. His concern was for the West; he didn't want to see it lost to the impending threats from the East.

Godfrey's thoughts were wandering quite a bit while jogging today. Whenever he thought of Tabitha, his chest grew warm. He felt the true happiness and love intertwined into one. Godfrey knew he couldn't live with this strong feeling much longer; he had to tell Tabitha the truth. His mind again reminded him of the consequences of that path. Inside, his stomach was churning—telling him to tell her. It was time to step out of the boat. It was time to live passionately again, Godfrey decided in himself. *All right, I am going to do it. When I get back, I will tell her.*

Godfrey did just that—he turned himself around and headed back to the house.

Chapter 41: A Shattered Heart

Tabitha was on the back porch. It was warm and sunny and like most girls in the South, she was outside sunbathing. She wore a red bikini. The red was a bright red, so bright it looked like it would glow in the dark. Her flowing brown hair hung down her back; she was lying down, facing up toward the hot sun. She had on no sunglasses, no tan lines—God forbid it. Sitting to the right of her was a small table with a pack of cigarettes and a cell phone. She had cut back, but hadn't quit.

Tabitha could hear her parents talking in the house. She guessed her dad was getting prepared for the next show. She felt sorry for him, because her dad was very well known. She could tell he was very stressed from what he said last time; it could be felt throughout the whole house. Then there was Godfrey—everything about him was weird. He claimed he was from the past, said he talked to angels, and now he was rich because some lady gave him a bunch of cash. On top of that, she felt confronted by personal doubts of her own—especially in seeing an angel, and then feeling the thick presence of God in the studio. Tabitha had these questions circulating around her head, but for now she wanted to relax and sit and enjoy the sun for a while.

She reached over and grabbed a cigarette and lit it. As she did, Godfrey came walking up. He was wearing black shorts and a gray shirt. He was covered in sweat from running, and his face was bright red from a mixture of heat, humidity, and breathing. He pulled up a chair beside Tabitha. She smiled at him as he did.

"Hey, Godfrey," she said.

“Hey, Tabitha,” Godfrey answered.

“You look kind of hot from the run,” Tabitha said.

“Yeah, nothing like the humidity. You’re sweaty yourself,” Godfrey said.

“I’ve got to keep up my tan, you know,” Tabitha said.

“Where I am from, that was considered a sign of a commoner, but now it is a sign of beauty,” Godfrey said.

“What do you mean by where you’re from?” Tabitha said.

“France, twelfth century,” Godfrey said.

“Oh…that’s right; I forgot you are from the past,” Tabitha said, doubtfully.

“What? You still don’t believe me?” Godfrey asked.

“I don’t know, Godfrey; it’s just a lot to take in. I try to be an open-minded person, which gets me into trouble quite a bit. But to say that you are from the past—I don’t know?” Tabitha said.

“You are such a doubter; you put Thomas to shame,” Godfrey said with a chuckle.

As they spoke, Godfrey’s heart was telling him that he should confess his love to Tabitha. It felt like unsettled waves crashing against the shores inside him, flaring up, then flaring down, burning with a message that he did not want to speak. Godfrey watched and listened to Tabitha go on about her day. He analyzed her with his eyes, and captured every detail about her body and movements. She moved with absolute grace. He watched as her giggle reached its pinnacle; her lovely eyes smiled and sparkled. Godfrey could feel his heart reaching for her again; it was like a ghostly stream of energy flowing toward her. This was madness, complete torture. His thoughts were racing; he felt complete concern for her. He worried about her, he desired her, he loved her, and he would die for her.

Tabitha reached for another cigarette to light it.

"You shouldn't smoke," Godfrey said.

"And you shouldn't be alive, time traveler," Tabitha responded.

"You got me there," Godfrey answered.

Tabitha lit the cigarette, exhaled a light cloud, and smiled at Godfrey. A few seconds passed and an awkward silence set in, as it always did. Godfrey went deep inside to find some confidence and came out with it.

"Tabitha? Have I ever told how beautiful you are?" Godfrey asked.

Tabitha got choked up a bit by the smoke and answered, "No, actually, you haven't, but thanks for the compliment."

Godfrey carried on, "You are not just beautiful, but you are the most beautiful creature in God's creation."

Nervousness and tension started filling the atmosphere. "Well, Godfrey, thank you very much for that comment, but where are you going with this?" Tabitha asked, as she put the cigarette out.

"I know this sounds strange, but everything about me is strange so I am just going to say it. I love you. I have fallen completely in love with you. You are mine, and I cannot live without you. When I see you, time stops; my heart flutters passionately for you. You have plagued my dreams and thoughts daily. I cannot get over you, and I want to marry you," Godfrey continued on until Tabitha interjected.

"Hold on, Godfrey, you have got to stop talking. This is way too much. This only happens in the minds of writers and movies. Love takes time to build; it is not random. You may love me, but I don't love you. Don't get me wrong; I am attracted to you, but this stuff takes time," Tabitha said.

Godfrey could feel a tear beginning in his chest. "Listen Tabitha, I cannot deny what my heart tells me about you. This is hard, I know, but who cares? Take a chance," Godfrey said.

Tabitha sat up and turned to the side of the chair, facing Godfrey. "Godfrey, don't get me wrong. You are a handsome man, but I have been hurt so many times, and my heart tells me not take chances because I might get burned. Just give me some time to think about all of this."

Godfrey just stared ahead, searching for some kind of comfort for the pain that was rooting inside. He felt his chest collapsing; his soul was trying to hide, but could not get low enough.

"You don't believe me?" Godfrey forced out.

"I guess I do; you don't seem to be a liar, but I don't have these same strong feelings you have. Maybe I will one day, but not right now," Tabitha said as pleasantly as she could.

"This feels so right to me, Tabitha; I just want you completely. God has given you to me," Godfrey said.

When Godfrey brought God into the equation he set off World War III. If there was one thing that Tabitha Maxwell didn't want to hear, it was that God was controlling her life. Tabitha was deceiving Godfrey. She did feel the same way he did. But for some reason, she was holding back because she felt that if she accepted Godfrey, she was also accepting God. Now she pulled all the way back and became defensive.

"God? What is that supposed to mean? God has nothing to do with me; I control my own life, and no one else. I admit I have seen some strange things since you have been around, but you are starting to completely freak me out now!" Tabitha snapped back.

"Man, I didn't see this going this way at all," Godfrey said.

"What? Did you expect me to jump in your arms and say, 'Take me to Tara, Rhett!' No way! I'm sorry, Godfrey, but this is the real world, and it does not function that way," Tabitha said as she stood up and walked into the house.

Before she did, Godfrey reached for Tabitha's hand and pleaded one more time. "Tabitha, just think about it, will you?" Godfrey asked.

"I'm sorry, Godfrey," said Tabitha, as she slowly walked away.

Godfrey continued to sit there, hoping that all that just happened was just a bad dream. He kept trying to wake himself up, but it did not work. It was all too real. He felt completely alone in the universe. Inside was silence, except for the toothache pain in his freshly shattered heart. Godfrey watched the clouds pass by one by one.

God, please let me go back in time and undo all of this.

At first, Godfrey tried to keep his faith up and kept reminding himself that this was just a minor step toward being with Tabitha. This approach, though, was slipping fast. Godfrey didn't know where to go from here; for once, he was at a halt in the vision for his life. It was like time kept moving, but not for him. He was left behind to pick up the pieces and try to make sense of it all.

Chapter 42: It's Time to Move On

Shortly after Godfrey expressed his feelings for Tabitha, life began to go sour for him. He was not doing what God had told him to do anymore. It felt like he had barely any faith inside him. His inner pillar of knowing what God said had been shaken tremendously. Godfrey's pain of being rejected was causing him much discomfort. The rest of the house quickly picked up on this. Godfrey or Tabitha never told anyone the conversation they had, but anybody with a bit of discernment could tell that there was tension between them. Godfrey knew he could not take being around Tabitha, especially living in the same house and working at the same place. It was just too much for him, and so he decided to move out of the Maxwell house. Godfrey moved back to the hotel with Grace. She gave him a room free of charge.

All eyes were now on the Maxwell house, especially those of Belial and his servants. Now that the champion was temporarily out of the picture, and disobedient to God, they could plan something really good to disrupt and discourage this family.

Belial was standing in front of the Maxwell house. He was meditating on how he would approach getting inside the house.

"The mother and father are following their Christ faithfully, so there is not a lot that I can do to them. It would take too long in the courts of heaven to finally find something on them. Ahh, yes, I know how. The daughter, the little doubter. We can get in through her. We just need to examine her past and see how we can do this," Belial said.

Tabitha pulled up in her car, blasting some country music. She stepped out, not knowing what was watching her. She was walking toward the door in the direction of Belial. Tabitha walked right through him. When she did, Belial read all her memories, because she was an open book and he had access to her. Tabitha started swatting at a bunch of frenzied flies that came out of nowhere.

"Gross! Nasty flies; they act like there is a dead body here or something," Tabitha said.

Belial was pleased with himself. He watched Tabitha go into the house that was closely guarded by Zadkiel posted by John and Meredith's prayers.

"You are mine, little angel; I will drag you to hell by your beautiful hair," Belial said, as he disappeared into a swirling tornado of black dust.

Chapter 43: Dismal Outlook

John and Meredith Maxwell were at their ministry office. John was receiving call after call from his powerful preacher friends from around the United States. Some were calling to condemn him for heresy; others were saying he was making the right move by telling the truth. Either way John was feeling the pressure. John was at his desk while Meredith was sitting on the couch with her legs crossed and her right hand under her chin, deep in thought.

"I've got some bad news, hon," John said.

"What's wrong?" Meredith asked, looking up.

"Godfrey said he is not painting on the show anymore—something about needing some time alone," John answered.

"It must have something to do with whatever is going between him and Tabitha. She won't tell me anything about it," Meredith said.

"And then for him to move out all of a sudden; that was just strange. I had become accustomed to him in the house," John said.

"Yeah, me too. I owe him my life for saving me," Meredith said with a hint of sadness.

The office phone rang, breaking up the discussion over Godfrey leaving. John picked it up.

"John Maxwell, how can I help you?" he asked. "What?" John answered the caller. "Are you kidding? No, sir, you were misinformed," John answered. "No, I am not a Mason, and no, I am not privy to what the Bilderbergs are planning. I'm sorry sir, you were misinformed; goodbye," John said, as he hung up the phone.

Meredith began laughing at John for being so perplexed by the call. "What was that all about? Who are Bilderbergs?" Meredith asked.

"I have no clue, but evidently I am a part of that group, and we are planning world domination," John said with a snicker.

"Well, you have been caught, my dear. The secret is out," Meredith said.

John stood up and walked over to Meredith and said, "Well, that means you are caught too." Meredith cowered as John went over and started tickling her. He then hugged her and kissed her. "I love you, darling," John said as he looked Meredith in the eyes.

"I love you too, John," Meredith answered back with a soft kiss.

The two love birds were soon interrupted by John's secretary, Tina. She popped her head in and excused herself, but told John he needed to turn on the television.

"What is it?" John asked.

"You need to watch it," Tina said.

Meredith turned on the television to the local channel. On it was Alex Levonson; he was in front of his church giving a speech. There were hundreds of people attending—a miracle for a small town like Athens, Georgia. John's heart sank as he watched the young preacher give a speech resembling one of Hitler's. The main topic of the speech was John Maxwell and his ministry. Alex was carrying on and on about how John had ruined the city and Christianity. John stood up as if he saw a ghost. "Look, do you see her?" John asked.

"Who?" Meredith and Tina answered simultaneously.

"Tabitha, look! She is attending that speech," John answered.

John, Meredith, and Tina were stunned to see Tabitha listening to the hate speech being given by Alex Levonson. They all wondered why in the world she was there. Meredith remembered that Tabitha had gone to school with Alex when they were younger. In fact, John had been friends with Alex's dad, Jason, before he had passed away. John had tried reaching out to Alex a few years ago when Jason had died, but John hadn't liked Alex when he met him. John thought he was the creepiest and weirdest little man he had ever met. Seeing Tabitha attending this locally broadcasted hate speech was chipping away at John's nerves.

"That girl has some explaining to do," John said to Meredith.

"Now John, don't get mad. She might have a good explanation," Meredith said, attempting to defend Tabitha.

"I don't think so, dear; I have a really bad feeling about this," John said in a worried tone.

Chapter 44: I Adore You

Tabitha was in the crowd of curious people who were listening to Alex Levonson. His speech was powerful and full of conviction. He stomped his feet and his fists on the podium; the crowd was amazed by him. They were drawn by his seductive and persuasive power. Tabitha had heard about the meeting through Henry Adams, the policeman. After his encounter with John, he decided to go to Alex for help. When he contacted Alex, he told Henry to attend the meeting and afterward they could talk.

Tabitha ran into Henry at a coffee shop, he recognized her as John's daughter. So he told her that Alex's speech was going to be about her father and his ministry. It was something new, so why not? Either way, she liked the way this guy spoke. He was very good.

Alex's speech ran like this:

"I am so sick of this man and his ministry of profit and doom raping our town of its goodness! No more! No more I say! We will not put up with this clown and his cohorts tearing down Christ from His cross and replacing Him with the glorious American dollar! John Maxwell is a Pharisee! John Maxwell is another Judas Iscariot dipping his fat little fingers into the pockets of God's people! I say we chop those fingers off for good, and run him out of this town!"

Most of the crowd was screaming praise and agreement; the rest were shocked at what was being said. Tabitha was not shouting in agreement, but in her heart, she believed every word Alex was saying. In just a matter of minutes, Alex Levonson had turned the people of Athens attending the meeting against John Maxwell.

After the speech was over, Henry and Tabitha were standing around talking to each other. Alex saw them and told them to meet him in his office. A lot of the crowd wanted to go in, but Alex had turned his congregation into a police force, and they stopped everyone from entering.

Tabitha and Henry walked to the back of the church to Alex's office. The church had been painted and cleaned up on the inside. It didn't look worn out and rundown anymore. Tabitha noticed a huge banner on the wall that said, "Praise the Light-Bearer." The church had a strange feeling to it, Tabitha thought. It felt like the church had a warm, welcoming feeling, but behind it, she sensed a touch of darkness. She didn't think that way about Alex though; she thought he was magnificent and charming.

The two entered the office; Alex was sitting at his desk, talking on the phone. He was talking to the local newspaper; they wanted an interview.

"Of course, I'll do it; the truth must be proclaimed," Alex said, as he motioned the two to sit down.

"All right, tomorrow then, okay, bye," Alex responded as he hung up. He leaned forward, interlocking his hands together, and looked right into Tabitha's eyes. Tabitha's heart started to flutter; she felt like Alex was inside her, reading her innermost being. He studied her carefully, and asked, "So, how can I help you?"

"It's actually me that needed the help," Henry said, as Alex broke his hypnotic gaze off of Tabitha.

Alex looked at Henry and asked. "What seems to be the problem? Henry, isn't it?"

"Yes. Well, I keep having these terrible nightmares. They keep me up all night, and I have all my lights turned on at night because I am so scared of seeing black shadows running down my halls or around my bed. I am starting to get scared right now, just thinking about it," Henry said.

"You seem to be really bothered by this." Alex said.

"Yes, I am; I am having a hard time," Henry said.

"I am here to tell you, Henry, that it will not happen again. As a matter of fact, your sleep will be so peaceful tonight that you will thank me tomorrow," Alex said, with absolute confidence as he leaned back into his chair.

"What makes you so sure about that?" Henry asked.

"Well, Henry, it is a matter of power and rank. You understand rank, don't you?" Alex asked.

"Yeah, of course. I'm a cop and a veteran," Henry answered.

"You see, when it comes to spiritual matters, I am high in rank; if I say that what is happening to you will stop, it will stop," Alex finished, with a slight smile on his face.

"For some reason I believe you, Mr. Levonson," Henry said, as he relaxed.

Alex looked at Tabitha again, and asked, "I believe I went to school with you, didn't I?"

"Yeah, I believe you did, but you look so different that I didn't recognize you," Tabitha said.

"I was fatter and somewhat of a nerd then. I was always the butt of jokes because I was a son of a preacher and I wore black all the time," Alex said, thinking back.

"I remember that; you look so good now. You must be really taking care of yourself," Tabitha said.

"Thanks, I try. The past has taught me to become stronger when faced with adversity and mockery from others," Alex said with a wicked smile.

"So, what's the deal about my dad?" Tabitha asked.

"It's not your dad I have the problem with; it's the mega-ministry and the gospel they preach. I totally respect your father, and I am sure he is a good man, but I believe that the mega-ministry is corrupting him. In order to save him from himself, he needs to get away from it," Alex said.

Tabitha was slightly upset with Alex for talking about her father, but she did agree that the ministry was his problem. She thought that the ministry was the cause of all of her family problems. Even though everything seemed to be coming together since Godfrey came to town. When she thought of Godfrey, the memory of the meeting they had had outside her house came back to her. She knew her response had hurt him, but she wasn't ready to be with Godfrey. She did like him and was attracted to him, but for some reason, she was holding back.

"Alex, I do agree with you. That ministry has been our problem from the beginning. I believe if we had been a normal family, life would have been a lot easier," Tabitha said.

"These mega-ministries are nothing more than a plague on Christianity. They do nothing but corrupt the body of Christ. I say we first save your father from OBN ministries, and then we take down the other monsters on the block," Alex said.

"Wow, are you really serious about this?" Henry asked.

"Yes, very serious. It is my calling in life," Alex said.

"Maybe you should talk to my dad and let him know what you're talking about," Tabitha said.

"Yeah, I could do that; how about you and I meet tomorrow and have lunch," Alex said.

Tabitha wanted nothing more than to be asked out by Alex. She was turning red a bit from her excitement and embarrassment. "Yeah, let's do that. Sounds good," Tabitha said.

Alex pulled a card from rack on top of his large desk and handed it to Tabitha, and said, "Just call me up and tell me when to meet you."

"Okay," Tabitha said, perplexed because usually it was the guy who called the girl, but she didn't care because she felt very attracted to this Alex.

"Henry, I guarantee you will not have any more problems with your dreams, but I must get back to business. I have a lot of meetings today, so I must bid you two farewell," Alex said, very politely. Tabitha and Henry stood up like two little children that had just been instructed by their favorite hero and headed for the door.

"Tabitha, I hope to see you tomorrow then," Henry said.

"Yes, of course; I call you up," Tabitha answered, stuttering a bit.

"All right. See you tomorrow," Alex said, smiling as he picked up the phone to make a call.

Tabitha and Henry went outside; they were both happy. Henry didn't have to worry about being scared, and Tabitha had met someone she really liked.

Chapter 45: Broken Wings

As the days went by, a dark cloud of depression set in over Godfrey. He was staying in one of Grace's hotel rooms. Godfrey was lying on the bed, staring up at the ceiling, watching the ceiling fan turn round and round. He listened closely to the annoying humming sound that the fan made. He could also hear the people walking by, talking, and the even flow of traffic. He could hear all of this on the outside, but inside, his soul lay silent. It would not move and would not speak. Godfrey felt devastated by the fact that Tabitha had wholeheartedly rejected him. Godfrey could not understand why he could feel the way he felt about her, without her having similar feelings toward him. Then, to put the icing on the cake, he still felt the same about her. He knew this had to be some kind of mistake. There had to be some kind of explanation.

He finally sat up on the side of the bed; he looked ragged. He had not shaved in several days; a dark beard was beginning to form. He stood up and walked over to the mirror, staring at himself, wondering why this had happened to him.

Why did You let this happen to me, God? I did what You told me to do, but she did not listen to me. Why did this happen to me? Why am I going through this? I heard what You said! Why did You hurt me? Why did You leave me in the dirt?

Godfrey reached down and turned on the water and began to wash his hands and face. After washing his face, he looked back up to the mirror.

Why! Why did You forsake me? Why did You allow this to happen to me?

Godfrey punched the mirror, shattering it instantly. Pieces of glass flew everywhere, hitting Godfrey in his face and body, leaving small cuts. His knuckles were torn to pieces from the sharp mirror. Once Godfrey ran out of mirror, he ran to the television and flipped it over. There were pictures and another mirror on the wall; he knocked off the pictures, and head butted the mirror.

Why? Why did You leave me to rot in this hell?

Godfrey fell to his knees; his head was down. Tears and blood mixed together as they dripped to the ground. Godfrey let out deep sobs; it was the only thing that helped his deep hurt. Behind him stood two angels; they each had a hand on his shoulders, speaking words of comfort and strength into Godfrey's spirit.

Godfrey felt a warm presence in the room with him; being a man accustomed to supernatural occurrences, it didn't startle him. Godfrey could feel his heart wanting to hate; rage was brewing deeply within it. Hardness was at the door and wanted to set in and shut the gaping, fresh wound. Godfrey knew he could not let it set in; when it did, it would be like a long, cruel winter that would not go away. After the angels had strengthened him, they disappeared and went on to the next assignment. When they left, Godfrey sat in silence and welcomed the quiet and cold darkness of his room.

How will I get past this, God?

"I feel myself slipping away into something more powerful than me. God, deliver me from myself," Godfrey prayed with little more than a mutter. Godfrey felt a surge of anger that flooded his whole body; he jumped up and screamed to the top of his lungs, "Why are You silent when I need You the most! Speak!"

Godfrey then reached for his painting supplies and started creating an image on the freshly cleared wall. He worked with anger and passion mixed with pain. The image was crude, but it was quickly forming into an angel—sitting on its knees, having its wings ripped from its back. After the painting was done, Godfrey leaned against the wall and slid down. He rested his head into his paint-covered hands.

Chapter 46: Delightful Spells

Sitting in the dark cavern that was now his lair, Alex Levonson was preparing to pray. He was sitting in the middle of one of the pentagrams on the stone floor. He had one of the many books from his library in front of him; he was examining them for a spell to put on Tabitha. He wanted to put a spell on her that would make her dumbfounded when it came to him. He wanted her to be like a sheep going to the slaughter—completely unaware and absolutely willing. She already liked him; he had acquired an unnatural charisma that could reach out and touch everyone he came near. He turned through the ancient pages. They had a crispy feel to them, like they had been soaked in coffee. Alex thought of how many men had come before him, and how many men had jumped down the hole. Alex glanced over at the mouth of hell beside him. It gave off a subtle, deep growl that sent chills up his back. Sometimes he couldn't even go near it because of the immense heat and an invisible force field that protected it.

Alex started to recollect his memories as a child and a teenager. He remembered Tabitha very well. She had always been beautiful, and he had always had a crush on her. She had not been stuck up or anything like that; she had given him enough attention to make him feel noticed. That was as far as it ever went. She was the type of girl who went from one group to the other—a bit of an outsider herself; being the child of a big-name preacher carried a stigma that was hard to hide. Everyone expected her to be good, but she did bad things just to squash the reputation that her father's image placed on her. Alex knew how it was to be a preacher's son; it was horrible and it had been much worse for him. He was fat, pale, strange looking, and quiet. Alex could remember back and say he honestly had never had even one friend. Some people were nice to him, like Tabitha, but most were cruel.

One person in particular was very cruel to him—Billy Ferguson; he had been especially mean. Billy would go out of his way to do horrible things to Alex every day at school. Alex hated Billy so much, he would imagine Billy being run over in the street. As he cried out, begging Alex for help, Alex imagined himself walking up and soaking him in gasoline. Last of all, he threw a match on him.

Today was Alex's lucky day. Billy had seen him on television, and he still lived in town. Billy was feeling bad for mistreating Alex and sought him out to ask forgiveness. Billy had just recently quit drinking, and one of the steps in Alcoholics Anonymous was to apologize to the people you had mistreated in the past. Alex was definitely one of them.

"How you doing over there, Billy?" Alex asked, as he thumbed through the book.

Bound to the ground facedown, Billy lay naked. He was trembling; the ground was cold against his skin. Over the years, Billy had become quite fat, and Alex had him tied down so tight that Billy's blubber was bulging out like a balloon between the straps. Billy tried to move, but Alex was efficient with his bindings.

"I, I, I, I apologized to you. I'm sorry for the way I treated you. I'm so sorry; please don't kill me!" Billy pleaded. Billy's breathing was in short spurts because of his panic and the lack of movement the straps allowed. Alex sat there in deep thought; he was imagining Tabitha. He kept turning through the pages, not even acknowledging poor Billy.

"Oh, you're talking to me, aren't you? You are not getting out of this, Billy. You've been chosen," Alex said, breaking the silence.

"Listen, man, I've got a daughter. Please, I just got my life back on track," Billy said, stretching his neck as much as possible.

"You've got a daughter, huh? Where is the mother?" Alex asked, acting concerned.

"We split a long time ago because of my drinking. I want to get her back. Dude, are you going to let me go, or what?" Billy asked.

"You know, Billy, you caused me a lot of pain growing up. I couldn't even be myself because of the worry of being tortured by you," Alex said.

"I know, man, and I am sorry for that. Just give me a chance; I am truly sorry for the way I treated you," Billy said, feeling as if he got his point across.

"You sound sincere, which is good and noble for you, at least. Because hopefully some Higher Power is hearing your repentant heart, but that someone is not me. All I want is vengeance and justice; I want your blood to be soaked into my skin, and if you do not shut that fat mouth of yours, that tongue will be the first thing cut out!" Alex blurted out.

Billy started crying, "I don't want to die, man. I just want see my child again. Please have mercy, for God's sake, have mercy," Billy begged.

On top of the hell mouth lay a short, razor-sharp samurai sword. The sword had been sitting there for a while; it was nearly red hot. The hell mouth was making hot, popping sounds, and the short sword was sizzling. Each time a random pop happened, Billy would jump from the sound; he didn't want the hot pieces of metal and rock to land on him.

Billy was sweating and very tired. Alex had been looking at the books for hours; he was not in a hurry. Billy kept fading in and out; when he did, he saw images of his daughter. All he wanted in the world now was to see her again. He wanted his family back—the one he had sold for the bottle. *This is fate I guess. I should have never have come here. Man, I am so stupid. I finally wanted to do something good and this is what happens. Reaping what you sow—I remember preachers telling me that. I should have listened, I should have listened, damn it all to hell, I should have listened.*

Another wave of sobs came up from Billy's gut. His eyes were hurting from crying; he had never cried this much in his whole life.

"Just let me stretch a little bit. Let me move around some," Billy said, with crying hiccups like a child.

"All right, I think I have it. Tabitha, my dear, we will join my lord in his infernal kingdom. You will be my bride, and our children will plague the millennium to come," Alex said as he stood up. He walked over to the desk and grabbed rope and a piece of cloth that had been used to clean up blood from other animals and people. He stood over Billy. Billy had a streak of hope go through him. "Are you gonna let me leave? I knew you would; I knew you wouldn't kill me. I promise I will not tell a soul," Billy said.

"Open your mouth; I've got some food," Alex said.

Billy did, not seeing what was in Alex's hand. Alex crammed the cloth into Billy's mouth and then wrapped the rope around his mouth. He tightened it fiercely. Billy gagged from the taste of blood and dirt.

"I told you to shut up, and make your peace with your god. Your about to meet him or her," Alex said, walking over to the hot blade.

That night Alex got his long awaited vengeance on Billy. Alex did his evil deeds, and Billy never saw his family again. Alex didn't know that Billy had lied to him; he did tell somebody where he was going. Billy had called his ex-wife and told her about asking forgiveness to everyone he had hurt, because she and his daughter had been first on the list.

Chapter 47: The Riot

John Maxwell pulled up to the OBN studio; instead of being able to find a parking spot with no problem, he found crowds of people screaming at each other, holding signs up. They were obviously protesting about something. One stuck out to John like a neon sign; it read "Burn the Heretic." Another one read, "The End is nigh." There were cops in front of the crowds; they were trying to contain them; at first the crowds were just screaming, but when they saw John had arrived, that all changed. People started throwing rocks, tomatoes, and their signs at John's car. John ducked when one of the rocks smacked right into his windshield; the rock left a massive crack that spread across the glass like a streak of lightning.

"Hey!" John screamed as he tried to edge his car forward.

The crowd was on each side of the parking lot. From all John could see one side was for him, and the other side wanted him dead. On the side that was for him, one sign said, "Keep Preaching, Prophet." Reading that gave John a sick feeling because he was not a prophet and never would claim to be. He finally got to a spot to park; he tried to get out of the car, but a very large man ran up and slammed his body against the door, causing John to fall back into to the car. The man started screaming, "Boy, you'd better stay in dat car. 'Cause if you get out I'm-a stomp you flat like momma's pancakes."

John saw the size of the man and figured it would be best to stay in his car. He hit the lock button on his door and sat, wondering how he had been caught in this mess. He decided to call Meredith; she picked up almost immediately.

"John, are you okay?" Meredith asked.

"Yeah, I'm okay; I just had a guy threaten to stomp me into the pavement," Jon answered, looking at the guy who said it. He was still staring at him.

"I saw what is happening on the news; they did a camera shot from a helicopter. There has to be over two hundred people there," Meredith said.

"This is crazy, Meredith; I wasn't expecting this! This has to be from that baldheaded preacher, Alex Levonson, and to think my daughter was there listening to his crap," Jon said.

"I'm sure she has her reasons, John; I'll talk to her when I see her," Meredith said.

John and Meredith kept talking. To John's left, a fight broke out; it was the fat man who had threatened him and a nearby policeman. They smacked up against Jon's car, wrestling each other. The fat man was pounding the cop left and right with jabs and uppercuts. The cop was doing his best to block the blows, but surprisingly, the heavy man was quick and methodical with his punches. John could feel his car shake from the punches that the poor cop was absorbing. Finally another cop came from behind and smacked the man in the back of his head with a night stick; the big man turned, making a growling sound and started attacking the cop who accosted him like he was a honey-glazed holiday ham. The cop that had been against the car being pulverized looked at John with a bloody nose and screamed, "Get inside! Before they kill us all!"

John ran inside without hesitation. He heard objects smacking against the wall as he ran. Through all the chaos, he forgot he was still on the phone with Meredith.

"Are you there, honey?" John asked.

"Yes! What happened?" Meredith asked.

"I had to run inside; at least I'm safe now. I hope that crowd is gone by the time I leave," John said, walking to his office.

"They will be. They will call in riot control," Meredith said.

"I hope you are right, love," John said, sitting down in his office.

"Have you heard from Godfrey at all?" Meredith asked.

"No, nothing," John answered.

"God, I hope he is okay," Meredith said.

"He is our painter for the show; we need him," John said, turning on his computer.

"I haven't heard a word since he moved out," Meredith said.

"Maybe we should check on him," John said, beginning to scan his e-mail.

"I think I will today; he is staying at that hotel again," Meredith said.

"I would go, honey, but I don't think I can leave the office anytime soon," John said.

"I know. On the news, they are showing a ton of people there, being arrested," Meredith said.

"Oh, wow, listen to this e-mail. 'I hope you burn for what you stand for, prosperity preacher. You are going to choke on all that money of yours. Your time will come. Sincerely, Sister Rita.'"

"Sister Rita? You mean one of the old ladies from church?" Meredith asked.

"Yep, it also says we are not welcome at church anymore. But I kind of figured that was coming," John said.

"John, I hope we are doing the right thing," Meredith said with a worried tone.

"I know we are, honey; if we weren't, there wouldn't be this much opposition against us. It is very hard, but a good sign," John said, surprising himself for the jolt of faith that went through his bones.

The two spoke a little longer, and then hung up. John began making plans for his show, and Meredith got ready to visit Godfrey.

Chapter 48: A Conversation with Crows

Belial sat in a dead tree that was still standing against the force of time and age. There were several blood-covered buzzards in the tree with him; they were resting from a feast they had had on a pregnant doe that had been hit by a car just several yards away. The large tree had a light gray color; it appeared to be hollow from the look of it. It had a giant hole that formed in the front of it; a possum had turned it into a home. All the trees that surrounded it were alive and thriving, but not this one; it was dead to the world.

"I love religious intolerance," Belial said, petting one of the buzzards.

"These people, why does God even waste His time with them? They are so stupid; I can manipulate them to do anything. It's not fair really; everything in this world is used against them. It must be some type of cruel experiment of God's," Belial said, scratching the chin of another buzzard.

Belial looked down at the deer carcass and noticed that a group of crows was eating what was left of it. They always got seconds to the buzzards. They cawed at each other, flaring their wings, showing dominance.

"That's all this mundane life is for the human race, a show of dominance. They kill each other, starve each other, and steal from each other. They know nothing of loyalty and respect. It was the same in their beginning; Lucifer purchased their innocence and freedom over a piece of fruit," Belial said, leaning back against the tree. The crows flew up to the tree to join them; they were to the right of Belial, and the buzzards were to the left of him.

"Ah, my children, my death eaters, you understand my quarrels with life. My life is much different from yours. When you die, that is it for you, to the dirt you go. As for me, it is the fire for me. I hear there is already a plot laid out for me, to sit and roast and be on display for all creation to see what rebellion gets them. That is my destiny, to be a fume in the nostrils of God, angels, and men," Belial mused, petting the back of a crow. Its head bobbed down and arched with his hand.

"I wonder…were we just experiments as well? My kind and I, the fallen angels, the most despised of all except Lucifer himself. Was it all just a simple test of will? Why did we follow him? We were his loyal army, and he was so charismatic. He made us believe he would win; he made us trust him. Just one mistake, my little crow, and your life can forever change," Belial said.

"I forgot what love was a long time ago. Rage, hate, vengeance, and pain are what fuel me now. Knowing the end before it comes ignites the flames inside me, my black-feathered friends. I wish for this entire planet to burn up and explode into nothing. I want it to become just a memory like my previous life. Just a memory of what could have been. I hate man so much; I want to stack their carcasses to the sky. I truly do," Belial said casually.

Belial and his feathered friends were interrupted by a light gray dove that landed in the tree with them. Belial coiled back like a snake, and the crows and buzzards flew away in a frenzy. The dove just sat there, peacefully looking at Belial.

"What do you want? We have won this little battle. Your champion lies in a bed of suicide; he cries and wonders why his God has broken his heart. He has disobeyed, and is now open game for us," Belial said confidently.

Out of nowhere a giant brown hawk landed on the tree with the dove. It flared its wings at Belial, showing no fear. Belial started backing away from the birds.

"I will kill your champion! I will kill his wife! I will kill his dreams and I will kill his destiny! His pathetic life will amount to nothing. He will be another scum that could have been and never was," Belial hissed.

Behind Belial, a large brown and white owl landed behind him. Its black eyes examined him intently. The tree began to make a cracking sound. The roots were giving in. Belial was outnumbered; he pointed his bony finger at the dove and whispered, "You will not win this one, I promise you."

The hawk suddenly let out a blood curdling scream. The scream got louder and louder; it was like waves that kept getting bigger and bigger. Belial couldn't handle the power of its voice. The waves were literally destabilizing him, but the hawk kept screaming and screaming. Belial watched the hawk's beak; he saw its tongue, vibrating up and down. The power that was in it, he couldn't take anymore; he had to go.

"Stop it!" Belial reared back, covering his face as if he were choking. Finally the tree began to collapse, and Belial disappeared and retreated from the birds.

Chapter 49: Suspicious Minds

Henry Adams was at the Clark County police station; it was early morning. He had a cup of black coffee in his hand, and he and the other cops were sitting in a conference type room. The chief was going to talk to them about what to do for the day. The conference room's walls had a dull yellow look, like they had been stained for years by smoking. The police station was old, and the entire building showed it. Outside the conference room, where all the offices were, the walls were wood panel, and the ceiling brownish looking sheetrock. The office was not that big; there were only about thirty cops or so. Athens was not a large city, but recently with all the killing that had happened, they had all been on their toes. The mayor was breathing down everyone's neck to stop all of the trouble that was plaguing Athens.

"All right, gentlemen," the chief said, walking into the room behind the brown podium.

Low grumbles could be heard going through the room.

The chief was a fat man. His stomach stuck out so far it looked like it would explode at any minute. Whenever Henry was really bored with listening to the chief, he would imagine his stomach actually exploding and colorful confetti going everywhere.

"It looks like we have got plenty to do today, fellows," the chief said. "Thompson, Grayson, Franklin, I want you three to stand post at the John Maxwell's office. They had a riot yesterday, so that means he needs an escort again."

"Oh, great," Franklin said.

“We get to protect the preacher everyone hates,” Thompson said.

“I’m sorry, what did you say, gentlemen?” the chief asked.

“Yes sir; we will get right on it,” the three mumbled, walking out.

The rest of the room shifted in their chairs to listen up for their assignments. “Adams?” the chief yelled.

“Yes, sir,” Henry answered, sipping his coffee.

“We’ve got a missing persons report, and I’d like you to look into it; seems like foul play. A Billy Ferguson has been missing since two days ago. Told his wife he had to meet with somebody; after that, no one has seen him at all,” the chief said.

“Yes, sir, I’ll get right on it,” Henry answered.

“Watch out for white vultures, Adams,” Roger Clemmons said from the back of the room. The rest of the officers started laughing.

“Kiss my ass, Clemmons; I might stop by and visit your wife on the way,” Henry said, smiling. The whole room laughed at that one.

Clemmons answered back, “Tell her to cook tacos tonight, will ya?” The whole room was rolling in laughter by now.

“All right, all right, get out of here, Adams,” the chief said, calming the room down.

As Henry was walking out, he overheard the chief tell Clemmons, “Since you’re such a comedian, you get to talk to elementary kids today on why not to do drugs.” Clemmons was not happy about it at all.

The chief gave the address to Henry; it was the address of Billy Ferguson’s wife. It was the last contact that Ferguson had before disappearing. From what Henry could find on his laptop in his squad car, this Billy had a record. His list of offences was the following: public drunkenness, assault and battery, DUI, and loitering. Billy had been locked up quite a few times for getting too rowdy in the local bars.

"I bet this guy got into a fight with the wrong person and was left somewhere for the crows to eat. That's the thing with these types of rednecks; they get a little bit of alcohol in them and they turn into a super hero," Henry said.

Henry was feeling a lot better since his meeting with Alex Levonson because ever since then, he hadn't had one bad dream or nightmare. He did not get that feeling of fear at all anymore in his house.

There must be something legitimate about that guy, but he was a strange character though. Bald with a well trimmed goatee, sort of creepy.

He reached the home of Billy's ex-wife. It was a small house right outside of town on a half acre of well-manicured grass. The house was a yellow one-story structure with white trim. The driveway was small and composed of gravel mixed with dirt. Henry stepped out of his squad car and headed for the porch. He knocked a couple of times and waited patiently. A little blonde girl with blue eyes answered the door. Henry guessed she was around four or so.

"Have you found my daddy?" the little girl asked.

"Not yet, but I will do my best," Henry answered the direct little girl.

She smiled through the cracked door. Henry noticed her mother walking behind the girl. She opened the door wider. She also had blonde hair, but her eyes were brown.

"Hello, officer!" the woman said. She was not totally grief stricken, Henry noticed, but she did appear to be quite worried.

"Hello ma'am, I'm Officer Adams, and your name is?" Henry asked.

"Joanne Fer—I mean, Taylor. Joanne Taylor," she answered. "Come on in, and have a seat," she said as Henry entered the house. "I guess you are here because of my ex-husband," Joanne said as they sat down as her kitchen table.

"Yes ma'am. You reported that he was missing," Henry said.

"Yes, he was supposed to come back and we were going to talk about some things," she said, looking down.

Henry saw the pain in her eyes; she loved this guy—whoever he was. "Your ex-husband has quite the record; he must have caused you a lot of grief," Henry said.

"Yes, Billy liked to drink, and he liked to fight. He has been like that since we were teenagers," Joanne said.

"Is that why you two split?" Henry asked.

"Yeah, I tried living with him and his ways for a while, but eventually I could not take it anymore, especially after we had our daughter," Joanne said.

"I can understand that," Henry said.

"I tried staying with him; I hoped that after our daughter was born, he would straighten up. He tried for a while, but all he did was hide his drinking. Finally, I told him it was enough and made him leave," Joanne said.

"How long ago was that?" Henry asked.

"I guess about three years ago. I hated to do that because I wanted my daughter to have a father, but I just couldn't take it anymore," Joanne said.

"So why was he coming over to talk to you?" Henry asked.

"Billy had begun AA; he was going through the program, doing the steps. He had not been drinking for a while. He told me he wanted to change; he said he wanted a family again. Of course, I didn't really believe him, but I wanted to for my daughter's sake," Joanne said.

"I'm sure," Henry said.

"He was taking the program seriously; he went from drinking every day to not drinking at all," Joanne said.

"How long was he off the drinking?" Henry asked.

"A few months; I'd say about six months or so," Joanne said.

"Joanne, do you know where he was going the last time you spoke with him?" Henry asked.

"You know that preacher who has been on here TV lately? Alex Levonson?" Joanne asked.

"Yeah, I know him," Henry responded, leaning in and becoming more intrigued.

"Well, Billy and I went to school with Alex. Billy was a jock, and a bully at that. He used to give Alex a really hard time as a kid. Billy was really mean to Alex; I felt so sorry for him, but I didn't do anything to stop it. I just laughed like everyone else," Joanne said, staring off into space, thinking about the past.

"Billy felt bad for what he did to Alex; when he saw him on TV the other day, Billy thought it was a good idea to seek Alex out and apologize to him," Joanne said, reiterating what was already said.

"Joanne, thanks for your time. I think I have enough information for now," Henry said as he stood up from the table.

Joanne stood up as well, and the two of them headed for the door. "Officer Adams, please find him. He said he had changed; my daughter needs her father," Joanne said, with a desperate tone in her voice.

"I will do what I can; I'm sure we'll find him," Henry reassured her.

As Henry walked out to his squad car, the little blue-eyed girl was waving at him. Henry waved back. Henry was thinking about the information about Billy; he decided the next step was to ask Alex about Billy's whereabouts.

Chapter 50: Black Clouds Follow Me

The hotel room had become a disaster area. The walls were covered with strange paintings of angels having their wings torn off and people being executed with swords; they looked like memories of Godfrey's first life. The only light in the room was from one of the lamps from a nightstand that had been kicked over. The lamp was on its side. Beside the angry paintings were a bunch of random quotes from the book of Job. One in particular was Job 3:5-6, "May darkness and gloom reclaim it, and a cloud settle over it. May an eclipse of the sun terrify it. If only darkness had taken that night away!" Godfrey was sitting on the end of the bed; his hands were resting beside him; his head was leaning down, staring at the floor. Godfrey's arms and chest were covered in slashes and wounds from his angry sessions in the room. He had lost at least twenty pounds because he had not eaten anything for days.

He was not sleeping either; throughout the night, he was tormented with demonic dreams. Whenever he woke up in the middle of the night, he saw spirits floating around his room, tormenting him and trying to scare him. One night he woke up and the entire room was engulfed in fire; in front of his eyes, he watched past scenes of himself being tortured in hell. Still, Godfrey did not care. Inside, he felt like he had been filled with concrete.

Godfrey began to lift his hands out like he was reaching for something in front of him. The only thing there was a broken mirror that showed a twisted version of himself.

Hell was bad, but this sucks too. I can relate to Job. What exactly did Job ever do wrong anyway? I never understood—it was like he was just a toy chosen to be tortured between Satan and God. A good man, who loved his God with all his heart—in return, his world melted away in the flames of a bet. Dark days are around me, dark times follow me, dark ways consume me, dark thoughts plague me.

Godfrey stood up to get a drink of water from the sloppy, dirty sink. He found a glass that was not broken and turned the sink on to get something to drink. He sucked the contents down slowly as if his throat hurt from the water going down it. Just the thought of eating or drinking made him feel sick. He finished his first cup, and went to pour himself another one anyway. He was interrupted by the room turning dark and the heat within it rising in intensity. Godfrey set his glass down and turned around. The room was in flames again. He walked over to his bed and lay down. His entire body was covered in sweat; the room felt like it was 120 degrees inside. Godfrey was starting to feel really tired in the seducing flames. His vision was fading in and out. Finally the fire put him to sleep.

It did not last long because he woke up to Lilith standing before him. She was wearing a red dress that exposed every curve on her body. It looked as if the dress was stitched to her. She was smiling, while holding the end of a long cigarette holder in her mouth and hand. One foot was on the bed while the other hand rested on her curvy hips.

"Hello, Godfrey, how is life treating you these days?" Lilith asked with a twisted smile.

Godfrey felt almost paralyzed from the trance-like state he was in; he couldn't tell if he was dreaming or not. The heat was real, Lilith's seductive countenance looked real, and Godfrey's tormented heart still felt real.

"I've seen better days, I could honestly say," Godfrey responded, closely watching Lilith.

"Did your little sweetheart reject you? Did she deny your undying love for her?" Lilith asked, laughing hysterically at the thought.

Godfrey shifted slightly, but that was all the movement his body would allow. As Lilith was laughing, a deep, nagging, itching pain hit Godfrey's heart. Godfrey just stared with the numbing thought of what he confessed to Tabitha; the memory burned like kissing hot coals. Small, subtle waves of pain hit him like a slow drum beat. The fire was crackling and licking the walls intensely. Lilith watched Godfrey's eyes as the words tore into him.

"I watched you tell her, Godfrey. I watched it all. For some reason, I have a personal attachment to you. Since you escaped my grasp in hell, I thought I would personally come and see you to offer you a deal," Lilith said as she casually smoked her cigarette.

"Really, another deal, huh? Am I that dangerous to you?" Godfrey responded to Lilith.

Lilith laughed sarcastically and said, "Look at you, Godfrey; you are not a threat or danger to anyone. You are barely existing, and doing a horrible job at that, I must add. We offer you anything you want or desire; we can make you one of the most powerful men in this world. All you have to do is kiss the ring of Lucifer. God has promised you long life, so you can spend it however you want it—through darkness or light."

"Why would I want to do that? Turn my back on the One who guides and protects me?" Godfrey asked.

"Did He protect you from this pain that you are going through? It looks like He hasn't done a very good job at all of taking care of you, Godfrey. Is that love? Your God is a cruel one; He really hates mankind. He places stumbling blocks before His children just to watch them fall into traps. You are nothing more than a failure, a false hope, a false messiah, Godfrey," Lilith answered back.

"I do not have all the answers to your accusations, and I do not understand why I am being put through all of this. But I know one thing—God will vindicate me. He will protect me from you and your wicked followers. I have hope, but you face the grave, fallen queen. Your fate is set—to the flames you will go, to the flames you will stay," Godfrey said.

"Do you know, Godfrey, that Tabitha wants to sleep with Alex? She wants to pleasure him with her body. She doesn't want you, but him—a fat bald man who was given everything he ever wanted from Lucifer. You could be the same, Godfrey; all you have to do kiss the ring too. Bow and kiss the signet of the dragon," Lilith said.

"What is it with the wicked?" Godfrey asked.

"What are you talking about, Templar?" Lilith asked, becoming annoyed.

"The wicked hide behind things, materials. They try to control men by offering substance and power. I am sure you already know, dead queen, that nothing goes with you to the grave. Empty-handed you were born, empty-handed you will die," Godfrey responded to Lilith.

"Really, Godfrey, have you become some kind of philosopher?" Lilith said as she put the end of her cigarette out on the tip of her tongue. "I know what you want, Godfrey. Tabitha is what you want. You can play Mr. Righteous all you want, but the fact is that we all have a price. We all have a temptation—idols from the beginning," Lilith said as she began to crawl on the bed toward Godfrey's body like a cat about to pounce on a mouse.

Lilith was right over Godfrey; she began to kiss him on his chest and neck. Godfrey hated it, and could not stop her. But as much as he hated to admit it, he was enjoying it. Despite everything, Lilith was very seductive and gorgeous.

"Is this what you want, Godfrey, touch from a female? Do you want to explore my garden of Eden?" Lilith said as she faced Godfrey.

As Godfrey looked her in the eyes, Lilith's face and body changed into Tabitha. Godfrey gasped, but still couldn't move. Lilith began kissing Godfrey on his cheeks while saying, "I can be Tabitha for you tonight, Godfrey. I can be anybody for you, just kiss the ring."

Godfrey was not responding, so Lilith began kissing him on the lips. She was whispering quietly in his ears, speaking seductively. Godfrey's mind told him to fight Lilith's advances, but his body told him different. For a minute, he forgot about Lilith and was thinking he was kissing the one he loved, Tabitha. The two caressed each other for a few minutes. The flames were still burning in the background. Godfrey forgot who he was for a second; for just a split second he felt like Tabitha was on top of him. For just a minute, his broken heart went silent.

It stopped. Godfrey's eyes opened. He saw Tabitha smiling at him, and she said, "Just kiss the ring, Godfrey, and I will be yours."

Godfrey lay there, still unable to move. He knew what he had to do. Hesitantly, he looked at her and said, "No deal; I will not kiss any ring or sell my soul to you or your master."

The fire in the room began to blaze with more intensity, and Lilith changed back to her true form. Her eyes were engulfed with rage and matched the burning fire surrounding the room. Lilith sat up and said, "You dare deny me? You dare reject me? You are a fool, Godfrey! I am the queen of hell! I offer you everything you could ever dream or want, and this is what you say?"

Godfrey had a hard time responding because as much as he knew it would cost him, the offer was tempting. Everything he ever dreamed of was laying at his feet—power, wealth, women, revenge, the pride of life—it was all there on the table. To have it, all he had to do was give his soul to hell, and even after experiencing the horrors firsthand, the temptation was there.

Lilith rose in the air, levitating. She began to scream with a horrible sound; as the sound intensified, little black shadows began swirling around the room. They swooped down at Godfrey; he closed his eyes and tensed his face up. Lilith came down like an eagle catching a fish and grabbed Godfrey's face with both her hands. Godfrey's eyes were wide open as Lilith's face was right in front of his.

"I will kill you, Godfrey; I will kill your future, I will kill your destiny, I will melt your dreams in the palm of my hand. You will taste my wrath firsthand," Lilith said, as she licked Godfrey's face from chin to forehead. It felt horrible; it was like being licked by a cat with a dry calloused tongue. She gave him one last kiss on the lips, and vanished with a loud popping sound like a sonic boom.

Godfrey opened his eyes to an empty room. He sat up but had no energy. *Was that a dream?* Godfrey had experienced many dreams, but his gut told him that this was no dream; if anything, it was a vision. Godfrey stood up and went outside to get some fresh air. It was wet, windy, and rainy. A ferocious thunderstorm had settled over Athens. All Godfrey had on was a pair of shorts. The rain was pelting down on him like little BBs being shot at him. The rain was good for him because he had not bathed in few days. In a strange way, Godfrey felt that his depression was lifting. Clarity was settling in his soul again. It felt good to breathe again. Godfrey stood outside for a few more minutes, then went inside his room and started cleaning up the mess he had made.

Chapter 51: The Date

Tabitha was in her room at home, drying off from a shower. She was getting herself nice and cleaned up for her date with Alex; it was their second one. They were going to a restaurant. Tabitha had butterflies in her stomach. She dried her tanned body and put on all of the necessities for smelling good. She put on her undergarments and began to blow dry her hair. The bathroom was still misty from the shower.

I can't believe I am so nervous. I haven't been nervous about a man in a long time. To think, Alex used to be so nerdy and such an outcast. Now, he is making his way to the top of the world.

Tabitha began painting her toenails red and putting rose-scented lotion on her legs and arms. She found a dress in her closet that had not been worn in a while. It was only worn for special occasions. It was a black summer dress with a bunch of different colored flowers on it. As Tabitha was doing the finishing touches of her make-up, her phone vibrated. She went over and looked down; it was a text from Alex, saying, "On the way." A sudden jolt of joy hit her heart to add to the mix of different emotions she was already experiencing. *I wonder if he's the one. That would be difficult since he called my dad a prosperity preacher who is nothing more than a plague that has to be wiped out.*

To be sure, Tabitha saw a conflict that would eventually rise between Alex and her parents. Alex was extremely driven and headstrong. Her dad was devoted to his ministry, and of course her mom hated everything she did. It didn't matter what it was, nothing seemed to be good enough for Meredith Maxwell. Just the thought of that made her want to go smoke a joint.

"Tabitha?" Meredith said as she knocked on the door frame of Tabitha's room.

"Oh, hey, Mom. What is it?" Tabitha answered as she put her wallet and phone in her purse.

"What are you getting so dressed up for? I haven't seen you like this in ages," Meredith said, leaning against the door frame.

"A date," Tabitha responded with a smile.

"A date! Wow! I thought you had given up on that," Meredith said.

"Yeah, me too, but it looks like luck is shining my way for a change," Tabitha said.

"That's good; who are you going out with?" Meredith asked.

Wanting to dodge the interrogating altogether because of the reaction Tabitha's mother would have, she answered, "A friend."

"Oh, does this friend have a name?" Meredith asked.

"Alex," Tabitha answered, breathing heavily.

"Is this the Alex who was on television mocking your father? The one we saw you standing with?" Meredith asked with a slight increase of volume in her voice.

"Yeah. He's not against dad; he is just against the false gospel of prosperity," Tabitha responded defensively.

"What? What do you know about the gospel? Are you suddenly a believer of some kind?" Meredith asked.

"I know enough to realize it's a bunch of crap. It's a bunch of fat Americans who think they can hide in their massive churches and not have to deal with real life—while those who don't fit in are left to fend for themselves on the outside," Tabitha answered.

"Your dad is not like that, and you know it. He is a good man," Meredith answered.

"Dad may not be, but his board of directors is, and so are most of his viewers," Tabitha answered.

"Listen, Tabitha, I don't want to fight with you. You know your dad is not going to like the idea of you going out with this guy," Meredith said, trying to restore peace.

"Mom, I know that, but I really like Alex, and I think you will too. Plus dad is changing his message, so I think this will all work out," Tabitha responded.

"I hope so, but I have a bad feeling about this," Meredith said as Tabitha looked at her phone to read a text from Alex that said, "I'm here."

"Don't worry, Mom; there is nothing wrong with Alex," Tabitha said, giving her mom a reassuring hug.

"Just be careful, dear," Meredith said.

"I will, I promise," Tabitha responded as she headed outside to meet Alex at his car.

Chapter 52: What Lies Hidden

Henry had just pulled up to Alex's church. It was a small place, but recently since Alex's electrifying popularity, more people started coming to the church, and more people meant more tithes. Money for new construction was flowing in, and it appeared that a lot of cosmetic work was being done on the outside of the church. It was around eight o'clock; Henry had another hour of daylight. The parking lot was empty, so Henry decided to pull around to the back of the church so no one would see his car from the road. There was no one else at the church.

I guess Alex is not here. Must be busy doing preacher stuff. That is one job I would not want, being a preacher. Sitting in front of a bunch of old farts and listening to them say "amen" to everything I say like mooing cows.

"Mooooooooooo!" Henry said out loud with a chuckle.

He parked his car and looked around a bit; he then went to the front of the church and knocked on the door. No one answered. As Henry started walking back to his car, he noticed a white flash move quickly in the thick woods behind the church. Henry just blew it off and continued for his car, but he saw it again.

"What was that?" Henry said.

Out of pure curiosity, Henry began to walk into the thick canopy of woods after he pulled out his flashlight. As he walked, his silhouette disappeared into the dark shadowy woods. All that could be seen from the outside was the brightness of his flashlight. It was like the woods were a world of their own; suddenly new sounds could be heard. Twigs were breaking from furry creatures walking on them, and birds were chirping. Henry looked down on the forest floor; it appeared to be trail leading further into the woods. It almost looked as if someone had been dragged through here. Henry dismissed the thought; it could have been a path for rain water. He kept following the trail without seeing anything; as he was about to turn around, the white flash appeared again. Henry turned around to try and catch it with eyes, but to no avail; it was gone again. Henry's heart started to increase its beating; chills were manifesting on his arms, back, and neck. A touch of fear was creeping into his mind once again.

"Get a hold over yourself, stupid," Henry said as he walked further into the woods where he saw the white flash. "I hope this is not some kind of weird UFO sighting, because if it is, I'm not telling a soul," Henry said as he calmed himself down.

The perspiration on Henry's back and neck felt a cold, quick breeze fly behind him. Henry reacted by pulling out his gun and pointing it at nothing. He felt it behind him again, causing him to turn once again. Henry looked up and saw the white vulture. Its eyes were glowing red like a bleeding heart; this time, instead of having two eyes, it had several like spider. The size of the vulture had increased; it was bigger than before. For the mockery that Henry went through before for saying that he had seen this thing, he decided he was going to show this bird to everyone as a trophy.

Pow! Pow! Pow! The gun fired at the white bird; Henry's aim was impeccable. Cold, methodical shooting, but to no avail; the bird responded by hopping off its perch and flying right toward him. Henry got off a few more rounds before he had to duck. The bird swooped down, then turned around, and flew deeper into the woods. When Henry ducked, he noticed a cell phone on the forest floor. He picked it up, put it into his pocket, and ran toward the behemoth fowl.

“You’re not getting away today, stupid bird!” Henry screamed at the vulture.

Henry was running nearly at full pace, which was hard in these woods. He kept getting caught in vines, small trees, and briers. Henry kept his eyes focused on the target, but he thought his eyes were playing tricks on him because it looked like the massive bird was a hologram of some kind, passing through the trees. Henry reloaded his gun while running. This was his last magazine; he only had two magazines of twelve on him.

Should have brought more, should have grabbed the shotgun.

It was getting dark; all Henry had was his flashlight and the red glow of eyes from the vulture to guide him. The bird stopped again; Henry was thankful because he was getting really tired and would have had to stop himself. Henry was panting heavily; he just wanted to sit down and catch his breath. Discipline stopped him though; he kept his aim on the target. The bird kept still as Henry came closer; the multiple eyes blinked nonchalantly, waiting, focused on Henry.

“Say goodbye, birdie,” Henry said as he unloaded the whole clip on the vulture. All twelve rounds passed right through the feathered creature. Henry stopped after he was out of ammo because of the empty clicking sound the gun made. He stood there, stunned and shocked; cold sweat was beading down his whole neck. Henry was starting to get scared.

“This ain’t no real bird, oh shit…” Henry whispered to himself. He started walking backward, wanting the nightmare to end. Henry turned and started trotting quicker and quicker as deep laughter began bellowing out of the vulture. Henry’s speed increased.

“Run! Run! Run, boy! Run as fast as you can!” the vulture said, as if it were directly behind Henry’s ear, licking it like a snake inspecting something new.

Henry thought he was home free until he fell into a large hole. Instead of hitting dirt or grass, he landed on stone steps that spiraled down at a sharp angle. Falling, falling, and falling some more down the steps, Henry felt every hit, every knock against the walls and the steps. The momentum from the fall caused every hit to be harder and worse than before. Finally he landed at the bottom of the staircase. His head was killing him. His radio was smashed, and his left leg and right arm felt broken. Henry tried getting up but the pain would not let him. The sudden throb of pain made him want to pass out. He looked around at his surroundings as he spun himself on his back; he could see a prison cell, bookshelves, and a huge fire pit that roared as if it were alive. On the ground he noticed some blood, and then he saw a lot more blood that trailed to a large white carcass that had been filleted from behind.

"Ohhhh…where am I? This place stinks, uhhh…death. Help…" Henry said as the pain was finally too much and caused him to close his eyes.

Chapter 53: The Curse

"You are so beautiful, you know that," Alex said as he reached and kissed Tabitha's hand.

"Well, thank you very much; you're so kind to say so," Tabitha responded, smiling at the bald man with the evil grin.

Alex looked sharp tonight. He was wearing an all white suit. All he needed was a cane and top hat and he could pull off the world's finest Caucasian pimp. Alex leaned back in his chair as they waited for their soup. He was still holding Tabitha's right hand. She loved every minute of it.

"So how are your parents taking us seeing each other?" Alex asked.

Tabitha got a little nervous, but responded, "My mom knows, but my dad doesn't yet."

"I bet he will get angry about this," Alex said with a slight snickering tone in his voice.

"Yeah, well…I am quite old enough to make my own decisions about who I want to date. They should be happy for us; at least you are a Christian. I mean, that is what they've wanted for me their whole lives," Tabitha answered.

"That is true, at least I am a godless, uh, I mean, a godly man," Alex said as he leaned back for the waitress so she could set their soup down. The waitress was a young, beautiful blonde girl; she looked no older than eighteen. She was either graduating high school or just starting college.

“Looks good,” Tabitha said as she took a bite of the crab bisque. “So, Mr. Levonson, man of mystery, how is it you have changed so much since our teenage years?” Tabitha asked with her usual curiosity.

“Well, I guess I decided I didn’t want to be a loser anymore. Life had made me that way, and lack of parental love and understanding only caused those patterns to worsen,” Alex said while he wiped his mouth with his napkin.

“I remember you; you would not talk to anybody at all. The teachers had to force you to say anything,” said Tabitha.

“I know. Don’t remind me. It was a hard time that only made me stronger and all the more ambitious,” Alex said as his decreased in volume.

“I’m glad you changed, Alex, and came out of your shell; it seems you’ve have the world at your feet now,” Tabitha said.

“It’s been a long time coming, but I am content with whatever happens to me or anyone else around me for that matter,” Alex responded.

“I’ll toast to that,” Tabitha said as she raised her glass of wine, waiting for Alex to do the same.

“I will give a toast with you, but not to contentment. To power. The power to make a change in this town and in the world, to make it better suited for a new way of thinking,” Alex said.

The two slightly banged the glasses together. They continued eating their course and kept chatting away.

“This place has really good food; do you want to try my gumbo?” asked Alex.

“Sure, why not?” Tabitha responded as she moved closer to Alex.

Alex fed her spoonfuls of his gumbo while their eyes met. The two inched closer and closer in the circular booth until they kissed softly and slowly.

“Wow, I have never felt a kiss like this before,” Tabitha said, looking away from Alex slightly embarrassed.

“Can I tell you something, Tabitha?” Alex asked.

“Yeah, what is it?” Tabitha answered.

“I have to tell you in your ear; it’s a secret,” Alex said, smiling seductively.

“Okay,” Tabitha responded, intrigued, while she leaned her ear closer to Alex’s mouth.

Alex cupped the right side of her face and stuck his mouth beside Tabitha’s left ear. She was giggling at first because the whispering tickled her ear. Tabitha’s countenance went from enjoyment to a serious face like she had heard something that she didn’t want to hear.

“From the beginning and until the end, you and I will be one in our sins. By blood of children and virgin brides alike, our lust will never die. Sanctified not by holy words, but bonded with the dark and condemned of hell. With the might of the lord of light, this curse will never end, and will begin this very night,” Alex whispered, leaning away from Tabitha.

When Alex was done reciting his curse, nothing had physically happened, but scales went over Tabitha’s eyes and a dark shadow covered her mind so she couldn’t think clearly anymore. She was herself, but yet she wasn’t. It was like running on autopilot in her mind. The only emotions that she felt the strongest now were the ones she had for Alex, and they had increased dramatically.

Tabitha didn’t want to eat anymore; she looked at Alex and kept saying, “I love you so much, I love you so much.”

“I know you do, love; eat your food. There is plenty of time for loving each other,” Alex answered while sipping on his soup.

The waitress came back with their main entrees. She balanced both of the plates like a pro. The restaurant did not have a lot of people in it, but it was an expensive one.

"Here you go ma'am, the salmon," the waitress said, but Tabitha just gave her a lazy nod, feeling jealous because another female was near Alex.

"And here you go, sir, the roasted lamb," the waitress said.

"Thank you very much; you are doing an excellent job," Alex said, smiling at the waitress.

The waitress smiled back at Alex, but Tabitha caught the smile with a glance, and jumped up, "You better get away from my boyfriend before I smash your pretty little face in!"

"Calm down, Tabitha," Alex said, grabbing her arm.

Tabitha sat down, red in the face, laughing as the waitress ran off to the kitchen, embarrassed and crying.

"Well, she deserved it, flirting with my boyfriend in front of me," Tabitha said, pleased with herself.

Alex cut his lamb and ate a piece; it was pink inside and soft and juicy. "I see it worked," Alex said, nodding his head in agreement.

"What worked?" Tabitha asked.

"Oh, nothing. Eat your food, dear; it's getting cold," Alex said, pointing at her food with his knife.

Tabitha reached over and grabbed Alex's leg. Alex looked up at her, surprised by the sudden interest in physical touch she was displaying. Their eyes met again, smiling at each other. Tabitha was so mesmerized by Alex that if she were a cat, she would have been purring by now.

"What did you want to do tonight?" Alex asked.

"I thought we could go to your place tonight," Tabitha said, smiling seductively at Alex.

"That sounds like a very interesting night, but we must keep our appearances, dear. I will get you home tonight at a decent hour so your parents don't start hating me," Alex said.

“They already hate you,” Tabitha answered.

“I’m sure, but we don’t need to add fuel to the fire,” Alex answered, taking a sip of his drink.

“All right, if that’s what you want to do,” Tabitha said with a pouty look on her face.

“Think about it, Tabitha. What would your parents think if you went home with me on our second date? That is not good manners Tabitha; we will have to wait for that later,” Alex said like a parental father.

Tabitha just nodded her head in agreement, not wanting to talk about any more; the two finished up the romantic meal and walked around a lake in the park before Alex brought her home. She made him promise to call her that night before she went to bed.

Chapter 54: Cooking in the Pot

Godfrey was cleaning up his wrecked hotel room. He had managed to break nearly everything that was in the place. All of the lamps were destroyed; the television would not turn on anymore—it had a crack that went down the middle of it. Godfrey had gotten most of the destroyed furniture off of the floor; he made his bed and cleared the table of food and drinks. He had several trash bags full of the destroyed items in the hotel room. The mirror in the bathroom was hopeless; it was in shattered into a million pieces. Some of the pieces had to be pulled out of Godfrey's skin. The walls were still covered in paintings, and Scriptures were scribbled all over the place. There wasn't a vacuum, so Godfrey had one of the cleaning ladies come and vacuum a bit. He heard her say, "Señor Loco."

What a mess; Grace is going to kill me for this mess. I'll tell her that I will pay for all the damages.

Godfrey not only cleaned up the hotel room, but he cleaned himself up as well. He shaved his beard, walked down the street and got a haircut, and took a nice long, hot shower. Godfrey sat down and repented for everything that he had said and thought the past few days. Sitting on the bed, he thought long and hard about his life. He remembered when he was a child, and when he became a man exposed to war, death, and politics. Then he thought about heaven and hell, the two places that stuck out to him the most. Godfrey couldn't believe, after seeing the beauty of heaven and experiencing the glory of God, that he could be brought to his knees by one woman, Tabitha. No one on earth had been through what he had been, and it was almost in vain because of one heartbreak.

"I nearly lost my salvation and my mind because of her," Godfrey said. "One woman, who played my heartstrings, nearly cost me everything. For what? Love? Companionship? Sexual desire?"

It wasn't just that though, Godfrey knew. He had felt that God wanted him to pursue Tabitha. Godfrey was intimidated by this unction, but he had done it anyway, not expecting the results. He had hoped that it would have been different. He wanted to obey God, but he also wanted Tabitha because he thought she was his. Now, by revelation of Lilith, Tabitha was with this guy named Alex, who apparently had made a deal with the Devil. Godfrey knew this was not good. It was finally dawning on him that this was all happening because his enemies were doing their best take him out of the picture. Then they could successfully destroy John's family, credibility, and ministry. Godfrey had to force himself to get through the pain, the agonizing pain of rejection, and do what he was supposed to do, and that was to help John with the hard messages that God wanted him to share with His people.

"Lord, I repent for the way I have been. This trial was a hard one; it was one that I didn't think I would get through. Somehow I did; from now on, I will keep my eyes focused on the mission at hand. Let Your will be said and done. In Your name I pray! Amen," Godfrey prayed out loud.

There was a knock at the door of Godfrey's hotel room; he went to the door and answered it. Grace and Meredith were standing outside with sunlight beaming from the warm beautiful day. Grace was wearing an orange summer dress with sandals to match, and Meredith was wearing a white business suit and brown shoes.

"Hey, Godfrey," Grace said, giving him a tight hug on the neck.

Right after Grace was done, Meredith reached in and gave him a hug as well and said, "It is great to see you, and you look so well and at peace."

"Thanks, I have been cooking in the pot a while and finally made my way out. But before you two come in, keep in mind, Grace, I will pay for all the damages and paint," Godfrey said nervously.

"Damages! What did you do to my hotel?" Grace asked as she fanned herself like she would pass out from the heat.

"I'll go in first," Meredith said, smiling with as much enthusiasm that she could muster.

Godfrey opened the door completely so the ladies could enter. First came in Meredith, and then came Grace. Godfrey closed the door and opened up the blinds to let some more light in. The two women did a scan of the room; its walls were full of strange paintings and Scriptures—many from the book of Job. The room didn't look all that bad now, since Godfrey had been cleaning it up all day.

"It's not that bad, Godfrey; whenever you leave though, I will have to have the walls repainted. I don't want our customers to see scenes from medieval wars and angels killing each other," Grace said in a calm voice.

"These pictures are really good, Godfrey, but I agree with Grace. They are not family friendly," Meredith answered.

"I know, I'm sorry. I just had to deal with some extreme emotions and painting this stuff seemed to help," Godfrey said.

"You look good. How are feeling, Godfrey?" Meredith asked, sitting beside Grace on the bed.

"A lot better; it has been a rough few weeks. But I have made peace with God and am getting myself revamped and refocused on the task at hand," Godfrey said.

"That sounds great, honey," Grace said, still scanning the walls, looking to where the mirror used to be. She noticed there were drops of blood on the wall.

"What is your task exactly, Godfrey? If you don't mind me asking?" asked Meredith.

The two women focused their attention on Godfrey, waiting for him to answer, because seeing the paintings of scenes from what appeared to be war from a thousand years ago intrigued the two. They both knew that there was something peculiar about Godfrey that they couldn't put their fingers on. Everything had happened so fast that they really didn't have the time to ask Godfrey any questions. Grace believed that he was an angel sent to speak to her, and Meredith thought he was a hippie artistic type from out West who could paint really well. Either way and with each theory, it appeared that Godfrey was going to tell them. Godfrey sat down at the small table and chairs that used to be scattered across the floor.

"I have some things to tell you about myself," Godfrey said, looking at the two briefly.

"What is it, Godfrey?" Grace asked. Meredith nodded her head in agreement.

"I am not from here," Godfrey said.

"Where are you from, Godfrey?" Meredith asked.

"France," Godfrey answered.

"France! But you have an American accent," Meredith questioned.

"Not just France, but eleventh century France. I am from the past sent here by God to help John," Godfrey said reluctantly.

The two women sat there, quiet and stunned with both of their mouths open. It was like the information Godfrey was giving them wasn't truly sinking in. Godfrey waited patiently for them to say something; they didn't, so he kept on with his story.

“I was a Templar knight who was involved in the sacking Palestinian cities. We successfully defeated Muslim rule in a large portion of the Middle East. The Holy Land was put into the hands of Christian knights. I am sad to say that we did not do a good and righteous job at it. It was bad for everyone there; power and corruption had no bounds. Even in the home of Jesus,” Godfrey said, until he was interrupted by Grace.

“Hold on, honey, are you telling us you are from the past?” Grace asked, giving him a perplexed look.

“So God sent you all the way from the past just so you could help John? Couldn’t God just have someone from here to talk to John? Why go through all this trouble, Godfrey?” Meredith asked.

“I don’t know why God does the things He does. I don’t presume to know why God does certain things and not others, either. But what I tell you is the truth, and it gets a lot weirder,” Godfrey responded.

“How so?” Meredith asked.

“How is that?” Grace said in unison with Meredith.

“I was murdered in the deserts of Palestine by Muslim Saracens. I died fighting, I am glad to say, but I died nonetheless. I left my body and descended into hell; it was the scariest and most horrible experience ever imaginable. Thankfully, I was released from hell by God and was summoned to heaven. There I learned why this all happened to me; I learned why I was born, and I learned what I am supposed to do. It is an out-of-the-ordinary destiny, but it is the destiny chosen for me. So I must do everything I can to see it happen,” Godfrey said.

Meredith got up and grabbed some soft drinks out of the small brown refrigerator; it didn’t have much in it. As a matter of fact, there were only a few drinks in it and some condiments. A half-empty jar of pickles and a small bottle of mustard.

“So you have been to hell and back?” Grace said, laughing a bit.

“Yep,” Godfrey said.

"That is amazing, Godfrey. Are you sure this is real, Godfrey? Maybe it was just a really vivid dream," Meredith speculated.

"Listen, I wish it was all a dream, but sad to say, it was not. My death was real, going to hell was way too real, and I am proud to say that heaven is real as well," Godfrey said casually and confidently.

"Amen brother! If you say this all happened, then I believe you! I can't wait to go to heaven to see my daddy!" Grace exclaimed.

"Wow! That is all I can say, Godfrey. Wow," Meredith responded, taking a sip of her cola.

"So, why do you have to help John?" Grace asked.

"The world is changing; the tsunami that hit the Caribbean is just the beginning. Everything will be shaken, kingdoms, thrones, and all avenues of life for humanity will be shaken. Where it will begin is His church, and that is where John will come in," Godfrey said.

"What does John have to do exactly?" Meredith asked.

"His message of prosperity and the easy life has to change; he has to warn God's people of what is coming. It is going to be hard; it has been already," Godfrey said, interrupted by Grace.

"Money is no longer what we will seek—a lot of people will not like that. There are a bunch of preachers who have made a good living off of that message," Grace said.

"Poor John, why him? He is not a confrontational man—prosperity and an easy message is all he knows when it comes to preaching. Just saying what he did with the first message a couple of weeks ago nearly gave him a stroke. Now his daughter is siding with the mouthpiece of opposition that stands against him," Meredith said.

"I know; the enemy is doing his best to disrupt John's task. That is why I am here, though, so I can help him in this endeavor so that what must be said will be said," Godfrey responded.

The overwhelming information that Godfrey laid before Meredith and Grace made them feel like they were treading in flood waters. But Godfrey knew what he had to do—pain brought clarity. His broken heart showed him what he was made of, and after the house inside him had burned down, the foundation still stood. Godfrey stood up, grabbed his supplies, and said, "Ladies, let's go talk to John about his second message."

The three headed out the door and made their way to OBN.

Chapter 55: Fish in the Frying Pan

Henry woke up to immense pain coming from his leg, ribs, and arm. It took a while for his eyes to focus and for his mind to remember what had happened to him. The more he blinked, the less blurry his vision became. There was not a lot of light in the cavern, but if the smell gave off a light then it would be like sitting in front of the sun. Someone had gone through the trouble of putting a makeshift splint on his leg. *It's a pity they didn't give me something for the pain, but I'm assuming whoever runs little place isn't bothered by my pain.*

Henry was not alone in the cell; the flabby, white, filleted corpse he saw before he passed out was lying next to him, leaning against the wall. The corpse's head was leaning over with its mouth wide open like it had been screaming. Henry recognized the eyes and facial structure; they were the same as the picture he had seen when he began his search.. Henry was pretty sure this had to be Billy Ferguson. Scattered on the stone floor were skeletons of every shape and size—some adults, some children. Most of this collection was from the previous tenants from past generations. A few of the skeletons still had clothes on; there were a couple of skulls that had strings of hair attached to them. This cave had been used for evil purposes for many an age, it seemed. Henry's mouth was dry, it made a smacking sound when he opened and closed it. His body was most likely hungry, but the pain killed any kind of hunger in him.

Henry slowly checked his belt for his gun; it was gone and so was his police belt and radio. He checked his pocket for the cell phone;

surprisingly it had not been taken—probably because it was so small and thin. Henry quietly opened it to check to see if it was on; it had one bar left of power. Henry quickly turned the cell phone off and decided to save that last bar for a call that would hopefully matter.

Sitting at the desk, Henry could see someone reading something through the bars. The person was wearing a brown, hooded cloak that had a rope tied in the middle like a belt. Henry assumed it was Alex, but wasn't sure. The man sat over there for hours, reading and writing with a few small red candles for light. He did not seem to be in hurry about anything; there was no noise in the place except for the roaring fire pit that came out of the floor like an old watering well. Just thinking about a well made Henry thirsty. *What I would do for a tasty sport drink right now.* Finally the man spoke to Henry.

"Are you awake over there?" the hooded man asked.

"Barely. Who are you?" Henry responded.

"Oh, somebody that you used to know," the hooded man answered.

"You must enjoy killing; that means some big guys in prison are going to get to know you," Henry responded, coughing a bit.

"I'd hate to go to prison; what would my mom and dad think?" the hooded man said sarcastically.

"You're a sick bastard," Henry said, closing his eyes from sudden fatigue.

Henry must have fallen asleep because he woke up suddenly to someone throwing cold water in his face. His eyes opened and slowly came into focus on the hooded man. His thoughts were true; it was Alex Levonson, smiling at him through the bars. He had a metal bucket in his right hand; there was the handle of a ladle inside the bucket.

"Thirsty?" Alex asked, smiling.

"Yeah," Henry answered.

"Then crawl over here and get something to drink," Alex said, picking up the ladle and pouring the water back into the bucket.

Henry's body cringed at the thought of moving, but he started inching his way over there to get something to drink. *I hope it is just water.* Henry finally reached the other side of the bone-infested cell; it felt like miles, but it was only a few feet. Alex poured one cup of very warm water into Henry's mouth and poured the rest out of the bucket.

"They will come looking for me, Alex. Your little chamber of horrors will be found and you will be executed," Henry said.

Alex went over to the middle of the chamber and began pouring salt around the pentagram on the floor. After that, he lit a few black candles that were evenly spaced out around the five pointed star; as he put out the lighter, he responded to Henry.

"They have already come here looking for you, Henry, and I told the concerned officers that I hadn't seen you. Don't worry about your car; it is already gutted and repainted. The church will sell it and put the profits in with the tithes. Nothing like blood money, huh?" Alex said, laughing at his sick joke.

Henry's thoughts were bleak; he knew he was probably not going to make it out of this scenario. Henry was not afraid of death, but when it came with a feeling of certainty and time, it was a different. The only string of hope he had was the cell phone; whenever he had a chance, his call had to matter. It was a matter of life or death.

"Are you hungry, Henry?" Alex asked, looking up.

"I guess," Henry responded, breathing with resentment.

"Well, eat up; time is a-wasting," Alex answered, pointing at Billy's corpse.

"You've got to be kidding me," Henry responded.

"Why do you think all of those skeletons are in there? They had to eat each other to survive," Alex answered.

"I'm not eating a dead guy you sick little bald man," Henry said.

"That is all you have, Henry; you need to eat him before he gets too rotten. He has plenty of fat and meat on him yet; go ahead. I won't judge you. It's survival," Alex said.

Henry's stomach was growling, but the thought of eating a person was not pleasing to him at all. Tiredness fell on him again and he closed his eyes to slip into another slumber. Henry woke up from a horrible dream of the white vulture with many eyes eating Billy Ferguson's body. The bird sat up with torn flesh in its mouth, it swallowed it whole, and said, "Henry, it's easy; just don't think about it."

The chamber was darker than normal; the only light in the place was from the candles that Alex had lit earlier. Alex was in the middle of the circle, chanting something. Henry could not hear what it was that Alex was saying; it just sounded like continuous mumbling. As the chanting from Alex increased, wind blowing inside the chamber increased. It was swirling around and around, causing goose bumps to come up all over Henry's body. A thick presence of fear came over Henry; it pushed him down to the ground. Whatever it was, it was an evil Henry knew. Henry looked up from the ground and saw something floating in the air in front of Alex. It had wings and a red cloak on that was torn and haggard looking. Boney spikes were sticking out everywhere on the floating manifestation. What sounded like millions of flies were buzzing around the spirit; the monster turned to look at Henry, but he hurried up and closed his eyes. Alex and the manifestation began talking.

"It is time to move ahead with the plan," Belial said with many voices.

"The girl is mine; the hexes have worked. I can take her whenever I want now," Alex responded.

"Good; she will be a good sacrifice," Belial said.

"What about her dad and mom?" Alex asked.

“Once they know what has happened to their daughter, they will quit everything in their grief and sadness. It works every time,” Belial said.

“What of this Godfrey character?” Alex asked.

“He is the only factor that is giving us problems, but he too will fall when his beloved is soaking in her own blood,” Belial said. “Are your followers prepared for the day of fire?”

“They are preparing the final stages; just a few more days and we will be ready,” Alex said.

“Everything is moving swiftly; our lord will be pleased,” Belial responded.

Henry could hear the whole conversation; it was the scariest thing he had experienced yet. They were going to kill Tabitha so that John would give up on his ministry altogether. Henry did not know what the day of fire was, but it must involve Alex’s brainwashed army of a church. They were planning something very big and horrible, and there was nothing that Henry could do. Henry sat quietly as the two continued in conversation; something big was going down. Tabitha was in a lot of danger that she knew nothing about, and her parents were too. Henry was a doubter before, but now he knew that evil was real, and it never slept. *I wonder what the guys at the station think of me disappearing. Somebody must be wondering where I’m at. Man, I don’t want to die like this,* Henry was thinking as his stomach growled more and more for nourishment.

Henry began thinking about his family; they did not live in Athens. They were from Atlanta. He did not see them a lot anymore, because of work. The only time they did get together was on holidays. Henry’s family was like the typical American family; everyone was busy with something else besides each other. It was just how things were. After Iraq and Afghanistan, Henry kept himself from getting close to his family because when he got home he felt like a stranger to them. It was like the desert took something away from him, and Henry was trying to figure out how to get it back. Now, sitting in this cell with bones and a corpse, it appeared to Henry that he would not get the chance to rekindle his relationship with his family.

He started coughing because of the thick humidity and stench, and that got the attention of Belial. Henry watched as Belial began floating toward the cell; he moved like a runaway balloon that was losing helium. Henry backed himself further against the wall, scared of the spirit coming his way. Belial made a low humming sound the whole time. Henry thought he would stop at the bars, but he was wrong. Belial came right through them with no trouble at all. Millions of flies were buzzing around everywhere in the cell. Henry closed his eyes and was swatting at them because they were trying to get in his nose, ears, and mouth. The next thing Henry knew Belial was face to face with him; he could feel the hot breath on him.

"I know you," the many voices said.

Henry kept his eyes closed, and answered, "I doubt that."

"I never forget such a smell—the sins in the desert, sins you thought were hidden from all eyes. I see them, I taste them, I love them," Belial responded with many tongues.

"I don't know what you're talking about, demon," Henry responded with his hands over his face.

"Yes, you do, boy; I see what your squad did to that family of helpless desert dwellers. You should be ashamed of yourself. At least Carlo had to guts to hang himself for his crimes. You hide yours, hoping they will disappear. I'm sorry Henry, but that is not how it works; even Abel's blood cried out to God when Cain beat him to death," Belial said, laughing.

Henry finally built up the nerve to open his eyes; when he did he saw into Belial's mouth. His mouth was the shape of a dog's snout; but inside his mouth, there was an endless hole with flies going in and out of it. Belial's long dry tongue just hung to the side, motionless. Henry closed his eyes again and kept them shut. Belial soon disappeared; Henry knew this because the loud buzzing flies were gone. Henry fell back to sleep, hungrier and thirstier than he was earlier. *I wonder if this is the kind of thirst you experience in hell*, he thought as he fell back into a deep sleep.

Chapter 56: Terrible Twos

John Maxwell had just gotten off the phone with his board members. They were mad about the comments and the sudden loss of viewers to OBN. Apparently telling American Christians not to seek after prosperity but to get prepared for disasters of every kind was not a popular message. John could understand their point of view; he had built this ministry on the prosperity message. Not only that, but the promise of the good life. No problems, no stress at all, the art of positive reinforcement and all could be yours was the way John preached. This simple message had made OBN the biggest and most popular of all the American Christian networks. John had met everyone—all the big names and pretty faces that were in the Christian world.

Why is it in America that we turn everyone into celebrities? Even Christian leaders are made into celebrities. Is this pleasing to God? Can a beggar on the street approach one of these spiritual fat cats and see Jesus in them? Or would they walk right by and pay no attention? Thoughts had begun to bother John a lot lately. He was beginning to realize he was a giant hypocrite, no better than a Pharisee in Jesus' day.

The board was beginning to flex their muscles with him; in twenty years, John had never had a problem with them. But now, when the boat started to rock a bit, the underbelly of Christian television started showing its ugly face. John got up from his desk and began pacing around his office; he started praying to God about his next message.

John said, "Lord, I will say what You want me to say, no matter what the cost. What should the next show be about?" John waited, pacing and running through subjects that he would think God would want him to teach about. Suddenly an epiphany hit him; the word stuck out in his mind and would not go away until he said it, "Marriage." John sat down, suddenly intimidated by the subject at hand.

"God, do You really want me to talk about marriage? I mean, I am not exactly the best man to be talking about it. Just a few weeks ago, I was in danger of getting a divorce. I will be honest, Lord, I don't know the first thing about marriage. How can I teach others about it when I have no clue about it myself?" John prayed out loud.

People think we preachers have it easy, but God makes us say and do everything that we do not want to do and say.

John had noticed something different about himself. He felt happier and more at peace with himself. Was it because the Lord was actually leading him with the ministry? John began to feel sad because of the years he had gone without letting God lead, but instead going his own way. Realizing he had been wrong most of his life caused John some grief; but on the flip side, he found joy that God had not given up on him. John wanted to make things right, so he sat down and began to write down what was coming to him about marriage.

John had been sitting at his desk for hours when he realized his hand was cramping from writing and typing. He sat back and shook his hands like they were covered in cobwebs. Then he started rubbing his eyes because of how dry they felt from the hours of staring at the computer screen. To his right, his phone vibrated with a text from Meredith. It read, "I talked to Godfrey; he is back on board with painting. We are on our way home; he needs to talk to you."

John sent back to Meredith, "Okay, love, I'll be home in a bit. Love you." Normally John would have ended up staying in the office or falling asleep on his brown leather couch. But Meredith had laid down some rules since the rekindling of their marriage. The first rule was no staying over at the office. John promised that he wouldn't anymore. Before he finished up his e-mail and small things at the office, Tabitha came walking in. She appeared happy, but drained at the same time.

Tabitha was wearing a pale white skirt that was just above her knees, and a white blouse with purple flowers. Tabitha's hair was tied back into a bun. She looked very elegant and beautiful.

"Hey, Dad," Tabitha said.

"Hello, beautiful," John said, smiling and rising to give her a hug.

When he touched her, he had a sick feeling in his stomach like something was wrong, but he didn't know what it was. The two sat down and began talking.

"Where have you been? I haven't seen you in a while," John asked casually.

"Oh, I've been around here and there. What about you?" Tabitha asked with a strange smile.

"Working, and being hated by everyone in Christendom. But I can't complain, at least my marriage is doing better," John said.

"That is good. You and mom have worked through all the kinks you two have had," Tabitha responded.

"So I hear you are dating one of my enemies," John said, waiting for a response.

"Oh…you mean Alex. He is not your enemy, Dad; Alex wants to help you," Tabitha said as if the subject did not affect her at all.

"Really? He is not my enemy? You were there when he told the town of Athens to burn me at the stake, but he is not my enemy?" John asked.

"No Dad; Alex is against mega-ministries. Not you. Just look at our Christian celebrities. They are giant puffed up balloons, full of hot air. It is easy to say God is good when there is plenty of money going around and everyone loves you," Tabitha said.

"Honey, I understand what you are saying, but that is not true at all. I wish I never had any problems, but the fact is we all have our fair share of troubles—even the celebrity Christians who go around preaching prosperity. Besides that, whatever happened to loyalty? I am your father, and the one you are with is against me physically and spiritually," John said.

"Dad, we are on the same side. I just think the mega-ministry is causing you, Mom, and me more problems than anything else. Then there are all the people who watch and are led astray by what is being taught," Tabitha said until she was interrupted.

"Hold on! Since when did you care about what was being taught to Christians? I don't remember you ever becoming one," John asked, looking at his daughter.

Naturally, Tabitha's blood would be hot right now and she would fire right back, but she kept her cool. She did not lash out like John expected.

She responded, "I wouldn't say I am a believer yet, but I have warmed up to it since hearing what Alex has to say about the way of the light."

That information hit John like a ton of bricks because he was hearing his daughter say that his example, his faith, and her upbringing did not help her at all when it came to understanding God. It made him feel like a failure of a parent. John felt like he was losing his appetite. This was probably the worst news a Christian parent would ever want to hear from their child.

He took a minute to gather his thoughts, and said, "I don't want you seeing Alex; I think he is hostile toward me, your mother, and you." Tabitha started laughing a bit, like it was some kind of funny joke her dad told her. Then John responded again and said, "I'm serious, Tabitha."

"Dad, I'm 25. You don't tell me who I can date and who I can't," Tabitha said, still giggling.

John stood up; his face was red with anger. He said with a louder voice, "Tabitha, I am your dad; I should come before some boyfriend who is teaching you to stand against me. Now come to your senses, girl, and break up with this cult leader!"

"No," Tabitha said as smooth as water.

She stood up and headed for the door, as John gently grabbed her by the arm and said, "Don't go Tabitha, I didn't mean to yell."

Tabitha pulled her arm away and said, "I'm going to see Alex, and I quit this stupid job. 'Bye Dad."

John watched as Tabitha walked out. He had to sit back down, because he knew this was bad. John was worried because his daughter did not seem the same at all; it was like she had no emotion whatsoever. The other thing that worried him was what Meredith was going to say when he told her that Tabitha had quit her job and was going to this bald, mouthy fanatic's church. He stood up and gathered his stuff and went home.

Chapter 57: The Garden

"There are so many beautiful trees here," the little green toddler told his mother.

"Yes, this is the envy of the world, my son," Lilith told Abaddon as she reached down and caressed his crusty, green face.

The toddler smiled at Lilith, showing its black pointed teeth; when she turned away the baby bit down on her fingers.

"Ouch!" Lilith screamed, responding with a back-handed slap to the toddler's face.

Abaddon growled at his mom and flapped his small wings. He flew away from his mother's cushioned chair. The rest of the demonic brood of children that were surrounding Lilith started laughing at Abaddon. They all scurried away, kicking and fighting with each other, disappearing in the forest of trees. Lilith was sitting in a mobile golden chair that had two poles in the front and two poles in the back. Slaves were attached to the poles by collars and chains. All the weight was on their necks and shoulders. They were not large men—some were fat and some skinny; they had to stand and hold up the seat the whole time. Lilith would not let them set it down; she didn't want them to get lazy. The slaves used to be very wealthy men on earth. They had exploited mankind and ruthlessly made people serve them their whole lives; now it was their punishment to serve as slaves in hell for eternity. The garden was the most beautiful part of hell.

Large ancient trees of every kind grew on green plentiful grass all around the hidden part of the underworld. Within the grass, red veins pulsed through the ground, while just enough light shone in from the great separation of Sheol. It gave the garden the feel of how it was on the surface in times past. It was said that when Adam and Eve had to leave Eden, Sheol opened its jaws and swallowed the garden whole, nearly intact when it came down. Not many came to the garden; it was kept for the ruling class of hell, the few who were not being punished, that is. Lilith would go there to reminisce and to have meetings with subordinates.

Through the trees, a large shadowy figure was gliding around with such ease that it looked like it was water trickling down a branch. Lilith sat, waiting for the figure to show itself, while the slaves shook from the weight of the chair but did not dare sit down. The figure slid on the ground, then coiled up like a bundle of rope, and stood up nearly twelve feet high. The Serpent blended with its surroundings because of its thickness and length; it looked like another tree. It had pale red and brown skin with black diamonds going down its back. The top of the Serpent's head flared out like a cobra, but on the back of its head were small black spikes that came out of the diamonds, making them look three dimensional. The eyes on the creature were enchanting; they looked as old as the world itself—light blue with gold and green specks.

Lilith had a long history with the Serpent; it was he that convinced her to become the queen of demons. This creature had taken many people down his path of rebellion and wisdom. The angels had Lucifer, and the animals had the Serpent. He came over and kissed Lilith's hand and backed away, flicking his tongue in one of the slave's ears. The slave just stood there, trying to stay still, twitching from the weight of the chair.

"I would reach out with my hand and kiss yours, my queen, but it appears I have lost them," the Serpent said, smiling.

Lilith laughed at the joke and responded, "It has been a while, my wise teacher. You seem to hide away in the garden, teaching my little children the ways of perdition."

"It is a busy task, I must say, my queen. But I am up for the challenge," the Serpent said.

"I am sure you are, my old companion, but it looks like our time is close," Lilith told the Serpent.

"Yes, yes, judgment and all. It is a nasty business. One that I never agreed with; to be fair, it is my choices that cause me to disagree with judgment. I guess because we are on the losing end of it," the Serpent said wisely.

"I know, but Lucifer still believes we will win. He doesn't even consider losing an option," Lilith said.

"Pride is a sickness that takes more and more reason out of a mind each day it spreads," the Serpent said.

"He is constantly working, that is for sure. He doesn't tell me half of what he is up to," Lilith said with a sad face.

"I remember when I first met the king; he was a remarkable creature. I was a student of Wisdom; I was taught everything by her. But it was Lucifer who showed me the path, the one that gave me access to all knowledge," the serpent said, reminiscing on the past.

"We have all had a part to play in what has happened to us and the world. Our fate is sealed, friend; if we burn, we will burn together," Lilith said.

"I'll toast to that, no pun intended," the Serpent said, laughing.

The garden was a quiet place; there was barely any noise in it whatsoever. Streams and rivers bled through the massive trees, meandering like a snake. The water was not clear, but black and murky. Lilith and the Serpent sat in silence, listening to the trickling of the water, when they were interrupted by the noise of Belial appearing before them. After his manifestation, the noise of his flies drowned out the trickling water. Belial took his hood off, showing his jackal-shaped head. He bowed to the queen and stood.

"My queen, I bring you the plans for the Maxwell family," Belial said.

"Oh, good. I hope to crush this family and be done with it. We've got bigger things to take care of," Lilith said, slightly annoyed.

Belial looked at the Serpent and nodded; he looked back at Lilith and said, "We've got the girl; our man Alex is planning what he calls the 'day of fire.' Godfrey, on the other hand, doesn't seem to be giving up like we planned," Belial said.

"I know. I hate that Godfrey. I tried to seduce him myself and he wouldn't budge. Knights and their honor—a load of dung if you ask me," Lilith snapped back.

The Serpent added, "You waste your time on Godfrey; he's God's man in this picture. Just worry about keeping him busy with everything else and go through with your plan."

"I hope this Alex has something worthwhile with this day of fire?" Lilith questioned Belial.

"Believe me, my queen; this will be a day that Athens will never forget. The town will burn John Maxwell, his wife, Godfrey, and the network on the stake by the time we are done there," Belial said with many voices.

"Sounds horrific…intriguing…delightful…but will it work?" the Serpent asked.

"It will, teacher, this is my best work yet. The master knew what he was doing when he chose this Alex character; that little bald man is evil and good at it. His tormented past and his desire for revenge make him the perfect pawn in our game," Belial answered.

"It had better work, Belial, or you will be the one suffering before your time," Lilith said with cold eyes.

Chapter 58: The Light

The small church was packed to its full capacity. Every pew was filled with white people, black people, and brown people. That was one thing for sure about Alex's church; it was not tolerant of racism. There were young people and old people alike; it was the new favorite church of Athens. It was hot inside because of all the breathing; to cool themselves off everyone had small hand fans. In the front pew sat Tabitha Maxwell, intrigued as ever with Alex's brimstone message. Inside the church, ceiling fans were turned on, and everyone was giving Alex amens every time he spoke.

"There has to be *change* in the way we are living! There has to be recognition of the *light* the Lord gave us! I am tired of watching godly folk giving in to the temptations of this world! We must change this. We must be an example of the *light* of the Savior! Only the *light* is what makes us different from this world; it is only the *light* that will keep us from the wrath to come!" Alex exclaimed, smacking his fist on the pulpit.

The crowd was responding with amens and heavy clapping. Some of the congregation stood up as if they were being electrocuted. One woman was walking up and down the aisle as if she couldn't sit down; she had to jump over another woman who was rolling up and down the aisle like she was on fire. It was an emotional church service, but exciting to watch. Tabitha had never seen anything like this, but kept all of her focus on Alex. His bald head was sweating; Alex would use a red wash cloth to dry off his head. Even his white suit had streaks from all the sweating he was doing.

Back and forth Alex walked behind the pulpit; he preached for hours and the people loved it. From the outside of the church, it sounded like a night club, thumping from all the music. The church was surrounded by cars and people were sitting outside on picnic tables and blankets. Children ran around, chasing each other, while some played basketball at an old hoop. There had to be a few hundred people in and around the church; there was a row of cars for sale placed near the church too—one was Henry's repainted squad car. Behind those vehicles, one of the church members was cooking on a giant grill, making hotdogs, hamburgers, and ribs. There was a long line of women, men, and children waiting to pay to receive their next meal.

Inside the church, Alex had quieted down a little, but he was still continuing with his message.

"The only thing that changes us is exposure to the light. The only thing that cleanses us is fire. It purifies gold and it will purify us, my children. We must walk through the fire that burns away the corruptible desires and ways that we are accustomed to. We must have living *fiiirre!*—holy, righteous, cleansing *fiiirre*! That will wash this city's enemies away. The enemies that I speak about are the enemies of God! I promise you, my children, we will walk through this fire unscathed just like Daniel's friends did in Babylon. The bringer of light will protect us, and he will guide us."

Alex went on for a little while longer, then he finally finished up his message by saying, "My children, we are the carriers of this holy fire that I speak of, and we must be the ones to bring it to this town. I will be speaking more about this in later messages, but for now our time has ended. You do not have to leave; there is food outside. Hang out as long as you like. God bless you, and may the light always shine on you."

When Alex stepped down from the pulpit, the congregation all stood up, giving him applause and chanting, "Prophet! Father! Teacher! God's friend!" Alex walked over to Tabitha and the two went back to his office while the inside of the church began emptying out. Alex sat down in his office chair worn out from the invigorating message he just preached. The two of them could hear the people talking about the message, with loud and excited voices. Tabitha stood behind Alex and started massaging his neck and shoulders. Alex gave in and let her continue; he had his head resting back with his eyes closed. He was enjoying the relaxing massage very much.

"Man, you are good at that, my dear," Alex said to Tabitha.

Tabitha responded by focusing more attention on the massage and said, "You did well in the service. It looks like you were born to preach."

"My dad was a preacher, and so was his dad. I guess it is in our genes," Alex responded.

"I talked to my dad yesterday; he didn't sound too happy about us seeing each other," Tabitha said.

"Oh really. That is a shame. I wanted to meet him to explain myself to him," Alex said.

"I don't know if that is possible or not, Alex. I kind of quit my job at the network too," Tabitha said, reaching down and kissing Alex on his cheek.

"Give it time; they will want to meet me, I'm sure. If you want, you can work for me," Alex said, reassuring Tabitha by grabbing her hand.

"What would I do?" Tabitha asked.

"Oh, we will find you something to do, I'm sure," Alex said, closing his eyes and laying his head back.

"Whatever you say, dear," Tabitha said.

"Can you get me something to eat and drink, Tabitha? I am just so worn out," Alex asked, resting.

"Sure. What do you want?" Tabitha asked, nearly hopping to attention when Alex spoke.

"I don't know—something cold to drink and hot to eat," Alex responded.

"Okay, I'll be right back," Tabitha said as she walked out of the office.

When she closed the door, Alex sat up in his chair and started thinking, *That spell really did work; she is doing everything I tell her to do. I couldn't ask for more. I wish I could keep her, but I know I can't. I have to fulfill my end of the bargain. Such irony! I get the girl I always wanted, and then when I do, I have to kill her. I wish there was another way of some kind. After everything is said and done, I have to jump down that hell mouth. I wonder what waits for me there. I will find out soon enough.*

Chapter 59: The Boss

I'm looking for Henry Adams," the tall, skinny man asked with a deep, slow, dripping molasses type of southern accent.

"Sorry, sir, I don't know who that is," the bartender answered back.

The bar was a little hole in the wall place that didn't have much business. From the outside, it looked like an old brick building that appeared to be sinking into the concrete. There was one door that had a barred window on each side of it with bright beer signs glowing. Inside, there was only one pool table and no women. Instead, just a few guys stood around drinking and staring at Don's giant white cowboy hat as he entered. When he walked in, his alligator-skinned cowboy boots made a repetitive thumping noise every time he took a step on the old wooden floor. Don was wearing tight blue jeans that went over his boots with a yellow short-sleeve buttoned shirt to match. He had a shiny gold watch on his left wrist and to two rings on each hand. Don's skin was tanned and leathery looking; on his face was a well-kept Fu Manchu goatee. When he smiled, all of his teeth were gold; they matched the giant belt buckle that covered most of Don's lower stomach. Don made his way to the bar and sat down.

"What can I get you, sir?" the bartender asked.

Don set his hat down, and then responded, "Let me get a double shot of whiskey."

"Coming right up," the bartender answered.

Don leaned on the bar sideways as he scanned the room behind him. The few guys who were watching him went back to their game of pool. When the bartender returned, he set down Don's drink and went to wiping down the bar.

"You boys got anything to eat in here?" Don asked, sipping his drink.

"Uh, we've got some chips and salsa, peanuts, and some pretzels," the bartender answered.

"What a huge selection you have; let me get some chips and salsa, spicy if ya got it," Don answered.

"Coming right up," the bartender answered.

One of the guys playing pool came up to the bar beside Don and asked for another beer as the bartender came back with Don's chips and salsa. He was a short, fat man, not well kept at all. He had a large blue T-shirt that had several holes in it. The man's gut filled in most of the old shirt.

"Here you go, Chase," the bartender said, handing him a beer.

"Where are you from, stranger?" Chase asked Don.

"Texas, God's country, born and raised," Don answered, crunching down on a loaded chip.

"Texas, huh? I couldn't tell by the cowboy get up you're wearing," Chase said sarcastically.

"Say there, Chase, do you know a boy named Henry Adams?" Don asked, making a mental note of the fat man's sarcastic overtones.

"Yeah, he's the local cop who's missing. I believe he was an army vet too. He used to come here sometimes," Chase answered Don.

"He's a family friend of mine; I was wondering what happened to him," Don answered.

"Now I remember him—he was a quiet guy. He'd come a couple times a week. He just sat, staring at his beer," the bartender answered.

"Oh, now you remember?" Don said to the bartender, giving him a look.

"What is your name anyway, stranger?" Chase asked Don.

"My name is Don 'the Boss' Warburton; you just call me Boss there, skinny," Don answered, finishing up his drink.

"I'll try to remember that, Boss," Chase answered, offended by Don's comment.

"There has been a lot of crazy stuff happening in our town lately. That guy Henry disappearing is just one of them," the bartender said to Don.

"Really? What else happened?" Don asked.

"Let's see, Hell's Angels being killed, mobs of religious people trying to stone John Maxwell, someone kidnapping Meredith Maxwell, EMTs being murdered, and several people missing. The town is divided right now; it looks like something bad is going to happen," the bartender said.

"Damn, sounds exciting," Don said, crunching on another chip. The salsa dripped down the side of his mouth.

"It's been a mess; I'll tell you that," the bartender answered as Chase shook his head in agreement.

"Why don't you be useful there, barkeep, and get me another shot," Don said to the bartender.

The bartender gave him an annoyed look and went to make another drink for Don. Chase, on the other hand, was still standing there, leaning on his cue stick. He looked like he was upset about something. Don sensed something was agitating Chase, and asked, "So Chase, just how long have you been so fat? Have you been this way your whole life or was it because of a mid-life crisis?"

"You listen here, cowboy! You don't come in my town…" Before Chase could finish his sentence, Don quickly stood up and leaned forward with a punch that connected with Chase's mouth. Chase's fat body fell to the ground; he was out cold. Don caught the cue stick that Chase was leaning on before it hit the ground.

"Sit down and shut up, you fat piece of meat," Don said, going back to his chips.

The bartender just stood there, stunned, holding Don's drink. Chase's two buddies saw what happened to their friend and decided to do something about it. Surprisingly, these two rednecks were skinny, but twice as ugly.

They responded with, "Hey! You cain't do that!"

"What are you two queers gonna do about it?" Don asked, still sitting down at the bar.

The first man ran at Don like he was going to spear him. Before the skinny redneck reached him, Don stood, turned around and pointed the cue stick at the charging man, hitting him right in the mouth. The few teeth he had quickly came out from the impact of the pool stick. The man's legs came out from under him and he fell to the ground, holding his mouth. Don stayed standing, and started rolling up his shirt sleeves. He put his watch in his hat.

"Come here, boy! You're next," Don said to the last man standing.

The two squared up and started throwing punches. The Boss looked like he was having fun. He countered each blow, causing the guy's mouth, nose, and eyes to bleed. The guy got mad and started throwing flurries at Don, but the Boss casually blocked them and danced around with him. Don finally got bored with the redneck and ducked low when he came in with a haymaker. Don responded with a left-handed punch to the back of the man's head. The redneck's neck made a crunching sound as he fell to the ground face first. The man slid so hard that splinters from the floor went into his bloody cheek.

Don walked back over to the bar and dropped three one hundred dollar bills and said, "Sorry for the mess, barkeep."

He finished his last shot, grabbed his things and headed outside. His boots made the same thumping sound that they did when Don had entered the bar. The bartender put the money in his pocket and ran over to the three guys and tried to wake them up.

Don was in his red pickup truck, cruising down the road. He was opening and closing his fists because of the recent scuffle at the bar. He was listening to some classic country music and singing as he drove down the road. On the front of Don's red pickup was a tag that said, "Born American, Southern by the Grace of God." The old Ford pickup looked brand new; old men turned and looked at it as Don cruised down the streets of Athens to get a feel for the town. Don drove around until he saw the giant sign that displayed the letters OBN.

"Looks like one of those stupid Christian signs," Don said as he went to pull in.

Before he did, Don noticed that a couple of police were parked in the parking lot. The police looked like they were on some type of security for the network. Don pulled up and tilted his hat to them to greet the police.

"How y'all doing?" Don asked in his courteous southern accent.

"Good, just pulling duty," one cop said.

The other cop just smiled and didn't say anything.

"That is good to hear, officers. I've heard about this place; I noticed the sign and was a little curious to see it up close," Don said, smiling.

"I'd say that there are only a few Americans who haven't heard of OBN, at least once," the other cop said.

"Yeah, I'd say that is true. Is that why y'all are here guarding the place?" Don asked the cops nonchalantly.

"Things have gotten pretty bad here in Athens as far as violence goes. There is a lot of religious unrest in the locals. John Maxwell, the one who runs this place, is loved and also hated here in town," one cop said.

"So I guess you guys have to keep an eye on him now, and his property," Don said.

"Yeah, it's like we are his personal security force," the quiet cop said with annoyance.

"I'm sure y'all boys are doing a fine job. What is going on about that young cop who's missing?" Don asked, lighting up a cigarette in his idling truck.

The two cops got quiet, and a sad look came over both of their faces. "You must be talking about Henry Adams; he disappeared a couple of weeks ago," the cop answered.

"I hate to hear that such a public servant is missing," Don said, taking off his hat to show respect to Henry.

"We are doing our best to find him," the quiet cop said.

"Why would he vanish like that?" Don asked.

"We don't know; he was having some problems, but nothing serious. He was on a case searching for a local drunk who is also missing. All of a sudden, he disappeared. We can't even find his car," the cop answered.

"He sounds like a tough kid, so I bet he will turn up eventually," Don said to the cops.

"That is what we are hoping," the other cop answered.

"What's the name of that drunk he was looking for? I bet I know him." Don asked.

"He was one of our local guys—Billy Ferguson," the cop said.

"Yep, I remember that boy. Nothing but trouble," Don answered smiling.

"That is definitely the truth," the cop said, nodding his head in agreement.

"If I come across anything, I'll let you boys know immediately," Don said like a concerned citizen.

"Thank you, sir, that will be much appreciated," the cop answered.

Don drove off slowly, making sure he used his turn signals and made complete stops so the cops would not have a reason to pull him over.

"Ole Billy Ferguson, where do you live, boy? I'm coming to talk to you," Don said out loud, talking to himself while country music played on the radio in the background.

Chapter 60: Moving Forward

"So you are telling me that you are from the past?" John asked Godfrey.

"Yes," Godfrey responded.

"Uhhh...are you crazy or something, Godfrey?" John couldn't help but ask.

"No," Godfrey responded.

"Meredith, love, am I crazy or am I just hearing things?" John asked Meredith.

"Most likely, but I think we are all crazy," Meredith said, lightening the mood of the house.

Godfrey had come back to the Maxwell estate to tell John about the visions that God had shown him, and to reveal to John his identity. In the living room, John was sitting beside Meredith, and Godfrey was sitting across from the two, drinking a glass of iced tea. Everything that Godfrey was telling John didn't shake Godfrey's nerves at all. John and Meredith, on the other hand, were a bit shook up. Godfrey was going into detail about the visions.

"There will be a second economic collapse. This one will be the end of American dominance in the world marketplace," Godfrey said.

John sat there, perplexed and shocked. Thoughts of "How can this be?" ran through his head.

"Not us; we are the USA. We are a Christian nation. We stand with Israel," John said, looking for some hope.

Meredith embraced her husband, giving him some comfort. She knew why this bothered John so much; he was the mouthpiece who must share this with the American Christian audience. John never enjoyed being the odd man out. He liked having attention on himself, but not negative attention. Life for John and his family had become quite stressful. Half of the town hated him; their local church told him it would be best if they stayed away for a while. It had really scared John when Meredith was kidnapped and nearly killed. It had also frightened John that a mob had tried to kill him at the studio. The police had to watch John's house on a regular basis now.

"This is what God has shown me. There are going to be a lot of natural disasters—hurricanes, earthquakes, tsunamis, rapid temperature changes—you name it, it's going to happen," Godfrey said.

"But I thought God would always protect America?" John questioned.

"This is not just an American thing, John; this includes the whole world," Godfrey said.

"America has plenty of sins and skeletons in its closet, just like all the other nations," Meredith said.

"Yeah, but I have to go on camera and tell everyone…again," John said breathing hard.

The three sat there for a while and went over the format. They even prayed a bit together to encourage John for the task. At the top of the house the angel Zadkiel stood watch. Looking toward the town, the angel saw heavy black clouds circling. Thunder was rumbling in the clouds, while lightning was brightening within them. The atmosphere was getting darker, spiritually and physically. Zadkiel looked up to heaven and saw his fellow angels flying back and forth at supersonic speed. Heaven was busy; Zadkiel could see that.

Along the trees surrounding the house, marching could be heard. The trees shuffled side to side like wind was blowing through them.

Zadkiel zoomed in to see and saw black hooded shadows with glowing eyes of different colors coming out of the tree line. Blue, red, green, yellow, and white eyes all stared at Zadkiel. Out of the thousands of shadows came an even larger one. This one had a crown on his head. It stood at the height of about fifteen feet. He came out from among them and raised his right arm in the air. The shadows yelled in adoration.

The shadow pointed at Zadkiel and screamed, "I want you, Zadkiel, captain in Michael's army! I will strip you of your wings and wipe my backside with them! The other shadows laughed hysterically at the giant's joke.

The showdown is coming. Real faith that's refined in the fire will be tested for this family.

The shadow king had long chains connected to his hands by shackles. They looked like they were his weapons of choice. He kept whipping them back and forth, making threats toward Zadkiel. The shadow king had four arms coming out of its torso so there were four chains coming at Zadkiel one after the other.

Zadkiel stood there watching the encroaching hordes of hell. He could not risk a fight yet; it was not time yet. This was just a trick to entice him to answer the challenge. The enemy had become bolder. To answer the arrogant shadow king, Zadkiel lifted up his spear just in time to catch one of the chains which were flying in the air. The spear caught the chain, pulling it into the opposite direction, causing it to wrap around the shadow's neck, knocking him to the ground before the spear finally found a home in one of the trees. The shadows didn't laugh when the big one got up because of fear; he was so mad that he grabbed one of the smaller shadows and ripped it in half. The poor thing screamed, and then all the shadows laughed at the spectacle. One particularly small shadow stepped out; it was wearing a jester's suit and it drew a line in the dirt. The line emanated a neon green color. The jester started laughing and dancing around with his bells jingling, doing cartwheels. Finally the shadow king had enough of the spectacle and punted the poor jester well into the surrounding trees. The crazy jester was laughing as he sailed in the air like a cannon ball.

"Cross that line, angel! Cross it and I will send you to oblivion!" the shadow king was screaming.

The surrounding shadows were beating on shields and the ground, making pounding noises. The army was growing restless, and Zadkiel knew he would have to answer their challenge eventually. The clouds released their rain as the night grew darker at the Maxwell house. Godfrey stood at the window, watching the rain pelt ferociously like a hurricane coming from the sea. Godfrey didn't see what Zadkiel saw, but the eerie feeling that everyone sensed in the house was enough to signal that something strange was happening in the atmosphere.

"All right; tomorrow we will do the show. This I'm sure will be the end of my public life," John said.

"God's people will wake up," Meredith said, trying to encourage John again.

Godfrey was still standing and staring out the window. His eyes followed the raindrops going down the window seal. He started tapping the window, trying to knock the traveling raindrops off on the other side. They all sat in silence as the storm slowly passed.

Chapter 61: Am I Dead?

Henry sat in the putrid cell that Alex had made so comfortable for him. He had dirty water to drink, and still nothing to eat. Henry couldn't remember how long he had been in this rotten place. He had accepted the fact that no one would find him here. Alex was in and out, and so were a slew of demons and spirits. Henry had gotten so used to seeing them that they did not really scare him anymore. Of course, they all taunted him ferociously, but even that had gotten old. The corpse and the skeletons were still in the cell with him. It smelled so bad that even after being in the cell for as long as he had been, Henry still couldn't get used to the fumes of death. Henry had lost a good bit of weight—at least 15 to 20 pounds.

To keep himself active, Henry would stand up and try to walk around a little bit, but the pain was still overwhelming and sent waves of sensation to his brain, causing him to pass out at times. Sitting in the dank, dark, and humid cell, Henry felt himself starting to get sick as well. The lack of nutrients wasn't helping. Alex had offered him food, but it was pieces of human and animal flesh freshly sliced off the bodies, not even cooked, but raw. As much as his ravenous hunger tempted him, Henry couldn't make himself eat anything that Alex offered him—especially a person's flesh.

Henry was dreaming a lot again because all he could really do was sleep. If he was awake, the pain and hunger bothered him. But while asleep, Henry forgot the horrible situation he was in. Henry was having a hard time breathing and was coughing a lot too. It felt like his lungs were full of phlegm, but Henry couldn't cough it up. One day Henry felt himself suffocating; he got worried that he was going to die so he stood up and forced himself to walk around again. It was to no avail because his breathing didn't get any better; his vision started blurring, and he started losing consciousness. Next thing Henry knew, he felt himself hit the ground. Henry's eyes closed and all went black.

Henry woke up in an extremely lighted area, but the light wasn't yellow like the sun, but all white. Henry wasn't sure where the light came from, but it was everywhere at once. Henry noticed that there were very tall beings walking around him. Some looked like women, and some looked like men; there were children as well. They had on white garments, and each and every one of them shone with an even greater brightness of white light than the background light. It was peaceful, and Henry wasn't scared at all. The first thing that Henry noticed was that he had no more pain in his body. When he sat up to look at himself, he noticed that he was wearing a garment as well. Henry was lying on a marble slab that looked like some kind of ancient surgery table. All the people around him began greeting and hugging him. Love emanated from them, but Henry didn't recognize any of them.

Then a thought came to Henry: *We are one here, we are family here, and we know you.*

"Am I dead?" Henry asked out loud.

Almost, answered a thought.

"Is this heaven?" Henry asked out loud again.

Yes, answered a thought.

Henry sat up on the slab of marble and looked around a bit. There were thousands of marble slabs with people on them. Henry noticed the floor was gold—tightly fitted gold bricks that showed anyone's reflection who looked into them. Surrounding the giant room of slabs was a giant amphitheater full of the bright beings. They were all talking and pointing and laughing with the sweetest joy Henry had ever felt or experienced. Past the entrance to the amphitheater was a massive city of buildings of every kind; beyond the city was a large mountain. It was the biggest one Henry had ever seen. Henry continued walking into the city, but looked back from where he had come from; at the top of the entrance was a sign that said, "The Hospital." People were everywhere, millions upon millions of people, walking together toward the city, and leaving the city to the green fields that surrounded the place.

Henry came to the entrance; there were two giant men with wings, guarding the gate. They had golden helmets with small golden wings on them. They had wings made up of white feathers. They looked extremely fierce from what Henry could make of their countenance, but when they spoke it was gentle and loving.

"Hello, fellow warrior," one of the angels bellowed to Henry.

Henry felt awkward and responded, "Hello to you too. My name is…"

"Henry, we know," the two angels responded in unison.

"What am I doing here?" Henry asked.

"We are not permitted to answer your questions, but enter the city and all will be known," the two angels responded.

With that Henry entered the enchanting metropolis of gold, marble, diamond, jasper, and ruby. Henry walked and heard, felt and tasted music everywhere. Colors sparkled in his eyes that he had never seen on earth. There were many different people walking around, every race from earth, and other races of beings he had never known, plus several different species of animals that were walking and talking with each other. They were all friendly to him, waving, talking and smiling. Henry did not want to leave; he had just decided in his heart that he wanted to stay instead of going back to being tortured by Alex. Henry sat on a bronze bench that was as comfortable as any recliner on earth and sat back to watch all the people. While sitting, a man came up to him and asked if he could sit by him.

"Sure, have a seat," Henry responded.

The man was very tall and old. The man didn't look weak, but regal and dignified. Henry thought, *This is what a king would look like.* The man had a dark olive complexion. He was wearing a crown. It was covered in jewels. Not everyone Henry saw wore a crown, but there were a few scattered in the millions who did. Some crowns were more dignified than others, but the people here didn't seem to be bothered by that. They just seemed to be happy to be here in heaven. Henry was beginning to understand why. The man was carrying a pail of water and offering people a drink of water as they passed.

"Hey, my name is Henry," Henry said, half expecting the man to already know his name.

"I am Constantine," the man answered with a rich Mediterranean accent.

"Constantine? That sounds familiar. Are you someone famous?" Henry asked.

"I am known on earth, for good and bad. But that is all chaff to me now. I am home," Constantine answered.

"Weren't you an emperor?" Henry asked.

"Yes, the first Christian Roman Emperor. Constantine the Great," Constantine said in a joking manner as people came up for a drink from the pail.

"Wow. I am talking to an emperor. That is amazing," Henry said to himself, totally surprised. "Shouldn't you be doing something more important than handing out water?" Henry asked.

"Nothing is more important than serving the Lord's people," Constantine said.

"You know, from what I have heard about Roman emperors, I thought you guys would have been the last people to be in heaven," Henry said.

"We are definitely one of the minorities in heaven," Constantine said.

"I didn't think I would have come here either," Henry said.

"You know, Henry, I was in the military and I had to kill people and ordered men to kill too. I have more blood on my hands then most. But God gave me a chance to change, and I did. The faces of the men I was responsible for haunted me night and day, but God's grace is plenty sufficient for anything done under the sun," Constantine said, as he passed out water.

"I know what you mean, but I am nothing compared to you, Constantine," Henry said.

"Killing is killing; it doesn't feel any better or worse whether it is one or a thousand," Constantine answered.

"I can't seem to forgive myself for what I've done," Henry said.

"Let God forgive you, and His Spirit will heal you in time," Constantine said.

"Thanks, I'll try that," Henry told Constantine.

"Of course, you will; that's an order," Constantine said, laughing and smiling at Henry.

"Roger that, sir," Henry responded, while standing up and walking over to Constantine.

"Here have a drink of water, Henry; it is delicious," Constantine said as he handed the ladle to Henry.

"Sure, why not," Henry answered.

As Henry drank the water, he could not help but feel the thick, intoxicating liquid pouring down his throat and igniting every sensation in his body at once. Henry had to sit back down because he felt drunk, not of alcohol but of joy—unhindered joy that kept bursting from his heart, causing him to laugh more than he ever had in his entire life. Henry closed his eyes and lay back on the bench.

As if coming out of a coma, Henry woke back up on the cold, wet stone floor of the cell he had been occupying for the past few weeks. It took several minutes for his brain to come back and register where he was. Henry felt like was dreaming now instead of entering reality; whatever had just happened felt more real than anything he had ever experienced. Henry found the strength to get his face off the floor and sat himself up.

He noticed that a bag with the logo from a burger joint was sitting in front of him. He thought he was seeing things so Henry closed his eyes and opened them again, just to be sure. To his surprise the bag was still there. Henry reached and grabbed the bag and examined the contents inside it. Two burgers and a large order of French fries were in the bag; beside the bag was a large drink. There was also a small letter inside the bag, neatly folded with cursive writing on it. He opened it to read the letter while he started nibbling on some fries.

The letter said:

Dear Henry,

I have decided to not let you die of starvation, so I have left you some food. From now on I will supply you with one meal a day until the time does comes for you to die. I've reasoned with myself that I want you alive to see the fate of this city and its people. You will get to see it all, firsthand.

No hard feelings, Alex

Henry set down the letter and said, "What an arrogant bastard."

Henry began eating all the food ferociously, and drank the ice cold large soda that what was left beside the bag. After eating, Henry looked at the phone he had found, and started contemplating when he would use it. Henry decided to wait, and to see what Alex had up his sleeve.

Chapter 62: Investigating

Don had followed the lead that the cops had given him about Billy Ferguson's wife. The poor woman was so distraught that Don couldn't get much out of her. She did tell him about Alex Levonson and where his church was. Don had done some research on him and found out he was some obscure preacher who had become a hotshot in the town. Alex had become the mouthpiece against John Maxwell, who was going to be the next person Don visited.

Don had arrived at the newly painted and upgraded country church that was Alex's. There were people walking around, looking at the used cars for sale. There was also a hot dog stand that had a couple of people getting food from it. Don parked his truck and started looking at the used cars. Henry's squad car was not there; it must have already been sold. Don walked around slowly and cautiously, examining the whole place. Don felt the atmosphere was different around the church. It felt awkward, like there was something hidden there, out of sight. Don walked over to the hot dog stand and decided to get something to eat. The guy making the hot dogs looked like a true blue idiot; he was wearing a white chef hat and an apron that said "Greatest Wife in the World." The man had a vertically striped red and white shirt on under the apron.

"How is it going?" Don asked in his thick southern accent.

The man was looking down, counting the hot dogs with his finger while singing some song that Don didn't recognize. It sounded like a simple children's tune of some kind.

"Hey! Boy! Did you hear me?" Don yelled at the simpleton.

"Right," the man answered looking at Don, smiling.

Don noticed the chef was missing most of his teeth. Before speaking, Don waited for his blood pressure to go back down, and then said, "I would like a hot dog, just chili and onions."

"Right!" The chef yelled, still smiling at Don.

Instead of making Don's hot dog, the man just stood there smiling, and then began to whistle. By this time Don had had enough and reached over the grill and grabbed the guy by the collar and pulled him to his face and said, "What the hell is wrong with you? Did your momma drop you on your head every day for fun or something?"

"No sir, my momma left me before I was born," the man answered.

"Oh, I see, we got us a good ole fashion smart aleck," Don said.

"Right," the chef answered.

"I tell you what, chef, if you don't start making my hot dog in the next two seconds, I'm

gonna make you swallow the few teeth that you do have," Don answered, pulling the man closer.

Despite all the threats and seriousness of the situation, the poor simpleton kept smiling and looking ahead as if he had no care in the world. Don saw this was getting nowhere and decided he was going to get the idiot's attention in some other way.

"So, you don't want to act like you got some sense, huh, boy?" Don asked.

"Right, coming right up ma'am," the poor chef answered.

Don grabbed the man by the back of the head and acted as if he was going to push his face into the grill. Instantly the man was screaming. He was howling like a dog. The grill was making a sizzling, popping sound that would make anyone cringe. Don pulled the guy away from the grill and pulled the chef's hat over his nearly burned face. He punched the chef in the face, and he threw him on the ground. There was a blood spot forming on the fool's chef hat where his mouth was bleeding. Don started making his own hot dog as the chef moaned in pain, wiggling around and hoping someone would help him. The few people who were there left in their cars and sped off. One old woman did a 360 turn in the gravel before speeding off in an old Cadillac. Don looked and waved; she responded with her middle finger. Don came around to the other side of the grill to talk to the simpleton.

"So boy, where is your preacher? This Alex Levonson," Don asked, eating the chili dog.

"Uhhhhh…in the woods. Ohhhh…call an ambulance," the chef moaned as he removed his chef's hat.

"Well, I see you don't have any problems hearing what I got to say now. Do you, boy?" Don responded.

The fool looked toward Don's direction and said, "Please…call an ambulance…I'm dying."

"You ain't dying, idiot; you just need some burn cream, and probably a dentist. Where in the woods is this preacher?" Don asked with a serious tone.

The man pointed to the back of the church and was going to say something, but saw Tabitha Maxwell walking up to the scene of carnage and suddenly shut up. Don couldn't help but notice how attractive this young lady was; he threw the rest of the hot dog on the chef and began walking in Tabitha's direction.

"Hello ma'am, I must say, you are as pretty as the sun," Don said smiling.

"Just what are you doing—beating up a handicapped man?" Tabitha said, staring Don in the face.

"That boy ain't retarded; he's just a bad actor and you know it," Don casually said.

"He is doing his job, and now he will have to go to the hospital because of you," Tabitha said.

"He'll be all right, but I'm looking Alex Levonson. Why don't you be a good secretary and page him out of those woods before I go in them and find him myself?" Don said.

"Alex is not here. What do you want with him anyway?" Tabitha asked.

"I'm looking for my friend, Henry Adams, and I heard he came here before he disappeared," Don said.

"Henry? I haven't seen Henry; he just vanished. Some say he checked himself into a mental institution because of all the crazy dreams and hallucinations he was having; he was my friend, but he didn't ever tell me he was leaving," Tabitha said with a sad countenance.

"So you knew Henry?" Don asked.

"Yes, we met Alex together. Alex helped him with some problems, and shortly after that I started dating Alex," Tabitha said.

"Dating the preacher, huh?" Don asked.

"Yes," Tabitha answered.

"Well, what do you know about John Maxwell?" Don asked.

"He's my dad," Tabitha answered.

"Really, this just gets more interesting by the minute," Don said.

"Are you a cop, or do I need to call them and have you charged with assault and battery?" Tabitha said, perturbed.

"No ma'am, just a friend looking for a friend. You tell Mr. Levonson I'll be in touch. Good day to you, doll. If you see your dad, tell him I'll be looking for him too," Don said.

Don turned around and headed for his truck. As he passed the fool on the ground, Don threw down five one hundred dollar bills on the chest of the idiot.

"This is for your silence, and your bad acting job," Don said as he passed the broken man who was still moaning and groaning from the whipping he received from Don.

Tabitha gave Don an evil stare. Don casually waved at her as he slowly drove off. The old truck made a low rumbling sound as it faded down the road.

Chapter 63: Nails for Breakfast

It all boils down to marriage," John said into the camera.

The set was nerve wracking; John was sweating from the content of the message. Godfrey was in the background finishing his large painting of heaven. John readjusted in his seat and went on with what he wanted to say.

"Our country is falling apart because of many things, but one is marriage—our physical marriages and our marriage to Christ. The two coincide and complement each other. The spiritual realm is connected to this physical realm; what happens here affects the other and vice versa. I am the last man to talk about this subject because I do not know what it is to have a good marriage. My wife and I almost came to getting a divorce just a few weeks ago, but God had mercy on us and we worked it out. I thought everything was fine. I was just going through the motions of running this ministry and life. Next thing I know, my family is falling apart right under my nose," John said.

This feels horrible—not only am I attacking marriages, but now I am sharing my personal struggles with the rest of Christendom. I feel like I am being cross examined. Oh man, God help me.

"We, as Christians, followers of Christ, have to get our houses in order, our personal houses and our houses of fellowship, instead of worrying about exploiting and selling Christianity with CDs, books, videos, and cooking shows. We need to get serious about judging ourselves before condemning the rest of the world. While we do not know it, we are simmering in the pot with them. To be separate from the world means to be separate from the world. God's judgments are coming very soon and we have to purge our hearts before we perish as well," John said.

He readjusted himself in his seat to alleviate some of the tension he was feeling; his mouth had become dry. He reached down and drank some of the water that was sitting in front of him in a blue cup. John noticed his hand was shaking the cup from nervousness. He attempted to hide the trembling from the camera's eye.

I used to be on this set talking about how God wants to bless His people with material things, and that He didn't want them to have any problems whatsoever. I used to say that life was to be nothing but good—with no struggles at all. What a fool I have been.

"God has shown me things that are coming soon. Yes, that is right; God showed me things in dreams and visions of the natural disasters and of human disasters as well. The first thing God showed me was that the stock market will crash again, but this time the American dollar will fade into history. Bartering and food rationing will be commonplace in America and the world. Los Angeles will be split in half. Much of the West Coast will be under water or under ash and lava. A hurricane will carve a new path through the northeast. Washington D.C. will barely survive the storm and rain waters. Assassinations of rulers will become common, mobs of gangs and disgruntled people will go to the streets, and turn peaceful cities into war zones. People will lose all hope in the government; anarchy will be championed for a while in some countries. God spoke to me and said His people must dive into Him while this flood of judgment is on the world so we can learn to trust Him, and only Him, instead of the fickle kingdoms of this world. We, as His bride, must be spotless. It is through trials and tribulations that we will be purged of iniquity. I know this is a lot of information, and it goes down like a rock sandwich. But this is what is coming to our planet, very, very soon," John said.

John paused for a moment, to let all the information sink in; he finished the show by saying that the next show would be about preparing for disasters and learning how to hear God's voice. "God bless you, and I hope to see you again soon. Good night," John said.

After the cameras were off, Meredith ran up to John and embraced him. She knew what he just said was probably the hardest message he had ever shared on camera. John just sat there, stunned, because he knew the board would be contacting him very soon. Godfrey came up; the paintings he had done in the background looked beautiful and realistic.

"How do you feel, John?" Godfrey asked, grabbing his shoulder.

"Like I've had nails for breakfast," John answered.

"You did what God wanted; that's all that matters," Godfrey said, smiling.

Meredith was hugging John closely, kissing him on his cheek softly. John sat for another minute and talked to the employees to see what their reaction was to his message. They were all perplexed by it—some agreed with him but most didn't. The last thing Christians wanted to hear was that their life was going to get harder. John couldn't lie to himself—he didn't want to hear this either. John's nerves still hadn't calmed down, but internally his heart was very calm and at peace.

John, Meredith, and Godfrey went to his office to gather a few things before leaving. They were all standing around when the phone rang. He picked it up and said, "Hello."

"Oh, hey, Ron," John said. "Yeah, I believe what I said," John said. "I know, but if I would have told the board, I wouldn't have been able to do the show," John said. "Right, I know the rules," John said. "Right, I understand," John said with a relieved look on his face. "No, God bless you, Ron. I'll see you around. 'Bye," John answered as he hung the phone up.

"Was that Ron from the board of directors?" Meredith asked.

"Yeah," John answered.

"What did he want?" Meredith asked.

“Oh, he just wanted to inform me that I am no longer the host of OBN. He told me the board will buy me out and give me a clean slate,” John answered.

Meredith ran up and hugged Jon tightly and started crying. They embraced each other for what seemed like an eternity. Godfrey sat there, stone-faced, distancing himself from the situation mentally so he could think clearly about what to do next.

“I’m so sorry, John, I can’t believe they did this to you. This ministry was your baby; we started it when it was just a small fellowship,” Meredith said.

“I know, love, but it is ultimately the board’s decision. Quite frankly, I feel great. As Godfrey said, I did what I was supposed to do. God will take care of us,” John said.

“We should probably get back to your home, John; I think it is going to get really dangerous around here for you,” Godfrey said.

“All right then; let’s go,” John said.

The three headed out the back door to be greeted by a mob of angry people. The police were holding the people back, but the people had hate and violence in their eyes. Rage had settled on the crowd.

“False prophet!” the crowd screamed.

John hugged Meredith to protect her as Godfrey pushed through the crowd. The cops were keeping the sides stable. People were trying to grab John, but the cops were doing their best to stop them. Meredith was frightened; she held tightly to her husband. The crowd was about a hundred deep with people; the closer Godfrey got to the edge, the more aggressive the crowd became. It was so rough, in fact, that one man attempted to hit Godfrey; Godfrey countered the punch by ducking, and grabbing the man’s arm and dislocating it. The man fell down, screaming in pain while being trampled on by the mob.

As Godfrey finally pushed through to get near the car, six men attacked Godfrey. At the same time, John realized his keys were still inside the studio. There was no way they were getting back through that gauntlet of a crowd. Godfrey was giving more than he got from the group of men, but they were distracting him enough so that a couple more guys came after John and Meredith. John put Meredith behind him, and prepared to defend his wife however possible. As the men charged John, a red pickup truck came pummeling through and hit them. The men that were hit went flying into the bushes. The man driving the truck screamed at John, "Get in!"

John didn't hesitate; he grabbed Meredith's hand and hopped into the truck. As soon as John shut the door, he locked it. Godfrey took down one guy before hopping into the back of the truck. The driver quickly backed out of the studio. Not moving for anyone, the crowd got out of his way; they did not want to be run over like the others.

As the four were driving down the road, the driver reached over and shook John's hand.

"Howdy, my name is Don Warburton," Don said, introducing himself.

"Hey, I'm John Maxwell, and this is my wife Meredith. Thank you for saving us."

"You're welcome. Who is that tough cookie sitting in the back?" Don asked.

"Oh, that's Godfrey. He is a family friend of ours," Meredith answered.

"I would hate to be on that boy's bad side," Don said, smiling.

"Yeah, he has been the biggest help I could ever ask for," John answered.

"I'll bet. You are not a well-liked man at all, John Maxwell," Don said.

"That's the thing; I used to be the most loved pastor in America. Now as you can see, it is the complete opposite."

"It looks like the table has turned on you, friend," Don said.

"Why did you help us, Don?" Meredith asked.

"Well, I'm looking for a friend. His name is Henry Adams, and I heard that he had talked to John a good bit before disappearing. So I wanted to ask some questions about him," Don said.

"Well, I'm glad you came, because that situation was getting really ugly, really quick," John said.

"Just in the nick of time," Don said.

"Well, I would be glad to answer any questions the best I can," John said.

"We can do that at the house," Meredith said.

With that, the four headed to the Maxwell estate. In the back of the truck, Godfrey noticed that black clouds hovered over the town again. They were much larger and thicker than before. The final gathering was now here. In Athens, Georgia, the battle was about to begin.

Chapter 64: My Burning Desire

It was night—pitch black and muggy. The clouds were rumbling again; the only light around the church was the massive bonfire that was built in the shape of a pyramid. Alex, dressed all in white, was standing in front of a podium that was built in front of the massive fire. The congregation of the small church was standing in front of Alex, listening to his tirade. The congregation was no longer small, but had grown exponentially with the sudden popularity of Alex.

"Listen, my children! We have walked through the desert together; we have struggled together; we have grown together. Now we must become one and stand against the darkness that has plagued our beautiful town. We have planned and waited, but now is the opportunity to take what is ours! We will burn idols, the people, the plague that has rested in our bones! This tumor must be removed and cast into the fire, and I promise, my children, this time is upon us. This tumor has been severed; now it must come into the fire!" Alex exclaimed.

The congregation was in an uproar. They had their fists raised to the air all chanting in unison. "Alex! Alex!"

Alex looked down from his stage and smiled at their worship of him. He loved every minute of it; it was more intoxicating than drugs. He waved his hand lightly in the air like a pompous pope, receiving adoration for just absolving everyone's sins.

"Now, my children, go out burn down the idols that have built themselves up in this town! Light everything up, make ash of everything that has made itself greater than the light! I promise you, when everything is ash, the phoenix will rise into the sky and glorify our bodies and make us one with the light! Once and for all, we will be one with the light, and eternal forevermore. Now go! Take down anyone who dares stop you! Because you are doing the work of the Shining One!"

The crowd left with much enthusiasm, ready for the next morning, the beginning of the day of fire. Alex stood in silence, watching his plans come to fruition. Tabitha walked next to him, amazed at how powerful and influential Alex had become.

"Hello, my dear; are you ready for what is to come?" Alex asked.

"Yes, of course, I am ready for anything with you," Tabitha answered woodenly.

"If that is the case, then follow me into the void, my dear," Alex said.

The two embraced with a hug and long kiss. Then Alex led Tabitha into the woods to his underground cavern to complete his diabolical plans for the day of fire. It was dark, but Alex had grabbed a torch from the church to lead the way. Tabitha had never been back this far, especially to the cavern. The only other people who had seen it were the poor souls who were murdered there and Henry who was still alive. The woods were strangely quiet and thick with fear of the unknown. Tabitha walked without a care in the world; normally, she would have been frightened, but the curse that was on her deadened her intuition and common sense. It was unfair and Alex knew it; he finally had the woman of his dreams, but now he had to fulfill his part of the bargain. She had to be killed as a sacrifice to bring an even bigger presence of evil into the town. Not only that, but her murder would crush her family and Godfrey. The destroyer would live up to his name once again.

They reached the entrance; it opened as soon as Alex stood in front of it. They walked down the dark spiraling steps. Alex spoke a word under his breath and all of the torches lit instantly inside the cavern. Sitting in the middle of the room was a wooden table. Tabitha saw

Henry lying in his cell and waved to him. Henry was half-conscious, but he recognized her.

"Hey, Henry, your friend Don was looking for you," Tabitha said, smiling.

"Tabitha, what is wrong with you?" Henry asked, very groggy.

"She is under a spell; she doesn't know what is happening," Alex said.

"Yes, I do," Tabitha said in a goofy manner.

"Of course you do, dear; take off your dress and come lay on this table," Alex said, kissing her and tapping his hand on the table.

Tabitha did as she was told; she undressed down to bra and panties and lay back on the table. Alex grabbed his shackles and chained Tabitha's hands and feet to the table, but she just lay there smiling at Alex, letting him do whatever he wanted. Alex bent down and kissed Tabitha one more time, and said, "I'm sorry for this, Tabitha."

Tabitha just smiled and said, "I love you, Alex."

Alex grabbed a gag and put it into Tabitha's mouth and tied it around her head. He gave her a shot of morphine to make her fall asleep until tomorrow. Within a minute, Tabitha was knocked out from the medicine and fast asleep. Henry, by this time, had woken himself up. Walking to the front of the cell, he asked. "Just what in the world are you doing?"

"Well, what does it look like? You have been in here long enough to know what happens to people when I bring them in here." Alex answered, staring at Tabitha's beautiful face.

"You can't mean you are going to kill her!" Henry yelled.

"Now Henry, don't act so ignorant. That is precisely what I am going to do," Alex responded.

"Don't do it, you sick bastard! Kill me in her place! She doesn't deserve this!" Henry yelled, coughing up fluid in his lungs.

"Sit down, weakling, and don't worry. I'm going to kill you as well. Your time will be soon, but first Tabitha must join me in the void," Alex said, as he walked out of the cavern.

"Nooooo!!" Henry screamed at Alex as he went up the spiraling stairs.

The cavern went dark again with barely any light in at all. Henry sat and looked at Tabitha's bound body, wishing he could do something to stop this. Henry sat back down; his head was hurting him tremendously. He closed his eyes for a while to slow the pain, then Henry remembered that Tabitha had said Don was looking for him. Don "the Boss" Warburton, his friend from the military. Meanest guy he had ever met. Henry reached for the cell phone that he kept hidden in his pocket. Henry had to stop for a minute to remember Don's number, but he did. Don's number was 542-5277, which spelled out "kick ass."

Henry turned the cell phone on; it still had ten percent of its battery left. He called Don's number and left a message; the message was, *Donnie, its Henry. I am located in the woods, underground behind that lunatic Alex Levonson's church. It is about a half a mile behind the church. Please come quickly, Alex is going to kill me and Tabitha Maxwell. Please hurry.*

Just as Henry finished the message, the phone displayed a message that said low battery, and it turned off. Henry put the phone into his pocket and began to pray to God that Don would be able to find the place in time.

Chapter 65: Burn, Baby, Burn

"I am so tired of watching this studio," the fat cop said.

"Yeah, me too; why don't we just kick John Maxwell and his family out of Athens?" the skinny cop responded.

"I don't know; no one ever does what makes the most sense," the fat cop said, nearly swallowing an entire jelly donut in one bite.

"This town has gone crazy, hasn't it?" the skinny cop protested.

"Yep," the fat cop answered, sounding like his mouth was full of cotton.

It was early morning; the two policemen had the night shift keeping watch over the OBN building. There had been so much rioting and violence there that twenty-four hour surveillance was now required. It was just the two of them; they would get relieved by two replacements in just another hour. It had been quiet throughout the whole night. The only excitement they saw was four stray cats, fighting it out over some scraps.

"You know, I am tired of being a cop," the skinny cop said.

"Why is that? You don't enjoy protecting the public?" the fat cop asked, licking his sticky fingers.

"Not really; nobody appreciates what we do. Plus we work for peanuts. I wish we would get a raise or something," the skinny cop said.

"Or at least a gift card or a free turkey," the fat cop answered, reaching for another donut.

The two venting policeman were interrupted by a Molotov cocktail that hit their windshield and exploded; fire was spreading all over the front of their squad car. The fat cop spit out chunks of donut from his mouth screaming, "What the crap!"

Before the two could get out of the car, several more cocktails shattered into the vehicle, causing the fire to seep into the cracked windows. The skinny and fat cop finally got out of the car, but when they did they were both greeted with more cocktails. The fat cop ran around on fire like a melting marshmallow from a children's campfire. The skinny cop never got off of the ground. The ones who were throwing the cocktails were several members of Alex's church; after killing the police, they set the studio ablaze, chanting "Praise be to the light."

The members of Alex's church were simultaneously setting all of the major buildings of Athens on fire—the police station, the fire department, city hall, as well as anyone who tried to stop them. Several policeman had been killed, and a few townspeople as well. Alex's brainwashed followers were shooting up the town and running people over, throwing Molotov cocktails at people walking or running down the street. It was madness, absolute chaos. The town mayor, Marcus E. Bradley, would have called the governor to send in the National Guard, but he was kidnapped from his home and sentenced to be publicly executed on Main Street. This had all happened within two to three hours early in the morning of the day of fire. It had been planned out with the utmost precision. It was now hell on earth for the town of Athens.

Belial was standing in the crowd of frightened townsfolk who had been rounded up by gunpoint to watch the mayor be executed by beheading. Belial watched in absolute amazement at what Alex had accomplished. He had successfully taken this whole town hostage. Belial knew this tale of carnage wouldn't last too long because someone would leak this out to the rest of the country. It was still a good show though. The people were terrified—some were crying while some were still confused on what exactly had happened. There were six hooded men wearing black standing behind the mayor; he still had his pajamas on and his hands were tied behind his back; he stood barefoot and confused.

"What is the meaning of this? Have you all gone mad?" the mayor exclaimed.

"We are bringing the light to this town, and to the world," the six men said in unison.

"What light are you talking about?" the mayor asked.

"The light of the light bearer," the six men said.

"Who is this light bearer?" the mayor asked, looking back at the six men.

"Lucifer, the god of all men, the god of power," the six answered.

"Lucifer?" the mayor asked, while one of the six men grabbed him by the shoulders and forced him to his knees.

The mayor turned white like a ghost as the crowd watched a glimmering sword appear from under the cloak of one of the black figures behind him. The hooded man raised the sword in the air, and the mayor began trembling from nervousness. He watched the crowd in front of him. Their eyes followed the sword as it was unsheathed and the blade was gently placed on the side of the mayor's neck.

"Do you have any last words, mayor, before you are thrown into eternity?" the hooded executioner asked.

The mayor had a hard time talking; the words that did come out of his mouth were so muffled and full of tears no one could understand him. Mayor Bradley was crying so much and shaking so hard that he could not speak. Just as the executioner drew his sword back, a gunshot rang out in the night. Everyone was looking around and ducking at the same time. The executioner's sword fell from his grasp. Then a second shot was fired. This time the executioner fell backward. The shot had hit him in the chest. The other hooded figures pulled AK-47s and started firing in the direction of the first two gunshots, and then ran for cover. The crowd being held at gunpoint started running in all directions, screaming, because their guards had turned to return fire at whoever was shooting. The mayor got up off his knees and ran to find some place to hide.

Up ahead there were two Humvees returning fire with .240G machine guns mounted on top of them. There were two squads of soldiers taking an offensive stance on the Luciferian terrorists. One was coming directly toward the terrorists, while the other squad was coming around the buildings to flank them. During the exchange, a few civilians were killed and some injured while a couple of terrorists were taken down. The heavy fire of the 240s and the constant advance of the National Guard caused the Luciferians to begin retreating in their vehicles. Despite the National Guard stopping more bloodshed, most of the town was in flames. Shortly after the troops showed up, firemen and paramedics came in from surrounding towns to help with the damages and injured. There were now helicopters flying over; images showing Athens burning to the ground and small gunfire exchanges were on national television.

All around town most of the terrorists were on the run; they were headed for Alex's church to make a final stand. The other place the Luciferians were rallying was the Maxwell's estate. Godfrey, John, Meredith, and Don were sitting in the basement of the house with all the lights off. Bullets were ricocheting off of the house and going through the windows; John thought it best to hunker down in the basement and pray that the cops outside could hold off the people intent on killing the Maxwells. There were four police cars with two cops in each of them set up hood to trunk in front of the driveway of the house. It was the only way in, but still men were trying to jump the brick fence. They were quickly brought down by the police. It was getting harder and harder for the police to hold their position because of the sheer number of the terrorists coming to the house.

Zadkiel was standing where the cops were holding their position. He was making a stand against the fighting hordes of shadows trying to take him down. Zadkiel was wielding a long sword; every time he swung the behemoth weapon it would take out fifty or sixty shadows. The shadows had circled around Zadkiel, but they were not getting near him. Every time they came close to overwhelming him, Zadkiel pounded the ground with his sword, causing massive tremors all around him, making the shadows fly back and fall to the ground. Behind Zadkiel there was an invisible force shield in the shape of a bubble that was protecting the house. None of the shadows could get near it; if they did, charges of electricity struck them like insects in a bug zapper. This was the hedge of protection from God given to the Maxwells. There was another angel dressed in a white cloak with a large hood covering its face. This angel did not have wings, but looked more human. The hooded angel was dancing in front of the house; every time his foot hit the ground, bolts of lightning came from the sky, hitting the massive horde of shadows. Large fireballs that looked like asteroids came from the dancing angel's hands, clobbering the charging shadow's weakening front. Zadkiel and the dancing angel were putting up a good fight, and so were the policeman against the Luciferian terrorists. If anything, in the physical and spiritual realm, the enemy was kept at bay.

In the basement, sitting in the dark, John and Meredith were praying for God's protection while Godfrey and Don were thinking of the best way of to get out of the house and to head to Alex's church. Don had received the message from Henry, but as soon he and Godfrey were planning to leave, Alex's men had begun attacking out front. When Godfrey had heard about Tabitha being held, he went berserk; he was going to run right outside, but Don held him back while Meredith and John calmed him down. Everyone was upset. Meredith was trying to keep it together, but she kept sobbing because she was so worried about Tabitha.

Meredith said, "I told her to stay away from Alex; there was nothing good about him."

"I know, dear, but Tabitha is an adult; we couldn't keep her from Alex. Now all we can do is pray that Don and Godfrey can stop this wicked scheme before it happens," John said.

"Listen, we've got to go and find this place and quickly," Don said.

"We don't have much time; we've got to risk it and get out the door," Godfrey said with the utmost urgency.

"There is a safer way out, but you two will have to run out and get a vehicle," John said.

"We can get my truck; my gun is in there. Something tells me we will need it," Don said.

"Godfrey, you are going to need a weapon too; I have a few guns," John said.

"We need to go too," Meredith said, still crying.

"No, it's too risky. It is much easier for two men to make it out of here alive than four people," John said.

"He's right, Meredith. You two need to stay here; it's safer. I promise you, I will bring Tabitha back," Godfrey said.

"Okay, Godfrey, I trust you. You saved me before; now you need to save Tabitha," Meredith agreed.

"So how do we get out of here?" Don asked.

"When you get your truck, head around back and go straight. Go through the field; there is a dirt path cut through a small patch of woods. It will eventually end at the main road that takes you right into town. There shouldn't be too many people out there. It is a pretty well-kept secret of mine," John said.

"All right; sounds like a plan. Now, let's go get some guns and send this sick puppy home where he belongs," Don said.

"Let's do it," Godfrey said.

John went over to his gun safe and opened the door. There were a couple of guns, some papers, and cash set to the side just for emergencies. The safe was taller than John, and dark green with a shiny finish. The safe had a golden handle on it. It looked so heavy that it would take some ingenuity and creativity for someone to try and steal it. John reached in and grabbed the .22 caliber rifle and the .40 caliber semi-automatic pistol there. Both were fully loaded. John handed the weapons and some ammunition to Godfrey and Don. John had another rifle, and tried to hand it to Don, but instead Donnie reached in and grabbed the 12 gauge pump shotgun that was lying there.

"This and my .357 is all I need, kemo sabe," Don said.

"All right; well, here are some shells for the shotgun," John said.

"Godspeed to both of you," John said as he grabbed the other rifle for himself. Even though John did not like the fact of having to keep guns for his protection, he knew it was a necessary evil.

Meredith hugged Godfrey and Don too. She told them to please save Tabitha and Henry. John shook both of their hands, and told them again that he would be praying for their success. The two men headed upstairs and to the front door; Donnie had his shotgun ready and Godfrey and his rifle ready. They both looked at each other, and agreed that Godfrey would lay down cover fire while Don got to the truck.

"On three, boy," Don said.

"Sounds good," Godfrey said.

"You don't seem to be bothered by nothing, Godfrey; you must be made out of nails like me," Don said, laughing.

"I guess so; death just doesn't scare me anymore. I guess it's because this is my second time living," Godfrey said.

"What?" Don asked.

"Never mind; if we survive this, I'll tell you a story you will never forget," Godfrey said.

“All right, can’t wait to hear it…three, two, and one,” Don said, opening the door while Godfrey came out from the side and started shooting into the mob of Luciferians coming up the driveway.

Donnie got off a couple of shots off while running to his pickup. Godfrey picked off several terrorists with ease. They were cold, calculated shots that hit the men and women who had made it their goal in life to destroy the Maxwells. Don had to keep his head down while he cranked the truck. The police didn’t even notice because they were too busy keeping themselves alive and trying to keep the house protected. Don whipped the truck around and motioned for Godfrey to hop in. Godfrey got off a couple more shots, bobbing and weaving, and trying not to get hit by any ricochets. Godfrey opened the truck door and slammed it shut.

“Let’s go!” Godfrey screamed.

The tires started spinning, slinging gravel behind the classic red truck. Luckily for the policemen, some of the National Guard had showed up and began hitting the local terrorists hard on their flank. In the meantime, Godfrey and Donnie went behind the house and followed the path that John had told them about.

Chapter 66: What Seals Us Binds Us

Alex was dressed up for the occasion that would be his final act. He stood over Tabitha with a shiny blade that had been used on many people and animals before her. It was bittersweet because Alex had always loved Tabitha from a distance. But now that he had her—physically and mentally—his god demanded her from him. Lucifer's blood lust was insatiable; it had to be fed without any personal feelings or reserve from his servants. Alex still felt a small piece of himself telling him not to do it, that there was still time to change his mind. Alex thought about the possibilities if he did decide not to kill Tabitha; that route of free will would most likely cause him an excruciating and painful death. Lucifer didn't appreciate cowards or turncoats; just like Hitler, he would hang traitors with piano wire for punishment. Alex was sure his punishment would be much worse. As the prison gang, the Aryan Brotherhood saying goes, "Blood in, blood out." Alex wasn't losing resolve, but there was still a string of humanity left in him that would occasionally pluck and make a faint sound.

The town was in flames; a lot of people were dead and his finale was coming to an end. After killing Tabitha, he would kill Henry and wait for further instructions from his lord to carry on more tasks if needed.

The day of fire had come; it was the beginning of the end for the Maxwells, OBN, and the small town of Athens. Alex had won; he couldn't believe it, but he had witnessed evil truly triumph over good. God was nowhere to be found.

"Are You under a rock? Did You hide in the trees? Could You possibly be on vacation? Where are You? *Where are You? I am all powerful, and You are nothing!* Nothing will stop me; I am a god in this town. They will worship me for who I really am, and You can't stop it!" Alex exclaimed, with his hands raised up, looking into the air.

Outside the church, there was another shoot out. Godfrey and Donnie had pulled up as far as they could. The roads were jammed with civilian and military vehicles. Some locals and the National Guard were exchanging fire with shooters who were defending the church from open windows and broken stained glass windows. The locals and troops outnumbered the terrorists six to one, but they just kept fighting. As one of the terrorists was shot, another person replaced him. It looked like they were hypnotized; they seemed totally oblivious to the fact that they were going to lose.

Don and Godfrey decided to go right into the woods from the road, circle the church, and find where Henry and Tabitha were being held. They were trying to avoid any gunfights, but to no avail. There were several people, sitting in tree stands, shooting at the two of them. Godfrey and Don had to lay low on the ground because these hunters were crack shots. Godfrey would raise up and shoot at the hunter to make him duck, and then Don would wait for the hunter to stick his head back out and blast it off. It was quite easy to get ahead after figuring out this strategy, because the tree stands didn't provide very much cover for the hunters.

It felt like it took hours just to get a few hundred feet into the woods. Godfrey could feel that they were getting closer because the intensity and thickness of the presence of evil was becoming stronger. There was only one more hunter in a stand, but a couple more guys turned up near what appeared to be the entrance to Alex's cavern. Donnie was reloading his gun while Godfrey laid down some fire on the hunter in the tree stand and the two guys behind the trees.

"Where did you learn to shoot like that?" Don asked, as he loaded his last rounds into his shotgun and .357 magnum.

Godfrey kept shooting, looking straight ahead, and answered, "In heaven."

"What? In heaven? They don't teach this at the pearly gates!" Don exclaimed.

"It's a long story that I promise I'll tell one day," Godfrey said, as he ducked to reload and let Donnie take over.

Don shot the last hunter in the leg. He fell down and rolled off the tree stand. The hunter's leg got caught in a limb and he was dangling in the tree, trying to reach for his gun. While Don and Godfrey hopped up in a leap frog pattern, Godfrey shot the man in the head because he had pulled out a pistol from the boot of the leg that wasn't caught in the tree limb. Godfrey quickly shot him, causing pink mist to splatter behind the man as he suddenly went limp.

Don and Godfrey quickly closed in on the other two men. They were entrenched and would not give up without a fight. It looked like the firefight would be a stalemate, but what felt like an earthquake started rumbling the ground ferociously. The ground shook so hard that a tree fell down on one of the shooters. While the other man hopped up to get out of the way of the tree, Donnie shot the man in the neck, causing him to turn sideways in the air.

As Godfrey and Don made their way to the entrance of the cavern, they noticed a huge blazing fire a distance away; they realized it must be Alex's church. Alex's men most likely set it ablaze as well. Godfrey looked at the pink sky and noticed that what looked like a planet that was twice the size of the moon was resting in the heavens. It was light purple, with white clouds at the top and bottom. There was a large moon in front of it. Glancing at the moon in front of the planet, he noticed what looked like a massive storm going across the surface of the purple sphere. Only half of the planet was showing; it looked like it was escaping a black hole.

"What in the world is that?" Don asked.

"That must be Neptune or some other planet," Godfrey responded.

"How did that happen?" Don asked.

"I don't know, but I bet it has something to do with the electrical discharges and earthquakes we've been feeling," Godfrey said.

"All right, boy, are you ready for this? We are gonna take down the boy, Alex. No questions asked; he is gonna die today," Don said.

"I was born for this moment," Godfrey said.

The two opened the trap door to the cavern and headed down the spiral staircase in silence. Inside the dark cavern, a great wind was blowing. Alex was in a trance holding a knife; his white cloak was blowing in the air from all sides. Alex was having a hard time standing because of the voracity of the wind, but he held his balance while saying his final prayer to his lord.

"What must be done will forever be written. What must be said will forever be echoed in the halls of hell. This soul which I've conquered will join me in the void," Alex was saying, staring straight into the air.

Tabitha was awake; she couldn't speak because of the gag. She couldn't really move because of the shackles, but even though she was under a spell, she was getting scared because of what was happening. The stones were starting to shake that were holding the cavern together. The ground was continually shaking, causing Alex to fall from side to side. The hell mouth began spewing out orange, hot lava all over the place. Even though Tabitha was a bit shaken, she still trusted Alex, holding the shiny, sharp knife over her. He was about to cut her bowels out and burn them as incense to his god.

Henry was up as well, but he could barely stand either. He had to hold himself up by grabbing onto the bars of the cell. He kept screaming at Alex, but it wasn't getting across to him at all. Alex was in a complete trance; whatever he was saying had completely locked in his consciousness on what he was trying to invoke. There were swirls of electricity and green fire going around Alex as he continued his unholy prayer.

"I speak to the most high of gods, Lucifer. The enchanted one, the true bright and morning star. Send us your presence; send us your power of life, death, and the true Christ. I give you my most precious gift, the love of my life; take her into your bosom!" Alex screamed as he came down with the knife. But instead of the knife going into Tabitha's heart, Alex dropped the blade because Godfrey speared him in the chest with the red-hot samurai sword lying nearing the hell mouth.

The sword went nearly all the way through Alex, but the handle stopped at the sternum of his chest; his skin began burning from the red hot handle. The room filled with the smell of Alex's flesh, cooking from the hot sword. Alex fell to the side, caught himself and then tumbled forward onto the ground near Godfrey and Don.

"No…it can't be…I am invincible…I won…" Alex said in agonizing pain while coughing up blood.

"Is this the little bald guy who caused so much trouble?" Don asked, moving the blade around in Alex's chest with his boot.

"That would be him," Godfrey answered, looking down at Alex to see if he was dead. "You wanted to serve hell so much, well guess what? You are going to spend eternity down there," Godfrey said, ripping the blade out of Alex and then picking him up and throwing him into the fiery hell mouth.

Alex's body faded away as it fell into the pit. As soon as Alex's body disappeared into the void, a sonic boom cracked across the sky, causing the feeling of oppression to lift. Outside the terrorists stopped fighting and began looking around at the carnage they had caused. At the Maxwell house, the dark shadows stopped fighting and began retreating in haste from Zadkiel and the Dancer. Suddenly Tabitha went from being still to jerking around, crying and wondering what had happened. Godfrey, of course, ran to her aid, while Don figured out how to get Henry out of the cell that he was in. Godfrey went over and removed the gag from Tabitha's mouth. She looked surprised, as if she honestly didn't know what was going on. Godfrey undid her shackles, and covered her with an old blanket he found.

It took Tabitha several minutes to speak. She held her head for a while like she was trying to slow down her thoughts. The cavern felt like it was going to collapse at any minute, so Godfrey carried Tabitha out while Don helped Henry out of the cavern. As the four escaped, the cave began falling into the ground, as it was sucked into the hell mouth, causing a massive crater where it originally stood. It was now a huge hollowed-out black crater, sealed in the middle where the hell mouth used to be open.

"Are you all right?" Godfrey asked Tabitha, holding her in his arms.

"I don't know. I feel like I have been asleep for too long a time," Tabitha responded.

"Alex said something about a spell he put on you; maybe that's what it was," Henry answered, coughing.

"Sounds spooky, but not as spooky as the giant planet in the sky," Don said.

They all looked up and were amazed to see such a sight. There were shooting stars going to and fro that could now be seen during the day because of the brightness of the planet.

"Wow, what is happening?" Tabitha asked.

"I don't know, but the world is going to get a lot stranger from here on out," Godfrey said.

"Godfrey, thank you for saving me," Tabitha said, starting to cry.

"I couldn't have done it without the help of Don and Henry's phone call. It was actually Henry you should be thanking," Godfrey said, holding Tabitha in his arms.

"Thanks to all of you then; this has been the worst year of my life," Tabitha said, crying into Godfrey's shoulder.

"It's all right; we made it out of there alive. We have a chance to learn from this and to move on," Henry said.

"That sounds great; let's get out of here. I think I have had enough of Georgia. I need to go back home to Texas," Don said, spitting on the ground.

"Let's go, we need to call your parents and let them know you are okay," Godfrey said to Tabitha.

"Okay, but first I need to do something," Tabitha said.

"What is that?" Godfrey asked before he was interrupted by Tabitha reaching up and kissing him. This was a surprise for Godfrey; it threw him off balance, but he answered back by embracing her and returning the long-awaited kiss. The four stood there under the new purple light that was emanating from the planet in the sky.

Chapter 67: I'm Home

It was so bright at first that it took a while for Alex's eyes to adjust to the light. Alex woke up on lush green grass that had little red veins of pulsating light running through them. He sat up and felt his chest where Godfrey had stabbed him. His chest was fine, no pain or puncture of any kind. Alex looked at his hands and noticed his flesh looked even healthier than before. Alex heard a bunch of different animal noises—birds, monkeys, wild cats, all sorts of wildlife seemed to live here. Alex stood up to wipe himself off and stood against a tree. Even the trees seemed to breathe and move with the life in this place. In the distance, he heard children, laughing and playing.

I was about to fulfill my destiny by sacrificing Tabitha until I was stopped by that wretched Godfrey. Then I was harpooned and thrown down the hell mouth. Then I woke up here. Maybe hell is not hot after all; maybe it is really a paradise. The world has got it all wrong; hell is where they want to go, not heaven.

"Hello Alex," a woman said behind him.

Alex turned around and saw the most beautiful woman in the world; he was instantly entranced by her. She had brown shoulder-length hair. It had a silver streak going through the side of it. The woman's skin was creamy white; she had red eyes that glowed lightly like a snake's. She seemed tall and slender like a modern-day supermodel. The throne she was sitting on was carved into a tree that looked thousands of years old. The woman had on a golden gown that exposed her arms, her back, and the top of her chest. She had green imps that were trimming her nails as she drank out of a crystal chalice.

"Who are you?" Alex said, dropping to his knees because of the indescribable beauty of the woman.

"I am Lilith, the queen of hell," Lilith responded, motioning to one of the imps to fill her cup.

"I did not know hell had a queen," Alex said.

"I've been a queen for a long time, Alex; I've been one on earth and now I'm one here," Lilith said, leaning forward.

"What kind of throne is that?" Alex asked mesmerized.

"This was hewn from the Tree of the Knowledge of Good and Evil. It is one of the living roots of hell. It is why we are all here," Lilith said, scratching the armrest.

"Wow! This puts everything into perspective. What a beautiful garden; it's not on fire and full of brimstone," Alex said.

"This is the garden of Eden, without the Tree of Life or God's presence," Lilith said.

"It is still very lovely," Alex said.

"It is just a remnant of its former self, but it is our home," Lilith said.

"What can I do for you, my queen?" Alex said, as he bowed down and kissed Lilith's feet.

"You must stay here in the garden with your other companions; it is a very important task that I have given you personally," Lilith said, smiling.

"Anything for you, my queen," Alex said, groveling before her.

"Good! I hope you remember that," Lilith said, leaning back into her throne, and motioning her hand for Alex to stand.

Alex stood up, waiting to hear what his new job would be. In the background, he heard the voices of children, chattering and laughing as they came closer. Alex stood there waiting to see what would happen next, but Lilith didn't say anything. Alex thought maybe he would be made some kind of prince or ruler in hell because of his courageous service and the utter chaos he had created on earth before being prematurely murdered. Of course, Alex had failed in his mission. Tabitha was still alive and now the hell mouth was closed off from Athens. He had also failed to conjure a larger, more powerful principality to rule over Athens. Nobody was saying anything about the details, so Alex figured Lucifer and his queen must reward valiant effort in any case.

"Alex, I want you to meet my children," Lilith said, as her little green demon babies showed their snarling teeth to Alex and Lilith.

"Oh, these are your children, my queen?" Alex said, getting a little nervous.

"Yes, aren't they precious?" Lilith said, while they were snapping their teeth at each other.

"What would you like me to do with them, my queen?" Alex asked, gulping as he did.

"My children must eat, and you must feed them," Lilith said, smiling as her snake-like tongue slipped out of her mouth, tasting the utter fear on Alex.

"Okay, how do I do that my queen?" Alex asked.

"Run," Lilith said, as her children started growling and facing Alex.

Alex turned ghostly pale as he began backing up in the garden. His back hit a tree, and he sat there stunned for a minute. Just for a second, he thought this was a joke and Lilith was just scaring him a bit. That all changed when one of the flying babies came out of the tree and landed on his head. Instantly, the baby started scalping Alex's bald head with its sharp teeth. The pain quickly kicked in and Alex tried to pull the baby off his head, but the little monster was as strong as an ox. Alex began running in the opposite direction of Lilith's throne. As he swung his arms, another baby latched on to his hand and began eating the flesh that was on it. The baby hung on like a piranha, crunching his bones.

The baby that was on Alex's head had made its way down his face; Alex couldn't see anymore except out of one eye because the baby was eating the other one.

Alex screamed and screamed until one of the other hundreds of children had locked on to his throat like a trained wolf. Now his screams were just wimpy wheezes, barely making it out of his mouth and nose. Half of Alex's body had been eaten, but he kept trying to run; he was dragging several of Lilith's children that had attached themselves to him. Finally he fell down to the ground and the children finished him up. Alex lay there like an antelope who had given up fighting and let the lions eat him.

Alex said, "It's over; now I can die," as a baby stood over him, smiling with bits of Alex's flesh and blood in its teeth.

Alex noticed the ground started shaking, and then he heard a roaring fire in the background. Suddenly the fire was on him; he began burning with extreme intensity; it felt like every atom in his body was splitting one after the other. His wheezy screams were drowned by the roaring of the fire. Soon enough the fire was gone. Alex sat up to see his body was back to normal; he had his healthy pale skin back again. Alex stood up and saw the red eyes of the children in the trees. They were Lilith's children waiting for Alex to regenerate his flesh so they could chase him down and eat him all over again.

"Noooo! I served you faithfully! I don't deserve this! Please—have mercy!" Alex screamed. He ran away from Lilith's children, only to be chased down and ravenously eaten, over and over again for the rest of eternity.

Chapter 68: The Exile

Belial stood motionless inside the frozen chunk of ice known as Titan, one of the moons of Jupiter. Instead of having him obliterated, Lucifer had exiled Belial to this no man's land until the final judgment came down from heaven. Lucifer knew this would be a far worse punishment for Belial since his only pleasure in life was murdering mankind and corrupting his ways. Now Belial could no longer be involved in the plans that his beloved king had for the world. Belial was actually in the center of Titan, in a frozen cell that could never be opened again. Complete solitary confinement. Belial's body was frozen too; the only thing that had motion was his thoughts. That is all the immortal being would ever have again—his memories to haunt him.

Thinking, thinking, and thinking some more, Belial played the recent scenarios over in his head. Inside his heart, he loathed Godfrey, John, Meredith, Tabitha, and OBN. He hated all of them; Belial imagined killing each and every one over and over again. Belial also hated Lilith; she was the one human who no one under Lucifer's banner could touch. She was all for Lucifer's pleasure; somehow, some way she had finagled her way to the joint throne of hell. It was Lilith's idea to have Belial put into exile. Of course, Lucifer listened to her, as he always did when it came to these matters.

Another Jezebel, we should have had her eaten by the dogs when we had the chance. Well, I guess this is it. I will just have to imagine re-killing all my enemies over and over again. I guess that's not so bad; where shall I start? Oh, I will start with Cain and Abel; I always enjoyed witnessing the first human bloodshed. Or maybe I can witness all the Hebrew babies being thrown to the crocodiles in Egypt, or perhaps I can watch Job lose his mind and become a raving lunatic. Ah…so many things to watch.

Left with his thoughts and his vast number of memories, Belial played them over in his mind for the rest of eternity, locked in his frozen asylum.

Chapter 69: Good News

Meredith ran out of the house to meet Don, Godfrey, and especially Tabitha. Henry would have been with them, but he had to leave in an ambulance from the remains of Alex's church because he was so malnourished. John quickly followed behind Meredith; they were both laughing and crying because Tabitha had survived the horrific ordeal that Alex had brought to the town. There had been at least seventy-eight people killed in this "Day of Fire." The three exited out of Don's truck, and Tabitha ran around to meet her crying mother's hug. They embraced tightly, while John came up and hugged both of them together, kissing them on top of their heads. Godfrey and Don were a little sore from all the fighting; John reached over and shook both of their hands vigorously.

"Thank you, thank you both so much for saving my daughter and this town," John said.

"You're welcome; I am just glad this mess is over," Godfrey said.

"Did you find Henry?" Meredith asked.

"Yes, he was locked up in the same place Tabitha was. We found him in the nick of time; he was weak from lack of water and food," Don said.

"It's going to take a long time for Athens to get over this; I believe I have my work cut out for me. Either we will be thrown out of town, or, hopefully, they will let us stay so we can help rebuild," John said.

Tabitha came over to Godfrey and hugged his side, giving him a light peck on the lips. John and Meredith looked at each other because they had seen this coming; both of them knew that these two should be together; it was meant to happen.

It was Godfrey's love for her that had saved Tabitha from the clutches of death. The Maxwell house was an absolute mess; there were bullet holes all over the front of the house, and all the windows had been shattered from gunfire. The well-manicured front lawn had muddy tire tracks all over it, while most of the white gravel had been spewed out of the driveway by the several police vehicles that had been there. As bad as it looked, the cops and military had held off the Luciferian terrorists; they had never set foot in John's yard.

On that day alone, the United States had several major earthquakes. One split Los Angeles in half; several thousand people had died, and many more were missing. There were widespread power outages across the world because of the mystery planet that was so close to Earth. The two planets kept exchanging electrical charges and these were destroying the power grid. The mystery planet was causing a lot of problems; it was beginning to pull the moon out of orbit from the Earth, causing the waves to get weaker in some parts and stronger in other parts of the world.

Around the planet a chain of volcanoes began blowing out massive amounts of lava, causing a good portion of ice on the earth to melt. Scientific experts were saying that the ocean levels would be much higher by next year; they were advising people to move away from the coasts and go inland. Astronomers had already sighted a few very large asteroids coming near the earth as well. Everyone had a wake-up call; the world had changed. It was time to adapt to this cold reality or to be killed by it.

"We are gonna have to start carrying guns; there will be looting and robbery from now on," Don said.

"I hate it, but you are right; men are going to become desperate. So desperate they will kill," John said.

"I don't like the sound of this," Tabitha said, looking at Godfrey.

"Don't worry, I'll protect you. This is a good opportunity to help people; we need to work together to establish peace in this chaos," Godfrey said.

"I agree, Godfrey; this is not the time to panic at all, but to seek God and trust that He will protect us from the hard times ahead," Meredith said.

"Let's go inside and get something to eat; you guys must be starving," John said.

"Sounds good, but first I need to shower. I feel disgusting," Tabitha said.

"I think I need one too," Godfrey said.

"You're going to have to let me borrow some clothes; this is all I have," said Don.

"Don't worry; we have plenty," John said as the five of them went inside.

While inside, Tabitha and Godfrey were in her bedroom getting ready for dinner. Tabitha was in the bathroom, washing her face and brushing her teeth. Godfrey was sitting on the bed, staring off into space. Godfrey was thinking of everything he had been through—the Crusades, death, hell, heaven, the present, killing Alex, now having the woman whom God had promised him. The scenario hadn't played out the way he had envisioned it in his mind, but everything that God had told him came to pass. Godfrey realized, like so many men of faith from the past had, that God's promises will endure all things, no matter what things looked like. Tabitha came over and sat in Godfrey's lap, put her arms around his neck, and kissed him.

Tabitha said, "I am so glad I have you. You didn't give up on me; you held out, Godfrey."

"You don't know how close I came to leaving; my heart aches just thinking about it now," Godfrey said.

"That doesn't matter now, Godfrey; we have each other now and forever," Tabitha said, while kissing Godfrey again. From then on the two never left each other's side without longing for the other one. They were quickly married and helped John and Meredith start a new ministry that was focused on preparing people for disasters and getting close to God in troubling times.

Chapter 70: Benjamin

The house was peaceful in the serene darkness of night. By now, everyone was accustomed to the large mystery planet that had recently been named Hydrea; it made the light during the day and night have a purple tint. Most people used their blinds during the night now because of it, but Godfrey and Tabitha left theirs open because of the beauty of the mystical planet's light. Godfrey and Tabitha didn't live that far at all from John and Meredith because these days families stayed close together, even in America.

Ever since the beginning of the end, as some called it, life became about survival and stretching everything one had. Nothing came in surplus anymore, except for suffering, violence, sickness, and death. The mindset of mankind had changed dramatically; three years had passed since the day of fire. John was offered his position back at OBN, but he denied it, and focused instead on his new ministry that helped care for the suffering and supplied food for the hungry. It was not glamorous like in the past, but life had changed. Christianity was no longer a beautiful queen dazzling in jewels; now she had become a servant. Most Christian ministries that focused on the easy life and material gain were gone. Thankfully, John had been warned ahead of time and had heeded the warnings God gave him. Most people didn't, and they tried to attack John about it, but John wasn't concerned about what people thought anymore.

Henry made peace with God and was back on the police force; he eventually became a detective and always helped the Maxwells with their ministry when he could. Don "the Boss" Warburton eventually went back home to Texas to take care of his family. Sometimes Don came up and everyone would camp out at the Maxwell house. A lot of people went to prison for what happened on the day of fire. Billy Ferguson's wife was told what had happened to her husband. Henry told her personally, but made sure she knew that the man who killed Billy was justly punished for it.

Godfrey and Tabitha bought the house they live in now with Godfrey's lump sum of money given to him by Grace. The rest of the money was transferred into Swiss francs, and kept in a Swiss bank account; the interest came in monthly. Tabitha had made her peace with God and finally realized that God was not against her, but wanted to love her and help her.

Godfrey and Tabitha were in bed, sound asleep. It was a cold winter night; it was supposed to snow, but rained instead. Godfrey had his arms wrapped around Tabitha who was facing the other way. Godfrey woke up from a chill in the air. He cracked his eyes open and noticed the window was open. Godfrey got himself up to close the window and to check on Benjamin, Tabitha and Godfrey's son.

Why in the world is the window open? It is the middle of winter. Who would have opened it? Strange, Tabitha is too cold-natured to do that.

Godfrey walked into Benjamin's room to see how he was doing. When Godfrey walked in, he saw the silhouette of a man with wings in the purple light shining through the window. The man was holding something. When the man stepped into the light, Godfrey realized he was holding Benjamin who was sound asleep. Godfrey's gut feeling was not a good one because he did not recognize this angel. He wasn't sure if he was an enemy or a friend. This angel was much larger than Shemiel or Jazrael. He looked older in the face, worn down from wisdom, but he had youthfulness to him. The angel had six brown wings, and wore red armor trimmed with gold. When the angel moved Benjamin back and forth in his arms singing lightly to the child, Godfrey saw the dragon crest on the front of the angel's armor. Godfrey's knees went weak; his stomach knotted and a sudden feeling of fear and dread washed over him.

"Who are you?" Godfrey whispered.

"You know who I am, Templar," the angel said.

"Lucifer, what do you want?" Godfrey asked.

"Come on, Godfrey, don't be rude. I just came by to see my favorite person's newborn child," Lucifer said charmingly.

"You've seen him; now leave," Godfrey said.

"Hold on a second, Godfrey; what is the rush?" Lucifer said.

"Don't you have better things to do?" Godfrey asked.

"Actually, yes, there is a kingdom to run, and I'm the head of it," Lucifer said.

"Just give him to me, okay?" Godfrey said carefully.

"Don't worry, Godfrey, I didn't come to harm anyone…not yet anyway," Lucifer said.

"So why did you come?" Godfrey said.

"You're too serious, Godfrey. I came to congratulate you for your defeat of my subjects. You beat us Godfrey; you stopped us from accomplishing our plans for you, the Maxwells, and OBN. You are a formidable foe; you even held back temptation from Lilith. I couldn't even do that," Lucifer said.

"I had nothing to do with it; God was the one who stopped you," Godfrey said.

"Yeah, yeah, when are you going to realize God could care less about you or me? We are nothing but little ants under a magnifying glass, pawns on a slanted chess board. Don't give Him credit; take your own. You beat me on your own," Lucifer said.

"Is that all you had to tell me?" Godfrey asked.

"No, I hate being beat more than I hate God or His son. You, Godfrey, are on my top ten list of men I will take down in their lifetimes; and if I can't get you, then I will get him," Lucifer said, holding Benjamin out with one hand.

"Put him down!" Godfrey screamed.

"I plan on it. Catch!" Lucifer replied, as he suddenly vanished into thin air.

Benjamin fell instantly, but Godfrey leaped in just enough time to catch him before he hit the ground. Benjamin didn't even wake up; Godfrey got up and held him tightly to his chest.

Tabitha walked in half asleep and asked, "What are you doing up?"

"I had to use the bathroom, and I checked on Ben," Godfrey said.

"Who were you talking to?" Tabitha asked.

"No one; I was just singing to Ben," Godfrey answered.

Tabitha came over to look at Benjamin, Godfrey wrapped his arm around her and held Ben with the other. Godfrey kissed Tabitha on top of her head and prayed to himself, *God, protect my family and protect my son. Guide our every step and shine light on our paths; keep us clear from the enemy's snares. Don't let us be caught in his traps, and don't let us be tempted by sin. Keep us holy, keep us Yours. Let the blood of the Lamb forever cover our door. God be with us, and let us always hear Your voice. In Jesus' name I pray. Amen.*

About the Author

A resident of South Carolina, Daniel spent four years in the United States Marine Corps before devoting his time to writing. He received this calling from the Lord after returning from his second tour of duty in Iraq and now desires to draw others to God through his stories. Daniel is employed full time and is a partner with Morningstar Fellowship Church. He is currently completing a bachelor's degree in theology through Regent University. He and his beautiful wife, Meredith, have been happily married for a year and reside in South Carolina with their German shepherd, Sheba.